To
Margaret Thomas
In memory of long friendship
and of days in Devon

CHAPTER
ONE

"So you wish the banns put up next Sunday, Polly?" Directed as it was towards the faded carpet of the Rector's study, and accompanied by a scorching blush, Polly's reply was practically inaudible. Fortunately she had her buxom and voluble mother to interpret and amplify it.

"Lift thy head, child, and answer Rector praaper! You mun axcuse her, sir — she'm mortal shy at this moment, as can be seen. Yes, if yu plaze, sir, to put en up for first time of axin next Sunday. 'Tes a pity her dear sweetheart come from furrin paarts, and so et can't be read out, 'both of this parish', which 'ud 'a bin more comfortin' like."

The Reverend Peregrine Carew showed some surprise. "You never gave me to understand, Mrs. Martin, that the young man of Polly's choice was not English! That is to be regretted. I should not have thought she would wish to marry a foreigner. And did you not tell me that he was called William Simpson? Such a name is — ah, I suppose you only mean that he is not Devon born?"

"That he'm not, sir! He'm from a plaace called — the maid has it writ down there. Read et out, Polly my dear."

1

Without consulting the paper clutched in her fist, the damsel, her face now like a glowing coal, mumbled out a word which certainly conveyed a suggestion of a wooer from Nijni-Novgorod or the steppes.

"Russian! William Simpson a Russian! Surely not!" exclaimed the astonished parson, looking from the prospective bride to her mother.

"Nay, sir, he'm no Russian — but he mought a'most as well be one, comin' from an island such a mort o' miles away; the Isle of Man 'tes called, us don't knaw for why."

"The Isle of Man? *Russian*. Can you possibly mean — Stay, give me the paper!"

Still murmuring that misleading word, Polly obeyed. As the Rector smoothed out the crumpled sheet his expression became less perplexed. "Ah, you mean *Rushen*, a place near Peel, I believe. Yes, that is it, and William Simpson, I see, comes from the parish of Saint —"

"He'm certainly a furriner," observed Mrs. Martin, as one well justified in a criticism. "Axin your pardon for interruptin' yu, sir."

A smile lit up Mr. Carew's kind and handsome face. In the year 1794, Manx territory, to the mind of an inland Devon rustic, was as far removed as were Sicily or Malta, and a journey thither about as likely to be contemplated. Further enquiries elicited that Polly Martin was not, however, to be transported after marriage to this remote isle, but was to bide in Devon, her future husband having found work on a farm over to Crediton — a solution satisfactory to all parties.

2

A few minutes later, sheep and lamb of his flock having made their respectful withdrawal, the Rector of Damarel St. Mary laid upon the mantelpiece the paper which the lamb had gripped so hard, and sat down in the winged chair by the hearth — fireless, since this morning of early October was remarkably warm. For a moment, as his hand played idly with the ears of the setter bitch lying there, he reflected on the sensation which a marriage with a genuine 'furriner' would have caused in this quiet and conservative village. It is true that he could scarcely imagine any of its inhabitants entertaining the idea of such a union, and would himself, when consulted, have thrown cold water on any project of the kind. Englishmen, in his opinion, had much better marry Englishwomen (or possibly Scotswomen); and indeed, in this secluded part of the country there was little likelihood of their doing anything else.

His eyes strayed almost involuntarily to the row of little miniatures above his mantelpiece. Competently rather than artistically executed, these little ovals represented, with a similarity too marked to arouse much faith in their truth as likenesses, the four surviving children of the Reverend Peregrine Carew and his wife Elizabeth, no less than five having died in infancy or early childhood. The two boys and two girls seemed in each case to have been painted at the immature age of two or thereabouts, and by the same hand. Yet at this present date the originals ranged from the Rector's eldest son Nugent's thirty-odd years, through the married Sophia's three and twenty to schoolboy Tom's fourteen and the ten summers of the small maiden Peggy, whose head was now so full of the imminent return of her elder, her sailor brother. For, as the Rectory household rejoiced to know, Captain Nugent Carew of H.M. 32-gun frigate *Callisto* was even now on his way home from hostilities against the French in the Mediterranean, and might arrive any day.

"You know that, Juno, my girl, don't you?" observed Mr. Carew softly, looking down into the setter's liquid eyes. "And," he continued, still addressing this appreciative audience, "I think my Lords of the Admiralty will not be ill-pleased with him, since he and his ship played their part in our recent capture of Corsica. Would you be surprised, my beauty, if, when the *Callisto* is paid off, he gets something larger than a frigate?"

The Carews were a very united family, but of his surviving children it was the firstborn and the last who were perhaps nearest to the Rector's heart. And soon, he reflected, that tall, lean, dark-haired naval son of his, whom even a mother's eye could scarcely connect with the chubby blond child of the first of the little portraits, would be sitting in this room with him, amplifying the letters which he had written home, with such regularity as he could compass, during a year and a half's absence in the Mediterranean. Indeed a good and a beloved son!

And it might be, thought Mr. Carew further, that if Nugent were not at once given another command, which, in spite of his own recent address to the setter, he could not help hoping might be the case, there

4

would be almost a full family gathering at Christmas, since Tom would then be home from Blundell's School at Tiverton, though the possibility of his elder daughter and her husband paying them a visit was ruled out by the fact that Sophia was expecting a second child early in the New Year.

The descendant of Cavaliers on the one side and of sailors on the other — did not Rear-Admiral Sir John Nugent, bluff and be-wigged, look across the dining-room at the love-locks and lace collar of that Peregrine Carew who, surviving Naseby, had lived to a ripe old age and the wearing, under William and Mary, of an even more full-bottomed wig than Admiral Nugent's? — the Rector of Damarel St. Mary had inherited that non-juring tradition which gave him a spiritual kinship with Jeremy Taylor and Bishop Ken. So that although he possessed an excellent seat on a horse, and often had a dog at his heels, he was by no means the hunting country parson of his day. Nor, on the other hand, did the notes which he had long been amassing for a projected treatise on the Fathers of the Egyptian Desert denote any personal leanings towards an existence such as theirs. On the contrary, 'Parson Carew' was known for miles round as one who had the spiritual and material needs of his parish sincerely at heart, and who did not spare himself in trying to meet them.

He roused himself now from his visions of a family gathering and pulled out his watch. It was nearly time for him to go and visit that crippled old Mrs. Dobbs, to whom there was also talk of soup being despatched by some other hand. He must ask Elizabeth about that before he started. He rose, the setter with him, but before he got to the door it opened, and in came, with considerable briskness, Mrs. Carew herself.

"George has just brought in the post-bag. And it has come, Peregrine, it has come!" She held up a letter, her eyes sparkling. Younger than her husband, and never more than passably good-looking, she had a face full of character.

"From Nugent!" asked the Rector, delighted. "Is it for you or for me?"

"For you. The postmark is Portsmouth, so he is back in England!"

"Excellent! Yes, Portsmouth it is. The *Callisto* is safely in harbour then." Smiling, he broke the seal with alacrity. "I wonder how soon we shall see him?"

"Will you not read it aloud, my dear?"

Slipping an arm round her, Mr. Carew complied.

"My Dear Parents, (*So it is for both of us after all!*)

"Here I am back in England, and more than glad to be so. And when the business of paying off the 'Callisto' is completed I shall immediately set out for Damarel St. Mary.

"As it is more than possible that the letter which I despatched to you from Leghorn before sailing may not yet have reached you, before proceeding further I will repeat the piece of news which it contained. I hope that it will not prove too disagreeable to you. For I should wish you to

6

know without delay that I shall not be returning alone."

"Not alone! Why, whom can he be bringing with him?" interjected Mrs. Carew, as her husband came to the end of the page.

"Some shipmate perhaps, or possibly one of our relations, the Mounseys, from Leghorn. We shall soon learn." He turned the page and continued . . . but not far.

"*I must in fact tell you that before leaving Leghorn I was* — What's this? "*I was married . . .*" He broke off, the letter wavering in his hand.

"*Married!* You must be mistaken, Peregrine!" Alarm in her eyes now, his wife clutched his arm. "It's impossible — it can't be true! Let me see — you have misread — or the word is blotted —"

Mr. Carew's eyes had raced on. "It is impossible . . . but it's true none the less!" said he, drawing a sharp breath. "My dear, had you not better be seated?" Drawing her to the chair he had just vacated, he put her into it, and continued to read on in silence.

"But how can Nugent have got married abroad?" cried Nugent's mother in incredulous bewilderment. "What English girl could he have met? Oh, Peregrine, tell me the rest quickly!" She made to get up from the chair, but the Rector, without looking off from the letter, laid a hand on her shoulder to prevent her. His face was grave, even stern.

"Better remain where you are, Elizabeth. It seems that our son was married at Leghorn before he left.

7

And his wife . . . You must prepare yourself for a shock. His wife, whom he has brought to England with him . . . But I had better read you exactly what he says:

"I was married in Leghorn on the seventh of September to a charming young French Royalist lady of good family, whom I am convinced, my dear Father and Mother, you will in a very short time take to your hearts. I am only too deeply aware that this unexpected news may come as a considerable shock to you — I wish it need not be so. I should also much have preferred the wedding to take place in England, but I could not bring Charlotte with me on board the 'Callisto', without female companionship, otherwise than as my wife."

"His *wife!* Nugent's *wife!*" faltered Mrs. Carew, white and stricken as few people had ever seen her. "My son married to a Frenchwoman!"

Her husband was still reading. Unopposed this time, she rose from the chair and laid her hand on his arm. "Where did he meet this girl, Peregrine?"

The Rector lowered the letter. "In Leghorn itself, it appears, at my kinsman Edward Mounsey's. She was engaged there in teaching their little girl, having fled from a relative's home in Toulon last December, when, as you may remember, we were obliged to give up the place in face of the Republican forces, and to remove our troops and fleet."

"Teaching Mr. Mounsey's little girl? Then she must at least be respectable — and educated."

"My dear Elizabeth, do you imagine that Nugent would marry a young woman who was not respectable?"

"But Peregrine, a Frenchwoman — so artful! Would he, also, know whether one was respectable or not? He cannot have seen much of this young woman! When was he previously at Leghorn?"

"After the fall of Bastia, in Corsica, last May, I think, when he took the *Callisto* to the mainland for water and so on. (I can look it up, for I have all his letters there in my desk.) And although he was not long at Leghorn on that occasion, it was presumably then that he met this 'Charlotte', for one cannot believe that he only made her acquaintance during his recent call at Leghorn before sailing for England. That would be too . . . too . . ." Mr. Carew found himself at a loss for the right word.

"Whichever it was," exclaimed his wife with vehemence, "she has caught him — our eldest son! And he is bringing her here, and we shall have to receive her!"

"Naturally," said the Rector, swallowing hard. This home-coming, to which they had so much looked forward — with what strange colours was it invested now!

"A Frenchwoman — one of the nation with which we are at war — an enemy!" continued Mrs. Carew bitterly. "How could he!"

"No, my dear, not an enemy. Nugent states that she is a Royalist. She would not otherwise have had to flee from Toulon when it fell to the Republicans. Let us not be unjust, Elizabeth."

"Still, she is French. And a Roman Catholic, no doubt. Have you thought of that, Peregrine?"

The bewildered sternness on her husband's face deepened. "It does not inevitably follow that she is of that faith. There remain still, I believe, some of the Huguenot persuasion in France."

But his wife shook her head as though determined to believe the worst. "I am sure she will turn out to be a Papist." And then, as another aspect of this distasteful union occurred to her, she said, in a tone tinged almost with horror: "Do you think it possible that they were married by an Italian priest?"

The Rector gave a rather dreary smile. "You sound, Elizabeth, as though you thought no ceremony at all would be preferable to that! Set your mind at rest. Nugent says here — I forgot to mention it — that the marriage took place before Mr. Udney, the British consul at Leghorn. He would be the proper person in the circumstances."

"Before the consul? One could hardly regard that as a real marriage. And perhaps," there was a perceptible lift of hope in Mrs. Carew's voice, "it actually is not legal?"

Mr. Carew shook his head. "I am afraid that it is." Then he caught himself up. "It would be more fitting for me to say that I am glad to know that it is. No, my dear, there is nothing for it but to make up our minds to a French daughter-in-law, and hope that the claims which Nugent makes for her do not exist merely in his imagination. I have always considered that he was blessed with a particularly sound and sober judgment — but then, as far as I know, there has never previously been a woman in the case. — Is there someone at the door?"

For the sound of the door-knob, turned apparently with some difficulty, had caught his ear, and Juno's too. As he looked towards it the door opened, and round it came the diminutive form of his younger daughter, chubby-faced and smiling. She was dressed for going out, and had a basket in her hand.

"Please may I take this broth when you go to old Mrs. Dobbs, Papa?" she enquired. "Mamma said that . . ." Then, quick to realise that something was wrong, the child stopped, looking at both her parents in some anxiety.

"Papa will not be going to Mrs. Dobbs for a little while, my dear," said her mother gently. "Take the soup back to the kitchen, Peggy; you shall carry it to Mrs. Dobbs later. — Wait, I will come with you." And, first giving her husband a glance to show that she would shortly return, she led the benevolent intruder from the room.

Standing there alone, the Rector of Damarel St. Mary put a hand for a moment over his eyes. Idle to pretend that he had not received a stunning blow. His elder son married out of hand to an unknown French girl met in Italy! And when, after a moment or two, he uncovered his eyes, his glance fell upon the sheet of crumpled paper which so short a time ago he had received from the village wench who was going to marry a 'foreigner' from the Isle of Man! Recalling his recent reflections on her case, he gave a short and bitter laugh. A genuine 'foreign marriage' had come, not merely upon the village, but upon his own family! So sudden and unexpected was the news of it, that he could still hardly realise that he already possessed a French daughter-in-law. To rush into marriage at all — still more, with a girl of another country, and a hostile country at that — seemed so out of keeping with the forthright, steady character of his son! Had Nugent somehow been entrapped into wedlock? The odious possibility was there.

The Reverend Peregrine Carew sat down to re-read the letter from Portsmouth. It naturally yielded no further information, and that which it did convey he still found hard to absorb. The only element which seemed real was the expression of regret, so obviously sincere, for administering such a shock, for in that he heard Nugent's voice. But there was unfamiliarity in the air of constraint which showed here and there, rendering the letter subtly different from those quite frank interchanges which had always taken place between father and son, although neither of them — least of all the son — was given to what a later age would have called sentimentality.

He sighed deeply, and folded up the letter which he would have given so very much never to have received.

CHAPTER
TWO

"I do trust, Mrs. Carew," said Lieutenant Robert Ommaney earnestly, "that you — and the Captain — will find these lodgings fairly comfortable? They are the best that I could procure, and I thought that for a short stay they might pass muster."

The letter which was to cause such consternation at Damarel St. Mary Rectory was still upon its way thither, when the third lieutenant of the *Callisto* stood thus apologetically with his captain's French bride in the parlour of what was to be her temporary home in Portsmouth — and at intervals her husband's also — until the frigate was paid off.

Young Mrs. Nugent Carew looked round the rather crowded first-floor room with a smile.

"But indeed there is no need to apologise," she replied gaily. "I like this room very much. It must belong to a sea-captain, I think. Those large *coquillages* — shells, I should say — and the paintings of ships! And if I should wish to look at the harbour, see, there is even a telescope!"

That staid young man, Lieutenant Ommaney, reflected (as he had reflected before) that the newly-made Mrs. Carew's slight foreign accent lent an undeniable charm to her speaking of English, which tongue she appeared to know well. He took his leave, glad that she seemed satisfied with the accommodation which he had found for her. Indeed, from what he had seen of her during the voyage home from the Western Mediterranean, his captain's wife was not hard to please. She had no 'French airs' about her. There was, he thought, little in her appearance or manners to prevent her from passing as English — to him a decided point in her favour.

Speculation as to the young lady's nationality was in fact already taking place downstairs. There in the kitchen Mrs. Osworthy, the comfortable relict of the erstwhile owner of the telescope and transporter of the large shells, was reporting her recent interview with Mrs. Carew to the sister who lived with her.

"Very taking she seems, the Captain's lady — young, and has that coloured hair I've always had a fancy for. But she speaks almost as if she was furrin, and when I asks her what she would fancy for three o'clock dinner — for it seems the Captain won't be here before this evening — she says she would like an Omelick. An Omelick!"

"May be she *is* furrin," surmised Miss Skinner musingly. "Omelicks is certainly furrin food. And what did you say to that, Eliza?"

"As you know, Selina, I never wish to disoblige, particularly when connected with the Navy, but serve any kick-shaws of that sort I can't undertake to do, only honest English vittles," replied good Mrs. Osworthy, happily ignorant that her disclaimer itself contained a

14

misrendering of a 'furrin' word. "But I didn't say that before the young Naval orficer. I said I hoped I could provide something she'd like better than an Omelick. I shall serve the boiled leg of mutton, with carrots and turnips. After all, if she is a furriner born, she'll have to be English now, married to the captain of a fine frigate like that!"

"I can't think somehow," observed Miss Skinner with a slightly condemnatory inflection, "that a Navy Captain would have picked up a furrin young lady for wife, seeing as we are fighting the furriners — leastwise the French."

"Ah, Selina," returned Mrs. Osworthy with a richly reminiscent sigh, "if you'd 'a seen as much of Life as I have, *and* Love, you'd not have uttered those words! *Sailors* — wasn't my Dick a sailor? . . . Likewise there's two kinds of French now-a-days, as you ought to know. There's those wicked Republicans as we are fighting against, and there's the Emigrants, that stood up for their King and Queen and lost their own property, and was sometimes beheaded themselves with that nasty machine of theirs; and them we allows in England. There's even some here in Portsmouth, looking, most of 'em, as if a good meal would do them no harm — instead of living on Omelicks! There'll be no Omelicks in this house, for, as you know, I've got a fine fat goose for the Captain and his lady this evening, and French or not, I'll warrant she won't refuse a slice!"

Ignorant of Mrs. Osworthy's culinary intentions, with hours yet to get through before her husband could leave his ship, the young foreign lady upstairs had laid aside her bonnet, and was looking with interest through the window. Of this, the first English town in which she had ever set foot, she could unfortunately see no more than the front of the modest dwellings of the small street in which Mrs. Osworthy's house was situated. Even the telescope over the mantelpiece could not have brought her a view of the harbour. A certain amount of noise and bustle might perhaps have penetrated to her ears from the Hard, which was actually not far away, had not the windows been shut. But shut they were, and firmly; and in any case it was raining — although as the *Callisto* had rounded the Isle of Wight the sunshine had been glinting on the chalk of the sentinel Needles.

Charlotte Carew, *née* d'Esparre, turned away at last from this unrepaying outlook, and once more studied the room in which she was. And to so many unfamiliar dwellings had Fate led her in the past twelve months, that she could summon up a sort of half-agreeable shrinking by trying to imagine what her feelings would have been were she here in England also as a refugee. But she was not a refugee: she was — however unbelievably — an Englishman's wedded wife!

Giving herself a kind of hug of pleasure, like a child, she went into the adjoining bedroom, to unfasten her baggage and take out some clothes. Her husband's kit also had been deposited there. She wondered whether it was expected of her to deal with at least some of this, but she was not sure that she could wrestle with the Navy's implacable methods of packing and securing what was packed; nor indeed that Captain Carew would approve such an action. For, after all, how very little she knew of him!

Nor was this remarkable, considering his lightning wooing (if wooing it could be called, since it had consisted in his practically ordering her to marry him, and that in circumstances hardly propitious to courtship), their hasty marriage on a soil native to neither of them, followed by a voyage — it could not be called a honeymoon — in a man-of-war in which, since he was the commanding officer, there were scanty opportunities for dalliance.

So, after she had laid out her own belongings, the bride, determined not to be idle, resolved to continue with some sewing begun on the voyage. Then she suddenly remembered that one day in the Bay of Biscay an unusually heavy plunge on the part of the *Callisto* had sent her thimble rolling away into some recess whence not even her special squire, Mr. Midshipman Vernon, had succeeded in recovering it. But, the rain having now ceased, the loss of this indispensable implement offered a good excuse for going out to buy another; for Charlotte had no fears about venturing unescorted into an unknown English seaport. She had had to take care of herself in an Italian one. All she needed to do was to put on her bonnet again and to ask her landlady the whereabouts of the nearest haber-dasher or milliner; and this she proceeded to do.

That excellent woman not unnaturally exhibited some surprise at so unusual and independent an action on the part of a young lady, even though a married one.

"The town's full of rough sailors, mam!" she said warningly.

"I am not afraid of English sailors," answered Charlotte with a smile. "My experience of them has always been a pleasant one!" And with Mrs. Osworthy murmuring that she hoped Mrs. Carew would not fail to be back in time for the good dinner she was preparing for three o'clock, Mrs. Carew herself sallied forth into the streets of Portsmouth to buy the thimble which coincidence was waiting for her to pluck from a finger of its proverbially long arm.

Portsmouth struck Charlotte as very different from Leghorn. It had none of the vivid colours of the Italian port, its brilliant sunlight and incessant shouts and chatter. Nevertheless the rain had been succeeded by glimpses of a softer sunshine; and if there was less conversation, there was plenty of noise. Young, unaccompanied and attractive, Charlotte did encounter appreciative glances, but they were none of them quite of the type with which she had become unpleasantly familiar in Italy, and she easily, almost unconcernedly, eluded a drunken sailor who, calling her 'Pretty Miss', suggested the bestowal of a kiss or two.

In the little shop to which she had been directed, where there was at the moment only one other customer, she found the broad Hampshire of the girl who served her difficult to understand after the cultivated English of her husband, and of her late employers in Leghorn. Yet, even while buying her thimble, she realised that the other customer, evidently a foreigner also, was in much worse difficulties than she, for this lady's English was inadequate to the demands made upon it, and she was helping herself out with French words which in their turn conveyed nothing to the puzzled owner of the shop. So Charlotte, enchanted to hear fragments of her own tongue again, went over to offer assistance.

Her compatriot, who appeared equally surprised and grateful, was a rather pretty dark-haired woman presumably in the early thirties, but thin-featured and somewhat querulous in expression. It seemed that she was trying to buy some pocket handkerchiefs for her husband, who was afflicted with a bad cold, for which 'the horribly changeable climate of this island' was to blame. And after the purchase had been carried through with Charlotte's help, the two ladies left the shop together, the elder profuse in thanks.

"Although my husband and I have been in England for some weeks now," she explained, as they stood talking outside, "and I understand the language quite well, I find it difficult to make myself understood sometimes. Indeed it comes more natural to me, if not to him, to speak German in a shop, since that is the country in which we have been exiles for the last three years."

"And I," smiled Charlotte, "had just now to check myself from speaking Italian for exactly the same reason."

"And yet you, Madame — or Mademoiselle?" protested the elder woman, "speak the English tongue so well that you have no doubt been for some time in this country! Is it permitted to guess that you are an *émigrée* like myself?"

Charlotte nodded. "At least" — she hesitated and coloured — "I do not know whether I should still call myself one ... for I am now married to an Englishman."

The other Frenchwoman's reaction to this was rather surprising. "Mon Dieu, what good fortune for you!" she said, with envy in her voice. "I have wished of late — but it is of course a vain wish — that it were possible for people like my husband and myself to become for a period English citizens — oh, only for just so long as the war lasts! But my poor Fabien does not agree with me. He says —" Here she broke off in surprise and even discomposure, as Charlotte suddenly gripped her by the arm.

"Did you say *Fabien?* ... is *that* your husband's name? ... and you were in Germany ... Where does he come from?" she demanded breathlessly.

The stranger stared at the girl's slowly paling face, while over her own there spread an unmistakable look of suspicion.

"My husband is the Vicomte Fabien d'Esparre," she replied rather haughtily. "It is hardly possible that you should know him ... Unless, indeed —" the look deepened.

As white as paper, Charlotte gasped out, "*Know him!* Fabien d'Esparre is my eldest brother, whom I have not seen since —" Then as the astonished face of her companion seemed to be dissolving beneath a haze of moving black specks, she prudently turned towards the door behind her, stumbled back over the threshold of the haberdasher's shop, and sank into a chair by the counter, while Mme d'Esparre, following her, called loudly in her own tongue for water and smelling-salts.

Charlotte d'Esparre, who was now Carew, was in fact the youngest child, and the only daughter, in the family of four who had grown up in the sunny old Provençal manoir of Esparre, near Arles. But both her parents were dead now, two of her brothers killed in the Revolutionary storm, and of that once happy group only Fabien, the eldest, and she remained. And about Fabien, who had emigrated to Germany early in the troubles and, it was believed, married there, nothing had been heard for a long while. All through her own refugee days in Italy Charlotte's hope — never fulfilled — had been to earn enough money to travel to Bonn in search of him. Soon she was to learn how last summer he and his wife had quitted Germany for Holland — not at all a happy exchange, as it turned out; and it was the alarming advance of the French Republican armies into the Netherlands which had caused their recent flight to England. Even so, nothing could have seemed more unlikely to occur than a meeting between Charlotte and her brother's wife on the very day of the former's arrival in the same country. Nevertheless, it had occurred.

Bending over Charlotte in the little shop, holding under her nose the bottle of smelling salts which the owner had hastened to produce, Mme d'Esparre mingled commentaries upon this astonishing fact with enquiries as to how the half-fainting girl was feeling. To this accompaniment was Charlotte restored to a full measure of the consciousness which she had never entirely lost; murmured her brother's name, sipped some proffered water, apologised for giving trouble, and, declaring herself completely recovered, asked this newly-found sister-in-law whether she might go to see that brother without delay.

Mme d'Esparre exhibited a certain hesitation. Her husband had so heavy a cold; he was hardly in a state to receive visitors. Later in the day perhaps . . .

"But *I* am not a visitor!" protested Charlotte. "And think, Madame, how many years it is since I have seen Fabien! I have not even known for certain that he was still alive! I implore you to allow me to come with you now!"

The plea could hardly be ignored, and so, after thanking the deeply interested shopkeeper and her assistant, they left the shop and began to walk in a northerly direction — not that Charlotte was in a state at that moment to recognise any point of the compass. At last she was to be reunited, and by the hand of Fate, not through her own efforts, to the brother of whom she had so often dreamt in the last few years. Of this new sister-in-law's talk as they went she really heard little, except when the latter suddenly exclaimed: "I have heard your Christian name, Madame many times from my husband — but, since you are now married . . . ?"

The girl came back to the present. "I am Charlotte Carew now," she said slowly. ("And hardly accustomed as yet to that fact," she might have added.)

All lodgings in Portsmouth were not, plainly, as well kept and cheerful as those of Lieutenant Ommaney's providing. The stairs up which the couple went were dingy; then Fabien's wife opened the door upon a room of moderate size, but dark and poorly furnished. At the further end was crouched over a meagre fire a man in a shabby dressing-gown. He did not turn his head at their entrance.

"Fabien," said his wife excitedly, "I have brought someone to see you! A . . . a young lady, whom you . . . whom you have met before!"

"In God's name, not *now!*" The indignant but stifled tone was in itself sufficient evidence of a bad cold. The speaker, ostrich-like, still presented nothing but his back.

Charlotte hurried forward. "But Fabien, I could not wait!" she exclaimed tremulously. "Oh, my brother — at last, at last!"

And a moment later she was sobbing in his arms.

II

"Three o'clock past, and the Captain's lady not returned, after all I said!" lamented Mrs. Osworthy. "That beautiful leg of mutton — a good thing I boiled it instead of roasting it! I hope nothing's happened to her, being a furriner."

But what brother and sister below middle-age, reunited in so remarkable a fashion after years of blank separation would give a thought to food when there was so much to tell and hear! By three o'clock Charlotte had forgotten not only the existence of the leg of mutton but even, for the nonce, Mrs. Osworthy's own. The three of them sitting round the scanty fire had for some time now been carrying on a vehement tide of narrative and — the two d'Esparres at least — of reminiscence also. These were memories which the Vicomtesse could not share, for it was in Germany that Fabien had met and married her. His own story was mostly of hardships, disappointments and *ennuis*, and indeed the lines on his face, and its expression, testified to an existence far from easy. Poor Fabien, who had once been the handsomest of her three brothers! Yes, it must be the disillusionment, and indeed — so Charlotte feared from what she heard — the actual penury of those years of exile which had given him the worried and discontented air which was even more marked in his wife. Charlotte fervently hoped that they would find better fortune in England, at Bath where, so she was told, an acquaintance had heard of a good opening for the teaching of French. They would indeed already have transferred themselves thither, had they not been delayed by Fabien's cold.

"But now," finished the victim, putting away his pocket-handkerchief, "I have great cause to bless this affliction, but for which we might never have met, my dearest Charlotte!"

24

"And if I had not lost my thimble on board the *Callisto* I should never have found out that you were in England at all, let alone in this very town! And your cold would have gone for nothing! But oh, how thankful I am that it was severe enough to delay your departure!"

Her brother pressed her hand, and, as he smiled at her, his face recovered for a moment the look it used to wear. "Now, enough of my affairs, dearest sister! It is time that we had your own story in more detail. You say that you and our poor mother, God rest her, left Esparre for Toulon just a year ago, and that she died after a short illness at Tante Ursule's house there? Then, when Toulon was abandoned by the English and Spanish that December, you fled, and eventually reached Leghorn in an English transport. But where, in that case, is Tante Ursule now?"

"In Toulon, I suppose — if she is still alive."

"She did not accompany you, then? Why not?"

A shadow came over Charlotte's face, and she looked down at the fire. "She would not consent to leave her house in Toulon, because it had been our grandparents'."

"But she surely did not allow you to make your escape alone?" And, as Charlotte was silent, her brother continued with some heat, "in that case she naturally placed you in safe hands?"

Charlotte Carew put her own hands over her face. When she dropped them the shadow was deeper still, and her voice came with a choke in it.

"Tante Ursule thought they were safe hands . . . That was why she forced me into marriage with —"

25

"Forced you into marriage!" exclaimed her brother, thunderstruck. "*Marriage!* In God's name, with whom? . . . But you are married to this English naval captain! Or are you not?" And he sprang up, dressing-gown, catarrh and all.

"Yes, indeed I am married to him," answered Charlotte firmly. "The unfortunate Creole gentleman, Monsieur de Marescot, to whom I was married at eight o'clock on the morning of that 17th of December, was dead at dusk — stabbed as we left the quay on that dreadful night by a Neapolitan soldier. He . . . Monsieur de Marescot . . . was trying to detain a boat and to help me down into it. It was on my account that he lost his life. And I . . . I had fought hard against marrying him: I hated it." The tears started down her cheeks.

For a moment the other two stared at her speechless. "Stabbed! Bon Dieu!" ejaculated Fabien d'Esparre after a pause; and sitting down again blew his nose hard, whether from emotion or a more purely physical cause was not clear.

"And after that?" enquired Mme d'Esparre eagerly.

"A boat — another boat — took me to Lord Hood's flagship, the *Victory*. There were a great many of us on board, but a great many more, I am afraid, were never able to get away from Toulon at all."

"And Tante Ursule — have you then no news of her?"

"None, though I wrote to her from Leghorn last spring. No reply had come when I was there again for my marriage to Captain Carew. It is probable that my

26

letter, which was to be carried by a naval vessel, never reached her."

"Ah yes, your marriage to this Captain Carew! We must hear about that before anything else," exclaimed Mme d'Esparre. "Where did you meet him, and how?"

"Wait a moment, Honorine," commanded her husband. "We shall come to Charlotte's second marriage in due time. Tell me first, little sister — though you are little no longer, and indeed were tall enough when last I saw you — tell me what happened to you when you reached Leghorn, before you met your present husband. Your wedding only took place last month, you said. What occurred in the interval?"

"It is true," interpolated Mme d'Esparre, "that one does not need to be told where Charlotte first met Captain Carew. It was, of course, on board this English flagship, before she ever reached Leghorn!"

"No, that is not so, Madame," corrected Charlotte soberly. "I met him first in Leghorn. When I landed at Leghorn in January," she continued, turning to her brother, "I thought that I was going straight to Germany in the company of a rich woman whom I had met on board the *Victory*, and so I was hoping to find and join you, Fabien But," she hesitated and coloured quickly and deeply, "the arrangement broke down. So I lived awhile in Leghorn with a good woman, a refugee like myself, and her son. They were kind to me, and I made a little money by helping her with her work, for she was a sempstress. But we were very poor, and so when the chance came my way of entering the family of an English merchant in Leghorn and looking after his little daughter and teaching her French, I took it. It was there that I met Captain Carew, who is a kinsman of Mr. Mounsey's."

"And it was there that he asked you to marry him!" exclaimed her sister-in-law. "A real romance. And what did the English family say?"

"Oh no, he did not ask me then." A sparkle came for the first time into Charlotte's amber eyes, and her mouth relaxed. "In fact he never asked me at all! He informed me that I was going to!"

Mme d'Esparre laughed, with a note of admiration. "I should have liked a wooing of that kind," she observed under her breath. "And still, what did the English family, his relatives, say?"

"They had no voice in the matter — luckily — for I know what Mrs. Mounsey would have said . . . what she did say, afterwards. But you see I had left Leghorn by then."

"Left Leghorn? Where did you go? But you just said that you were married in Leghorn!"

"So I was. I went back there from the island in the *Callisto*, Captain Carew's ship, and directly we arrived I was married."

"Island!" exclaimed her brother. "What island? You have told us nothing about any island!"

"Dear brother, I have not had time! I will be more explicit. Listen then! My employment in Leghorn came to an unpleasant end in July, because Mrs. Mounsey accused me of stealing a necklace of hers. (No, you had better not jump up again, Fabien, or you will upset that *tisane!* I learnt on my return that

28

the real culprit, my pupil. had confessed.) But when Mrs. Mounsey turned me out of her house the saints sent to my aid — Tell me, Fabien, had you ever heard our father mention a comrade of his in his soldiering days — a certain Baron Henri de Dieuzie?"

Muttering something about a damned English-woman the Vicomte d'Esparre shook his head.

"Well, when we met — I will tell you how another time — he recognised my name, and took me as his guest to the island of Farfalletta, off Corsica, of which he was governor. After the English had captured Calvi, and Corsica was theirs, the *Callisto* appeared one day off Farfalletta —"

Here Honorine d'Esparre almost clapped her hands as one applauding at a play; but her husband remarked dryly, "The vessel had not, I imagine, gone there on Charlotte's account."

"No, indeed," agreed his sister, "though unfortunately Monsieur de Dieuzie thought — or pretended to think — that she had! She had actually been sent by the English admiral to destroy the old fortifications of the island. And it was in the midst of this noisy business that Captain Carew announced that I was to marry him. And so, when we got to Leghorn, I did! For when you meet him — and I may bring him here, may I not, when Fabien had recovered from his cold? — you will see that he — in short, that one *does* obey him!" But her smile was not the smile of one really living under a tyranny.

"Dear sister!" said Fabien affectionately, bending forward and kissing her. "May you both be very happy!"

"I trust that Captain Carew is a Catholic?" observed Mme d'Esparre suddenly.

Charlotte shook her head. "He belongs to the Church of this country. His father is what, I think, one calls a parson — a priest of it."

No longer was Honorine d'Esparre the appreciative audience of a romance. "A heretic — and the son of a heretic minister!" she exclaimed in a horrified tone. "How could you —" But here her husband's frown checked her. "Then who married you, may I ask?"

Charlotte, a good Catholic herself, decided to be amused rather than indignant. This wife of Fabien's is evidently *fort dévote*, she reflected, and thereupon replied mischievously, "Mr. Udney, the kind English consul at Leghorn."

"The consul! The *consul* married you! But then, in the eyes of the Church, you are not married at all!" exclaimed the Vicomtesse, and she pushed back her chair a trifle as one withdrawing from contamination.

"Charlotte was brought up as good a Catholic as you, Honorine," said her husband reprovingly. "I cannot think that, whatever her husband's views, she was content with a mere civil marriage."

"Naturally I was not," replied his sister sedately. "And Captain Carew understood my scruples and respected them. We were married later in the same day in a Catholic church. I assure you, ma belle-sœur, that I am not without the Church's blessing!"

30

But even as she spoke Charlotte could see again the disfavour with which her husband had regarded the slovenly and unshorn Italian priest who had bestowed it — disfavour which she could hardly resent because she shared it.

"You do indeed relieve me," said Mme d'Esparre gravely. "And your brother too, I know. And now," she added in the tone of one turning to more secular matters, "if you will excuse me, I will complete my preparations for dinner — for we have no servant."

"Dinner!" cried Charlotte. "I had forgotten there was such a thing as eating! And speaking of a meal, my landlady bade me be back by three o'clock. What time is it now, Fabien?"

Her brother pulled out a shabby silver watch. "Nearly half-past. But in any case you will stay and share our meal."

For a moment Charlotte thought of accepting, but only for a moment. She had surprised on Honorine's face the look which, being of the same sex, she could easily interpret as meaning, 'If she does, there will not be enough to go round'. And the correctness of her mind-reading was shown when Fabien too, seeming to recollect himself, asked his wife with a tinge of uneasiness: "Is Monsieur Guillemin dining with us to-day, Honorine?"

"Yes, he is," answered she, the expression still more evident. "Indeed I think I hear him coming up the stairs now. I must fly!" And without giving Charlotte time to intimate that she would not stay to share the repast, nor opportunity to take farewell of her, she left the room, addressing as she did so a few words to some person outside.

"I will say good-bye for the present then, dear brother," said Charlotte affectionately as she rose. "No, indeed I must go. My landlady may be anxious about me as well as about her gigot. But soon, very soon, I shall come to visit you again. May I bring my husband, when he is sufficiently at leisure, to pay his respects to your wife?"

"But certainly. He will be welcome, and you, my dearest Charlotte, more than welcome." And he kissed her warmly. "Oh, pray come in, Monsieur Guillemin; we are expecting you."

Charlotte, turning, saw on the threshold a little, neatly dressed man wearing a cheerful expression, and carrying under his arm what seemed to be an unframed picture. He hesitated a moment.

"Am I not intruding, Vicomte?"

"Not in the least, I assure you. Come and let me present you to my dear and only sister, whom Fate has just restored to me in the most unexpected manner. Charlotte, this is our friend and fellow-traveller from Holland, Monsieur Guillemin."

Laying down the canvas upon a chair, the newcomer advanced briskly and kissed Charlotte's hand. "May I be permitted to offer my congratulations, Mademoiselle, upon so fortunate a reunion?"

Charlotte thanked him a little shyly, while Fabien explained that she was not Mademoiselle any longer, but Madame — or rather 'Mrs.' "For she is married, as I have but just learnt, to an Englishman. She is the wife of Captain Carew, who commands that fine frigate, just returned from the Mediterranean, upon which you were commenting this morning, Monsieur."

"Indeed!" returned M. Guillemin; and his already bright eyes seemed to gain an extra sparkle. "Perhaps then you could persuade Madame votre sœur to procure for me the permission of Monsieur le Capitaine Carew to make a painting of his ship. In this manner." And he picked up again and showed a brig in full sail on a blue, white-flecked sea.

"Monsieur Guillemin is a marine painter of much skill, as you can see, my dear Charlotte," explained her brother. "And already he has sold quite a number of his pictures here in Portsmouth. Do you think your husband could be induced to allow him to exercise his art upon his frigate?"

"One must live, you know, Mrs. Carew," said the little painter apologetically. "We exiles have very lean purses. If your good heart should incline you to ask your husband . . . ?"

Charlottle could not help smiling at him; he was like a hopeful robin. "I will certainly speak to him on your behalf, Monsieur."

"In that case," returned M. Guillemin with a gallant little bow, "I shall regard the permission as granted! You are kindness itself, Madame . . . May I ask the frigate's name?"

"She is called the *Callisto*. But I must warn you, Monsieur, that she is just about to be — I do not know the French for the expression — 'paid off'. Nor do I know what happens to her then."

"I should make but a quick study, Madame, if time is short. Afterwards I could work it up at leisure. I am afraid that we painters do not always complete our canvases on the spot. A harmless deception, I hope?" And with another bow he opened the door for her.

CHAPTER
THREE

When Charlotte returned, excited and apologetic, to Mrs. Osworthy's dwelling, she was admitted by the good lady in a fluster, caused not only by the spoiling (so she feared) of the leg of mutton, but far more by the arrival, about half an hour earlier, of Captain Carew himself, "expecting to dine with you, Madam, and now up there walking about and wondering where you was got to, me having no notion, except that you was gone to buy a thimble at Mrs. Shillitoe's. So with your permission I'll dish up straight away, for I am sure the Captain must be wanting his dinner, not to speak of you, Ma'am."

Indeed Mrs. Osworthy's attitude towards this august guest had a strong flavour of the probable reaction of the patriarch Abraham in like circumstances — that is, if upon the Angel of the Lord turning up unannounced at the door of his tent, some domestic hitch had delayed the choice repast befitting so exalted a visitant. And indeed 'walking up and down' held an ominous suggestion of an angry lion deprived both of meal and mate. Charlotte gave a sound of dismay and hurried up the stairs.

35

"Oh, mon cher Nu-gent, I am so sorry to be late . . . and so pleased to see you! But I did not expect you until this evening"

The tall, lean man in naval uniform on the other side of the table laid for dinner put down the telescope which he seemed to have been examining, and said succinctly:

"Evidently not, Mrs. Gadabout!"

Nature or the Navy, or both, had set Nugent Carew's face in lines that were undeniably stern; but if — which is doubtful — he had been trying to make his words sound sardonic, he did not succeed, because of the twinkle in his eye. The lion did not *sound* very angry, and anyhow his mate, if not his meat, had now arrived.

"It is impossible to be more penitent than I am!" declared Charlotte coming round the table to him, and taking off her bonnet as she did so. "But when you hear the reason for my unpunctuality, Nugent, you will forgive me at once. Indeed I am so sure of this that I think you may forgive me even before you hear it!" And she held up an animated face for the seal of this pardon.

"You are taking a great deal for granted, Madame!" retorted her husband. "You ought to be lectured first. Portsmouth is hardly the place for unescorted young ladies to be abroad in. However, I suppose I must pass it over." And he put a kiss upon the proffered cheek, adding, "I might not be so compliant if I did not know that you are no bread-and-butter Miss."

" 'Bread-and-butter Miss?' " repeated his wife slowly.

"What is that? Yes, I think I can guess what it means." Her smile grew teasing. "And in your heart you regret that I am not one, *monsieur le capitaine de vaisseau?* It is true, to be a suitable wife for a gallant English sailor I ought to faint at the sight of a spider, so that he can protect me!"

"I don't like spiders very much myself," admitted the gallant English sailor, with an unexpectedly boyish grin. "And I hardly think, my girl, that you are likely to achieve a swoon over any insect, considering how cool and collected you were, upon the whole, when we blew up the defences at Farfalletta!"

Charlotte's expression became demure. "But you see, Nu-gent, *you* were there! . . . And it was just after the great explosion that you gave me what I think you call in your profession "sailing orders'. So I *was* under protection — with the prospect of more to come!"

Her husband caught hold of her. "I will teach you to make fun of —" he was beginning, when a knock at the door heralded the arrival of the martyred leg of mutton. Charlotte too slipped from his hold and went into the bedroom to take off her walking pelisse and to smooth her hair, while through the open door floated the apologies of Mrs. Osworthy, and her husband's voice begging her not to distress herself for what was in no way her fault.

Making no comment upon its condition, Captain Carew dealt with the joint, Mrs. Osworthy handed round the vegetables and withdrew; and the meal had got well under way before he observed:

"And now, truant, you can tell me *what* you were doing when my back was turned. Something, evidently which has put you into good spirits. Why did you go out?"

"Did not Mrs. Osworthy tell you? To buy a thimble."

Captain Carew narrowed his eyes. "Was that all? It took the deuce of a long time to buy, then!"

"It was all I bought, I assure you. But in the shop . . ." She laid down her knife and fork. "Oh, Nugent, I hardly know how to tell you!"

"No need to tell me. In the shop was an expensive hat or bonnet which you want me to buy you, although you are not sure that I shall like it!"

Charlotte broke into delighted laughter. The captain of the *Callisto*, until so recently a mere bachelor, was trying to assume what he took to be the proper attitude of a married man towards a wife's purchases.

"Mon ami, you could not be further from the truth! It is no question of headgear. What I found in the shop where I bought my thimble led me to . . . to a man whom I have known for many years, whom I love deeply, and with whom, but for this" — she lifted her hand with its wedding ring — "I might be setting off to Bath in a few days' time!"

She had at least succeeded in making her husband lay down his own knife and fork. But she did not think that she had really deceived him, for he observed after a moment:

"I am glad to think that you had scruples about eloping with this old flame of yours, especially as you knew that I should be too much occupied to come after you. They do you honour."

"Besides, he had a bad cold," murmured Charlotte reflectively.

"I own I am relieved to hear that. It must have diminished his attractions. But if this former admirer of yours was not personally in the shop how did you come across him?"

"His wife took me to him."

This time there was no doubt that she had startled him.

"His wife! His *wife!* Confess now, Charlotte, that are you inventing this tale!"

"But no, not a word of it! It is all true. His wife is — my sister-in-law. Oh, mon mari, listen! I have found my brother Fabien, of whom I have spoken to you — the only brother I have left now. He is here in Portsmouth, not long arrived from Holland. It was by the veriest chance that I met his wife. Forgive me for trying to mystify you . . . but I hardly know what I am saying; this coming upon Fabien after so long is such a miracle!" And, her eyes suddenly overflowing, she hastily pulled out her pocket-handkerchief.

Nugent Carew got up at once and stooped over her. "My dearest Charlotte," he said very kindly, "don't cry, I beg of you! It is indeed a wonderful and happy coincidence. I must make your brother's acquaintance as soon as possible. Now go on with your dinner like a good girl. Even if the mutton is overcooked, don't let it it get cold into the bargain!"

Over the apple tart, reasonably restored to composure, she told her husband what she had learnt of her brother's existence in exile and how he and his wife had contrived to find their way to England.

"And by the way," she said at this point, "I met in Fabien's lodging a fellow traveller of his, a Monsieur Guillemin, who is trying to make a living by painting pictures of ships. When he heard that you commanded the *Callisto*, which he seems already to have seen and admired, he asked me if I could obtain your permission for him to make a sketch of her."

Captain Carew gave the request a moment's consideration. "I do not know," he said, "that there would be any objection to that, provided that he does not get in the way. But I wonder if he knows enough to draw a frigate correctly? Otherwise he will not be able to sell his picture — or any others of the kind — in a place like Portsmouth."

"But he has already sold some, I think. And I saw one that he had with him, of a ship with two masts. The sea was very well painted, I thought. But not being familiar with ships —"

"No, of course not, my dear. Why should you know a schooner from a brig? Well, tell this marine painter, or let your brother tell him, that he may immortalise the *Callisto* if he wishes to."

"Oh, thank you!" exclaimed Charlotte gratefully. "That will indeed be good news for the poor little man. It is often hard, you know, Nu-gent, for my unfortunate fellow-countrymen to make a living. My brother and his wife have, I fear, sometimes been in difficulties

40

themselves, therefore this opportunity of earning their livelihood — or so they hope — in Bath is very welcome."

"Monsieur d'Esparre is going to teach French in a school there, I think you said?"

"In more than one, he hopes. He hears that there are good openings."

"He and his wife must soon pay my parents a visit at the Rectory. Bath is only in the next county."

"You are too good, Nu-gent. But no," returned Charlotte shaking her head wisely and a little sadly, "it will be enough of strange for them to receive one French person. Not for a long time must Fabien and his wife visit your home."

"It is time, Mrs. Carew," said her husband with mock solemnity, "that you realised you are no longer 'a French person'. But I suppose that fact still seems to you 'enough of strange', as you put it. Perhaps — independent young woman that you are — you are already regretting it?"

There naturally followed upon this speech a brief interlude in which the suggestion was satisfactorily rebutted.

Two days later, on a fine, breezy morning, when the English weather was exhibiting its good qualities to a young lady who had recently been informed that she was English herself, Charlotte was conducting her husband to call upon her brother and his wife. She herself, not unnaturally, had spent most of the previous day in their company. Now, as Captain Nugent Carew had a few hours at his disposal, and M. d'Esparre's cold, judging from its improved condition yesterday, would permit of his receiving a visitor, she was about to bring together the two men she loved best.

Radiantly happy, the sun gilding the bronze-gold curls which peeped from her bonnet, her arm through her husband's, she was chattering gaily as they walked from their own very respectable and sedate street towards the less estimable quarter of Portsmouth where Fabien lodged. Anecdotes of her own childhood days, of Fabien's achievements — those indeed of a brother some fifteen years older than herself — flowed from her so rapidly that at last she checked herself.

"You should reprove me, my dear husband! I am talking too much, when I should be practising a more reserved deportment, as I am sure the English ladies do!"

Smiling down upon her, Nugent replied: "No, no — you do not need to copy other females! Indeed I love to hear you prattle; so continue!"

" 'Prattle'! Another strange word! I suppose it means — but we are nearly at my brother's lodgings. That is the house — the fourth, no the fifth. Oh!" She gave an exclamation of surprise. "There is the little painter coming out! I did not see him yesterday, and I forgot all about him and his request. Cannot we stop him?" And without waiting for assent she raised her voice a little. "Monsieur Guillemin, Monsieur Guillemin!"

And Nugent saw the small middle-aged man who, carrying some kind of a satchel under his arm, had just descended the steps of the house indicated, pause and turn his head. Next moment he had snatched off his hat and was hastening towards them.

"Madame Carew, what a pleasure to see you again!" he exclaimed in a gratified voice. "And this gentleman is perhaps . . ." He paused interrogatively, his head on one side, nore like a robin than ever, thought Charlotte — a rather shabby robin, yet somehow a neat one.

"Yes, I am Captain Carew, Monsieur." Nugent's deep voice contrasted noticeably with the painter's lighter tones. "I understand that you wish permission to make a sketch of His Majesty's ship *Callisto*?"

"If it were possible for you to give it, *monsieur le capitaine*," replied M. Guillemin, using his own native tongue (as Nugent had done). "Even an inadequate presentment of so beautiful a vessel would find sale here, I think . . . if you would allow me to exercise my art, such as it is, upon her."

"My wife has already approached me on the point" (here M. Guillemin beamed gratefully upon Charlotte). "I cannot see," said Nugent Carew, "that there is any objection, provided that you do not — to put it bluntly — get in the way of any work that is being carried on."

With a shocked air the robin deprecated the slightest intention of causing inconvenience of any kind. "I should be most careful on that score, *monsieur le capitaine*. And I am more grateful than I can say! To you also, Madame!"

"Very well, then that is settled," said Nugent, who had meanwhile been studying him carefully. "You can begin operations as soon as you please. Good morning to you!" And he prepared to walk on.

"But, sir," put in the Frenchman apologetically, "if you will pardon me for troubling you further, would it not be better for me to be furnished with something in writing? Just an informal permit or pass with your signature? Otherwise, if I have no authorisation to produce, I might well be stopped, particularly if you were not at hand to answer for me if required. I regret infinitely —"

"Yes, you are quite right," returned Nugent, slightly annoyed with himself for having overlooked this contingency. Producing his pocketbook he scribbled a few words, detached the page and handed it to the artist. M. Guillemin received it with renewed expressions of gratitude, stowed it carefully away, took a courteous farewell of the couple, and trotted away.

"Your painter seems an industrious little fellow," remarked Nugent as he and Charlotte stood together on the door-step which M. Guillemin had just quitted. "I wonder if he can really do justice to the *Callisto's* lines?"

Then they were admitted, and a few moments later Captain Nugent Carew and the Vicomte Fabien d'Esparre had made each other's acquaintance.

The last evening in the Portsmouth lodgings had arrived, and Charlotte was packing for the morrow's journey to Devonshire, being even entrusted with the bestowal of some of her husband's belongings. To-morrow, when she would set out to meet his parents, to see for the first time his home and the surroundings in which he had grown up — to-morrow, not the day of her arrival here in Portsmouth, was the real opening to her new life — hers and Nugent's. And with one of her slippers in her hand she knelt there, thinking about it.

"A penny for your thoughts!" said Nugent's voice, suddenly — and there he was, standing in the doorway, looking at her.

She dropped the slipper, rose and went to him. "I was thinking of to-morrow and all the to-morrows to follow it. Nugent, they will be happy, will they not? Not all of them, perhaps — that would be too much to ask — but most of them?"

He put his hands on her shoulders and looked down at her, and she returned his gaze with one as straightforward and hopeful.

"Please God, they will!" he said in a tone which left no doubt of his own conviction about the future, and he put a kiss on her forehead.

After this salute Charlotte went on more lightly: "Now that I have been so honest, and have really earned my penny, I will offer you one. What was in your mind an hour ago when you were sitting thinking, with this kind of expression on your face." She wrinkled up her own in an attempt to imitate it.

"Was I really looking so morose?" asked her husband, laughing. "I did not know it. But the penny — I will pay you yours presently — can properly be offered only for a person's thoughts at the moment, not for those in the past."

And even if he had been offered that inducement at the appropriate time he would certainly not have

accepted it, for, like not a few married men in the
history of the world, he had, at the moment referred to,
been thinking how much more attractive his wife was
than her relations. Not that he had disliked the Vicomte
d'Esparre, but he was not greatly drawn to him, and
very little indeed to his spouse. However he felt that it
was probably their years of poverty and exile which had
generated much of the seediness and generally
discontented attitude still more evident when the
couple had supped and spent the evening with them
yesterday. But he had consoled himself (again like many
another Benedick) by the reflection that, after all, he
had not married his wife's family. Indeed, save for a
remarkable coincidence, their presence in England
would have remained unknown both to Charlotte and
himself.

In reply to his refusal to qualify for her penny,
Charlotte now made a little grimace at him on her own
account. "I believe you were thinking what a sad
mistake you had made at Farfalletta when you told me
that I was to marry you! You were realising as you sat
there how much better it would have been if you had
behaved less *en Grand Turque*! Well, it is too late now!"
She went back and picked up her slipper. "It was
already too late on board the *Callisto* . . . .Dear *Callisto*!
I was sorry to take farewell of her this afternoon. — By
the way, I saw no sign of Monsieur Guillemin anywhere
near her, though my sister-in-law told us last night that
he was progressing well with his sketch."

"I had seen him earlier in the day," said her husband.
"I even went and had a look at his picture; it was not at

all bad. And now, my dear Charlotte, since you are to be a lifelong burden to me, I must try to lighten it by instilling into you *my* notion of how one should pack . . . as distinct from a lady's."

CHAPTER
FOUR

I

"How I wonder what she will be like!" It was by no means the first time that Mrs. Carew had thus speculated.

"As to her outward appearance, my dear Elizabeth," reiterated the Rector, "I can make a good guess. Rather under the middle height, with dark hair and eyes, and that vivacious manner natural to the French. And pretty, I suppose."

"Yes, in a French way, perhaps," qualified his wife.

The passage of more than a fortnight had done a little, not indeed to reconcile, but at least to accustom Mr. and Mrs. Carew to the idea of a foreign daughter-in-law. And now, as the autumn day drew towards its close, her actual arrival was at hand.

When the news had gone round Damarel St. Mary that Captain Carew was bringing home a bride, the enthusiastic villagers were for organising a triumphal reception. The Rector, however, had tried to quash this project, which he knew would not meet with his son's approval, by pointing out that, the bride in question being French — for this staggering fact must come out sooner or later, and in fact he discovered that scarcely a member of his flock but appeared to know it already —

would find such a ceremony strange and perhaps embarrassing. None the less George Cripps, his old gardener, had informed him this morning that there was a gurt big arch of green stuff a-putting up by the 'Clavering Arms', which was apparently to bear a painted legend in red, white and blue reading, 'God Bless the Captain and his Lady'.

But as dusk began to settle, and the chaise had not yet arrived, it seemed probable that the full splendour of this erection would not be visible to the bridal pair. The Rector had gone once or twice to the hall door to listen for the sound of wheels, but had each time returned unsatisfied to his wife's side in the big parlour, where a splendid fire awaited the travellers. Nevertheless there was a sentry upon the threshold — small Peggy, who had begged to be allowed to remain there on outpost duty; and was permitted so to remain, clutching her doll, her eyes shining with excitement, her ears strained to catch the cheering which was likely to be heard from the village. (Privately, however, she was just a little uneasy at an idea which had only recently occurred to her: would this new relation wish, or be expected, to give her lessons in French?)

Ah, what was that? A kind of roar punctuated by shriller noises was borne Rectory-wards on the windless dusk. One or two seconds to make sure, and Peggy scampered back to the parlour.

"They're here, Papa . . . they're here . . . they're coming through the village!"

Peregrine Carew and his wife gave each other a long look. Then he held out his hand to her, and so, preceded by the child, and a little, at that moment, like elderly children themselves, they went out to the threshold of their home to greet the — no, not 'the intruder', it was wrong to think of her as that — but their son's chosen wife.

They had not long to wait. The distant cheering had not quite died away when round the laurels of the sweep came the hired postchaise which contained the pair. Its lamps were already lit, but they served rather to emphasise the slight mist in the air than to give light, and the whole shape of the vehicle was quite plainly to be seen. The postillion checked the horses just beyond the door, and was quickly off his own, but not before Nugent himself, whose face had been visible for a moment at the nearer window, had jumped out to let down the step before offering his hand to assist his fellow-traveller out. (In former days, thought his mother with a pang which she tried to stifle, the moment his feet had touched the ground he would have hastened to take *her* in his arms, had she been — as she usually was — on the door-step to greet him.)

Instead, and all too soon, he was leading up the shallow steps a girl in a green pelisse and bonnet, trimmed with brown fur, a girl who was neither small nor dark, but rather tall and of a warm fairness, and, at that trying moment, surprisingly full of diffidence. There could be no doubt of that. It spoke in those amber eyes of hers, and in her whole bearing. So one at least of Mrs. Carew's fears — that of 'French assurance' — was removed.

"Father — Mother — here is Charlotte!" said their son's deep voice. And for all the pride and pleasure which rang in it, there was also a note of deprecation, almost of pleading, very rarely heard there.

Smiling a little, and colouring, 'Charlotte' dropped a curtsey. Mrs. Carew looked at them both and her eyes suddenly filled. "My dear!" she murmured, and had opened her arms to this unknown foreign bride even before she had embraced the son who had brought her there.

Quite soon they were all in the parlour, and Mr. Carew (whose guess as to her personal appearance had proved so remarkably incorrect) was urging his daughter-in-law to approach the fire, while Peggy, clinging to her brother's hand, stared up at her with parted lips.

"I am quite warm, thank you, sir," said Charlotte in her excellent English. Her smile and voice are alike sweet, thought the Rector; and what attractive eyes — almost auburn, like her hair!

"But she has a slight cold nevertheless," supplemented her husband. "She caught it just before leaving Portsmouth."

"Then she had better go to bed without delay," said his mother promptly. "In any case she must be tired after her journey. Come with me, my dear. I will have a meal sent up to you, and before you go to sleep you must take a treacle posset. Would not that be the best treatment, Nugent?"

"Much the best," returned Nugent decidedly, concealing his surprise that his mother should seek his

51

approval of any régime. It had never happened to him before. "I was in fact going to suggest it myself — if it was not inconvenient to you."

"It is, I am sure not, in the least inconvenient," said his father. "But it is regrettable, in that it deprives us of Charlotte's company this evening. — Good night then, my dear . . . daughter."

So the new daughter was swept away, and he and his son were left face to face. But not alone, for small Peggy was still holding fast to her brother. And as the door shut Nugent answered the pull on his sleeve by stooping and receiving a whispered confidence.

"What's that, Peg? You think Charlotte is pretty? Of course she is!" He caught her up with a laugh. "Do you think I should have brought you a new sister who wasn't?"

"But she is not my sister," objected Peggy, puzzled. "Not like Sophy."

"Well, no, not quite in the same way. She is your sister-in-law. But I think you will soon forget the 'in-law' part . . . As I think — I hope — that *you* will, sir," he added in a more serious tone, looking across at his father.

But the presence of a child, when, as in the first moments of a brother's return after a considerable absence, the child cannot be banished from the room — at least not under the kindly discipline prevailing at Damarel St. Mary Rectory — may prove hampering when there are matters to be discussed not suitable for childish ears. Because his little sister was there, Nugent Carew could not immediately express to his father the hope that his parents had forgiven him the shock which his letter must have caused them; and conversation turned to minor matters, from which Peggy was not excluded.

Meanwhile, up in the big candle-lit bedroom Mrs. Carew was poking the fire into a still brighter blaze.

"I am afraid, my dear, that your cold is due to our English climate. You must find it a great contrast to that of the Mediterranean. I hope that you will not feel this room chilly? The bed, I can assure you, has been thoroughly warmed. You will do best, will you not, to get into it immediately, and have your dinner there?"

(What an untold blessing, she said to herself, that the young woman seems to understand and speak English!) "Now, have you all you need? If not, ring the bell, and ask Betsy for it."

"You are too kind, too kind indeed!" said the 'young woman' gratefully. Now that her bonnet had been laid aside, Mrs. Carew could see her features better — and, still more important, her expression. ('She has a *good* face,' she told herself, 'I do not believe that she "caught" Nugent!')

"I am ashamed to give you this trouble, Madame," went on Charlotte. "I am sure that I have everything that I need. And," she added a little diffidently, "pray do not let me keep you a moment longer from your son, whom you have not seen for so long a time."

"Very well, my dear," replied Mrs. Carew, not ill-pleased at this consideration. "If you will promise to go to bed at once I will take you at your word. Betsy can help you if you desire it."

At the door she turned again. "I hope with all my heart that you will be happy with us, Charlotte!" A certain wistfulness tempered her usually brisk tones as she continued: "There is, you know, a place all ready for you here if you care to fill it. Mr. Carew and I miss our elder daughter very much."

The constraint of which both Mr. Carew and his son were aware had not been dissipated when Mrs. Carew returned to the parlour, where the situation still remained undiscussed. Still less could it be discussed at dinner — postponed from its wonted time of three o'clock until this twilight hour — for, in addition to the specially permitted presence of Peggy, there was also the intermittent one of Betsy, the maidservant.

But much could be asked and told about Nugent's naval experiences during the past eighteen months. Had not the *Callisto* played her full part in the capture of Corsica in the summer? Had not the Navy under Lord Hood and Captain Nelson — Nugent's immediate superior — in particular been mainly instrumental in bringing about the fall of Bastia and of Calvi? As a naval officer Captain Carew was bound to think so — and not, indeed, without reason.

"And in all this bombarding you were never injured, Nugent?" asked his mother at one point. "It is true that you never mentioned such a thing in your letters — but then you might purposely have refrained from doing so."

"I never received a scratch. I was luckier than Captain Nelson, poor fellow, who lost the sight of an eye at Calvi. The only misfortune which happened to me was a short bout of sunstroke, but it soon passed off."

Peggy laid down her spoon.

"What is —"

"It is what happens to people who go about on a hot day without hats," explained her father.

"As you have more than once been forbidden to do," completed Mrs. Carew.

"Then why did Nugent —"

"Get on with your pudding, child! It is time you were in bed."

II

"And now, my dear boy, sit down and tell us all about Charlotte, how you met her and so on," said the Rector, subsiding into a chair by the parlour fire. Mrs. Carew was already installed on the other side of the hearth. "Pull up that chair for yourself; I think it has grown chillier in the last hour."

His son obeyed, as far as fetching a third chair was concerned. But he delayed seating himself. "I should like first of all to say to both of you, my dear father and mother, how exceedingly sorry I was to inflict the news of my marriage upon you without any preparation. It was a necessity which I deeply regretted, and still regret, but which I could not avoid. Naturally I should have liked to give you more warning. I should have wished even more that you could have married us, sir."

"Oh, then Charlotte is not a Roman Catholic?" asked his mother with relief in her voice.

"Unfortunately she is. It was in deference to her beliefs that I went through the ceremony again in a church of her own faith. That was after the consul had married us in his office. There was no English chaplain in Leghorn at the time."

"You were married over again — and by an Italian priest!"

"But Charlotte would not have felt that she was married at all, it appeared, without the rites of her own church. It did me no harm, my dear mother," said Nugent with a smile. "And while we are upon this question of religion, sir" — he turned to his father, "I hope it can be arranged for Charlotte to go when she feels it necessary to the Shirleys' private chapel at Monks Damarel? We have discussed that already. She would not be happy cut off from the exercise of her religion, nor, fortunately, need she be, as long as she remains here — that is, if you give your consent to this plan?"

"I have no valid reason for refusing it," said the Rector, "and I will write immediately to Mr. Shirley about it." For he was on good terms with this old Roman Catholic family of the neighbourhood. "There will, I am sure, be no objection on their part."

"No, indeed," said his wife with some tartness. "I only hope that they will not expect Nugent to accompany Charlotte to service there!"

"Such an idea, I am positive, would never enter their heads, Elizabeth!"

"With Papists one never knows . . . So Charlotte will never wish to come to church with us, not even on

Christmas Day? She will never hear your father preach!"

Nugent leant across and took her hand. "I beg of you, my dear mother, not to distress yourself unnecessarily. We may not be able to attend the same church, but Charlotte and I firmly intend never to let the difference in our creeds come between us — any more than our difference in nationality."

"Quite right, quite right, my dear boy," said the Rector emphatically. "And as you know, or ought to know, in my view there is little real disparity between those creeds, since, like good Bishop Ken, I firmly believe the Church of England to be as much part of the Catholic Church as the Roman."

"But I very much doubt if Charlotte does!" commented Mrs. Carew dryly. "However, we must hope that as little scandal as possible will be caused in the village when an inmate of the Rectory is known to attend a Popish place of worship." And then, seeing her son redden slightly, she in turn leant over and patted his hand. "Forgive me, Nugent! That sounds unkind, I know, but we must look facts in the face. If it will make amends, let me say that there are two things about Charlotte which already please me much — that she speaks and understands English so well, and that her name is as English as Peggy's or Sophia's. She might have been called something outlandish like Célimène or Lucindde."

The Rector, with a twinkle, observed that Charlotte was a French name as well, and Nugent, smiling too, to show that he had forgiven the downrightness of his mother's previous remark, observed: "You must remember that your daughter-in-law comes from a quiet country home near Arles in Provence, and not out of a play by Racine or Molière."

Mr. Carew seized upon this topographical detail. "Arles? Ah, that perhaps accounts for the suggestion of the classical in her face! Arles, you know, was an important Greek colony, and I have read that something of ancient Grecian beauty has always survived among its women. The statement," he said, looking kindly at his son, "seems to me well-founded."

"Thank you, sir," said Nugent, returning the look. "You have a quick eye!"

"I certainly expected someone much more French in appearance," observed his mother. "But your Charlotte might almost be an English girl."

"She might — until she opens her mouth," qualified her husband. "But her manner of pronouncing English is not, I think, disagreeable. In fact I like it!"

"I suppose," said the Rector, "it was at the Mounseys' that she acquired her knowledge of the language? But tell us, Nugent — how did she reach Leghorn from Toulon — and why was she in Toulon at all if her home was at Arles?"

"Because she and her mother had to flee from Arles and took refuge in Toulon with an aunt, in whose house her mother died shortly afterwards. Then, as you know, the Allies had to evacuate the town, taking off as many of the Royalists as was possible. Charlotte fortunately was among these, and after a brief period in Lord Hood's flagship, the *Victory,* was landed from a transport at Leghorn, alone and almost penniless. As you know," added Nugent parenthetically, "the *Callisto* took no part in these operations; we were never near Toulon."

"Poor girl! But the aunt, what happened to her?"

"She elected to remain in Toulon — would not leave her house, I understand. Charlotte tried to communicate with her from Leghorn last spring, but without success — that is to say, she never received any letter in reply."

"And has she no other family — no relatives of any kind?"

"Her father died about three years ago and two of her brothers were killed fighting for the monarchy, one, I think, in the sack of the Tuileries. But the only remaining brother, the eldest — well here is the most extraordinary coincidence! She met him, neither knowing that the other was in England, the very day the *Callisto* reached Portsmouth!"

And the Rector and his wife found themselves hearing, with the amazement proper to its reception, the tale of this fortuitous but lucky encounter.

"And this brother and sister-in-law, do they intend to settle in Portsmouth?"

"No, they have just set out for Bath, where Monsieur d'Esparre hopes to get an engagement to teach French, for, like so many of these impoverished refugees, he must turn his hand to anything for a living. He had previously done something of the sort, I understand, in Germany."

"D'Esparre? Was that Charlotte's family name?" put in Mrs. Carew? "Do you know that you never mentioned it in your letter — not that the omission matters."

Her son looked slightly taken aback. "Did I omit it? Yes, d'Esparre was Charlotte's maiden name, and also the name of the place she came from."

"Well now," said his father, "go back, if you will, to Charlotte's landing at Leghorn, and tell us how you first met her, and when you decided to make her your wife. It all happened, I presume, at Edward Mounsey's villa there, where, as you told us, she was in charge of his little daughter."

But Nugent shook his head. "Far from it! I had my first sight of Charlotte in the public gardens at Leghorn, where the odious child had given her the slip, purely in order to cause her trouble. In running after the little wretch the poor girl had slipped and cut her hands on the gravel. I escorted her back to the Mounseys, where I contrived to see her once again. Otherwise my next sight of her — to my great surprise, I admit — was on the island of Farfalletta, to which, as I wrote to you at the time from Calvi, I was sent in order to demolish the old fortifications. I expect you will say, What on earth was Charlotte doing there! She had found refuge with the Governor, an old friend of her father's. Some day she will tell you all about it."

(When that day came, his parents would learn, what Nugent would never have told them, the personal risk he had run to rescue her from her room at the fort, in which she had got shut up, at the very time of the blowing up of its defences.)

"Poor girl! Poor child!" murmured Mr. Carew. "She shall not want for any care or affection from us, if you leave her here for a while, as I suppose you will be constrained to do."

"— For as long as you please," supplemented his mother. And, always outspoken, she added: "From the very little I have seen of your wife, I think we may get on well together. In time I believe that I shall be able to say, with thankfulness, that you have made a good — if an unexpected — choice."

"You are both very kind," said Nugent Carew a trifle hoarsely. "I know that I have sprung a shock upon you. But I would stake my life on it that you have gained as good a daughter-in-law as any you could have found in England — not excluding" (and here he smiled) "the elder Miss Clavering, whom I have sometimes suspected you of wishing to select for the position."

III

"Cossetting! That is what you are enjoying — though I doubt if you are acquainted with the word!" exclaimed Nugent Carew about eleven o'clock the next morning, looking down at his bride, still ensconced among her pillows. "Cossetting such as my sister Sophia was seldom privileged to receive — and all because you sneezed a few times in the coach yesterday!"

"And had, I am sure, a very red nose when I arrived," completed Charlotte. "Alas, I am sure that I

61

have it still!" She touched the organ in question, as though to ascertain its hue. "But how kind to me is Mrs. Carew! — What is that letter which you have in your hand, my husband?"

"A very tiresome, and yet a welcome one," responded he. "Listen, my dear girl. I am sorry to say that I shall have to leave you this afternoon, and go to London. But I shall be away only for a very few days, and when I return I shall hope to find you have quite got rid of your brother's legacy; for I cannot help thinking that you caught this cold from him."

The smile faded quickly from Charlotte's face. "You are going away — so very soon! When we have only been in your home one night!"

Nugent Carew sat down on the bed. "You cannot regret it more than I do," he said, taking her hand. "It may be, however, that I shall bring back some good news from London. This summons," and he could not keep the satisfaction from his tone, "is from the Secretary of the Admiralty, who wishes to see me without delay."

"The summons which you told me you were hoping for? And you hope too, do you not, that it means you will be given a new, a much larger ship to command? But if you must at once go to sea in her, that will be no cure for my red nose! And I shall have red eyes also!"

Captain Carew, R.N., had of course no choice about obeying the bidding of the Admiralty, as his wife well understood, and his parents, regretful yet pleased, still better. By noon he was gone, and Charlotte was left alone in the house of those parents, one of whom, owing to her yesternight's indisposition, she had hardly seen.

But from that indisposition — legacy from Fabien or no — she was by this time so nearly recovered that when Mrs. Carew came to pay her a visit she asked whether she might not get up and come downstairs. It seemed to her the more courteous thing to do, although she rather shrank from entering upon this (as it were) unexplored tract of country without her husband's companionship.

So at three o'clock she made a fourth at table opposite the wide blue eyes of her little sister-in-law. Commiserating with her at being so swiftly, if temporarily, bereft of her spouse, her new relatives did everything possible to put her at her ease; and afterwards Mrs. Carew showed her over the rambling, friendly old house. Then, since she thought Charlotte had better not venture out of doors yet, the two of them sat down in the parlour with needlework, an occupation apt to lead more easily and insensibly to intimacy than almost any other. And so Charlotte, embarking once more on her still unfinished piece of sewing, and using for it the new thimble which she had acquired in Portsmouth, was not unnaturally moved to tell Mrs. Carew to what an unexpected meeting the purchase of that thimble had led. Thence it was natural also that, after a little probing, she should confide some details about her family and bringing up. After which she spoke of her sojourn at Leghorn, finding, however, that her husband had already told of their first meeting and the final scene in the little Mediterranean island. But her own recital of these events was from another angle, and made with so much spirit, modesty and good sense, that her English mother-in-law was plainly well contented. And Charlotte herself, who so far had felt more in awe of her than of the Rector, became more at ease in her society.

Just then Mr. Carew himself looked in, in order, though he did not say so, to show the bride the little miniature of Nugent as a child. Declaring that he would not on any account interrupt her, he sat down, begging her to continue her recital.

"You were speaking of your time with the Mounseys, were you not, my dear?" he hazarded (but Charlotte had got further than that). "Edward Mounsey is a good fellow. I hope you found him so?"

"Yes, he was always very kind, sir."

"And his wife? I only met her once, and did not, I must confess, take to her at all. And Nugent spoke of the little girl, your charge, . . . well, not at all favourably!"

With Charlotte's smile, a trifle wry, went the first little 'French gesture' which they had yet observed in her, for she slightly shrugged her shoulders without saying anything.

"Poor Charlotte had a very trying time in Leghorn altogether, even before she entered Mrs. Mounsey's employment," observed his wife. "I have just been hearing about it."

"I am sorry to learn that. I have indeed been wondering . . . My dear," said Mr. Carew, addressing his daughter-in-law directly, "how exactly *did* you contrive to make your escape from Toulon?"

Charlotte had been hunting on her lap for the embroidery scissors which, with the malignity of all their kind, had in the space of a few seconds totally disappeared. But she instantly desisted. Her face had grown very grave, and she looked away from her questioner.

"Until . . . until the dreadful thing happened I was in the care of poor Monsieur de Marescot —" She broke off, fighting, it was clear, for composure, and Mrs. Carew saw the tears come into her eyes. Really Peregrine should not have revived those memories, whatever they were, which were obviously distressing to the poor girl! She was just about to say, "Never mind, my dear; tell us another time!" when Charlotte, still looking at the fire, went on unsteadily:

"He was killed, you know. I saw it happen — stabbed as he was trying to help me into a boat."

"Dear, dear!" exclaimed the Rector, now himself regretting his question, "how truly terrible! And you witnessed it — shocking!"

"But, Charlotte, who *was* he?" asked her mother-in-law — since this painful memory *had* been revived. "I mean, how came you to be with this gentleman in particular?"

"He was the man whom my aunt had made me marry . . . so that I should not be without protection."

The miniature of the infant Nugent dropped from the Rector's fingers and fell unregarded upon the carpet.

"Made you marry!" he exclaimed incredulously. *"Marry!* Then you . . . you have already had a husband . . . you were a widow when Nugent —"

Charlotte turned her saddened face from the fire. "But did he not tell you so? I supposed he had. Yes, I was a widow — though I was never a wife," she added in a lower key; and Mrs. Carew, her busy hands quite still now, repeated that disconcerting word "widow" under her breath. "I was married — at my aunt's desire, and very much against my own — to this Monsieur de Marescot at eight o'clock that morning. And before nightfall he was at the bottom of Toulon harbour, dead." Her voice was steadier now, but a little shudder suddenly ran over her.

For a long moment only the crackling of the fire broke the silence. The exact quality of that silence, even the stunned manner in which both her parents-in-law were staring at her, passed Charlotte by, for she was back on that nightmare quayside in Toulon.

Mrs. Carew was the first to recover herself. She got up — slowly enough, it is true — crossed over to Charlotte, and laid a hand on her shoulder.

"My poor child! How terrible!" She glanced then at her husband, who was still sitting thunderstruck, his lips moving as he repeated, softly but audibly: "A widow! a widow! Is it possible!" Then she saw what was lying at his feet, picked it up, and went back to her daughter-in-law, who by this time was dabbing at her eyes with her pocket-handkerchief.

"Let us not talk any more now of your experiences, Charlotte. It is too painful for you. And see what Mr.

Carew has brought in to show you. But I think you will hardly guess who it is."

Putting away her handkerchief, the girl accepted the miniature and was studying it when the door opened, and the voice of Betsy announced, "Mr. Clavering, Mam!" And on that there strode into the room the owner of Damarel Place, sturdy, jolly and sexagenarian, come, as it transpired, to consult his fellow J.P. about a smuggling affair. His advent at this juncture was by no means as inopportune as it appeared.

In Mr. Carew's study, to which the two gentlemen shortly afterwards adjourned, the Squire gave voice to his pleasure at meeting the new French daughter-in-law.

"Charming, charming! Lucky dog, Captain Nugent! Some romance behind it that the ladies would all love, I wager! Hope you'll allow my girls to come soon to call upon her — and Dick too if he may? How well she speaks English!"

Thought the Reverend Peregrine Carew after this breezy presence was withdrawn, "I wonder what Clavering would say if he knew that Charlotte was a widow when Nugent married her . . . and that he never told us!"

For that, he felt, was the sharpest thorn in the disclosure. Or was it not?

The subject could not conveniently be approached with his wife until Charlotte had gone to bed, which, at Mrs. Carew's recommendation, she did at an early hour. She was in good spirits again, and before retiring made them a grateful little speech. They were so kind and considerate, she could never thank them enough. And Mrs. Carew had kissed her.

"You have behaved better than I over this, Elizabeth," remarked her husband when they were alone again. "Perhaps the revelation of Charlotte's previous status did not affect you so strongly. I hope that was the case."

"On the contrary," replied Mrs. Carew, "I felt as though the ceiling had fallen upon me. But I did not want her to see it. And after all, Peregrine, it is not the girl's fault that she had been married already — if you can call it so merely to go through the ceremony! I do not know why we should instinctively hold it against her — especially as she apparently did not want this man for a husband. She evidently had not concealed the fact from Nugent, nor did she try to conceal it from us."

"No, it is not she who has done any concealing." The Rector sighed heavily. "It is Nugent's silence on the point which distresses me. Why, her name was not even d'Esparre when he married her! It was legally that of the murdered man — which I cannot at the moment remember."

"But, Peregrine, Nugent never stated that he married Charlotte as a d'Esparre. He only said that it was her maiden name."

CHAPTER
FIVE

I

It was in a deeply divided state of mind that Captain Nugent Carew was returning Devonwards from his visit to the Admiralty. On the one hand he had been most handsomely complimented on the *Callisto's* record during the blockade and capture of Corsica, and on his subsequent handling of the difficult situation at the little island of Farfalletta. And on top of these encomiums had come the promise of a ship of the line, when such a command should be vacant. Unfortunately this had to remain as yet but a promise; and so, at the moment, there was nothing but the prospect of inaction. It was true that something had been said about a dockyard appointment in the New Year. But Nugent did not want a shore post. Better that, however, than doing nothing on half-pay.

Of course — to revert once more to the favourable side of the situation — a speedy separation from his newly-made wife was not now as imminent as he had half expected, and as she had feared. As yet he had only had Charlotte to himself in snatches. Now they could enjoy uninterrupted companionship for weeks, and learn to know each other better. He must contrive not to allow her to guess the depth of his disappointment at

69

the temporary check to his career . . . and not alone to his career, to his desire to go on fighting the French.

So Nugent journeyed westwards through Hampshire and Dorset, resolved to put as good a face upon the situation as possible, in which laudable resolve he was assisted by an episode of his arrival. After he had left the local coach, which had brought him from Queensteignton and was walking homewards from Damarel St. Mary village, where only a few evenings ago he and Charlotte had passed under that embarrassing arch of welcome, he saw ahead of him in the lane two female figures of differing stature, a young woman and a little girl. They were picking some kind of an autumn nosegay from the hedge, to the accompaniment of a good deal of chatter and laughter. It was his wife and his small sister.

Excellent, thought Nugent, that they are getting on so well together. How Peggy had grown, by the way! Out of doors one noticed it more. Eighteen months since he had seen her — until the other day. Eighteen — nay, *eight* — months ago he had never seen Charlotte!

The two did not seem to have heard him approaching; at least neither turned her head. Nugent moved on to the grass verge so that they should be unaware of his presence as long as possible, for it pleased him not a little to contemplate them at their task. The afternoon sun, that benignant October sun, made a minor glory of Charlotte's hair under the wide-brimmed hat she was wearing, as, with one arm raised to the hedge, she bent her head to look at some find of Peggy's. And then Peggy caught sight of him.

"Here's Nugent, here's Nugent!" she cried, dropping some of her spoils and running towards him. He thought he would always remember the picture which Charlotte made then as she turned quickly round, her face lit with joy and welcome, a long trail of fruited bryony caught on her yellow gown.

With his wife on one arm, and Peggy on the other, he went home, the child chattering of all the things which she and Charlotte had done together since he left, and how she had shown her the owl's nest in the hollow tree and the toy wheelbarrow which Tom had made last holidays. Charlotte herself said little, but the pressure of her arm against his own spoke for her. It was altogether the pleasantest home-coming that he could have wished.

It was not until they were approaching the Rectory door and Peggy, detaching herself, had run up the steps, that Charlotte asked the result of his visit to London.

"Have you — have the Admiralty appointed you to another ship . . . are you going away soon?"

His answer enraptured her, as he had guessed it would. "Oh, Nugent how thankful I am! I have been so anxious about it!" Then the glow on her upturned face suddenly faded. "But — no post at all before the New Year? How selfish of me to forget your disappointment — for you are disappointed, are you not, though you have not said so? Oh, *mon cher mari,* I am so sorry!"

There on the steps of his home Nugent took her gently by the shoulders. "Do not be too sorry, Charlotte, or I might think you wished me gone before the New Year! And there is, after all, quite an inducement to stay at home just now! Perhaps you can guess what it is!" And, sparing of caresses though he was, even in private, he kissed her — in the open-air.

In face of their son's good spirits, more surprising to Mr. and Mrs. Carew, when they had heard his news, than Charlotte's — it seemed unkind to arraign him in any way that evening about his silence over Charlotte's previous marriage.

In the event it was Nugent himself who, next day, brought up the subject.

It was the Rector's custom to retire soon after breakfast for a while to his study, where sometimes, though not always, he strove for an hour or so to arrange his notes on early Church history on something like a manageable plan. He had not been long in that retreat next morning when the door opened and a voice said:

"Won't you come for a stroll, sir? It is a beautiful morning, and too early in the week for you to be meditating your sermon!"

Quill in hand (but the ink was dry on the quill) Peregrine Carew looked up from his writing-table. That tall son of his stood smiling in the doorway, the excited Juno at his side.

"And," went on the intruder, "there will probably be plenty of wet days later on this autumn in which you

72

can shelter in caves with those Desert Fathers of yours."

Mr. Carew got up. "Yes, I should like a walk." (It would give him a good opportunity of asking a certain question.) "But will not Charlotte accompany us?" (In that case the question would not be put.)

"No, Charlotte is learning the mysteries of an English stillroom, or something of the sort. We can leave her in my mother's hands."

The early autumn morning had all that season's unmatched and gracious charm. Hardly a tree had as yet taken on more than a touch of the warmer colouring which would clothe it later, or had lost more than a few leaves; smoke from Damarel St. Mary village rose straight and blue in the windless atmosphere.

"It is good to be back in Devon," said the returned sailor after a while, sniffing the air appreciatively. "I find these hedges, in the long run, a pleasanter sight than olive-groves. I believe that I even prefer a good field of turnips like this." He stopped, and looked over a gate, his father pausing with him. "This is Farmer Thorpe's field, is it not? He has an excellent crop."

"He has indeed. Although he is getting on in years now, he looks after his land as well as ever. He has even, to most people's surprise, taken to himself a second wife."

Nugent removed his hand from the gate. "Married again? That reminds me, sir," he turned and faced his father squarely: "I had fully meant to tell you days ago, what I now find that Charlotte has told you in my absence. You know now that before she married me she had already gone through the ceremony with some one else — a Frenchman who was killed the same day during the evacuation of Toulon."

The Rector's gaze was on the wide expanse of turnip tops. "Yes," he said, and his tone was not free from reproach. "Charlotte told us that, on the evening of the day you left. She thought you had already done so."

Under the Mediterranean tan, a little of which still lingered, his son coloured.

"I intended to have told you about it that very evening, and should have done so, had I not been obliged to start at such short notice for London. No doubt I ought to have informed you of it on the evening of our arrival, but I was deliberately reserving the disclosure until next day, since I felt that I was already causing you enough — I hope not distress — disturbance, for one day. Not, indeed, that the matter is of importance — at least I do not consider it so. In law Charlotte may have been the widow of this unfortunate de Marescot when she became my wife: but in fact she had only, as I say, been through the ceremony of marriage. As she has told you, the wretched man was murdered under her eyes on the quay that same evening."

"Yes, poor child! . . . Nevertheless, the revelation that she had been a widow was somewhat of a shock to your mother and myself. Yet, to be frank, my dear Nugent, what disturbed us almost more was that you appeared to be intending to conceal the fact from us altogether."

"Good heavens, why should you think that?"

74

"Because you gave the impression that Charlotte had never borne any name but d'Esparre."

His son bit his lip and appeared to reflect. "Now that I come to think of it, I fear that I must have done so . . . I wish I had not postponed telling you of her first marriage."

"If your original purpose, my dear boy, was to have told us the next day, there is no harm done."

"Not if you believe, sir, that I did most fully intend it."

"You have said so — and I have never known you to lie . . . Come, let us be getting on. We might walk round by the big spinney. By the way, I do not suppose you know that we have a new landed proprietor in these parts? A gentleman named Wilkins has bought Headleigh Court. Not the usual type of country gentleman either; Clavering says he cannot imagine why he should have settled himself in the country at all. A regular town-dweller."

This was not the only walk which Captain Nugent Carew took that fine autumn day. In the early afternoon he set out with Charlotte for a stroll which took them past the church, so near a neighbour of the Rectory, and through the village, where their progress was punctuated by many a curtsey and greeting, and by not a few chats, and where, of course, 'the Captain's French wife' was the magnet for every rustic pair of eyes.

"Do you realise," said Nugent, as they turned homewards (Charlotte not sorry that this ordeal, though agreeable, was over) "that this is the first real walk which we have taken together — since one can hardly count my escorting you, with your poor scratched little hands, back to the villa, that day we first met in Leghorn. And that reminds me" — he broke off and began to laugh to himself. "Charlotte, try to guess whom you might have had as a fellow-passenger in the *Callisto!*"

"Some friend of yours, I suppose, a naval officer on leave?"

"You could not be further from the truth. To begin with, you have the sex wrong."

"A woman? The wife of an officer then."

"Wrong again! Neither a wife . . . nor even a woman!"

Charlotte stopped, and, since she was on her husband's arm, he must stop too. "But, Nugent, *voyons donc!* Neither man nor woman! It must have been some animal, then. A race-horse, for instance — perhaps even a cow?"

"Neither would have shared your cabin, my Charlotte, as this young animal would have had to do."

"Young animal! How foolish of me! A dog, of course — a female dog, *une chienne*, like your beautiful Juno. I should not have objected to her — on the contrary! Oh Nugent, tell me!"

"Let us walk on then. *Eh bien* (as you would say) you might have had to share your cabin with someone much less amiable than Juno here . . . your late charming pupil, Arabella Mounsey!"

At this Charlotte stopped again. *"Arabella!"* she gasped. "Arabella a passenger to England! Without her parents, do you mean? Impossible!"

"Not at all. And she is welcome to come to England for all I care. All that concerns us is that the *Callisto* was not afflicted with her presence."

"Do you mean that the child did sail for England, in some other vessel? But how did you learn that?"

"Because when I was at Whitehall I ran into an old shipmate, just home from the Mediterranean in the *Diadem*, of which he is first lieutenant, and we dined together. I cannot quite recall how we got upon the subject, but he happened to mention that the captain of the *Diadem* had conveyed home from Leghorn a certain colonel of foot and his lady, who had in their charge a little girl, not their own, who was going to school somewhere in England — Wilberforce never heard where. This tomboy of a child was so rude and unruly, and made herself so much of a nuisance on board, that Wilberforce said he was sorry for any schoolmistress who took charge of her. And the hoyden's name was — Arabella."

"But there might be another —"

"Be logical, Mrs. Carew! There cannot possibly have been two wildly misbehaved little English girls called Arabella in Leghorn!"

"But, mon cher Nugent, when we were married there, only a few weeks ago, Mr. Mounsey never said a word about sending Arabella to an English school."

"And a mercy he did not — for if he had asked me to give her a passage, and you to take care of her, it would have been impossible to refuse. So you see how narrow has been our escape! It is true," added Nugent with a grin, "that I could have kept her below hatches as a potential mutineer. You see, the decision to send the child must evidently have been a sudden one, taken, luckily, after the *Callisto* had sailed. I suppose that our cousin Edward could stand his daughter's uncivilised conduct no longer. But I warrant he had a struggle to get his wife to part with her darling!"

II

As October and then November went by in these new surroundings, it began to seem to Charlotte Carew that, now her only channel of communication with her native land — Tante Ursule at Toulon — had failed (as had indeed long been obvious) her previous life in France was taking on the character of another existence altogether. Memories of that life were indeed as vivid as ever, for they were the ineffaceable memories of childhood and girlhood, and, since she was still only one and twenty, they were recent memories too. On the other hand those still more recent dark days at Toulon, with their tragic culmination, and her subsequent trying experiences at Leghorn and elsewhere, appeared to be no part of *that* world. Her brother Fabien, so strangely met again, belonged to it indeed, but save that she thought of him often, and had written to him once or twice, Charlotte knew herself becoming more and more absorbed into this happy and peaceful new life in her Devon village. In details and setting — above all in climate — it was unlike that other, but there was at the Rectory much the same atmosphere which had always prevailed in her childhood's home before the tempest of revolution had slain or scattered those who dwelt there.

Here too that tempest was felt now, but not its full force, only its eddies, for it was a wind of foreign war, not of revolution, which blew over England. Charlotte learnt before long how critical the situation was becoming for the British in Holland, where they had had to retreat behind the river Waal, whose floods in that very rainy November would serve as a barrier against the French advance. She heard too of the great efforts at home to raise recruits for the army, the success of which, to Nugent's disgust, were serving to stop the flow of those for the Navy. He himself, as she could see, was beginning to chafe wildly at his continued inaction, and every day looked for orders of some kind from Whitehall. But though Charlotte genuinely sympathised with him, she continually though privately blessed the Board of Admiralty for this respite. For she had known practically nothing of her husband before their hasty marriage; now in these weeks of companionship she had the opportunity of learning not only to love, but to know him, mixture of simplicity and reserve that he was. Up to a point he could behave like a boy, yet he could, she divined, be remarkably stern and uncompromising. The combination, added to his real though undemonstrative tenderness towards her, was all that she could desire.

So December too began to slip away, a severe December, not a little trying to a girl born and bred among the olive trees of Provence. And now, over in Holland, the flooded Waal was freezing over, and soon its value as a barrier would be gone — and what would happen then?

But at Damarel St. Mary it was difficult to realise war and hardship elsewhere. Charlotte sometimes wondered whether this was because she now lived on an island, with the sea between her and such scenes, but concluded it was rather because she herself was so happy. She had her husband's presence, the unvarying kindness of his parents, (even if Mrs. Carew occasionally showed a tartness of speech which, however, did not wound) the childish affection of Peggy; she was beginning to know the villagers, as well as the Claverings and other families of the neighbourhood. And, thanks to the existence of the Shirleys at Monks Damarel, she was not cut off from the exercise and privileges of her religion.

Yet as Christmas approached two changes in her life also came nearer. The more important was the probable departure of Nugent at the New Year for his temporary and as yet unspecified shore post; the other was the return of Master Tom from school. This was an event looked forward to by Peggy with much eagerness, but by Charlotte with just a tinge of apprehension. How would the boy react to the presence of his elder — his much elder — brother's wife? And one afternoon, when they happened to

80

find themselves alone in the fire-lit parlour, she confided her doubts to Nugent. But he pooh-poohed her misgivings, adding bluntly:

"If there is anything amiss with the young rascal's behaviour, he will soon have it knocked out of him! I'll see to that!"

There was both affection and amusement in the glance which Charlotte threw him.

"*Thou shalt not dislike thy sister-in-law*, in fact!"

"What's that?"

"Your attitude, *mon ami*, brings somehow to my mind the precepts of Moïse which so curiously hang in your church here. Forgive me if I was profane; I did not intend it."

The question of profanity was not taken up. "But why," asked her husband in surprise, "is it curious to have the Ten Commandments displayed in church? To me it seems very natural. I know that you don't have them in your churches, little Papist, at least not in Italy; and I cannot help feeling that the Italians and Corsicans, from what I have seen of them, would be all the better of a little study of the Commandments — and also if their churches had fewer images and candles and less of that lace stuff about. — But I don't want to hurt your feelings, my dear girl. You know I promised you that you should always have the freest exercise of your religion that is possible in this country, and that the difference in our creeds need never come between us. And, you see, I was only alluding to the dirty cumbered-up churches of Italy, not to those of France."

Charlotte hid a smile. Yes, for all that determined mouth and occasional quarter-deck manner, Nugent was in some ways as ingenuous as a child.

"I am afraid that you would often find the same in France, my dear. You see, we Catholics have a faith with more warmth in it than you Protestants — our churches are more of a home to us than yours seem to be to you."

"All the more reason, then, for keeping them clean and tidy," was the uncompromising reply. "And, Charlotte, don't apply the term of 'Protestant' to the Church of England in front of my father! He will certainly ask you to point out any place in the Prayer Book in which she calls herself so!"

"That I certainly could not do," replied Charlotte. Only once had she opened that volume. "But we have strayed some way, have we not, from the subject of Tom? It might be a good thing, I think, if you were to tell him directly he arrives that he need not be afraid that I shall insist upon giving him lessons in French during his holidays; for that fear, I found, was haunting poor little Peggy on her own account when I first came."

Charlotte need not have been nervous about Tom, nor Nugent have hinted at summary proceedings against him. After a little initial shyness it was soon evident that this well-grown, frank-looking schoolboy needed no injunctions as to his relations with the French newcomer. For the first day or two, it was true, this shyness, which revealed itself in a rather abrupt and gruff manner of speech, made him avoid her, but this abstention did not last.

It was over the matter of decking the hall of the Rectory with evergreens for Christmas Day that his defences went down, and with startling suddenness. Not her husband himself could have been more assiduous in attention when Charlotte pricked herself rather severely with some holly. It was true that the handkerchief which Master Tom produced to supplement Charlotte's own exiguous one was not over-clean, as Peggy instantly remarked with more shrillness than tact.

"Shut up!" commanded her brother. "Cleaner than yours, I'll wager — if you've even got one! I've only had this one since —"

"Pricked yourself, Charlotte?" enquired Nugent. "Here, let me see." And, pulling out his own handkerchief he advanced from the other side of the hall.

But Charlotte, considering that youthful chivalry should not be snubbed, even in the interests of cleanliness, said quickly: "No, no, Tom's will serve excellently," accepted a square of linen which appeared to have been in contact with something of the nature of tar, and let the boy, red with pleasure, tie it over her own improvised bandage.

A few days later Nugent was complaining that if Charlotte wanted a spaniel to follow her about everywhere he would buy her one, and willingly, for Tom in that capacity was a nuisance.

This was especially so because Nugent's own sojourn at the Rectory was, at last, coming to an end. The very day after Christmas he had received a communication from the Admiralty ordering him — to his disgust — to take up on New Year's Day a post in the dockyard at Plymouth. It was true that it was only to be temporary, and there seemed to be every prospect of his being posted to a ship of the line in about a couple of month's time. But it was tiresome, and more tiresome still was the fact that, although it was a shore appointment, he could not immediately take Charlotte to Plymouth with him, since the Admiral there, a crusty old bachelor, had a known and strong objection to wives accompanying their husbands. This prejudice would have to be overcome (if it could) before he could send for her to join him.

"If only I could walk into the old fellow's presence with you on my arm, dear girl," he said on the morning of his departure, "there would be an end of his woman-hating propensities! But I shall lay siege to him in as crafty a manner as possible, and at once. What will you wager that in less than a couple of weeks you are not posting along to join me?"

"But naturally I will not take your wager," answered Charlotte, "when I hope with all my heart that you are right! Meanwhile I could not be in a better anchorage (you see how nautical I have become!) than here in your own home, with Mr. and Mrs. Carew so good to me."

"And you must not forget," added Nugent half teasingly, "that Tom for the rest of his holidays will take special care of you. He has solemnly assured me of that — impertinent young beggar!"

CHAPTER
SIX

I

The day on which a moral thunderbolt elects to fall is often, until that shattering advent, of very ordinary texture. Or it may, on the other hand, be of a specially joyous and carefree complexion. For Charlotte Carew the 17th of January partook of both these natures, for, though it was in itself a day rather humdrum than otherwise, in which she was occupied with various small duties (so much had she become the daughter of the house at the Rectory) it was also irradiated by the knowledge that only a very few more such periods lay between her and Nugent's arrival to fetch her to join him at Plymouth. For the naval misogynist in command had been prevailed upon to lift the ban in favour of one wife at least.

It was towards the end of the winter afternoon that, with Tom at her side carrying a laden basket, Charlotte paused on her homeward way at the little village shop, which was also the post-office, to ask whether there were any letters for the Rectory. This enquiry would have been made earlier in the day, had not old George Cripps, whose business it was to fetch them, been laid up with lumbago, while the Rector himself was away at Exeter upon some clerical business. While she was asking this question Tom shot over to the cobbler's for a pair of his boots which were being repaired.

"Yes, my dear," said the old postmistress, going to some invisible receptacle behind the counter, "they'm tu letters for his Raverunce, and — what do ee think — one for yu! Simingly it come from over the sea — look, my dear!" And her gnarled finger pointed out the postmark. "'Tes from a plaace called . . ." She spelt it out, laboriously but correctly, "L-i-v-o-r-n-o."

Charlotte's heart gave a queer leap as she took this letter and those for the Rector. She had, she thought, recognised the handwriting on hers, which had very likely been brought in some British man-of-war. But what could her one-time employer be writing about? The letter felt rather thick, and the idea came to her that it contained an enclosure. Could this be, after all, the long expected communication from Tante Ursule at Toulon, which for so many weeks, when she was at Leghorn last year, she had awaited in vain, and for whose advent she had now given up hoping? Smiling at the old post-mistress she slipped it into her pocket, feeling that she must read it in private, and held out the other two to Tom, as he came in with the boots under his arm and saluted the old lady.

"Lawks, Master Tom, I'd scarce have known 'ee — so growed yu be!"

"Well, Mrs. Drew, you wouldn't expect me to have shrunk, would you?" retorted the boy, grinning. "But I've not grown too much for bull's eyes, if you have any?"

Although the letter was burning the proverbial hole in Charlotte's pocket she was resolute enough not even to look at it until she was upstairs in her own chintz-decked bedroom. But here she did not wait even to unfasten her redingote, much less to take off her bonnet, before she pulled it out, and, going closer to the window — for the light was beginning to fail — tore it open. Yes, there was an enclosure, very shabby and travel-stained . . . and it *was* from Tante Ursule! Intact though it was, she knew that from the hand-writing of the direction; and so, disregarding Mr. Mounsey's short covering note, she unfastened the seal with impatient hands. What news would Tante Ursule have to give of herself after this long silence? and why had she not written before?

Before? Why, by the date at the head of the letter, which was the first thing she looked at, it had been penned as long ago as last June!

As Charlotte knitted her brows for a moment over this strange fact, her gaze fell upon Mr. Mounsey's letter, lying unregarded on the window-sill and a sentence jumped to her eye:

". . . it arrived soon after you had left us — as we know now, but did not then — for the hospitality of Monsieur de Dieuzie at Farfalletta. I put it carefully away, being quite ignorant of your whereabouts, and by the 7th of September, when I had the pleasure of seeing you for a short space on the occasion of your marriage to my cousin Carew, I am ashamed to say that the fact of my having done so had slipped my memory. I cannot sufficiently ask your pardon for this oversight; and since an opportunity offers am dispatching the letter without delay."

So this letter of Tante Ursule's had really been awaiting her at Leghorn ever since last July! Well, she had received it in the end. Now to see what it said. It was fairly long, and Mlle d'Esparre's handwriting was fine. In spite of her uncompromising disposition, it did not seem as though she had been molested by the Republicans when they re-entered Toulon.

A quarter of an hour later Charlotte was still standing at the window in the dusk, as motionless (though upright) as if she had been Dame Margaret Clavering's recumbent effigy from the tomb in the church. But Dame Margaret's serene expression was not hers, for Charlotte's features were sharpened and frozen into a mask of incredulity and despair.

"I cannot think why Charlotte does not come down," said Mrs. Carew. "She is not usually late. Run up, Tom, knock at her door, and tell her that the meal is served."

"Charlotte says," reported the messenger on his return, "that she has a very bad headache. She asks you to excuse her, and not to trouble about her in any way, as she could not eat anything. I think she said she was going straight to bed."

II

During his rather chilly journey home from Exeter next day the Rector of Damarel St. Mary had thought more than once with satisfaction of his own warm hearth, not to speak of the welcome which was always his. But on arrival he had scarcely set foot in the hall when his wife came hurrying across it, before Tom, who was leaping down the stairs, could reach him, drew him into his own study and shut the door.

"Peregrine —"

"What is it, my dear? Something amiss, I can see. Not illness, I hope or an accident?"

"No, thank God! But almost as bad — worse, possibly. Charlotte has left us!"

"Left us! Elizabeth, what do you mean? Gone back to France? Impossible!"

Mrs. Carew, more discomposed than her husband had ever seen her, was bringing out a letter. "No, not that. She has apparently run away to her brother in Bath. Without a word to us — except this!"

"Run away to her brother!" reiterated Mr. Carew. "But *why*, in Heaven's name? Did she give no reason for such a step?" Here he saw the letter held out to him, took it, and glancing at it became aware of phrases: "*letter from France . . . very bad news . . . oh, forgive me but I cannot wait . . . must have my brother's advice . . .*" Well, that is Perhaps not so unreasonable —"

"Yes, Peregrine, it *was* unreasonable, and very wrong, to steal out of the house as she did, before anyone was awake, and to go off like a fugitive — our daughter-in-law, Nugent's wife! I should not have put any obstacle in her way if she wished to consult her brother, rather than her husband or us, seeing that this bad news from France must concern her own family and not ours."

"When did she go?"

"Early to-day. She had retired to bed early yesterday evening, saw no one and when Betsy went in to rouse her this morning her bedroom, was empty, though the bed had been slept in. No one heard or saw her leaving the house, so she must have stolen out before the maids were up — in spite of the cold. This note, addressed to me, was on her dressing-table. But she has not to my knowledge received a letter of any kind, let alone one from France."

"No letter? Yet she speaks of one. This requires careful looking into, Elizabeth," said the Rector rather sternly. "Such an extraordinary step to take — at least, as you rightly observe, such an extraordinary manner of taking it! There must be something seriously wrong for a girl like Charlotte to behave so. As to the letter from the Continent, we can easily ascertain from Mrs. Drew at the post office whether there was one or no; she would be sure to remember the fact. If so, this letter may have contained news such as the death of this aunt at Toulon who sheltered, and then, as it seems, turned her out."

"Perhaps," admitted Mrs. Carew. "But why should that make her creep out of the house at such an hour on a winter morning? It is no sufficient reason for such behaviour."

"I agree, I agree. But, whatever the cause of Charlotte's flight, she must be prevailed upon to return at once, before Nugent comes to take her to Plymouth.

Her knowledge of his impending arrival, to which she was so much looking forward, makes this action of hers all the more inexplicable."

"Indeed it does! But how is she to be persuaded to return?"

"I suppose that I shall have to go to Bath after her," responded the Rector with a sigh; and at last he sat down by the welcoming fire.

"Oh, my dear Peregrine, surely not! Write her a letter, telling her to return at once!"

"I feel that a mere letter would be of little use." Mr. Carew sighed again. "It will be quicker to take the stage coach to Shepton Mallet and then go post, rather than the mail coach route, which is less direct. What is the address of this émigré brother in Bath? I see she does not mention it in this note. Do you know it, Elizabeth?"

"No, indeed I do not. But Nugent probably does."

"That will not do. Charlotte must be back in this house before Nugent sets foot in it!"

"That is all very well, Peregrine; but what is the use of rushing off to Bath to find Charlotte without knowing where to look for her? Bath is not a mere village."

"No, that is true. But I remember her telling us that her brother or his wife, I am not quite sure which, had obtained work teaching French in a school or two there. There cannot be an unlimited number of such establishments. I suppose, by the way, that the children know about Charlotte's . . . flight?"

"It could not be kept from them. Tom is very much upset; as you know, he had become devoted to

Charlotte. And Peggy is quite bewildered, and has cried several times. I have tried, however, to hide my surprise and grief that Nugent's wife should treat us so, and to put the best complexion on her departure that I could."

"Very wise, my dear; as your actions always are."

Tom might be upset, but he was also excited, and of his youthful fancy had already been born a theory, not capable of very lucid exposition, that his French Royalist sister-in-law had been kidnapped by Republican agents and spirited off to some place of captivity from which, if permission and money were only forthcoming, it might be his privilege to rescue her. The letter which she had left behind, of which his mother had informed him, he dismissed as having somehow been extracted by *force majeure*.

But enquiries in the village next morning dealt hardly with this theory. A young female, somewhat heavily veiled, but recognisable as 'the Captain's lady', had come early the previous morning to the 'Clavering Arms' with an urgent request for horses to be put to a chaise without a moment's delay, so that she could catch the stage coach at Honiton. This had been done, and off she had gone as though Old Nick himself were after her. Yes, she had seemed in distress, and had murmured something about bad news.

Enquiries in another quarter revealed that Charlotte *had*, the afternoon before her precipitate departure, received from the post-mistress herself a letter with a postmark which that good lady, not liking to venture on

92

its pronunciation, was nevertheless able to remember and to spell out — 'Livorno'.

"So the letter was not from France," thought the puzzled Rector, on hearing this. "Livorno is the place we English call Leghorn, and that is where she lived for a time with the Mounseys. Perhaps the letter was from Edward Mounsey or his wife — or possibly from that Baron Somebody or other in that island. But, as we do not know what was in it, save that it contained bad news of some kind, there is nothing for it but to go at once to Bath to find out its nature, and to bring her back with me."

III

A grey rain-laden sky was leaning morosely over the city of Bath as Fabien d'Esparre walked homewards towards his modest lodgings that afternoon. He himself looked sufficiently morose also, returning as he was from instructing young ladies in the French tongue. But at the particular educational establishment which he had just left, he was at least treated — perhaps on account of his title — with a certain consideration. There, though the Young Ladies were in his opinion of a stupidity and frivolity inconceivable, he had never actually heard himself called Frenchy or Froggy, as had happened once or twice at the Academy for Young Gentlemen where he likewise instructed. Though he did not enjoy his present avocation, at least he was earning enough to support himself and Honorine. Bath too was a fine city, but he naturally had not the means to share in any of its social gaieties; and Honorine (partly for that reason) was more than usually irritable and low-spirited. He was really glad of the masculine and cheerful society of M. Guillemin, the little marine painter, who, turning up at Bath after they had settled there, was once more lodging in the same house with them, though at the moment he had gone off to Bristol in search of a possible market for the pictures which he had painted at another port, Plymouth.

His landlady opened the door to him. "Oh, sir, there's a young lady arrived about half an hour ago — from the stage coach, I think. She would not give her name, but seemed to know all about you and Mrs. Despair." (This was the nearest approach which Mrs. Gibbings could ever contrive to the name of her lodgers.) "So I took her upstairs to your apartments. Mrs. Despair is still out."

A young lady who knew them arrived by coach! It could be nobody but his sister Charlotte, paying them an unexpected visit. Much pleased he hurried up the stairs.

And it *was* Charlotte, sitting in her pelisse and bonnet, with a little valise on the floor at her feet, apparently just as she had arrived.

"My dear sister, what a pleasure — and what a surprise! You designed it for one, no doubt, as you did not give your name! But I guessed, I guessed!" He kissed a very cold cheek. "But you are frozen, Charlotte! and no wonder — the fire is out! Why did not Mrs. Gibbings . . . However I'll soon put that right!"

94

As he looked round for fuel, Charlotte caught him by the arm. "Pray leave the fire alone for a moment, Fabien! I must tell you, before Honorine returns, why I have come. I did not give a name because ... because ..."

Looking at her in alarm as she struggled for speech her brother put his other hand on her shoulder.

"My dearest sister, tell me at once what is amiss!"

CHAPTER
SEVEN

I

It was sleeting a little when the Rector left Shepton Mallet, where the stage-coach had deposited him the previous evening. The postchaise which he had hired there for the latter stage of his journey to Bath was cold and musty-smelling, and though it was presumably furnished with springs, they were singularly lacking in resilience. Worry and speculation however, kept him from noticing these inconveniences overmuch. *Why* had Charlotte fled from her home just when her husband was on the point of arrival there?

Between Shepton Mallet and Radstock the rain, which had succeeded the sleet, ceased, and a watery sun made its appearance, without much effect upon the spirits of the chaise's occupant. Realising that he could not now be much more than twelve miles from Bath, Mr. Carew began once more to reflect on the means whereby he should upon arrival set about discovering Charlotte's — or rather M. d'Esparre's — address. And, as he cogitated, the post-chaise which, without visible reason, had been slackening speed, suddenly came to a standstill. A shouted colloquy then took place between the postillion and some person unseen, and had hardly terminated before the former threw himself off his horse and appeared at the window.

"There's a cart here, sir, by the roadside, a carrier's cart, I reckon, wi' summat wrong to axle or linch-pin. I'd like to lend a hand for five minutes if so be you've no objection. The man says there ain't been no other vehicles come past for quite a while, this not being the mail coach road."

"Yes, lend a hand by all means," replied the Rector. "I will take the opportunity of stretching my legs a little."

Descending, he saw a short distance away a two-wheeled hooded cart which had been going in the opposite direction to theirs. The stout grey horse between the shafts was turning a mildly interested gaze on the postillion, who was already examining the near wheel, but the driver, a lanky fellow with a shock of grey hair, appeared to be engaged in an altercation with someone inside the vehicle — obviously, from what the Rector heard as he approached, a female.

"No Miss, I've bin a thinking it over, and I can't take ye no further! Don't know yet if I can get on meself. You go back to Bath now, like a good girl. If he's going there, as seemingly he is, the gentleman in this chaise here might —"

"I'm not going back!" interrupted a shrill voice. "Not with anybody! You promised to take me as far as Shepton Mallet."

The grey-headed carrier made a somewhat helpless gesture. "The more fool I, then! Why, if ever I got you as far as Shepton Mallet I'd likely land meself with a mort of trouble. They might say as I was a-kidnapping of you, Miss!"

"But you aren't!" retorted the voice, still more piercingly. It was a youthful voice. "And I'm not going back to Bath! I am going on a visit to Captain Nugent Carew of the Navy, who lives in Devonshire — I have the name of the place written down, as I told you. And you *are* to take me to Shepton Mallet as you promised!"

The Rector of Damarel St. Mary, who had received some considerable surprises of late, now really knew the meaning of the expression about not believing one's own ears. Who, in Heaven's name, was this shrill-voiced young female of Nugent's acquaintance who was proposing to descend uninvited upon his home? He must surely have heard wrongly. A few more paces and he beheld, leaning forward from beneath the hood, as in the mouth of a cave, a flushed and unattractive little girl of nine or ten, wearing expensive clothes untidily put on.

"Who is this child?" he demanded with authority. "And what has she to do with my — with a Captain Carew who lives in Devonshire?" It had come to him with a sensation of relief that perhaps some other Captain Carew must be meant — the name was not rare in the West Country.

Alas, this hope was soon dashed. The young traveller stared at him for a second or two and then announced: "Captain Carew is the cousin of my Papa. He came to our house in Leghorn and gave me a musical box. I am going to his home so that he can take me away from that odious school in Bath where Papa sent me."

Little short of petrified, the Reverend Peregrine Carew continued to stare also, ignoring the fervent rivulet of pleas from the worried carrier that, if he were on his way to Bath, he would relieve him of the young lady, and take her back there with him. As he was a living man he did not know till this instant that she had run away from school; she had told him a very different story. But the Rector was not listening to him; and he had to pour the rest of his recital into the more receptive ears of the postillion, who, abandoning his solitary examination of the wheel, had now joined the group.

"A young lady run away from school!" ejaculated Mr. Carew at last. "That is a most shocking thing to do! And what did you say, child, about Leghorn and your father's cousin? Is it possible that you are Edward Mounsey's daughter, whom —"

"Oh, do you know Papa, sir?" broke in the young lady. "Then you will help me, won't you? Make this man take me on to Shepton Mallet when the wheel is mended."

"I shall do nothing of the kind! On the contrary, I shall take you back to your school without delay. I am indeed upon my way to Bath," he explained to the carrier, "and as I am a kinsman of this young lady's it is quite fitting that I should assume the temporary care of her."

Fitting, perhaps, but evidently very far from welcome to the young lady in question — or, for the matter of that, to the Rector himself. Miss Mounsey's face grew very red, her lower lip protruded unbecomingly, and, holding on tightly to the seat upon which she sat, she fairly shouted, "I *won't* come with you! I *won't* go back to that place! I am going on in this cart — and I'll scream if you try to take me out!"

"No, indeed you're not going on, Miss!" retorted the carrier, greatly heartened by this opportune reinforcement. "And I don't care if you screams yourself hoarse. This reverend gentleman is the proper person to look after you anyhow, and sent by Providence, it's clear. Come now, get down, and don't let's have any fuss!"

"Listen, child," said the emissary of Providence hastily and rashly — anything to prevent this threatened screaming. "You cannot possibly go on if the carrier refuses to take you; moreover his cart has broken down. If you will come quietly with me now — I am Captain Carew's father, you know — perhaps you could visit us in the summer, when, I suppose, you have a holiday. And for the present, when we get to Bath, you shall have a pound of the best lollipops that I can buy."

It was evidently touch and go whether Miss Mounsey would lend an ear to these blandishments or whether, rending heaven with her shrieks, she would not have to be torn bodily from her perch. But, to the relief of those who might have so to tear her, her face now cleared a little. Not primarily however, at the prospect of lollipops.

"I can really come to visit you in Devonshire?"

"Yes, if you are a good girl now."

"And will Cousin Nugent be there?"

"Possibly. If he is on leave, that is. (What can my son have done in Leghorn to inspire this attachment?)

"Very well, sir, I will come with you," agreed the truant, wriggling. "Is your name Carew too?"

"Naturally. And what is yours — your Christian name, I mean?" For though he had elicited from Charlotte a certain amount of information about her late refractory pupil, he could not at the moment recall this detail.

"Arabella," replied the traveller. She prepared to descend, did so with the assistance of the delighted carrier — how, Mr. Carew wondered, not having paid attention to his narrative, had she ever persuaded him to instal her in his cart? — and very shortly she, and a small ill-secured bundle which she had with her, were settled in his own conveyance. The postillion reporting that five minutes of his and the carrier's joint labours would put the wheel of the cart right, though one man could not do this alone, the Rector allowed him the time, looking on meanwhile at the operation, though his thoughts were elsewhere. Then he regained his seat and the chaise continued its way Bathwards.

"And now, Arabella," said he to his new travelling-companion, "tell me, if you please, the name of your school."

Miss Arabella looked up at him sideways with a smirk. "Oh no, I shan't tell you that! I said I'd come to Bath with you — but not to that horrid Miss — to that horrid place!"

It was an age where all the emphasis was laid upon the duties and behaviour of children towards their parents and elders, and none at all upon their own wishes or whims. Although the Reverend Peregrine Carew had never ruled his own offspring by fear, yet a tempered discipline had never been lacking at the Rectory. And even to him it appeared scarcely credible that a girl — not even a boy — should not only be such a termagant as to run away from school, but also so lost to proper feeling as to refuse to reveal the name of that establishment when adjured to do so. Suppressing a strong impulse to shake it out of her, he replied after a moment, in what he hoped was a sufficiently firm manner:

"In that case I shall take you round to all the seminaries for young ladies in Bath until we arrive at the right one." (I shall have to do that in any case, he thought ruefully, and probably go to most of the boys' schools as well, if I am to pick up the trail of Charlotte's brother!)

But at this prospect Arabella giggled, and began to bounce up and down on the hard and dusty cushions. "What fun!" she exclaimed.

"You may not find it so. And do not fidget like that, child!" The Rector looked down severely upon his companion, deciding meanwhile upon an indirect approach to the subject of M. d'Esparre. "Tell me, Arabella, do you learn French at your school?"

"It's not my school, because I am not going back there," was the pert reply. But the bouncing ceased.

"I suggest," observed Mr. Carew, "that on your return there — for you shall return — you take a course of lessons in manners! Answer my question, if you please; did you there have French lessons, such as you used to have, I believe, in Leghorn from Mademoiselle d'Esparre?" For he had remembered that in the Mounseys' household Charlotte had always been known by her maiden name, and he was thus able to introduce it as a possible bait.

Arabella made a grimace, whether at the memory of past or present tuition was not clear. Then, looking up at him with a knowing rather than a childlike gaze, she put a question in her turn.

"Were you angry when Cousin Nugent married Mamzelle?"

"*What* did you say?" Taken quite aback, the Rector stared at her a moment. Then he recovered himself. "That is not at all a proper question for a little girl like you to ask!"

"Then you *were* angry!"

"If I had been, it has nothing to do with you, Arabella. You must learn not to be impertinent. But I was not." (No, not *angry*, he said to himself.) "And that is quite enough of the subject."

But the young lady did not see it so. "Mamma always said she was after Cousin Nugent," she commented, rousing in her companion the acutest desire to slap her which he had yet experienced. "I wanted to go with Papa to their wedding at Mr. Udney's, but Mamma would not let me." She paused for a moment and then added reflectively: "It's funny that the French teacher

103

at Miss P —" But there she broke off abruptly, turning scarlet — and with reason. She had obviously all but come out with the name of her schoolmistress at Bath which she was so sedulously withholding.

Nevertheless, though she still withheld it, she had unknowingly presented Mr. Carew with precisely (or almost precisely) the other piece of information for which he was angling.

"Do you mean," he asked trying not to betray too much eagerness, "that the French teacher at your school is also called d'Esparre? A relative, perhaps, if that is so, of . . . of your 'Mamzelle'?"

"I don't know," replied the runaway, with real or assumed indifference, beginning once more to bounce up and down. "And I don't care. He's only a Frenchman anyhow."

So far so good, thought the Rector, suffering the bouncing this time in silence. The as yet unnamed head of Arabella's school, when found, would almost certainly be able to give him d'Esparre's address, which this child was unlikely to know. Alternatively, if he should light upon the Vicomte's trail at some other school, before successfully returning Miss Mounsey to her seminary, then the Vicomte could direct him to that establishment, the name of whose head, as he had just learnt, began with a P. In any case he *must* get rid of the additional complication with which he was saddled before tackling the problem of Charlotte's behaviour.

In the interests of saving time he must therefore once more descend to diplomacy, if not to bribery. He cleared his throat.

104

"I said that you should pay us a visit in the summer, Arabella — but only if you do what I tell you now."

"That wasn't what you said when I was in the carrier's cart!"

"It was what I meant. Now listen! You will have to return to your school until your parents can arrange for you to go to another one, if they see fit to do so. As you dislike your present one so much, I will write to them about it; and I will also ask your schoolmistress to deal leniently with this extraordinary escapade of yours. But go back to her you shall. She must be indeed in great anxiety about you."

"And serve her right!" ejaculated the runaway with a snort.

"Therefore," went on Mr. Carew, disregarding this manifestation, "unless you tell me her name without delay there will be no visit to Damarel St. Mary. I shall naturally discover it in the end, but if you put me to the trouble of search I fear you will not stay with us in the summer." (Had he not now descended, even below bribery, to something like blackmail?)

Casting another of her sideways glances at him, the young blackmailee considered this proposal.

"You promise — you truly promise that if I tell you her name I shall come to visit you?"

"Yes, I promise."

"You won't say afterwards that you meant something different?"

"No," answered the Reverend Peregrine Carew, feeling slightly hot about the neck. This wretched child was altogether too shrewd. "You shall stay at Damarel

St. Mary if you tell me the name of your schoolmistress, and in what part of Bath your school is situated."

"And you will prevent her from punishing me? And write to Papa about taking me away?"

"I have already said that I would do so."

"I want the lollipops too!"

"You shall have them."

"The best ones, from the shop in Pulteney Street?"

The Rector realised that it was high time to assert himself, and not only because they were now entering the outskirts of Bath. "You will have what sugarplums I choose to buy you," he said severely. "Come, tell me what I have asked you without further loss of time."

Arabella must have recognised that the very extensive tether which she had hitherto enjoyed would stretch no further. After a moment's study of the floor of the chaise she announced sulkily:

"Her horrid name is Miss Frederica Polfrey, and her ugly old house is called the Min — Minerva Seminary for Young Ladies."

At last! Mr. Carew rapped loudly on the glass to attract the postillion's attention, gave the necessary orders (which, since he had been piqued by the recent reflection upon his good faith, included stopping at a pastrycook's to buy sugarplums without delay) and before long the chaise was entering the drive in front of Miss Polfrey's establishment.

It was a handsome building enough, standing in its own grounds, but was, he suspected, though he could not be sure, saluted by its returning inmate with a vulgarly protruded tongue. He prepared to get out.

"You will stay in the chaise, Arabella, until you are sent for. Do you understand? No pranks now, or when we part you won't get the sugarplums after all!" For those delicacies, though duly purchased, were still in his pocket.

"But you said —" began Arabella indignantly.

"Be quiet!" commanded the harassed Rector, turning away to constitute the dismounted postillion a sentry over the young lady, of whose truant proclivities he was already aware.

II

Mr. Carew had pictured Miss Frederica Polfrey as a tall, angular, and probably forbidding female. The reality was surprisingly different, for in a large and well furnished room, whose only scholastic touch was a marble bust of Pallas Athene on a stand, there greeted him a short roundabout gentlewoman of about fifty, becomingly gowned in dove-colour.

Yet even so, her appearance was to prove deceptive. A few exchanges soon, indeed, established the fact of Miss Polfrey's sincerest gratitude for the pains to which the Rector of Damarel St. Mary had put himself to return her erring pupil. She herself had of course been caused acute anxiety and been put to a vast amount of trouble since Arabella's disappearance early that morning. Such an escapade, or indeed anything remotely like it had never before occurred in her well-managed establishment. But then that establishment had never before harboured a child of so unruly a nature.

"I am not altogether surprised, Ma'am," observed her visitor, "to hear you give Arabella Mounsey that character, for I fear it is but too well deserved. Nevertheless I will ask you of your kindness to deal with her as leniently as you can. I am able to plead as my excuse for this request the fact that she is — as I find to my surprise — the daughter of a kinsman — a second cousin — of my own."

"*Indeed*, sir! Mr. Mounsey is a relative of yours?" For some reason Miss Polfrey's expression brightened perceptibly as she learnt this fact. "That is indeed remarkable; singularly fortunate, in fact. How strangely — and on occasions how beneficently — does coincidence invade our lives!"

Though considering this observation somewhat trite, the Rector could not gainsay it, and assented. And then, feeling the need both of a meal and of interviewing Charlotte as soon thereafter as possible, he asked if he might now bring in the captured runaway from his postchaise. He had already risen from his chair.

"Bring her in!" exclaimed Miss Polfrey, looking as if he had proposed to introduce a tiger or a cut-throat. "Oh *no*, Mr. Carew, not on any account! What purpose could that serve, since I have no intention of receiving back into my establishment a little girl — I cannot term her a young lady — of such deceitful habits, unbridled temper and flagrant contempt for authority? I should never have admitted her at all had I been aware of her true character."

The Rector felt as though the bust of Pallas Athene, helmet and all, had landed on his head. No utterance of Miss Polfrey's had prepared him in the least for this ultimatum.

"Not take her back!" he ejaculated. "But . . . what is then to become of her? Her parents, as you know, are in Italy. You cannot, my dear Madam, turn the child into the street!"

"Of that there is fortunately no question, my dear Mr. Carew," returned Miss Polfrey briskly, but with a smile. "Have you not just informed me that you are a kinsman of her father's? Who then more fitting — particularly since you are in Holy Orders — to take charge of Arabella until her parents can be communicated with?"

"Take charge of her until — But letters to Italy in this time of war — consider the delay, the uncertainty even of their ultimate arrival!"

"Arabella has other relatives in England, I believe," countered Miss Polfrey unperturbedly. "There is an aunt somewhere in Warwickshire, whose address must be known to her, since she received a present from her recently. You could no doubt arrange for this lady to receive the child later on, until her parents have made known their wishes concerning her."

"But, Madam," protested the Rector, struggling like a man in a quicksand, and as vainly, "surely you could give the child shelter in the meantime — it might not be for long — just sufficiently long to tide over . . . I do not know that my household arrangements will permit —"

Miss Polfrey, inflexible, allowed herself to interrupt him. "As for *temporary* shelter, you have just, my dear sir, expatiated upon the delay likely to ensue in correspondence with Leghorn! But even were this not so, were it even to be but the case of a single night, I could not admit Arabella Mounsey a second time into this establishment. My conscience, my duty towards the other young ladies under my charge would forbid it. I shall, naturally, write without delay to her parents, and inform them that I have placed her in your care. And, since she will be in such excellent hands, no one can accuse me of the slightest breach of humanity."

Mr. Carew, over whose head the quicksand had now closed, was not so sure of that — only in his view it was not the little girl who was the victim of barbarity. This implacable little partridge of a woman was saddling him with that obstreperous child just when his whole mind had to be given to the delicate problem of his daughter-in-law's flight. There was only one faint ray of consolation in the affair — he would at least have the assistance of Charlotte in coping with her on the homeward journey to Devonshire. (Provided always that he could find Charlotte.)

"Very well, Madam," he said at last, shortly. "I must of course accept your decision. I can do nothing else. You have not yourself the address of this aunt in Warwickshire?"

"I regret that I have not," replied the partridge. "But I think you will find that Arabella has. And now, sir, if I

110

may ask you to wait for a few moments, I will have the child's clothes put together." Receiving no sign of dissent, she rapidly left the room, presumably to give orders to that end, leaving the Rector plunged into a whirlpool of vexation, which was not mitigated by having to partake of a glass of what he considered very inferior port, accompanied by highly sweetened biscuits, which a maidservant brought in while he was waiting.

Miss Polfrey, as a matter of fact, returned sooner than he had anticipated, and signified that Arabella's trunk was ready to be transported to the chaise — so soon, in fact, as to suggest that the child's belongings were already packed up for despatch before his arrival.

"Before I take my leave, Madam," said the defeated Rector, "I shall venture to ask you a favour — which has nothing to do with your late charge."

"Pray ask, Mr. Carew," said Miss Polfrey graciously.

"Thank you, Madam. Would you be obliging enough to furnish me, if you know it, with the address of the French émigré gentleman who, I understand, instructs your pupils in that language? I believe that he is a Monsieur d'Esparre, and if so I have a particular reason for wishing to see him. I . . . I am acquainted with a near relative of his." Mr. Carew saw no reason, though the phrase was perhaps disingenuous, for admitting that this near relative was in fact his own daughter-in-law.

Miss Frederica Polfrey looked a trifle surprised but replied that, since she had it, she would willingly furnish him with 'the Vicomte's' direction; and, going to an escritoire, consulted a book therein. She then

111

wrote an address upon a sheet of paper headed with the name of her Seminary. Armed with this, the Rector took a somewhat stiff, yet subdued leave of the determined little lady, and left the Minervan threshold, followed out to the chaise by two maid-servants bearing Miss Mounsey's trunk.

He found the runaway, with a lollipop of her own providing in her cheek, engaged in making faces from the chaise at some of her late schoolmates, visible at an upper window, who were returning her grimaces with interest. The postillion, staid and middle-aged though he was, appeared to be concealing a smile behind his hand.

"Well, child," announced the Rector with a leaden heart when he had seated himself beside her once more, "I suppose you will be glad to learn that you are not to return to the Seminary. Your schoolmistress —"

Before he could get further Arabella, to his astonished displeasure, had flung herself upon him in an awkward embrace. "Oh, thank you, thank you, Uncle Carew!"

"I am not your uncle," returned he, trying to fend off these endearments, "and it is not I who am responsible for this turn of events. It is because after your most reprehensible conduct in running away, and your general behaviour, Miss Polfrey absolutely refuses to receive you back into her establishment."

"Hurrah! hurrah!" shrilled the outcast. She then, to the Rector's dismay, thrust her head out of the window and shrieked up to the watching young ladies: "I'm not coming back! I'm not coming back!" After which she turned to him and said with a grin: "You will have to take me home to Devonshire with you, Uncle Carew, and not wait till the summer! Oh, how glad I am that you made me get out of that old cart!"

The Rector groaned inwardly. That action of his, unavoidable though it had been, caused him no gladness. And it was with unusual severity that he looked down at his travelling companion, as the chaise wheeled out of Miss Polfrey's domain, and said: "Now listen, Arabella! As I have important business in Bath, I shall leave you in charge of the landlord's wife at the 'Pulteney Arms' while I go about it. But mind you, no tricks in my absence, or you do *not* return with me to Devonshire!"

A vain threat, as he well knew; for what else, for the time being, was he to do with this small incubus, save take her back to Damarel St. Mary with Charlotte?

CHAPTER
EIGHT

Fortified by a good meal, shared with Miss Mounsey, at the "Pulteney Arms", Mr. Carew set out about an hour later on foot for 121, Eglinton Terrace. Under the sun which had now fully emerged, the better quarters of the city of Bath looked, as they usually did, dignified and charming; but these epithets could hardly be applied to the quarter which housed M. and Mme d'Esparre. This brother of Charlotte's must have decidedly straitened means, thought the Rector uncomfortably; well, of course, poor fellow, he would not be here teaching French to little wretches like Arabella Mounsey unless that were the case.

"I believe that Mrs. Nugent Carew is here upon a visit to Monsieur and Madame d'Esparre," he said to the woman — respectable enough — who answered the door of No. 121. "I am the Reverend Peregrine Carew. Will you ask her to receive me?"

Mounting the narrow but clean stairs behind the landlady he heard himself announced:

"Madame Despair, here is a reverend gentleman to see Mrs. Carew."

In the small sitting-room there rose hastily from a chair a dark thin-featured lady who must be Charlotte's sister-in-law. She was almost exactly the Rector's idea of a typical Frenchwoman — but not, somehow, his idea of a French aristocrat. He bowed, and after a penetrating look at him, she curtseyed slightly.

"I am Charlotte's father-in-law, Madame," he said. "I understand that she has come here because of some bad news she had received from abroad."

He hoped that Mme d'Esparre understood English, even if she did not speak it — his own case with regard to French. Evidently she did; nay more, she replied in English, though with a very marked French accent, which transmuted all her th's into z's or s's, and made away entirely with her h's.

"But no, Monsieur," she qualified. "The news Charlotte receive', one cannot call it *bad. Mais elle lui a porté un coup* — 'ow do you say, a shock."

"The news was, perhaps, the death of her aunt in Toulon?" hazarded Mr. Carew. "Although, in that case —"

"Alzo you do not compre'end, n'est-ce pas, why ze death of 'er aunt should make 'er run away from your 'ouse? But it is not a death which make 'er run." The Vicomtesse d'Esparre paused, and added with something between a smile and a grimace, *"Au contraire!"*

Now what did she mean by that? The Rector did not pause to enquire, but said firmly, "I should like, with your permission, Madame, to see Charlotte herself without loss of time."

The Vicomtesse looked at him doubtfully. "She is vairy much prostrate' by this so unexpected news. I do not know if —"

She paused, and the Rector gave her no time to go on. "I have posted up from Devon, Madame," he said still more firmly, "and I am not going back without at least having speech with my daughter-in-law, and learning from her own lips the reason for her flight from my roof. That, I think, is not an unreasonable attitude."

On that Charlotte's sister-in-law gave way. "*Très bien, monsieur le pasteur.* I will tell 'er that you are 'ere. Pray to seat yourself." Waving her hand at a chair, she left the room by a side door.

But Mr. Carew did not sit down. Instead he took a turn or two among the shabby furniture. What was this mystery, and what did Mme d'Esparre mean by saying 'on the contrary' when he had put forward a query about a death in the family? The contrary, the opposite, of death was *birth*. Wild speculations were on the point of invading his mind when the door at the side of the room opened once more and Charlotte herself came in, alone.

She was so greatly altered, such a pale shadow of her usually smiling self, with reddened and dark-rimmed eyes, that every word of the pained remonstrance which he had intended left Mr. Carew at once. For the moment he could not find any words at all. Bad indeed — nay, shattering — must be the tidings from abroad to have brought about this distressing change!

It was Charlotte, therefore, who spoke first. And what she said shocked him almost as much as her appearance.

116

"Oh, sir, I did not think that you would follow me!
. . . How did you discover . . . But I beg you to go back
at once!"

"Go back!" exclaimed Mr. Carew. "My dear
Charlotte, how can you ask such a thing? Whatever
blow you have suffered — and I can see that it has been
severe — have I not a right to learn what it is, and to
help you to bear it?"

Motionless by the door, Charlotte shook her head
mournfully. Even her auburn hair seemed less bright. "I
have no claim on you now, sir."

"Because you have . . . run away? Nonsense, my
dear!" He went to her and took her cold, passive hand.
"What was in that letter which you received? Come
now, my dear, tell me!"

His daughter-in-law withdrew her hand, but rather
as if she did not know what she was doing. "I
cannot bring myself to tell you, Mr. Carew. You had
better read the letter yourself." And, pulling out a
paper from her dress she put it into his hands, went
past him into the room, sat down, and buried that
tragic face in her hands.

Increasingly perturbed, the Rector took the letter
over to the window. It was long, and its folds rubbed
as if it had known considerable travelling. The
heading was 'Toulon', not 'Leghorn', and the date,
he noticed, was as long ago as June of the previous
year. He turned to the end to see the signature; it
was, as he had half expected, 'your affectionate aunt,
Ursule-Marie d'Esparre.' And he began to read what
that lady had written.

My dear Charlotte,

No words can express the relief which your letter from Leghorn has afforded me. It was delivered to me yesterday by the captain of a small trading vessel, who received it from an English sloop of war which had hailed him off the Hyères coast. How often during the past months have I not longed for news of you, and longed also to write to you. But this I could not do, since I did not know where you were or what had befallen you.

Of the dreadful fate of your husband I had heard. But now — prepare yourself, my dear niece, for wonderful news! M. de Marescot is alive after all!

The Rector broke off with an exclamation. Like Charlotte when those same words had first met her eyes, he stood petrified.

"But this *can't* be true!" he said, finding utterance at last. "Your husband — your first husband, that is — alive all this time. Oh no, Charlotte, it is impossible!"

"Read on, sir," said Charlotte in a trembling voice. And, too stunned to do anything else, Mr. Carew complied.

Though desperately wounded, he survived the Italian's dagger, and, by the mercy of God, was picked up almost immediately from the waters of the harbour into which he had fallen, by some fishermen of one of the Iles d'Hyères who

118

happened to be there with their boat. He was unconscious, and in the turmoil of that dreadful night there was no means of establishing his identity — that they only did later — but they took him back to Porquerolles with them and there nursed him back to health, a long business. At the time I naturally knew nothing of how you had fared on your escape; I could only hope that you had both contrived to reach the Spanish flagship, as M. de Marescot had planned.

The first news of your husband's survival was brought to me by the men about the beginning of February together with a letter from him (or rather, a dictated letter, signed by him, his right-hand having been badly crushed between two boats in his fall). Directly I learnt that he was safe and recovering, I wrote and implored him to come to Toulon for a period of convalescence. I also sent him the sum of money for which he asked, since one of the two packets of assignats which he carried with him had somehow been lost, after the murderous attack made on him. This sum he needed in order to recompense his rescuers, and to defray the cost of several visits from a surgeon whom these charitable fishermen had procured from the mainland.

On a second visit to Toulon about three weeks later the fishermen brought news of good progress, but reported that the poor gentleman had such a perfect horror of Toulon after his terrible experience there, that he preferred to remain where he was until complete recovery. Indeed the letter they brought, which told me that he needed a further sum of money for the surgeon and other expenses, more than hinted at this. I regretted his decision, but could understand his aversion. As I am expecting another visit from one or other of these good fellows in a few days, I shall most joyfully take the opportunity of despatching by them to Porquerolles the good news of your safety and present whereabouts in Leghorn — the best incentive to complete recovery which M. de Marescot could receive! Expect therefore soon to see, my dear Charlotte, the bridegroom from whom you were so tragically parted on your wedding day, come to claim you after all! Heaven indeed watches over you both, to reunite you after great trials on both sides. May the rest of your life together be as happy as its beginning was calamitous!

I am myself in good health, and unmolested, so far, by the Revolutionary authorities.

At last, in the heavy silence, the Rector reached this last sentence. "Good God!" he said under his breath — and sat down heavily in the nearest chair. Never, in his speculations over Charlotte's flight, had he imagined a cause for it such as this.

Charlotte raised her head and looked at him with a desperate gaze. "My aunt says that . . . that Heaven has watched over me! She means it . . . though she knew well that I . . . that I would have given the world not to

120

marry Monsieur de Marescot. To me it seems" — she stifled a sob — "as though Heaven had abandoned me!"

The Rector did not make the rejoinder (which his cloth might have dictated) that Heaven never abandoned anyone. He said, in tones as leaden as his heart:

"If this is true — *if* it is true — you are not Nugent's wife."

"No," said Charlotte dully. "Only his mistress."

Coming out like that, and in such circumstances, the self-applied epithet shocked Mr. Carew into a renewed repudiation of the situation. "You must not use that term of yourself, Charlotte! And there must be *some* mistake. If it be true that Monsieur de Marescot is still alive, why did he never come at any time to Leghorn to claim you? He would have had the Mounseys' address from your aunt. Yet it is clear that he never did any such thing, either before your marriage to Nugent last year, or since: for in the first case Edward Mounsey would never have allowed you to go unknowingly through the ceremony of which he was a witness; and in the second —"

But Nugent's wife — or mistress — broke in with almost a note of hysteria.

"It is true that Mr. Mounsey was a witness at our marriage — yet all the time this letter, which made the marriage a mockery, was lying forgotten at the Villa Nespoli. See what he writes!"

Mr. Carew took his cousin's letter and read the apology which it contained. A further degree of consternation showed itself on his face; and under his breath he made somewhat condemnatory remarks.

"Not like Edward Munsey to forget a thing like that — most unfortunate — but naturally he was unaware of the contents of the letter."

"So you see," broke in Charlotte for the second time, "that from the very first moment my happiness has been built on sand — but I did not know it!"

(Yes, thought the Rector, and if Edward Mounsey had not been so criminally careless, there would have been no marriage at all.) Then he pulled himself together for further argument.

"Listen, my dear Charlotte, and let us try to be logical. Painful as it is to you to learn that this letter was already awaiting you in Leghorn at the very time of your marriage, the fact does not make the accuracy of its contents one whit more probable. That remains (in my view at least) just as debatable then, as it was when the letter actually reached your hands four days ago. For Monsieur de Marescot, if living, would certainly have arrived at Leghorn to claim you (or if still unable to travel, would have written to you) neither of which has he ever done. In either of these cases Edward Mounsey would certainly have communicated with you (he would be anxious to atone for this lapse of his) and would also have been particular to give him your present address. Yet Monsieur de Marescot has shown no sign of life whatever, though more than a year has passed! If he really be living, how do you account for never having received even a letter — no message of any kind?"

122

"Because of the difficulties of communication in these times of war, and the great risks of any letter miscarrying," answered Charlotte miserably. "The fate of this letter of my aunt's, already more than six months old, is a proof of this. Monsieur de Marescot may have written more than once — my having received nothing from him is no proof of his not having done so. So any day now I may receive one — worse, he may any day present himself at Damarel St. Mary to claim me as his lawful wife, and to take me away. He has but to apply to Mr. Mounsey for my address, and find a ship to bring him to England."

"Yes, if he be alive. But I am convinced that he is not," reaffirmed Mr. Carew with fervour. "Granted that he survived the assassin's dagger, for that seems from your aunt's letter to be an established fact, I incline to believe that in spite of the report of his partial recovery brought by these fishermen in the second visit to which she refers, Monsieur de Marescot must afterwards have suffered a relapse, and died in this island to which they had taken him. Remember that Mademoiselle d'Esparre never had the opportunity of seeing him in person, and forming an estimate of his actual physical condition, nor does she appear to have got into communication with the surgeon who attended him. Come, my child, terrible as this shock has been to you — and to me — I am convinced that the situation which would arise if the news of your first husband's survival were true, has not, and never will come to pass. You are still what you have always been — Nugent's lawful wife and my dear daughter."

"I may be," agreed Charlotte in a very hopeless voice. "I pray to God many times a day that I am. But, with that letter in my possession, how can I take comfort in a 'perhaps'? As long as he may be alive, and whether he ever comes to claim me or not, I cannot regard myself as anybody but Charlotte de Marescot."

There was a heavy silence. The worst of it was that in his heart the Rector knew that she was right. "My poor boy!" he thought. They had been such a happy pair! He had seen enough, during the past three months, to be convinced that they loved each other sincerely, that the marriage after all had thoroughly justified itself. This black storm-cloud, passing though it must surely be — for he could not bring himself to think otherwise — was of such dimensions that it was no wonder Charlotte had lost her head, poor child. No longer did he blame her for her impetuous flight. But she must return quietly with him now, and quietly must they all try to face this menace until the hour when, please God, it should be withdrawn. Leaning forward, he spoke with all the persuasion of which he was capable.

"Charlotte, my dear girl, you will come back with me to-morrow, will you not? You shall not, I promise you, hear a word of reproach for having left us so suddenly."

"Oh, Mr. Carew, you are too good!" She caught at a sob. "It was wrong, it was very unkind of me to do that. I saw it afterwards . . . But I cannot come back now. I am too much ashamed."

"Ashamed of what?" asked the Rector. "You have been in no way to blame, my child. You had every reason to believe your first husband killed. And no one

124

save ourselves, in Damarel St. Mary or elsewhere, need ever know of this . . . this uncertainty about your marriage. We must do our utmost meanwhile to obtain proof one way or the other — write immediately to Leghorn for instance. And you shall write to your aunt in Toulon."

Very near to tears, Charlotte shook her head. "No, sir, I cannot return."

"Come now, dear child, why not? You are being cruel to Nugent. Imagine his feelings when he arrives to take you back with him to Plymouth and finds that you are not at the Rectory. (Your return there with him will have to be postponed for a while, I grant.) But think of his distress, his disappointment!"

"That is just why I cannot go back with you," cried Charlotte, weeping. "Because Nugent is coming there. I cannot face him — it is too hard! I love him too much . . . and yet he is not my husband!"

There was another silence, broken only by her sobs. The Rector got up and went slowly over to the window. He was face to face with a situation which, to an ordained priest like himself, admitted of no compromise, and there was no way of escaping that fact. Breach of the marriage law there had certainly been — if this more than disconcerting news from Toulon were true — yet it had been, up till now, a perfectly innocent and unconscious breach. Henceforward, on the contrary, it ran a serious risk — Mr. Carew would not put it stronger than that — of being neither innocent nor unconscious. It would be wrong, impossibly wrong, for him to do anything to sap his French daughter-in-law's

125

resolution to take the proper course in this matter, and break off relations with her present husband, though she seemed to be breaking her own heart in taking it. (Irrelevantly it flashed across his troubled mind that the position she was taking up did not exactly fit in with the popular English idea of a nation which held the marriage tie in far too light esteem.)

He turned away at last from the window and saw that Charlotte, tolerably composed now, had risen from her chair. He went to her and took both her hands in his.

"I respect your attitude, my dear child," he said gravely and kindly. "And I can guess the cost of it to yourself. Remain here then, with your brother and his wife, for the present. I am convinced that before long you will hear, perhaps in another letter from Toulon, that the news of your husband's survival is false. As for my poor son — have you, Charlotte, broken this hard tidings to him already, or does it fall to me to do so?"

"I wrote a short letter to him before I left," she replied. "It . . . broke the news. I also told him that I was going to Fabien at Bath; he had the right to know that. But I did not give him this address, of which I think — I hope — he is ignorant. I feared that he might come after me, to try to persuade me. (I do not know how you, sir, discovered it.) So I implore you, if he comes to Damarel St. Mary, or if he writes to you instead, not to give him my direction but rather to use every means in your power to dissuade him from coming here. I could not bear it! Promise me, promise me, Mr. Carew, to do your best in this!"

126

Nugent's father shook his head. "My best will not be of much avail, I fear. If he means to come here I doubt if I can prevent him. But if, upon reflection, I think it right to do so, I will try."

"Tell him that I cannot see him if he does! It is too much to ask from me!" declared Charlotte a trifle wildly, and she in turn began to walk up and down the room, twisting her hands.

The Rector followed her sadly with his eyes. "Is it not too much to ask from *him*, Charlotte, that he should never hear this most distressing story from your own lips, never be able to discuss its truth or falsehood with you, the person most concerned, save himself? Is he to be content with a mere letter?"

But to this thrust Charlotte was saved a reply, for just then the door opened, and her brother walked in with a bundle of his pupils' copybooks under his arm.

CHAPTER
NINE

"So that was Charlotte's English father-in-law," remarked the Vicomte d'Esparre to his wife about an hour later, when Charlotte had withdrawn to her room. "He reminds me a little of the then Bishop of Arles, whom I used to admire in my boyhood."

"Oh, surely not!" expostulated Mme d'Esparre, presumably on doctrinal grounds alone, since she had never at any time set eyes on that prelate. "It is true that I did not look very closely at this Monsieur Carew, for I was in the room with him but a moment or two. In fact, I regretted that I was at home when he came. To me, as I have said from the beginning, the mere idea of a man in Holy Orders — however invalid — having a family is repellent. And how much more the idea of marriage with a member of that family!"

"But if Monsieur Carew's Orders are invalid, he is a mere layman, and you have no cause for repulsion."

His wife paid no attention. "A mixed marriage is bad enough, but to have a kind of ecclesiastic, even heretical, for a father-in-law — it outrages every right feeling! A Church with a married clergy — how can it call itself a Church at all!"

Fabien d'Esparre said rather wearily: "The Orthodox Church seems to find no difficulty in doing so, and in being recognised as a Church."

Honorine shrugged her thin shoulders. "The Orthodox Church is schismatic."

"In any case," observed her husband, "we know — though for poor Charlotte's sake I wish we did not — that, if Tante Ursule is right in what she has written, there has been no marriage with the son of a quasi-ecclesiastic. In which case, my dear Honorine, there is no need to enlarge so much upon your scruples."

"You mean that they are uncalled for because it is not a question of a marriage but of a liaison?" enquired his wife spitefully.

Fabien coloured with anger. "You will oblige me, Honorine, by not using that word in connection with my innocent sister! You know perfectly well that she and Captain Carew went through the marriage ceremony — and before a Catholic priest, too — in all good faith. There could be nothing further from a liaison than their union! Moreover Charlotte instantly left her husband's home on receipt of Tante Ursule's letter — left it despite the personal suffering the action caused her."

"She is young; she will get over it," pronounced the Vicomtesse carelessly. "And when she is able to view the situation more calmly, she will perceive how much better it is not only to be the legal bride of a French Catholic instead of the wife of a foreign heretic, but to have married a man of wealth and position instead of a mere naval officer dependent, probably, upon his pay. For you remember, Fabien, that Monsieur de Marescot, as Charlotte told us at our first meeting with her, has large estates in Louisiana."

"Where the poor girl has no wish to live," completed d'Esparre with some warmth. "Above all as the wife of de Marescot! You cannot have forgotten how she also told us that she had been most unwilling to marry this Creole gentleman, however rich he may have been. Tante Ursule practically forced her into it; Charlotte said so. Your picture of her possible future is rosier than it appears to my poor sister herself!"

"*Forced!*" exclaimed Honorine seizing on the word with an odd emphasis. "No, I do not remember Charlotte's using that term. It is too strong. *Persuaded,* perhaps. Otherwise she could —" She stopped abruptly, glanced at her husband, and went on rapidly: "But, to leave the question of Charlotte's matrimonial entanglements, is it to-day or to-morrow that Monsieur Guillemin returns from wherever he has been the last few days?"

"To-morrow, I believe," answered Fabien. "What were you going to say about Charlotte?"

"Oh, nothing of importance. And I wished to know about Monsieur Guillemin because, if he had been supping with us to-night, another cover would have to be laid. — We were talking of Monsieur Guillemin, Charlotte," she explained rather loudly as the door leading to her sister-in-law's bedroom opened. "He has been away for a few days."

130

Almost wraith-like, the girl came in and sat down. She did not at first appear to take in Honorine's words. Then, with an effort, she said:

"Monsieur Guillemin? Does he still live with you, as he did in Portsmouth?"

"He never precisely lived with us, my dear Charlotte," explained her brother, "nor does he now. He lodges under the same roof, that is all, and for the sake of our landlady's convenience his chief meals are usually served here with ours. And we are pleased that he should again have his headquarters in the same house."

"But there are no ships to paint in Bath," objected Charlotte — since she must say something.

"No, but he has been going round the country making pictures of them in other ports, I believe. At least until recently he has been doing so. But of late, finding, I understand that his marine pictures were not selling so well, he has taken to other subjects. My dear Charlotte, you look worn out! This has been a day of great strain for you. Will you not now retire to bed, and Honorine shall bring you some supper there?" And Charlotte was only too glad to follow his suggestion.

She went about next day like a creature condemned to death, grateful for Fabien's real sympathy, but little relishing her sister-in-law's attempts to cheer her, for they were underlaid by a subtle and most unwelcome flavour of "perhaps it is all for the best," although the actual words were never uttered. It did not lighten her misery that their evening meal was shared, as foretold, by M. Guillemin. It was not that she felt any personal dislike of him, but that the presence of any stranger seemed an intrusion on her grief and her desire for privacy. Fortunately it was quite unnecessary to offer him any explanation of her own presence there, save the very natural one that she had arrived to pay her brother and his wife a visit.

"But how delightful!" exclaimed the little painter, as he stooped in the most courtly way over Charlotte's cold hand. "And *monsieur votre mari*, Madame, is he in Bath also?"

"No, Monsieur, he is in Plymouth."

M. Guillemin's eyebrows lifted a little. "Ah, indeed! I had pictured him at sea again, on the deck of some fine ship . . . It is good of him, in that case, to have allowed you to visit Monsieur and Madame d'Esparre. Perhaps," he added after a moment's pause, "he intends to join you?"

The question had on Charlotte the effect of a knife being twisted in a wound . . . "No, I do not think he will," she murmured, and was grateful to Fabien for remarking quickly that the soup was getting cold, and incontinently steering her to a place at table.

Perhaps he intends to join you. The words rang once more in Charlotte's ears as she again lay sleepless in her little room that night. She knew that Nugent would intend exactly that, but that, starting directly from Plymouth, he could not easily carry out his intention, since he did not know her present address. All at once, however, with a gasp, she sat upright in the dark and the cold. She was wrong — he *could!* One day last autumn (it came to her now) she had told him, in reply

132

to his enquiry, where Fabien lodged in Bath, and he had written down the address in his pocket-book. She recalled the incident distinctly — so distinctly that she now wondered miserably why she had ever thought it worth while to beg Mr. Carew not to communicate the address to him. Nugent had no need to go, or write to Damarel St. Mary to discover it, nor need she in her despairing little letter to him so carefully have abstained from giving it. He had it already, and would come straight here from Plymouth; she was certain of it! So there was only one thing to be done, though it broke her heart anew to contemplate doing it. She lay down again, and sobbed herself at last to sleep.

Next morning she put the case to Fabien and Honorine. For a time at least she must leave their roof, and that as soon as possible. Was there not some place, not too far away, where she could find a temporary retreat? Fabien, like her father-in-law, was inclined to tax her with unkindness. Could she not accord her husband even a short interview? Surely it was her duty, as well as no doubt her secret desire, to do so? In any case he, Fabien, could think of no suitable refuge, since he supposed she would not wish to stay unaccompanied in some strange hotel or inn?

But Honorine's attitude was quite different. She strongly upheld Charlotte in her resolve to avoid an interview which would be both painful and fruitless. And she knew the very refuge for her — a refuge which had the advantage of being only a dozen miles away, and of providing in addition spiritual consolation for a soul in distress. This was a little community of French

Ursuline nuns at Bristol, of which a pious émigrée acquaintance of hers had told her. These nuns, on the testimony of Mlle Lemonnier, occupying a house much too big for them, would gladly receive any Catholic lady desirous of a short stay, nor would it be necessary to write to them beforehand to ask hospitality, for they were always ready to receive any suitable applicant for it. Nothing could be more convenient or more beneficial.

"I will go there at once — to-day, if it is possible," said Charlotte feverishly. "It is only about twelve miles to Bristol, you say. There are stage coaches, I suppose? But, Honorine, neither you nor Fabien will mention to Monsieur Guillemin, will you, the true reason for my leaving you again so suddenly? I could not bear him to know it."

"Most certainly we shall neither of us do such a thing," replied her sister-in-law with emphasis. "On the other hand we must not excite his curiosity by making a mystery of your temporary absence. If the question should arise, the best thing will be to mention your destination. To anyone of Catholic upbringing — though it is true that I suspect Monsieur Guillemin of free-thinking tendencies, indeed there was a time when I even believed him to be a free-mason — it would seem quite natural that you should take advantage of this rare opportunity of spending a few days in a religious community. For in this heretical country," she explained, "there are no such communities save those who, like the nuns at Bristol, have been driven out from the continent, and have sought asylum here like any other refugees."

So it was settled. Charlotte should start for Bristol early that same afternoon, Honorine obtaining of the landlady that dinner should be served a good deal earlier, an arrangement to which it seemed M. Guillemin had no objection, though Fabien d'Esparre, away imparting the French tongue, would come off rather badly on his return.

The meal had not been long in progress when M. Guillemin (necessarily informed of the reason for its unusual hour) expressed a hope that when Mme Carew came back again — he understood with pleasure, he said, that her absence would be short — the weather might be less inclement, so that she could view in comfort the architectural beauties of Bath, its crescents, its public buildings, its fine vistas. He was himself embarking on a series of modest water-colours of those beauties.

"In particular," he finished, "I hope to make a sketch of the Pump Room of Monsieur Nash while there is still the opportunity to do so — for I hear a rumour that it may soon be pulled down."

"You must show my sister-in-law your new sketches when she comes back Monsieur Guillemin," said the Vicomtesse. "She could not fail to admire them."

"I should prefer," said the artist modestly, "to show her the originals, if she were inclined to vouchsafe me that pleasure on her return from . . . Bristol, is it not?"

"Yes, Monsieur," admitted Charlotte; and then, mindful of Honorine's counsel, deliberately added, "I

135

am taking advantage of being so near that city to pay a short visit to the convent of the French Ursulines there."

"Ah, indeed? I did not know that there was one. You are to be envied, Madame Carew. It will be like visiting a small corner of our own beloved France!"

"And also", completed Honorine, with her most pious air, "a time of spiritual refreshment."

M. Guillemin inclined his head. "I do not doubt it. And in what quarter of Bristol are the good Sisters established?"

"Not, I believe, in the city itself, but on the outskirts," replied Mme d'Esparre. "In some mansion standing on that side of Bristol where there is some very romantic scenery — or so I have been told — a deep gorge of some kind. The convent, though not far from the city, is on the way to this spot."

M. Guillemin seemed so much interested in this somewhat vague topography that he laid down his knife and fork for a moment. "Then I believe I know the very mansion," he said slowly. "For when I was in Bristol last autumn, sketching merchant vessels in the river, I visited that gorge. But it was too grand a subject for my humble brush."

And for the rest of the meal he was somewhat silent, and seemed to be reflecting perhaps upon his own artistic faintheartedness. But when it was over, and Mme d'Esparre was devoting herself to coffee-making, he said to Charlotte, in a deprecating manner, "I have been wondering, Madame, whether, since you are going to that particular district of Bristol, I might venture to ask you to do me a favour?"

Charlotte roused herself from her own unhappy thoughts. "If it is anything in my power I shall be pleased to do it, Monsieur."

"You are too kind! It is this then. There is a small painting of mine — oh, quite small, and a water-colour at that — which I have promised to send to a gentleman and his wife who live on the very side of Bristol to which you are going, quite close indeed to the Ursuline convent. I was intending to take the picture myself when next I visit the city in an attempt to sell some more of my wares, but as yet I have none suitable. If it were possible, madame, without overburdening you ... indeed I hardly like to ask it ... but this Mr. O'Connor is flatteringly anxious to have the picture as soon as possible. He has a rich friend shortly coming to see him, to whom in his kindness he wishes to show a specimen of my work ... and that, Madame, as you will understand, is a chance which a poor painter would not readily miss! Might I then throw myself upon your amiability so far as to ask if it would be possible for you to convey this little water-colour to Bristol with you?"

"But naturally," replied Charlotte pleasantly. "I will do so with pleasure."

M. Guillemin beamed. "I do not know how to thank you. I will at once show you how little of a burden the picture will prove. If Madame d'Esparre will excuse me for a moment, as I see that her excellent coffee is not quite ready . . ." And he hastened from the room.

"But what," asked Charlotte of her sister-in-law, "am I to do with this picture when I arrive in Bristol?"

"Monsieur Guillemin will doubtless arrange for that," replied the latter, setting down a cup of coffee before her. "But even if the commission causes you a little trouble, even if the painting is not so light as Monsieur Guillemin declares, I beg you to oblige him in this, for we are indebted to him — in various ways."

Charlotte had barely time to speculate on the nature of these obligations when M. Guillemin was back again, carrying a picture — as at her first sight of him in Portsmouth. But this one was enclosed in a slender gilt frame. He handed it with a bow to Charlotte.

"To make it still easier to place in your baggage, madame," he said apologetically, "I could remove the glass if you wished — and indeed the frame also. I would do anything to make it less of a burden!"

He looked so wistful, so anxious to have his painting delivered as soon as possible to this patron of his — and indeed it was not heavy — that Charlotte instantly protested she could not think of such a thing. "The picture might get damaged. Look at it, Honorine — is it not pretty!'

The little painting was certainly very different, in subject as well as in medium, from his former maritime canvases. Here was a charming thatched and rose-clad cottage on the borders of a stream fringed with bulrushes, the whole bathed in sunlight. But lest any critic should think the scene too unrelievedly rustic, the proper romantic element had been introduced by the hint of a ruined castle and a waterfall in the distance.

138

"Oh, it is not a picture of a ship!" was Honorine's exclamation.

"I *can* paint other things," responded M. Guillemin smiling, "though I admit that I am more at ease with marine subjects."

"Nobody would think so, Monsieur," said Charlotte, with some of her lost animation. "In fact, this picture is so charming that I shall quite regret parting with it. And so, Monsieur Guillemin, if you hear in a little while from this gentleman in Bristol that the picture has not arrived, you will know why!"

"My sister is only jesting," said Mme d'Esparre. "I am sure that she will deliver it most punctually."

"Deliver it!" exclaimed Charlotte, a little startled, for she had not anticipated this. "But — how shall I find the house not knowing the neighbourhood at all? Will there not be some gardener or servant at the convent who could convey the picture to this Mr. O'Connor — was not that the name?"

"But, Madame Carew, I could not trust a gardener or the like any more than I could the carrier, and I should not dream of sending it by *him!*" M. Guillemin's tone held a hint of reproach, and there was even anxiety in his expression. "Mr. O'Connor's house — he is a shipping agent for wines, with a charming wife who would give you a warm welcome — must be within a very short walk of the Ursulines, or I would not have asked you this favour. And neither is in a quarter of Bristol where a lady need fear to go out unaccompanied. If you could possibly, at your own convenience, convey the little picture yourself, and

139

deliver it into the hands of Mr. or Mrs. O'Connor, my gratitude would know no bounds!"

"But of course Charlotte will do so!" put in Honorine quickly, giving Charlotte a meaning look. "She is not timid or afraid to meet strangers — she who went through the siege and evacuation of Toulon! And so, Monsieur Guillemin, you may be quite certain that your picture will reach its proper recipient. For servants are often careless, and dishonest too. We understand perfectly that it is of moment to you that the gentleman should receive his purchase undamaged, and be able to show it to his rich friend when the time arrives."

Hemmed in between the evidence of her recent adventurous past, and the fact that, having already agreed to convey the picture, she was almost committed to the little extra trouble of delivering it to its new owner, Charlotte promised that she would do this and at the first opportunity. Profuse in his thanks, M. Guillemin then tied a piece of paper over his picture, and Charlotte took it forthwith into her bedroom. Honorine, she reflected as she did so, does indeed seem anxious to oblige M. Guillemin; she made herself almost more the mouthpiece of his desires than he was himself. I wonder if it means that he has lent them money?

140

CHAPTER
TEN

I

"Now, my dear child," said Mother Marie-Agathe, "I hope you will be happy here. Comfortable you may not be, for we are very poor, although we have a large house — too large, indeed! But one must not complain of what the good Lord gives us, even if He sees fit to be somewhat inconsiderate at times, as St. Theresa of Avila once pointed out to Him, you will remember! And it was undoubtedly a great grace that He should inspire a Protestant merchant of this city to put a house of any kind at our disposal!"

Small, old, shrewd but sweet-faced, and dignified like all nuns by her habit, she stood with Charlotte in the bare and carpetless bedroom which, though of moderate size, had already taken on the look of a cell, and which, even had the community been better off, they would not have furnished differently.

"And you will see a little of France here and there," added the Mother Superior, and her old eyes rested affectionately on the little holy-water stoup of gay Breton ware hanging on the wall. And Charlotte smiled at the sight of it too.

Even to enter that austerely clean bare parlour downstairs, with its smell of beeswax and its stiffly ranged chairs, where the Reverend Mother had first welcomed her, was to be swept back in an instant to her own convent girlhood at Arles, even though there the Order had been a different one. But all convent parlours breathed the same atmosphere . . . Altogether, this place was a haven where the surge of the sea outside could only be faintly heard, a hidden haven too, where no one would find a sheltering craft. Nugent would not sail in here . . .

Before she surrendered herself to its healing peace, however, Charlotte decided to carry out the errand which she had undertaken for M. Guillemin. Enquiries revealed that Mr. O'Connor's house was not indeed above three-quarters of a mile away, and so next morning, in sunny and frosty weather, she set out with the little picture under her arm.

How very pretty it was on this side of Bristol, outside the real city limits, where the river came flowing down from the deep gorge which, she had learnt from the nuns, was one of the sights of the neighbourhood. Before long she found herself approaching a cluster of neat houses, neither small nor large, which with their gardens and shrubberies almost recalled those she had known at Leghorn; and after enquiries of a passer-by, was quite soon walking up to the door of one of these dwellings. Having asked — she thought it better — for Mrs. O'Connor, she was ushered into a cheerful, well-furnished though slightly untidy parlour. When she gave her name she added that she had come by request of Monsieur Guillemin, though feeling sure that the maid-servant would be unable to transmit his name correctly.

She had to wait some considerable time before the door opened smartly, and there almost ran into the room a smiling, good-looking lady in her thirties who, in a perceptible Irish accent, greeted Charlotte as if she were an old acquaintance.

"Ah now, to think I've kept you waiting, and you coming from that French painter — sure I can't pronounce his name any more than Sally could! Is it a message about a picture ye've brought from him, me dear — indeed I don't think the girl is after saying your name right neither!"

"My name is Carew," said Charlotte, rather overwhelmed by this exuberance, so unlike the usual English reserve. "It is not a message that I bring you, Madam, but the little picture itself."

"The painting itself!" beamed Mrs. O'Connor, and her eyes went to the package which Charlotte had deposited upon the rosewood table near her. "Ye have it there, and ye brought it all the way from Bath? Isn't that the kind act, now! Sit down again, Mrs. Carew me dear, and we'll all have a glass of me husband's very best Madeira. I'll be calling him to come, for as luck has it, he never went to his office this morning. And pleased indeed he'll be to know the picture's come, and what a pretty young lady has brought it!" On which speech she left the room almost as tempestuously as she had entered it.

Mr. O'Connor, with whom she returned, was plainly not the product of the same florid mould as his wife,

143

for there was something grave, almost prim, in his air. But he was pleasant enough, and, presented to Charlotte, thanked her warmly for her kindness, and hoped that M. Guillemin was in good health. Wine and biscuits were brought in and dispensed, Mrs. O'Connor never ceasing to chatter or every few minutes, to push back locks of her pretty but negligently arranged dark hair. All the while the picture lay shrouded and unviewed upon the rosewood table. 'I might have brought the wrong one for all the notice they have taken of it,' thought Charlotte . . .

"If I may make a personal remark, Madam," observed Mr. O'Connor, as he relieved her of the wine-glass which she declined to have refilled, "you pronounced our friend the painter's name as he pronounces it himself — and as I fear nobody else in this country is likely to do!"

"But you see, sir, I also am French," explained Charlotte, "so that the name gives me no difficulty."

"It's married to an Englishman ye'll be then, Mrs. Carew, to bear the name ye have!" exclaimed her hostess.

"Yes," answered Charlotte; and then grew first red, then pale. For why was she here in Bristol at all except that she was *not* really so married?

But the couple seemed unaware of her discomposure.

"It is a pity, Madam," went on Mr. O'Connor, "that you will not allow me to fill up your glass so that we may all drink success to your compatriot and his art. I am afraid that the poor gentleman finds it none too easy to make a livelihood by his brush."

144

Charlotte said she feared it also, and that it was the same with many of her exiled fellow-countrymen.

"So you also, Mrs. Carew, are, like him, a Royalist emigrant?"

"Why, yes, sir! How else could I be in England?"

"Mr. O'Connor means, I think, me dear," explained his wife, "that an Englishman meeting a young lady as pretty as yourself in France, might be bewitched the way he'd forget to enquire into her politics, and be marrying her out of hand, the lucky man!"

As it happened, there was a good deal of truth in this complimentary interpretation, but now — it stabbed rather than gratified.

"And how, if you will forgive my curiosity," said Mr. O'Connor, coming and sitting down by her again, "did you make the acquaintance of Monsieur Guillemin, and in consequence so kindly make yourself his messenger?"

So Charlotte gave a brief account of her two encounters with the artist, and had barely finished before Mrs. O'Connor was saying: "Sure, Phelim, Mrs. Carew will be thinking it strange if ye don't unwrap the picture and look at it!" — which was in truth just what Mrs. Carew *was* thinking.

"Indeed you are right, my dear," agreed her husband, getting up; "and it seems ungrateful to Mrs. Carew as well — which indeed I am not. Let us be opening it at once. I admired Monsieur Guillemin's art very much when he first showed me some specimens, but I see enough of ships in my business here, so I asked him would he paint me something quite different." He had the wrappings off now and was holding up the little water-colour. "And, by the saints, he has certainly done so!"

"Oh, Phelim, isn't it the beautiful landskip!" exclaimed his wife admiringly. "Will ye look at the roses that's in it! I wonder where we'll be hanging it now, the way 'twill be best seen?"

A brief discussion ensued, at the conclusion of which Charlotte took her leave, refusing Mrs. O'Connor's pressing invitation to pay them another visit, and Mr. O'Connor's to show her the port of Bristol. She excused herself on the ground that she had come thither in order to spend a few days in seclusion with the Ursulines, and this explanation the O'Connors, Catholics themselves, immediately accepted as valid. With reiterated thanks for her obliging behaviour in bringing M. Guillemin's production, they conducted her to the door, and Charlotte found herself with her face once more set in the direction of the convent.

A coldish wind pressed against her as she walked, and she had not gone a quarter of a mile before she was obliged to search in her muff for her pocket handkerchief, only to find that it was not there. Nor was it in her pocket. She must have dropped it at the O'Connors'. And on that she came to a standstill. At the cost, perhaps, of a few intermittent sniffs, she could quite well have continued without it, but that embroidered pocket handkerchief had been bought for her by Nugent in Portsmouth in those first happy days of their married life (she still must think of it by that term) and she could not bear for the handkerchief to pass so easily into the casual ownership of Mrs. O'Connor. The circumstances of its purchase were still too vivid in her memory for that. She would turn back and ask the maid-servant to look for it in the parlour she had just quitted, and need not herself trouble Mrs. O'Connor by entering the house again. All the way back she thought of that day in Portsmouth; it was the last but one of their stay . . .

This time Charlotte had to wait longer upon the doorstep of the villa. At last she heard hurrying footsteps; then, somewhat to her surprise, the door was opened by Mrs. O'Connor herself, who also showed a not unnatural astonishment.

"Mrs. Carew! Now I hope this will be meaning that ye've thought better of it, and will dine with us one day after all? Sure the good Sisters would wish ye to have a little relaxation!"

But Charlotte smiled and shook her head, explaining apologetically the real purpose of her return, adding that the handkerchief in question was 'a favourite one'. With exclamations of sympathy Mrs. O'Connor thereupon swept her back into the parlour; sure, they'd soon come upon it, she declared. And so they did, almost immediately, for the missing object was lying in the corner of the sofa on which Charlotte had been sitting.

With renewed apologies for her carelessness, Charlotte was just taking her leave, when she was mildly astonished to perceive upon the table not merely the discarded wrapping of M. Guillemin's painting, but also its frame and glass. This seemed so odd that she glanced twice in that direction; but she had not been mistaken. Only the empty chrysalis was there; the actual butterfly had gone. Presumably the O'Connors thought the picture worthy of a more elaborate or at least a different frame; if so, they had lost little time about the exchange. But it was none of her business if they had; and she made no comment. Mrs. O'Connor, however, seemed to become aware almost at the same instant of what her visitor had seen, for she suddenly flushed up and made a half movement as though to gather up these relics, then she checked it, and said wheedlingly:

"Ah now, Mrs. Carew alanna, let you not be telling the French gentleman that —"

She never finished, for from outside the open parlour door came the voice of Mr. O'Connor calling loudly: "Molly, Molly, why the devil have you gone off just as I'm needing you to pour out the boiling water while I mix in the —"

"Whist now, Phelim!" cried his wife equally loudly, and running to the door cut short this invisible and annoyed inquiry. "Sure I'm here in the parlour with Mrs. Carew, who came back for the pocket handkerchief she'd left behind! Let you wait a moment!" Turning back into the room she said to Charlotte, laughing: "Will ye believe it, me dear, if Mr. O'Connor can get the kitchen to himself, as he has at this moment, Sally being gone off to the market, he'll be trying his hand at some dish or other! But 'tis always meself has to go to help him out in the latter end."

148

"Then pray do not let me keep you any longer," urged Charlotte. "For it is plain that Mr. O'Connor is in real need of your assistance at this moment."

"Ah, not at all!" declared that gentleman negligently, now appearing in the doorway and bowing to Charlotte. "I heard what my wife was saying to you, Mrs. Carew, about my culinary experiments, but like most of her sex she exaggerates. She —" Then somehow his gaze, too, fell upon the picture-frame and its accompaniments, and he came to a stop.

"Ye're right, me dear," said Mrs. O'Connor instantly. "Mrs. Carew has seen that we've taken the picture out of its frame, and I was just after beseeching her not to tell the poor man of it. Sure we'd not be wanting him to suffer in his feelings, for 'twas no doubt the best frame he could lay his hands upon. But we are after putting it in a much finer one," she went on, turning to Charlotte once more; "and being mad Irish, ye know, and impatient, nothing would serve Phelim there but he must do it at once."

(But I understood that he was trying to cook, thought Charlotte; though indeed he does not look as if he had been — or were ever likely to.) "No, I promise not to tell Monsieur Guillemin," she said with a smile, and was thereafter conducted once more by the couple to the front door, and a cordial leave taken of her.

Yet if Charlotte could but have seen, that door had barely closed behind her before Mrs. O'Connor, quite without smiles now, drew a long breath and looked at

149

her husband, who returned the look in silence. It was Mr. O'Connor who broke it.

"If you are most damnably careless, Molly," he said in a tone of grudging admiration, "at least you have a damnably quick wit!"

"And 'tis yourself was damnably careless too, coming screeching after me and then, when ye got into the room, looking the way ye might be seeing a banshee or the like! Ah well, there's no harm done, please God!"

"You do not think the girl had left her pocket handkerchief behind the way she'd be obliged to come and fetch it?"

"I do not — any more than the babe unborn!"

On which the two returned, not to the kitchen, but to Mr. O'Connor's private sanctum, where M. Guillemin's carefully painted and belauded little water-colour lay rather forlornly on a table.

II

It was Sunday, the third evening after Charlotte's departure, and the trio occupying Mrs. Gibbings's rooms in Bath were unusually cheerful over their supper. Fabien d'Esparre had just secured a rise in salary, on the strength of which the Vicomtesse had bought a game pie at a pastrycook's; and M. Guillemin — who, however, was nearly always in good spirits — had produced a bottle of wine which he had brought back from Bristol — a present from his new patron, Mr. O'Connor, the wine-shipper. The meal was nearly over, and conversation was flowing freely under the stimulus of this gift, when there came a knock at the door and the voice of Mrs. Gibbings saying: "A gentleman to see Mr. and Mrs. Despair."

"Admit him!" said 'Mr. Despair' in a somewhat lordly manner, and the gentleman was incontinently ushered in. It was Captain Nugent Carew.

Honorine d'Esparre gave an audible gasp. So he *had* come after her! Fabien rose from the table; M. Guillemin also.

"Captain Carew! An unexpected pleasure! Will you join us — or at least take a glass of wine after your journey?" (It was best to begin with the requisite courtesies, however this far from welcome interview was likely to terminate.)

"No, thank you, Monsieur," replied Nugent briefly. His eyes had already told him of Charlotte's absence. "Not, at least, until I have had speech with my wife. Will you, Madame, be good enough to take me to her?"

"I regret, Captain Carew, that my wife cannot do that," said Fabien. "Charlotte is not here."

"Not here? But she came here, surely! That was her intention; she told me so!"

"She did come here, yes. But she is not here now."

"You cannot mean that she has left you," said Nugent in a tone of disbelief. (M. Guillemin during these exchanges had retired to a corner of the room, where, presumably that he might be considered as still further withdrawn from participation in the family affairs of others, he produced a book from his pocket.) "You cannot mean that she has left you!" he repeated.

151

"For a short time she has done so. But only for a short time."

"Where has she gone?"

"I am afraid that is just what I cannot tell you."

Nugent confronted his French brother-in-law much as he might have confronted a mutinous crew — had he ever had to face such an unlikely gathering. "That statement I do not believe," he answered roundly. "You must know perfectly well where Charlotte is. And my belief is, that in anticipation of my arrival, you are concealing her somewhere in this house — misguided girl that she is!"

"No, no, zat is not so!" exclaimed the Vicomtesse, coming forward to her husband's side. "You shall look, Monsieur, if you wis', in all our rooms — zey are not many — in Charlotte's *chambre-à-coucher*, everywhere! N'est-ce pas, Fabien?"

"Certainly," responded he. "And no doubt our landlady, when she learns of Captain Carew's errand, will allow him to search the rest of the house also."

"Thank you, Monsieur," replied their visitor, with no abatement of his grimness. "I shall accept your offer." And, Fabien immediately going to the door by which the Rector had seen Charlotte enter, he followed him.

The brief investigation was conducted almost in silence. In his heart Nugent knew that the offer would not have been made had it been likely to yield any fruits. Charlotte's bedroom was palpably unoccupied. And he reflected that there had been no fourth place laid at the supper-table. It did indeed look as if she were not here.

152

Nevertheless, he then went downstairs and closely questioned Mrs. Gibbings, who, in a flutter, confirmed this conclusion. The young lady, Mrs. Carew, had indeed left No. 21 last Friday afternoon, but she did not know for what destination. She readily offered to show Captain Carew all the other rooms, including her kitchen and bedroom, and did so, excluding only one, to whose shut door she pointed apologetically.

"That there's the other French gentleman's room, sir. It will be locked, I expect — yes, it is. Takes his meals and often sits with Mr. and Mrs. Despair, he does, along of its making less work for me. But if you was to ask him, sir, I'm sure —"

"Yes, yes," said Nugent a little impatiently.

"And you don't think, I hopes, sir," finished the good woman rather tearfully, "that I'm still a-hiding of the young lady somewheres? Never would I do such a thing — and from her own lawful husband too! Nor Mrs. and Mr. Despair aren't a-hiding of her neither, for I see her with my own eyes go off with her little valise on Friday."

Nugent pressed some money into her hand and mounted the stairs again. When he re-entered the sitting-room the d'Esparres were talking in a low voice to M. Guillemin, no longer in his corner; but broke off at his appearance, what sounded like an argument or remonstrance. The painter fellow ought to have taken the opportunity to withdraw altogether; not that, at this stage, Nugent much cared whether he were present or not.

"You are convinced, I hope, Captain Carew, that my sister is not concealed anywhere in this house?" asked the Vicomte, not without a tinge of satisfaction in his voice.

"With the exception of one room, where I admit I should not expect to find her, yes," replied Nugent, glancing at the tenant of that apartment.

"Indeed no!" responded M. Guillemin with emphasis. "But I shall willingly unlock the door for you, sir!"

"Very well. As I leave the house, then — a formality merely. And so, Monsieur d'Esparre, as Charlotte is apparently not under this roof, I demand to be told where she is — and why she left!"

"That at least I can tell you," his recalcitrant brother-in-law answered. "It was just because she half feared that you might come here after her, and she wished to avoid an interview . . . in the present distressing circumstances."

Nugent Carew received this information outwardly unmoved. But his mouth tightened still more. "If she could take such an unbalanced view of the situation, then it must have been under pressure of some kind. Whether I see her personally or no, I must be told where she is, and satisfy myself of her safety."

"Charlotte is safe enough, Monsieur!" intervened Honorine d'Esparre. "Verree safe! She could not be in a better place. And it ees 'er own wish zat zis place should not be known."

"I have only your word for that, Madame," retorted Nugent. "That she was coming here she informed me by letter. Her present disappearance has therefore very suspicious elements about it. You will kindly tell me without further subterfuge to what 'place of safety' you have sent, or induced my wife to go!"

"If she were indeed your wife, Captain Carew —" began Fabien.

"I think you will find that she is quite sufficiently my wife in the eyes of the law!" returned Nugent with extreme grimness. "A six-months'-old letter from Toulon with rumours of the survival of a man killed more than a year ago will not much impress an English magistrate. And to a magistrate I shall go without delay, and lay a charge against you both of conspiring to keep my wife from me."

"A magistrate, what is zat?" asked Mme d'Esparre in an uneasy whisper of M. Guillemin, in whose reply only the words 'juge de paix' uttered in a rather apprehensive tone, were audible to Nugent. That, and the temporary hush in the room showed that he had secured an effect.

"Surely," protested Fabien at last with a gesture, "you cannot contemplate, in so delicate a matter . . .

"I am not threatening what I do not mean to carry out," said Nugent quietly. "In this country, at least, the assistance of the law can be claimed against those who interfere between husband and wife."

"Forgive me for pointing out that it is a question of whether you indeed are husband and wife! I also," went on Fabien, "have some standing as Charlotte's nearest relative by blood — her brother, in short — and some right to protect her interests and reputation. Until, therefore, this most painful situation is cleared up, it is

155

my plain duty to withhold information as to her present whereabouts — which I assure you on my word of honour are completely suitable."

"Very good," returned Captain Carew. "Then, Monsieur d'Esparre, you will know what to expect. I wish you both good night."

He was too angry, as he left the d'Esparres' room, to realise that M. Guillemin had followed him out, and had reached the head of the stairs before he heard a voice close behind him saying: "Allow me now to show you my room, Captain Carew!"

He turned. There was the little painter, with a key already in his hand.

"Unnecessary, thank you," replied Nugent and began to descend the stairs. The Frenchman hopped after him and laid a hand on his arm.

"Pray give me a moment, Captain Carew!" he said earnestly in a lowered voice; and Nugent paused. "It grieves me," went on M. Guillemin, "it sincerely grieves me that you should be kept in ignorance — even with the best intentions — of the whereabouts of your young wife. But to take the matter to a magistrate will mean further delay, will it not? And the affair will then get abroad . . . You will not reconsider your threat?"

"Not unless my demand is complied with," answered Nugent impatiently, wondering why the devil this little man, whose tactless remaining in the room throughout the recent encounter had not exactly gratified him, should now betray what sounded almost like a personal interest in the affair.

156

"In that case, then," said M. Guillemin, lowering his voice still further, and giving a quick backward glance at the door of the d'Esparre's apartment, "to save my friends there from unpleasantness, — and also because you, mon capitaine, were so obliging to me at Portsmouth . . ." He paused suggestively.

"You know where she is!" exlaimed Nugent in considerable surprise. "Out with it then quickly, if you please!"

"From gratitude I tell it to you," repeated the delineator of the *Callisto*. "But I pray you not to betray me to the Vicomte or to Madame — especially not to Madame!" He came still closer and all but whispered: "Your wife is on a visit to the convent of the Ursulines in Bristol, *religieuses* who fled from France a few years ago."

CHAPTER
ELEVEN

Her mission to the O'Connors fulfilled, Charlotte had expected to be able to surrender herself to some measure of peace in her refuge, her fortress, with the Dames Ursulines. In the chapel she sometimes succeeded, but nowhere else. Sure as she was that she was doing right, the cost, at times, seemed more than she could pay. Yet here she had all the armoury of the Church to help her against her own desires, she was immersed in an atmosphere of prayer and renunciation. And indeed, though she felt sometimes that these exiled nuns had no struggles of their own — except to make both ends meet — that atmosphere, joined to the religious teaching which she herself had known from early childhood, did more, possibly, than she realised to help her maintain her difficult resolution to see no more, for the present, of the husband who was perhaps no husband at all.

And then on Monday the battle entered on a much sterner phase. She had come from the chapel and had just re-entered her chilly and austere room when the sister portress came to tell her that a gentleman was waiting to see her on urgent affairs in the parlour. He would not give his name.

Charlotte's heart seemed all at once as cold as her room itself. The nun had left before she could question her on the visitor's appearance. It could not be Nugent, for she knew that he would never have been able to induce Fabien or Honorine to inform him where she was. It must — she had to face it — it must be M. de Marescot, her real husband, arrived at last in England, and sent on from Damarel St. Mary Rectory to Bath, where — to him — her whereabouts would willingly be made known. Yes, it was Oreste himself, risen from the dead, risen from Toulon harbour. And she must go with him . . . how many thousand times more unwillingly now than on that dreadful day which had seen their hasty wedding. She knelt for a moment before the crucifix on the wall, then, pulling her resolution round her like a cloak, went down to the parlour. "I must greet him, after all he has suffered, as though I were glad to see him — I must, I must!"

But when she opened the parlour door she uttered no greeting at all, only a little cry. For it was Nugent who was standing there.

Yes, it was Nugent, and not as she had nearly always seen him, in naval uniform, but in civilian attire; sterner, too, than she had ever known him look — though she knew that he could look stern. Her heart went to meet him, but her body, more obedient, stayed where it was, just inside the parlour door, which her hand unconsciously closed. He too made no move.

"How . . . how did you find me? Did Mr. Carew —" She heard her own voice; it fluttered uncertainly. Any words would have been difficult to bring out, and these were not what she most desired to say.

"I have not been to Damarel St. Mary. It was through that French painter in Bath," answered her husband briefly. "Your brother and his wife refused to tell me where you were. Was that by your desire?"

His tone was frigid in the extreme. Charlotte bent her head. "I feared that you might —" This time the words tailed off into nothing.

"Come after you, you mean? Your apprehension was well founded. I do not surrender my rights as a husband as lightly as you forget your duty as a wife!"

It was like being stabbed with an icicle. The only way to endure the pain of it was to parry with what weapons she had.

"But, Nugent," she answered, struggling with the difficulty in her voice, "it is just because I do remember my — my duty as the possible wife of another man that I came away. Surely in your heart you know that to be the only reason — and you must admit that it is a weighty one!"

"Weighty!" repeated he. "You consider that word 'possible' a weighty reason, a justification for stealing secretly out of my father's house, and for conspiring with your relatives to hide yourself away in this fashion, as though you were some Clarissa Harlowe, and I a Lovelace!"

Charlotte flushed. She was familiar with Richardson's famous novel. "Believe me, I did both against my will, Nugent! But until I hear once more —"

"Until you hear! You may never hear! This disastrous rumour upon which you have chosen to act so precipitately has taken — how many months? — to reach you? For how many more do you intend to await its confirmation or denial? I may soon be going to sea again, perhaps for years. Am I to sail knowing that my wife believes she is not married to me?"

"No, no!" exclaimed Charlotte in great distress. "I do not *believe* that — I only do — I only do not know!" She put her hands over her face.

Next moment she felt them gently but firmly taken in his. "Charlotte! Look at me — and say that you will return to the Rectory! I do not demand any rights — I do not even ask you to return to Plymouth with me — I only beg of you to come back to the people who have grown to love you. And because we also love each other! — Or do we not?"

The tears were running down her face now. "You know we do, you know we do! And that is why, if I came back . . . No, no, I cannot return until I know for certain that Monsieur de Marescot is not alive."

"He is *not* alive!" declared Nugent with emphasis. "I would stake my own life on that! If he were he would certainly have come to England to claim you — even if, in the whole year and more that has passed since that night in Toulon, he has never communicated with you. Why has he never come? Mounsey would not have withheld your address. It is because he is dead."

"I have weighed all that," said Charlotte faintly. "I have gone over all those arguments until my head reels with them. But there is another which you may not have taken into account, and that is, that my aunt may in the end have lost touch with him. Perhaps the fishermen never paid another visit to Toulon as she expected, and so she could not send a message to him about me. Perhaps he himself, as a Royalist, was unable to enter the town, if he tried to do so. Tante Ursule was the only possible channel through which he could learn that I had gone to Leghorn; and if he was ignorant of that fact he could do nothing to trace me. No; that he has not written nor appeared in person does not prove that he is not living — living but still without news of where I am. Oh Nugent, Nugent, if only I could see it otherwise!"

He had dropped her hands, and now remained looking down at her sombrely. "I see. There is then no end to the separation to which you condemn us — and all for the sake of a man who never really was your husband! I cannot believe that the mere ceremony is binding!"

"I cannot see it in that light," said Charlotte, still more faintly. "We *were* married, and marriage is a sacrament."

"But not *our* marriage, I suppose!" And here Nugent seemed all at once to become conscious of the implications of their surroundings. "It is this Romish religion of yours!" he said, half to himself . . . and the words sounded very much as though they came out from clenched teeth. "And I believed once that it would never come between us!"

But Charlotte heard and took up the challenge, even with her handkerchief at her eyes.

162

"Yet if your sister Sophia were in my unhappy position, would not your Church uphold her in her resolution? If it would not, then surely it . . . But I am sure it would. Your father did not — could not — condemn my attitude."

He made no answer to that, but recurred impatiently to his previous argument.

"Charlotte, your scruples are all based upon an impossibility! Why, you saw de Marescot killed before your eyes! It is so wrong-headed, what you are doing. I had thought you more sensible." With these last words a new idea seemed to strike him, and in the tone of one who believes that he has at last lit upon the solution of an enigma, he exclaimed: "These fancies! My dear, is it that you are going to have a child?"

"Oh no, no!" she exclaimed, taken by surprise, and with an emphasis which was unfortunate.

"You mean," said her husband instantly, and with a return to his bitterer mood, "because, according to your ideas, it would be born out of wedlock!"

He was trying to hurt her — had succeeded, and saw it. Catching her hand again he said penitently: "Forgive me, forgive me! I did not mean that . . . But Charlotte, my dear, dear Charlotte, you will at least return with me to Damarel St. Mary, will you not?"

She was so tired of fighting against him, and against her own deep desire, that all she could do was to shake her head and whisper, "I cannot, Nugent, I cannot. Oh, do not press me so! I cannot act against my conscience."

That austere and unpleasant word dropped between them on to the waxed floor-boards of the convent parlour almost as a round-shot might have done. It seemed too, that to Nugent Carew it *was* the final shot in this unsuccessful engagement. He drew off from the encounter and reverted to his stiffest.

"Very well. Only, before I take leave of you, pray assure me of one thing — that your coming to this place does not mean that you have any intention of solving the problem by becoming a nun?"

Even in the midst of her misery and fatigue Charlotte felt a prick of amusement. How could he ask such a question! "Such an idea never entered my head for a moment!" she replied instantly. "And even had I wished to do so — which indeed I do not — I could not, unless —" There she stopped, regretting that she had said so much.

"Unless what?"

"A married woman," said Charlotte slowly, "cannot take the veil unless her husband enters religion also."

"Indeed! Is that the arrangement?" observed Nugent sarcastically. "I am glad to hear that there exists that much safeguard. For though I cannot of course answer for the phantom of Monsieur de Marescot, I can assure you that I am not likely to take such a step!"

And at this very unnecessary declaration, Charlotte, despite her wretchedness, was most perversely seized with half hysterical laughter. To Nugent her mirth obviously appeared as heartless as it was unexpected. His angry astonishment was plain on his face as he looked at her; then he crossed the room again to pick up his hat. And Charlotte's untimely merriment abruptly ceased.

So this was the end. She had won — at what a cost — not he. But she was not going to let him depart in anger, not even if she had to bar the way to the door behind her, and refuse to let him pass until he had forgiven her. Yet before she could get out a word of any sort, before she could take a step either backwards or forwards, that door suddenly opened from without, and the voice of the lay portress said in French:

"If Madame will be so good as to wait here I will inform Mrs. Carew — oh, *pardon!*"

But the deed was done. Charlotte had turned in dismay, and beheld advancing upon her a lady in a flamboyant hat — Mrs. O'Connor.

She too was brought up short. "I beg your pardon, Mrs. Carew! I fear I am intruding?"

"Not in the least, Madam, I assure you," said the other visitor, advancing. "I was upon the very point of departure." And he bowed to his wife. "I have the honour to take leave of you, Mrs . . . *Carew*." Another bow to the intruder, and he was gone.

None but the most obtuse of women, and Mrs. O'Connor was not that, could fail to perceive that her call was being paid at a most unfortunate moment. For young Mrs. Carew was standing there like a creature that's been knocked on the head, thought the Irishwoman.

"Me dear," said she quickly, laying a hand on her arm, "the gentleman's gone before he intended! 'Tis

165

my fault — no, 'tis the portress's. See now, let me go after him and call him back — he'll not have gone far!"

Charlotte in her turn laid a hand — a restraining hand — upon Mrs. O'Connor's arm. "No, no, it would be quite useless — unnecessary, I mean. Pray do not think of it. We had finished . . . our conversation."

(But oh, her heart cried, if only Mrs. O'Connor had not been ushered in just at that moment!)

"Is that so? Still, I'll not be keeping you long, me dear." The visitor went on with words which passed Charlotte by until she forced herself to listen, when she gathered that Mrs. O'Connor had apparently come merely to repeat the invitation to call upon them again which Charlotte had already twice refused. Was it for *that* she had been forced to allow Nugent to depart in that bitter and unrelenting mood?

"I am sorry, Madam," she replied dully, "but I intend returning to Bath immediately . . . possibly indeed this afternoon." It was on the impulse of the moment that she spoke, but directly the words had passed her lips, she knew that she desired never to enter this convent parlour again.

"Ah now, wasn't I half afraid of it!" returned Mrs. O'Connor in a voice of regret. "Me husband will be sorry indeed. I wonder, now," she went on, hesitating a little, and looking at her with almost a coy smile, "I wonder, if ye're returning to Bath immediately, would ye do him another kindness — you that's been so kind already, I declare 'tis a shame to ask it?"

"Yes," said Charlotte almost mechanically. "Anything that I can do . . ."

166

A letter now emerged from Mrs. O'Connor's many-coloured reticule. " 'Tis this letter — if 'tis not troubling ye too much to take it back with ye and give it to the painter gentleman, into his own hands? Sure it's to thank him for the little picture, but it's to pay him for it too. Phelim thought that with a banker's draft in it 'twould be safer with yourself than with the post. And there'd be no franking to pay — we all have our little economies these days, haven't we, me dear?"

"Certainly I will take the letter and give it to Monsieur Guillemin." She held out her hand for it.

"Ye're sure 'tis not troubling you too much, Mrs. Carew — and it having money in it?"

"I shall remember that, and be very careful not to lose it." If only Mrs. O'Connor would go!

But there were more expressions of regret and gratitude to be uttered before that lady did indeed take her departure. Charlotte went out with her to the hall, saying little. And after the portress had let the visitor out and had gone away herself, she still stood there as if her body would no longer obey her, her eyes fixed on a vast painting of some civic function or other, a relic of the mansion's former aldermanic days, which had never been removed from the hall. She was not really seeing it, but her ears were listening, as if with a life of their own, for some sound which might, in spite of all, announce Nugent's voluntary return. But there was no such sound; he had really gone, gone in anger, and it was she who had sent him away. It was infinitely worse than if he had never come.

What did at last break the silence was the rattle of
Mother Marie-Agathe's long, hanging rosary as she
came across the hall.

"My child, my child, do not stand there like that!
Come into my room. I guess what has happened, and if
you want to cry, you shall cry there. No one, not even
our Blessed Lady herself will blame you if you do."

CHAPTER
TWELVE

I

Mrs. Carew had been smoothing her hair in her bedroom, which overlooked the Rectory drive, when she heard the sound of wheels, and hastened to the window. Yes, it was the chaise from the 'Clavering Arms,' and she could just see that Peregrine was not alone in it. Thank God, he had succeeded then in his mission, and had brought Charlotte back with him. What a relief!

It took her a moment or two to adjust her cap upon her head again, so that by the time she reached the hall, pondering over the exact temperature of her greeting to the runaway daughter-in-law, the travellers were already there. That is to say, the Rector, to her astonishment, was just leading in a plain little girl of nine or ten with a markedly sticky mouth, who clutched in one hand a paper bag and looked about her with a mixture of excitement and distrust.

"Who is this, Peregrine?" asked his wife, bewildered. "And where is Charlotte — still outside?"

"This, my dear, is Edward Mounsey's little daughter, whom I have brought upon a visit. Charlotte is . . . not returning at present. I will tell you more later.

Meanwhile this young lady — make your curtsey to Mrs. Carew, Arabella! — must be hungry."

"Not if you have been feeding her all the way on sugarplums, Peregrine," retorted Mrs. Carew, on whom the visible traces of this form of nourishment had not been lost. "However, I expect *you* are." The disappointment had hit her hard, and not only on Nugent's account. Was this ugly little creature, moreover, to be placidly accepted as a substitute for Charlotte? And why was she here in any case?

At this point Tom and Peggy came racing along the landing above with cries of "Charlotte's come back, hurrah!" But that was before they had turned the corner of the stairs. A moment later they were standing by their mother's side staring mutely and suspiciously at the small newcomer, who eyed them with an equally hostile expression.

"This, children," said Mr. Carew, putting his hand upon the shoulder of the unwanted guest, "is your little cousin Arabella Mounsey, and you must be very kind to her, for her parents are a long way off, in Italy."

As if these words had been a cue, Arabella's besmeared mouth promptly took a downward curve, and she broke into a howl interspersed with speech. "I want to go back to Leghorn! I want Mamma!" And then, abating the lamentation a little, "I want Cousin Nugent! Where is Cousin Nugent?"

"I told you, Arabella, that he was not here," said the Rector in an exasperated voice. "Elizabeth, I think this child had better be put to bed at once. She has had a long and tiring journey."

170

"I cannot imagine why she ever made it," commented his wife with undeniable asperity. "But come with me, Arabella," she added more kindly. "You shall sleep with your cousin Peggy." And the young traveller, suddenly becoming more amenable, was borne away.

Their father having bethought him that the postillion was still unpaid, the boy and girl left alone in the hall gazed at each other in dismay. Both found themselves saying: "Why has Papa brought this Arabella here?" to which was added by Tom in a disgusted tone, "I did think it was Charlotte come back!" and by Peggy in a rather tearful one, "I don't *want* her to sleep with me!"

"Well, Peregrine," said Mrs. Carew, entering her husband's dressing-room about ten minutes later, "so Charlotte has not returned with you! And you have not yet told me the reason for her flight?"

"I could not, before Tom and Peggy. It is," said the Rector, "a very grave reason indeed, and you must prepare yourself — I cannot disguise it — for a great shock. The letter which she received from Leghorn was one from her aunt in Toulon forwarded by Edward Mounsey. And it told her that — at least at the date when it was written — her first husband, the Creole, was still alive!"

It was a shock; it could not be other. Mrs. Carew was deprived of speech, merely staring at her husband with a slowly paling face. Only after a full half-minute was she galvanised into protest.

"Alive, the Creole *alive!* Her first husband not dead after all! — Oh no, Peregrine, it can't be true, it can't!"

"I myself see what I trust are good reasons for doubting its truth, though Charlotte will not recognise them. Nevertheless we must face the fact that it *may* be true.

"*May be!* It *may* be true that Charlotte is not Nugent's legal wife! . . . Then was she lying from the beginning, lying to him in the first place, when she said that she saw her first husband killed, while all the time she was only covering up the fact that she had run away from him? You remember that she said she was married against her will."

"No, no," said Mr. Carew with emphasis. "You are too impetuous, Elizabeth! You should not allow yourself to harbour such an unjust and baseless idea! I am not only satisfied that the poor girl told what she was convinced at the time was the truth about her first husband's fate, but that it *was* the truth. In spite of any evidence to the contrary, everything, in my opinion points to the fact that Monsieur de Marescot was killed that night in Toulon!"

"Yet Charlotte would not return with you! That does not look as if she had much faith in any of your arguments!"

"I did my best," said Peregrine Carew, turning away rather dejectedly. "But in the end I could not find myself justified in combating her convictions any longer. If Nugent is not her legal husband, because her first husband is still living, then she cannot, she should

172

not be forced to return to him. The stand she takes is right. But she is quite heartbroken over it — make no mistake about that, Elizabeth!"

"And how long does she intend to keep up this attitude?"

"Until she knows more certainly what her real status is."

" 'Until she knows'! — Poor Nugent!"

"Yes," said her husband heavily, "poor Nugent! I suppose he knows by now. She had written to him."

"He will not easily accept the situation; one may be sure of that. I cannot yet grasp it myself . . . There is another matter — vastly less important, I admit — which I cannot grasp either. This child you have so astoundingly brought here — how came you to encumber yourself with her?"

"Most unwillingly, I assure you! I will tell you the story later. However," he added, trying to sound less depressed, "I hope we need not keep her long."

"I hope not indeed. As a substitute for Charlotte . . . Oh, my dear Peregrine," cried Mrs. Carew, suddenly remorseful, "here I am almost scolding you, when you look so tired, and have, I know, done your utmost about Charlotte! Come and have your supper at once! The children have had theirs already, and Betsy is attending to that disagreeable-looking Arabella. To think that she is Edward Mounsey's daughter!"

"But also Emilia Mounsey's!" said the Rector with a wry little smile.

The reactions of the younger members of the family to 'Edward Mounsey's daughter' were, unfortunately for her, very much the same as their elders', and a good deal more bluntly expressed.

"Good Heavens, why did Papa ever bring that frightful little girl here?" grumbled Tom to his sister, the very next day. And a few days later he has adding to this *cri de cœur*: "She's always bleating after Nugent, too. I wish he would come home and give her a good whipping!"

"Nugent won't come home, I espect, till Charlotte does," sighed Peggy.

No, Miss Arabella Mounsey had failed to commend herself to the younger members of the Rectory household; in fact they detested her. The only appeal which she held for Tom, and that was of brief duration, because she boasted so much of her feat, was that she, a girl, had actually run away from school. She was more than ready to furnish him with details of her escape, details which his father (though secretly curious) had thought it more consonant with an attitude of disapproval not to enquire about.

Towards the Rector and his wife Arabella comported herself with some circumspection, for Mrs. Carew, though never unkind to her, kept a very firm grip on the reins: and this was so surprising to a child whose mother had never held any reins at all, that she rendered a — for her — remarkable measure of obedience ... as long as any deflection from the prescribed path was likely to be found out. Mr. Carew, for his part, did not cultivate her society, for, as he remarked to his wife, two days of almost unbroken companionship with the young lady, and a good portion of that time penned up with her in the confines of stage-coach or chaise, had surely earned him some respite. He had not suffered a day to elapse before writing to Arabella's aunt in Warwickshire, whose address Arabella *was* fortunately able to furnish, to enquire when she could relieve him of the child. The lady, however, did not hurry to reply, and when she did it was to say that circumstances made Miss Mounsey's reception impossible at present.

Her enquiries after Nugent, which Tom found so distasteful, had begun on the day after her arrival. That their encounter the previous year in Leghorn had roused in the little girl's breast a sort of coltish worship for his elder brother only dawned upon him gradually — arousing in him when it did, no little scorn and disgust. There were also other queries with which he dealt — and, it must be admitted, in none too amiable a manner. Why wasn't Mamzelle here, if she wasn't with Cousin Nugent in Plymouth? Because she had gone to visit her brother in Bath. In Bath — what, that Mossoo d'Esparre who taught French at the Minerva Seminary? And why had Mamzelle gone to visit him. "Why? Just *because* he is her brother, you goose! And what business is it of yours, anyhow?"

Thereafter, if Charlotte's prolongation of that visit was a source of sadness to the Rector and his wife, to Arabella it was a riddle which she was for ever trying to solve. She was acute enough to guess after a while that there was some real mystery connected with Mamzelle's absence. Before long, well served by her inquisitive ears, ever pricked at meals and outside half-open doors, she had gathered that it had something to do with 'that letter from Toulon'. She was not clear whether this was a letter which had already been received, or which was expected in the future. It even seemed to her as if there must be two letters, one past and one, perhaps, to come. She remained, therefore, very much the 'little pitcher' of nursery parlance; but she was astute enough to put very few, if any, direct questions on the matter which was exercising her. She did venture one on Tom as to the reason for the Rector's visit to Bath (without which she herself would not have been at the Rectory) for she could not but suspect that it had something to do with 'Mamzelle's' presence there. From him, however, she got nothing but advice to mind her own business.

Peggy was less oyster-mouthed; and indeed she had never been told not to reveal that Papa had gone to Bath for the purpose of fetching Charlotte back if possible. And when one day, finding her alone in the nursery, Arabella seized the most treasured of her dolls and announced that Belinda was going to have her head cut off like the Queen of France, Peggy's frantic appeals for mercy resulted in her being allowed to ransom her darling in exchange for the desired information — which she would not have withheld in any case.

It so happened that Tom came upon the aftermath of this little scene when the prime agent had taken her departure. There crouched poor Peggy, sobbing quietly, the reprieved Belinda strained in her arms. Being very fond of his little sister, the boy, instead of telling her not to be a cry-baby (which indeed Peggy rarely showed herself) asked the reason of this grief, and was hotly indignant when he heard it.

"Little sneak — that's what she is! Always trying to find out something about Charlotte, I believe! Never mind, Pegs, it doesn't matter what you told her. But look here, if after I've gone back to school next week, she tries to bully you again, you must stand up to her. Give her one in the eye!"

Tears still upon her cheeks, his small sister looked up at him rather piteously. "But she's as old as I am, and much bigger. Even if I stood upon a foot-stool —"

"Well, kick her on the shins then, or even scratch her, if she goes for you. *You* can do that, because you're only a girl. And she's a coward really. But I wish I weren't going back to Blundell's while she is here."

The very next day, though at a certain cost to himself, Tom Carew's wish was granted. And Arabella herself was the cause of its fulfilment.

Although this was the exceptionally severe winter which was proving so cruelly disastrous to the retreating British in the Netherlands, there was suddenly in that corner of Devon a remarkable interlude of open weather with sun and very little frost. And so, early on the next afternoon, the three young people were all in the garden, Tom engaged in the finger-chilling work of directing, by means of a decidedly messy clay dam, some of the water of the little stream into a miniature reservoir at the side. The purpose of this construction was that in the spring and summer Peggy should have a pool into which she could dip her little watering-pot, in order more easily to refresh the childish garden which last year had proved such a sad disappointment. This labour, in which Arabella declined to participate, she after a while ceased contemptuously to watch and, unregretted, went off by herself to another part of the Rectory garden.

Muddy, more than a little cold, but well content, brother and sister were still squatting by the streamlet when a series of shrill yells of alarm was borne to their ears.

"That's Arabella," pronounced Tom after a second's listening. "In some kind of trouble, too. I suppose I'll have to go or Papa will be disturbed. Bother her!" He left his hydraulic operations and ran off, guided by the outcries and the wild barkings of Juno, with Peggy trotting after him.

Since the elms at the side of the lawn were bare of leaf, the reason for these outcries, now increasing in stridency, was soon apparent. For one of them, to Tom's genuine amazement, bore a fruit in the form of the visitor standing on a bough about ten or twelve feet up, clutching another bough with both hands and bawling with all her might, "I can't get down! I can't get down! Somebody come and help me!"

"Why, you little fool!" shouted up the ungallant Tom, "if you got up there, you can get down again — Be quiet, Juno! — That's not a difficult tree to climb! Turn round and take hold of that crooked bough behind you — no, not there! Of course you'll never get down if you set about it in that way!"

But Arabella, her nerve completely vanished, after one or two clumsy efforts to follow his instructions, desisted, and screamed alternately for 'Papa' and a ladder.

"A ladder! Fancy wanting a ladder!" exclaimed Tom Carew scornfully. "Oh well, I suppose I'll have to climb up and show her where to put her silly feet."

He started to swing himself up rapidly — a trifle too rapidly, as it turned out, since he was forced to take an untried route up a tree which otherwise — like most of those at the Rectory — he knew by heart. He did not want to arrive at precisely the spot occupied by the present vociferating adventurer, and so he trusted too much of his weight, inconsiderable though it was, to an untested branch, which, having the unreliability of elm branches, broke beneath his feet. And the boy, after a struggle to retain his hold on another which, fortunately, he was gripping with one hand, was obliged to let go altogether, and half fell, half dropped, almost on top of his terrified little sister.

The result was a broken left arm, and a considerable extension of his holidays.

III

"Dere Charlot," ran Peggy's laboriously formed letters, "Tom has broakn his arm he fell out of the hellum he

179

climed up to get Arrabeela doun he canot go back to scole he dos not mined and I am glad Bellinda sends you her love wen are you comming back."

When indeed, thought Charlotte, her eyes smarting a little. And out of what place or object, she wondered, had Tom fallen — for she did not recognise the influence of old George Cripps's vocabulary upon Peggy's. The child's missive, read first, was enclosed in one from the Rector, brief but sad. "I wish that I had a letter other than this to enclose to you, my dear Charlotte, but nothing has come from the Continent. I am at a loss how to institute more enquiries. We are well, save that Tom has broken his arm through falling from a carelessly climbed tree. Your former charge, as you see, is still with us."

Charlotte laid down her correspondence with a sigh. Muffled in a shawl, she was sitting in her cold little bedroom in Fabien's lodgings. In a happier climate and warmer time of year it would have been the siesta hour, after the midday meal which she had helped her sister-in-law to prepare and to remove. It is true that there was a fire in the sitting-room, but there was also Honorine, whose company she was coming to find more and more of a trial, even when mitigated, as now, by Fabien's. She could hear her high querulous voice echoing at this moment through the communicating door, in complaint or argument. And yet Honorine had something to occupy her, something to do, a husband to look after; whereas to Charlotte herself, though she made herself useful in every way she could, the days appeared pointless as well as unending — a mere matter of waiting and waiting. Sometimes it seemed to her that she would wait thus until the end of her life.

Not so did Honorine d'Esparre view the situation. In her eyes each of the succeeding days which dragged so slowly for her sister-in-law was 'another day nearer the hour when your lawful husband comes to claim you', an attitude which, as well as greatly annoying Charlotte, stabbed her also with its probable truth.

On the other side of the door Fabien d'Esparre was suffering too. It was difficult to correct his pupils' exercise-books while his wife, mending a shirt by the fire, continued so unceasingly to deplore the scarcity of vegetables, the high price of meat, the disobligingness of Mrs. Gibbings (which existed only in her imagination) above all, the calamitous delay in the arrival of M. de Marescot, which, she more than hinted, saddled them in their straitened circumstances with an extra person's maintenance.

And at that Fabien laid down his pen and looked at his wife in exasperation.

"You speak, Honorine, as though Charlotte did not contribute to our household expenses and, in addition, help you in every possible way! Moreover, since I for my part have come to believe, as both the Messieurs Carew believe, that Oreste de Marescot is dead, and will never come to claim her, and as, even if he is alive, she could get the marriage annulled, you had better ask her to leave us if her presence is so —"

But at that word 'annulled' his wife, after an alarmed glance at the communicating door, had hastily risen, and was now at his side.

"For God's sake, Fabien, moderate your voice! And what in the name of all the saints, are you talking about? *Annulled!* How could Charlotte's union with Monsieur de Marescot be annulled! You know as well as I that marriage for us Catholics, is indissoluble — the least instructed knows it!"

"Sit down for a moment," commanded her husband. He had the air of a patient man roused at last. "Sit down here and do not pretend that you, who all your life have frequented ecclesiastical circles, do not know that in Charlotte's case there is not merely one valid ground upon which her marriage could be declared null, but two! She was forced into it against her will, and it was never consummated. The first ground alone renders it no marriage at all in the eyes of the Church, to which you are so fond of referring — and I can see that you know it!" He looked hard at her as, with bent head and slightly heightened colour, she fidgeted with his abandoned pen, and went on: "If Charlotte has not already been enlightened on this point (and she appears indeed to be ignorant of it), then she should be told."

"Oh no, no!" exclaimed his wife, raising her head. "No, leave her in that ignorance! It is better so, much better!"

"Why? Is it better that she should go on suffering, poor child?"

"Suffering in a good cause is never thrown away," replied Mme d'Esparre with an uplifted expression. And as her husband gave an impatient exclamation she continued: "And it is so much better that when Monsieur de Marescot arrives — for I have every right

182

to differ from you in your assertion that he is dead — she should go to him with —"

"You know quite well that even if he has survived she could get her freedom!"

"Only by appealing to Rome! And how could that be done in the midst of a war which every day shows signs of spreading further? It would be cruel to hold out that hope to her. And since she has been given the grace so promptly to cut herself off from Captain Carew and his family, ought we not to see in that an indication of Heaven's will for her future?"

"You interpret Heaven's will as meaning that if Monsieur de Marescot appears she should, in ignorance of how she might well act otherwise, acquiesce in his claim upon her? When the very fact that Tante Ursule forced her into the marriage invalidates the sacrament?"

"We have only Charlotte's word that she was so unwilling! And . . . ought we not to consider a little her worldly prospects too? What are they as the wife of a mere British naval captain? Monsieur de Marescot has a fortune. And you yourself — a Frenchman of noble birth — how much more of your life are you going to spend cramming the elements of our beautiful language into these thick-skulled and clumsy-tongued English masters and misses? In Louisiana —"

Fabien pushed back his chair. "So *that*," he said slowly, "that is the real reason for your pious anxiety that de Marescot should survive and the first marriage stand! You think that we could conveniently become his hangers-on? I tell you, Honorine —"

But his wife, glancing nervously towards the communicating door, gripped his arm warningly. He too saw the handle turn, and said no more.

CHAPTER
THIRTEEN

Another, though minor, result of Arabella's exploit —
an exploit which had endeared her still less to the rest
of the household — was the overt admiration for Tom
which now began to replace in her youthful if savage
breast her former farouche attitude towards him, and to
oust her unrequited devotion to the absent Captain
Nugent Carew. When after a few days the boy appeared
downstairs again, somewhat pale and with his arm in a
sling — and intensely desirous that as little notice as
possible should be taken of this adornment or its cause,
for he was not at all proud of having fallen from a tree
— it was highly distasteful to receive from Arabella
(who had in the end been rescued by the gardener with
a ladder) almost fawning tributes to his bravery, and to
feel himself surrounded when in her company by an
atmosphere of dog-like devotion. It revolted Tom to the
marrow when Arabella asked: "Shall I fetch so and so
for you, Cousin Tom?" for, as he would explain gruffly,
he had the full use of his legs. And to be asked in that
squeaky voice if his arm was hurting him, a question
which his mother or father were scarcely suffered to
put, drove him to such plain-spoken frenzy that the

Rector had to give him a private lecture on his behaviour.

His injury was already some weeks old and doing nicely when Arabella stood alone in the empty hall of the Rectory eyeing with a metaphorically watering mouth the tempting object lying on the table there. This was the shabby flat leather satchel in which letters were transported to the Rectory from the village. But the mail had arrived late to-day, so that George Cripps had brought in the bag after the family had dispersed, and no one had yet attended to its contents.

This bag was almost more of a symbol than a secure repository for the Rectory correspondence, since its clasp had for some time been out of order, a fact already known to Arabella, while quite a long period had elapsed since the loss or mislaying of the key. There was no one about, so that the temptation to seize this heaven-sent opportunity was acute. Yet she had not quite the courage to plunge her hand directly into the bag and pull out the letters to examine them. But what if she were to tip its contents on to the floor? Then, if anyone caught her handling them, she could say that she had accidently knocked the satchel off the table and was just picking up the letters to replace them. (If Juno had only been with her she might have declared that the setter had knocked the thing off with her tail.)

Arabella sidled a little nearer to the table; then, after having listened carefully for any sound of approaching footsteps, she took up the leather bag, tilted and shook it — and was rewarded by seeing two letters slide out on to the floor. Over these she stooped quickly — and only just suppressed an exclamation. On one of them, to her great surprise, she recognised her own father's handwriting.

A letter for herself — how right she had been to investigate! Thrusting back the other letter, which was for Mr. Carew and seemed of no particular interest, and restoring the bag exactly to its former place on the table, she took another hasty look at the letter before retiring with it upstairs — and received a shock of disappointment. The letter was not for her at all; it was addressed to Mrs. Carew. Then it almost certainly contained some directions about the new school to which she anticipated being sent sooner or later. Arabella grew red with anger at the thought . . . Inside, however, there would surely be a letter for her as well, either from Papa or Mamma — perhaps from both of them. Still, she dared not open Mrs. Carew's letter in order to find out. It would have to go back into the bag. And she was just going to replace it, when she made a fresh discovery which stayed her hand. The name on the letter was 'Mrs. Nugent Carew'.

A flame of jealousy was instantly added to the little girl's anger. Why should Papa be writing to Mamzelle — who wasn't even here. He ought to be writing to *her* — not to her ex-governess. And for a moment Arabella's fingers really itched to tear the letter to pieces.

But — sudden brilliant thought — might not a letter from the place vaguely called 'the Continent' to Mamzelle have some connection with the mystery which she herself was always trying to penetrate? There was, at least, a very good chance of this. Jealousy and curiosity conjoined to stifle the voice of conscience in favour of another voice, very suspect in origin, which whispered that in this case she had a *right* to open her own Papa's letter. And in a trice she had slipped the missive into her pocket, meaning just to read it in privacy, seal it up again with one of the wafers with which Mamma had provided her, and replace it in the letterbag as soon as possible, a procedure which should be quite easy now that it did not fasten properly.

Stealing up the stairs, Arabella reached the bedroom she shared with Peggy. It was empty, as she had hoped. With the scissors from her work-box she prised up her father's seal without causing it much damage, and, crouching by the window, proceeded to investigate her booty.

To her satisfaction she found that Papa had merely written a brief covering note to 'Mrs. Nugent Carew', informing her that he was sending on with as little delay as possible the enclosed letter which had arrived recently at the Villa Nespoli. Eagerly she opened that travelstained enclosure. And then indeed her heart leapt up in triumph — for it was headed 'Toulon', and was from someone who signed with the name of d'Esparre. 'Hurrah, hurrah' she whispered to herself. Now she would learn before anyone else the secret which they were all so tiresome about, and be able to gloat to herself over her knowledge!

And so indeed Arabella might have done — had she been able to read French with any ease. Unfortunately for her, the one or two children's books in that tongue on which Charlotte had once pastured a refractory lamb afforded little clue to the meaning of the communication in Mlle. d'Esparre's flowing but not very decipherable writing. Little indeed could that determined and autocratic spinster have imagined that the first eyes to fall upon this second epistle of hers — if not precisely to read it — would be the gooseberry orbs of a little English girl whose patchy knowledge of French was just sufficient to enable her to realise that it was about some matter of importance to its proper recipient, without being able to make out what that matter was.

The sight indeed of M. de Marescot's name, which occurred fairly soon in it, excited Arabella's curiosity to a high degree, since she knew that he, Mamzelle's original husband, had been murdered on a quay at Toulon in a dramatic and horrible manner highly satisfying to the blood-thirsty instincts of the young. Yet now that she had the actual 'second letter from Toulon' in her possession, before anyone yet knew of its arrival, she found that she was profiting little in the way of information. Whatever could the word 'scélérats' mean? And 'veuve' what was that? And 'trompée'? 'Mari' was a word which seemed more familiar, yet she could not fit a meaning to it. Could it signify 'married'?

Angry and disappointed, Arabella put down the purloined letter. She *must* try to find out what it was about, which meant delaying its return to the leather bag. And unless she could find some means of interpreting its contents her misdoing would be

189

fruitless. Yet she could obviously not lay the letter before anybody, nor would it be at all advisable to ask Tom (supposing that he knew any French) or either of his elders, the meaning of some of the words. Her only hope was to find a French dictionary.

And that was why Tom, coming a little later into the old nursery, found the young visitor sitting in a corner feverishly turning the leaves of a small battered quarto which he recognised as a discarded Latin dictionary, once the property of his elder brother.

"You surely can't be wanting to learn Latin, Arabella!" he exclaimed in tones of horrified scepticism. "Anyhow, if you do, you can't learn it from a dictionary!"

The investigator grew red and pushed the book away. "I *don't* want to learn Latin."

Tom picked it up. "Then why did you take this out of the shelf?"

"To find out . . . some words.

"Latin words? What were they?" enquired Tom. "Come on now, and I'll help you, though I can't think why you should bother about *mensa* and so on, when, being a girl, you needn't!"

Arabella gave her usual sign of embarrassment, a wriggle. "They were French words. I used to learn French in Italy."

"You can't have learnt much if you don't know the difference between a French and a Latin dictionary! Ask Papa to tell you what the words mean — he knows French."

But Arabella shook her head, muttering that it wasn't worth while, and turned the conversation, she hoped successfully, on to something else.

She received a nasty shock, therefore, when at dinner that afternoon Tom, who, it must be admitted, never missed an opportunity for scoring off his second cousin once removed, came out with:

"Fancy, Papa, I found Arabella this morning trying to look up French words in Nugent's old *Latin* dictionary!"

"A praiseworthy if misdirected attempt on her part," observed the Rector genially. "And, after all, the French language is derived from the Latin. What were the words for which you were searching, my child? There is, I fear, no French dictionary in the house, but I have a fair though somewhat rusty knowledge of the tongue."

Arabella, crumbling her bread vigorously, was understood to say that it didn't matter.

But Mrs. Carew interposed. "If you show Mr. Carew after dinner the book you were reading, Arabella, and point out the words which you do not understand, I am sure he will help you."

Further unintelligible mumblings from the recipient of this offer conveyed a refusal to take advantage of it.

Said Mrs. Carew at this, with severity: "It is very improper, Arabella, for a little girl like you to decline with so little civility an offer of help from her elders. You will take the book to Mr. Carew directly dinner is over — and apologise."

"I haven't got any French book, Aunt Carew!" said the goaded child. "They were only some French words

I s — I heard one day. But I don't really care what they mean." And she darted a black look at the grinning Tom.

"But where did you hear them? In Bath?"

"Yes . . . I mean, no . . . In Leghorn. But I don't —"

"Still, we might as well know what they were," broke in the Rector.

"The child may have picked up some very undesirable expression, Peregrine!" warned Mrs. Carew.

"If she has, I need not translate it," replied her husband. "Now, Arabella, let us hear your problem."

"There was," said the cornered Arabella after a pause, kicking the legs of her chair, "a word like 'scalyrats'."

Tom immediately went off into a hoot of laughter. "Scalyrats! Oh Lord!"

"A very remarkable word to occur in the French language," observed Mr. Carew with a smile. "You must write it down for me afterwards. What else?"

" 'Tromp'," emitted the student unwillingly, ignoring accents. "And 'viewve'."

The Rector shook his head. " 'Tromp' suggests the verb 'tromper' 'to deceive', or, in the passive form, 'to be mistaken.' The other word conveys nothing to me. Peggy, my child, don't stare like that, but eat your pudding."

After this discomposing episode, it was a relief to Miss Mounsey that the only apparent result of her unwilling disclosure was the delighted adoption by Tom of 'scaly rat' as a strictly private nickname for her. Nevertheless it was to have more disturbing consequences.

For an evening or two later, after the younger members of the party had gone to bed, the Rector was reading by the fire, Mrs. Carew sitting sewing on the other side of the hearth, when he laid down his book and gazed throughtfully into the logs.

"Do you know, Elizabeth," he said after a moment, "I believe that I have solved the meaning of one of those very curious French words which Arabella mispronounced (or so I apprehend) the other day. I conjecture that 'viewve' is her rendering of 'veuve', widow."

Mrs. Carew continued to sew. "That may well be . . . I was much displeased with her rude behaviour over the matter. Her manners are indeed . . . I remember that Charlotte . . ." She broke off with a quick sigh at the mention of that name.

"Yes, even Charlotte," said the Rector, and his voice too was sad, "even Charlotte was unable to undo in a brief time the results of years of faulty upbringing. Ah well, the child will soon be leaving us now." And he returned to his book.

It was Mrs. Carew who was next visited by an illuminating thought.

"Peregrine," she exclaimed suddenly, and her needle-work slid to the floor, "I am much afraid that Arabella, in addition to being exceedingly ill-mannered, is a consummate little liar as well! How could she possibly have heard, even in Italy, the French word *veuve* pronounced 'viewve'? On the other hand, is not that exactly the way an English person — an English child for instance — not well instructed in French might pronounce it if she had seen it *written?* Possibly the same applies to that absurd and rather objection-able term 'scaly rat', which I fear that Tom has now taken to using?"

Struck with this idea, the Rector gazed across at its originator. "How quick-witted you are, my dear Elizabeth! Of course you are perfectly right! And that means that Miss Arabella *has* in her possession a French book — or at any rate something printed (or written) in French. And if she is so anxious to conceal the fact . . ." He shook his head.

"You mean that it looks as if the book or paper is an undesirable one, and that she knows it? Yes, I am afraid it does."

"On the other hand," objected her husband, "it is extremely unlikely that any pupil of the eminently respectable Miss Polfrey's should get hold of undesirable French literature; nor that, if she did, it would make any appeal to a child who, as seems evident, could not read any French book with ease!"

Mrs. Carew picked up and resumed her needlework. "Nevertheless I must go into this matter thoroughly. I shall question Arabella to-morrow, and if necessary examine her possessions."

Silence fell anew. But after a while, glancing at him, Elizabeth Carew saw that her husband's book was on his knee, and he was looking once more into the fire. She knew from his expression what he was thinking about — the subject which was never far from either of their minds. And at last, without removing his gaze from the flames, he said:

"I wrote a line to Charlotte this morning."

"To say that no letter had come for her yet?"

He nodded. "As you know, I do not believe that one will ever reach her. And how long is this situation to go on between her and Nugent? Oh, I know, none better, the answer she would give — 'until some definite news can be obtained one way or the other about — '"

"About that unfortunate Creole gentleman," supplemented Mrs. Carew, as he paused. She knew how he shrank from using the term 'husband' in this connection, even if qualified by 'former' or 'late'; and she herself was not always able to remember the name correctly.

"Yes. But how can such news be obtained? Writing to Edward Mounsey — though I have done so — is of little avail. For this Monsieur de Marescot may well be in a Republican prison, or in some other situation in which he can neither leave France nor despatch a letter to Charlotte, and therefore this dead silence, this seemingly hopeless suspense, may possibly continue for years! And both Nugent and she breaking their hearts!"

A little later than Mrs. Carew — that is to say, early the following morning — Miss Arabella Mounsey also came to a decision. Since the purport of the letter from Toulon still remained hidden from her, and its retention was not without peril to herself (it had for instance, to be kept carefully from Peggy's eyes in the room which they shared) she determined to restore it to the bag at the very first opportunity. Rising, therefore, before Peggy woke, she fastened it up again inside her father's letter to 'Mrs. Nugent Carew' and, not without comments from her companion, contrived to dress quickly and to be downstairs before any of the rest had assembled for family prayers. She was hoping to find the post-bag in the hall or even (as occasionally happened) on the breakfast-table.

Alas, it was in neither place. All that happened was that the Rector rallied her on her unusual punctuality.

Perhaps there were no letters to-day? Or perhaps the bag would be brought in soon after breakfast? On one pretext or another Arabella managed to slip into the hall again and to hang about there, Peggy and Tom being the only difficult people to avoid, since the Rector went straight to his study and Mrs. Carew to her house-keeping. And once again luck was with her. She had no companion but the cat, with which she was pretending to play when old George suddenly lumbered in with the post-bag, laid it on the hall-table, and then caught sight of her.

"Good morning, Missy! Will 'ee kindly take this here into Rector?"

"Yes, certainly," replied Arabella, exultation in her heart. If she were caught handling the post-bag now nobody could say anything to her. The moment that George had taken himself off, but not before, she rushed to the table, pulling out the letter from her pocket. A couple of seconds, and she would be relieved of her dangerous possession.

Alas, she had been over-optimistic! The leather satchel was not closed in its old haphazard fashion at all. Evidently the clasp must have been repaired. Laying down the letter Arabella took two hands to it; but the catch would not budge. It almost seemed as if the Rectory post-bag, which for so long it had been difficult to keep shut, was now impossible for any unauthorised person to open, that the lost key must have been found, and used. If that was the case . . . 'I can't put the letter back! I can't *ever* put it back!' thought Arabella to herself in panic.

She had not recovered from this stunning blow when Mrs. Carew came down the stairs. (But before she had reached the bottom the letter had been crammed into the child's pocket.)

"Ah, there you are, Arabella! I have been looking for you. Come into the parlour for a moment; I want to speak to you."

"I . . . I was just going to take the letter-bag into Uncle Carew's study. George asked me to."

"Never mind that now. Come in here!"

In spite of the kind though firm intonation Arabella entered the parlour full of apprehension. Why had Mrs. Carew been looking for her? She kept her hand in her pocket as though the letter, like a captive snake, might emerge of its own will.

Mrs. Carew shut the door and opened fire at once.

"I feel sure, Arabella, that you are not telling the truth about those French words which you mentioned the other day. And it is a very dreadful and wicked thing for a little girl like you — or for anyone — to lie so deliberately!"

She paused. Arabella merely glowered at the carpet and shifted from one foot to the other.

"Now tell me truthfully," went on Mrs. Carew, "— you need not look so frightened! — tell me truthfully, have you not after all some French book or paper in your possession?"

"No, ma'am, indeed I have not," gulped Arabella, still crushing down the hidden viper. Her demeanour could scarcely have been more guilt-ridden.

Mrs. Carew looked very hard at her. "Take your hand out of your pocket, child! I should prefer to believe you, but I find it hard to do so. In any case it is my duty to find out whether you are lying to me or no. If you are telling the truth there is nothing to fear. Come with me to your bedroom. I am going to look in your trunk and your chest of drawers."

Without more words she opened the door and went out, followed, very slowly indeed, by Arabella. The worst had happened, and the accused was quite certain that when no contraband literature had been found elsewhere, her person would be searched. Then not only would something French but something stolen be revealed. Where, where could she hide the letter while the inquisition was in progress?

At this tense moment the procession to the scaffold was suddenly held up. In the hall Mrs. Carew perceived the letter-bag confronting her upon the table, and gathering it up bore it into her husband's study. As yet Arabella's leaden feet had not quite carried her over the threshold of the parlour, and it was now that her eyes, sharpened by desperation, caught sight (not indeed for the first time) of the discoloured old porcelain monster, half dragon and half toad, which

198

squatted on a little table in the corner by the door, and which very likely had squatted there since an earlier sailor member of the family than Nugent had brought it from the East. This grotesque, which had always tickled her fancy, now struck upon her senses like an answer to prayer . . . There was just time to tug the letter from her pocket, to thrust it into the creature's wide, leering mouth, and to hurry into the hall to rejoin 'Aunt Carew'.

The search which then took place upstairs caused her to congratulate herself upon her foresight; for, no receptacle having yielded anything incriminating, she was made to turn out her pockets At the conclusion of the whole operation she did indeed find herself reinstated in 'Aunt Carew's' good opinion, but she was nevertheless read a short lecture upon 'looking people in the face' and being straightforward in every department of daily life.

Yes, she had escaped the letter's being discovered upon her; but what if someone were to see even a corner of it showing in the mouth of the dragon before she could pull it out of his interior again? The big parlour was in constant use, and she was not at all sure whether in her haste and agitation she had pushed the document sufficiently far in. It might yet be that the direct penalties would fall upon her . . .

Several times that evening, while Mrs. Carew was reading aloud to the two little girls by the parlour fire, as she sometimes did before despatching them to bed, Arabella's eyes slid furtively towards the Chinese dragon in his corner by the door. She could however, see no trace of anything white protruding from his mouth. Nevertheless she heard singularly little of the improving tale about the naughty boy who disobeyed his good parents, and the results thereof. She was turning over in her mind the unwelcome thought that, as long as the purloined letter reposed inside the monster, she would be letting slip the chance which *might* unexpectedly present itself of replacing it in an unlocked letter-bag. And since neither she nor her possessions would be searched again, it was now quite safe to fish out the letter when an opportunity offered.

So, next morning, having shaken off Peggy (never a very difficult matter) ascertained that Tom was in the stables, Mrs. Carew in the kitchen and the Rector out visiting parishioners, Arabella slipped into the empty parlour and softly closed the door. Then, breathing rather hard, she inserted her hand into the dragon's mouth . . . only to find that, child's hand though it was, she could not thrust it in quite far enough to grasp the letter in his interior. And yet the letter was not lying flat on the bottom of his anatomy, for she could touch a corner of it with a finger-tip.

But several determined efforts to get hold of the document proved as futile as the first. The dragon's mouth was wide indeed, but it was also shallow, affording easy passage for a paper, but not for any human hand smaller than a baby's. He seemed to be saying, with that leer of his, that he had no intention of giving up what she had forced him to swallow.

A little whimper escaped the child. She was frightened, for she had never intended this. What was she to do now? . . . There was nothing she could do, except to confess her crime, an idea she did not entertain for a moment. And every second the creature grinned up at her more like a malignant toad than ever.

"Horrid beast! I hate you!" she exclaimed under her breath, forgetting the service which it had rendered in her hour of need. Nevertheless the letter — and her part in its disappearance — was extremely unlikely to be discovered, unless by some ill chance the dragon were to get broken, when the room was dusted, for instance. But the old thing looked fairly strong, she thought, even though there was a crack running across him.

It was while she stood considering its durability that the door at the far end of the room, which led to Mr. Carew's study, opened, and the Rector himself, presumably returned from his visiting, looked in.

"Are you there, Elizabeth? — Ah, it is you, my child! I thought your aunt was in here. And what may you be doing there all by yourself? Studying ceramics?"

At the sound of his voice Arabella had backed hastily away from a dangerous neighbourhood.

"Is that what it's called — that ugly china animal?" she faltered, instinct having warned her to say something or other.

"Well, no — not this specimen exclusively. And it *is* an ugly old piece," said Mr. Carew kindly, coming and looking down at the dragon. "I only keep it because an uncle of mine brought it home many years ago. — Had you not better run away now and find Peggy? And I must find Mrs. Carew."

He went out into the hall, whither very shortly Miss Arabella followed him, leaving the creature from China to digest the entombed letter and leaving also (though this she could not know) in her 'Uncle Carew's' mind the germ of an idea which he was to put into practice on his next visit to the city of Exeter.

CHAPTER
FOURTEEN

I

March had come, with crocuses in the Rectory garden, but with no Charlotte in the house. But Tom was still there, for, though his arm had knit, an epidemic of measles at Blundell's School had still further delayed his return thither. On the other hand Arabella's aunt in the Midlands had signified at last her willingness to relieve the Carews of the charge of her niece, before she went to the school about which arrangements had now been made by her parents. And Arabella, somewhat to everybody's surprise, appeared quite prepared and even anxious to leave. Mrs. Carew indeed, if not her husband, had observed of late a noticeable diminution in the child's hoydenish behaviour, and hoped that she might assign it to the lecture which she had given her after the 'French words' episode. The problem of getting Arabella to Warwickshire, a task which neither Mr. nor Mrs. Carew was at all anxious to undertake, was solved by the happy fact that the Claverings, who happened to be setting out for London in their own chaise, had offered to take her with them as far as Basingstoke, where a trustworthy servant of her aunt's would meet her.

There was joy in the hearts of Tom and Peggy when this departure was announced to them, joy which was much increased when about the same time a letter came from Nugent informing his family that he proposed to spend a night with them on his way from Plymouth to visit the Admiralty, in accordance with instructions given him some ten days previously. The summons, he had been given to understand, was connected with his being posted, at last, to a ship of the line, the sixty-four gun *Defiance*. It was certainly ironical that his arrival should take place — as it evidently would — on the evening of the very day fixed for his youthful admirer to leave the Rectory. It had indeed been hinted to Tom and Peggy by their father that Arabella had better, if possible, be kept in ignorance of this fact, lest she should make a scene; but as the young Carews had not been actually forbidden to mention their brother's visit, Tom found himself yielding to the pleasure of doing so almost before he realised the fact.

"Guess who is coming here to-morrow, Arabella — *after* you have gone!" he whispered teasingly later in the day. "Nugent, — your dear Cousin Nugent! Aren't you sorry that you won't see him?" And, as Arabella grew very red, he added with mock sympathy, "it does seem a pity, after you have been wanting so badly to see him all these weeks!"

"I don't want to see him now," muttered Arabella sulkily. "I'm glad I shan't be here."

"Do you expect me to believe that!" exclaimed her tormentor. "It's just sour grapes!"

Curiously enough, Arabella was speaking the truth. In the last fortnight two events had badly shaken her, and contributed to that subdued demeanour which had attracted Mrs. Carew's attention. The first was the abrupt and unexplained disappearance of the china dragon (with its stomachic contents) from the parlour. One day there as usual — the next, gone! The occurrence caused the little girl both alarm and relief, but less of relief than alarm. The second was that, over-hearing — by chance and not through eavesdropping — a fragment of a conversation between the Rector and his wife on the subject of Nugent and Charlotte, she learnt at last what was keeping the latter apart — the lack of definite news about that first marriage in Toulon, and whether the assassinated M. de Marescot really had survived, as was said. This made her wonder very uncomfortably what had really been in that French letter, now vanished she knew not where. She was afraid to ask why its repository had been removed from the parlour; the subject was too dangerous; and no prowls round the house had revealed the squat monster anywhere. Yet it could hardly have been broken, since the letter would then have come to light, and enquiries about its curious habitat have been set on foot — which had certainly not happened.

At the same time, that overheard conversation had suggested to her mind the possibility that, in dealing as she had done with the letter from Toulon, she had injured her whilom idol — about injuring 'Mamzelle' she cared little. Because of her guilty conscience, therefore, she was well satisfied to be leaving before his arrival on the scene, since she could do nothing — or so it seemed to her — to repair her misdeed. She could not have told him what was in the letter — and now the letter itself had disappeared.

Tom, rather disappointed at the reception of his news, sauntered off again. "I thought I should have got a good bellow out of her," he confided later to Peggy. "But I didn't."

The morning of Arabella's departure broke bright and clear — too clear perhaps for permanence. For the Rectory household the weather seemed to fit the day, and what that day would bring — the long overdue removal of a tiresome guest and the advent of a very welcome one.

But it also brought a less pleasant happening. The party had hardly finished breakfast when a groom arrived with an urgent summons for the Rector. Mr. Charles Pelley over at Dodsleigh, ten miles away, who had long been ill, was dying, and as an old friend had expressed a wish for his ministrations. The messenger reported his master as unlikely to live twenty-four hours. Mr. Carew at once gave orders for his horse to be saddled, and prepared to accompany the man; and while Mrs. Carew could not suppress a regret that the summons had come on the very day of Nugent's visit, she expressed a hope that her husband would be back by nightfall.

"That depends, my dear," said he, "on how long poor Charles holds out. If he lasts till this evening, and is conscious, and wishes me to stay, then stay I must.

206

Our friendship goes back many years, though I have not often seen him of late . . . I had better take leave of that child before I go. At what time did you say the Claverings would call for her?"

Twenty minutes later he had ridden off, and Miss Mounsey, dressed for the journey, stood in the hall with Peggy and Tom, awaiting the chaise which was to remove her. Juno, observing baggage, wandered uneasily to and fro; but Mrs. Carew, who was originally of the group, had been called away by some domestic emergency, and Tom was free to exercise his unkind humour upon the departing guest, despite the fact that she already looked tearful.

"I can't believe, Arabella," he began, "that you aren't sorry to miss your dear Nugent!" (To this there was no response.) "Who knows, perhaps he was bringing you a valentine, though it is past the time. Haven't you left one for him — not even a pretty message?"

Half as though she were driven by impulse, and half as though she wanted to keep back the words, Arabella said hoarsely: "I . . . I did leave . . . there is something . . . but I don't know what has become of it."

"You got him a valentine and lost it, you goose? Perhaps Pegs and I can find it before he gets here. Where did you see it last?"

Arabella gave a scared glance round, and moved further away from Peggy, who in any case was not listening, but trying to reassure Juno. "Come over here! It's a great secret!" Then, as Tom obeyed, she went on feverishly: "It's not a valentine. It's something —" again she stuck for a moment — "something Cousin Nugent ought to know about . . . important . . . nobody else knows about it but me . . ."

"Something important that only you know about," repeated Tom, half amused, for he had no belief in the importance of any revelations from this source. "All right, tell me what it is, and I'll pass this great secret on to Nugent, if that is what you want me to do."

Arabella nerved herself. She had one eye on the hall window; very soon, no doubt, the Claverings' chaise would arrive to deliver her. "Papa sent on a letter . . . it was from that place in France, Toulon."

Tom's grin faded. Indeed he looked at her for a moment with his mouth open. Then he recovered himself.

"But that's no secret to Nugent, you little stupid! Charlotte had that letter weeks ago, and that was why —" He pulled himself up, remembering that the young lady was not supposed to know the reason for Charlotte's prolonged absence.

"I don't mean that letter, but another," said Arabella desperately. "There was another — a little time ago. But it was in French, so I couldn't understand it."

"Another letter! And you *opened* it!"

"It had Papa's writing outside," retorted the culprit sulkily.

"But it wasn't addressed to you — a letter from Toulon! It couldn't have been! It was for Charlotte. Now, wasn't it?" In his eagerness he had seized her by the arm.

"Yes," muttered Arabella, struggling to free herself. "Ow, you're hurting me!"

"You jolly well deserve it!" flashed back Tom. But, though a tease, he was no bully, and he released her. "Charlotte's letter — and you opened it, and then couldn't read it! Couldn't you even make out who wrote it?"

A mumble. "Someone who had the same name as she used to have."

"Her aunt, then. How did you get hold of the letter anyway?"

"The post-bag fell off the table," said Arabella, utilising her former bright but unused idea. "It wasn't fastened, so the letter fell out on the floor there. I saw Papa's writing —"

"Don't say that again!" ordered Tom angrily. "Tell me at once what you did with the letter, you little sneak! Where is it now?"

Arabella's mouth went down convulsively. "I don't know. I said so."

"*You don't know!*" exclaimed the boy, thunderstruck. "You don't know!"

"It's not my fault," protested Arabella, sniffing loudly. "I tried to put it back into the bag . . . but it was locked . . . and Aunt Carew frightened me . . . so I . . . I poked it into that old china dragon which used to be in the parlour . . . And then" (her voice began to get shriller) "I couldn't get it out again! . . . And now the dragon has been taken away, and I can't find it anywhere!"

"Taken away!" exclaimed Tom vehemently. "I should think it had. It's been *sold!*"

Miss Mounsey's knuckles went on her eyes, and she began to whimper outright. "I didn't know ... I couldn't help ..."

"Sold — with that letter still inside it, I suppose! If you could not fish it out again, you little fool, why didn't you tell someone about it? You surely didn't mean to hide it for good — you *couldn't!*"

"No, no," gulped the delinquent. "I didn't, I didn't. I only put it in there for a little because Aunt Carew would have found it in my pocket ... when she looked for a book in French. And if I had said, when I found I couldn't get it out, that it was in the dragon, I should have been punished for taking it out of the letter-bag!"

Tom's aspect became very threatening, though he managed to restrain himself from shaking her. "*Punished!*" he repeated. "And rather than that, you horrid little coward, you have let this letter, which may be so very important to Nugent and Charlotte, go heaven knows where! How shall we ever find it again? ... And you can't even tell us what it was about! If you weren't a girl I'd punch your head to a jelly!"

But at this diatribe Arabella broke into the full-fledged howl which had for some time been brewing. It brought Mrs. Carew back to the hall.

"My dear child, what is the matter? Don't cry so!" She spoke with more gentleness than she felt, just because, like her husband, she was glad to see the last of the weeper. "I think I hear Mr. Clavering's chaise, so dry your eyes, like a good little girl."

Mrs. Carew was in fact more anxious not to deliver a sobbing charge into the care of Mrs. Clavering, than to

210

enquire too particularly into the cause of the charge's lamentations. And some instinct of chivalry, whether misplaced or no, must have restrained Tom from revealing Miss Mounsey's two-fold enormity (with its perhaps irretrievable results) until she was no longer under the Rectory roof. So all that the Claverings concluded, as their weeping travelling-companion was helped up into their chaise, was that the child seemed heart-broken at leaving the Carews — which was creditable to both parties.

But when the carriage had disappeared, Mrs. Carew was suddenly visited by a suspicion, and she remarked a little severely, as her son closed the hall door again.

"I believe you had been teasing Arabella. That was very unkind of you, just as she was leaving us. It was thoughtless towards kind Mr. and Mrs. Clavering too, who will have to put up with the dreadful noise she was making."

"Teasing her!" exclaimed the boy. "It was her own bad conscience made her howl! You do not know, Mamma, what a terrible thing she has done. She had just let it out. Listen!"

The effect of his disclosure was certainly all that he could have wished — had he been thinking merely of terms of creating one. His mother, who in his experience rarely showed discomposure, stared at him for a moment in horror and disbelief.

"She told you that there was a letter from Toulon — and she stole, opened, and finally made away with it! — for that is what it comes to! No, Tom, I can hardly credit such a tale! Surely even that child . . . No, she must have made up the story!"

"She wouldn't have bellowed so hard if she had, Mamma," replied the logical Tom. "She was so upset, as you saw, that I am sure it is true."

"Then you should have told me about it before she left, or at least asked her more about it! Oh dear, we cannot do that now! . . . When did she get hold of this letter?"

"She did not say exactly, but if it was before the key of the letter-bag was found again, it must have been about three weeks ago."

His mother took an agitated turn about the hall. "All this time wasted, and now the letter has vanished, perhaps for ever, and *unread!* For the wretched child could not make it out, you say?"

"No, but that was where she got 'scalyrats' from, and — what was the other word?"

"*Veuve*," replied Mrs. Carew almost mechanically. "Yes, the story must be true. I was only too right in feeling sure that she had something in French concealed. Why did I not search more thoroughly!"

"But, Mamma, when you looked, the letter was already hidden inside the Old Toad — or so Arabella made out."

"And every day we have been hoping and praying that a letter would come — and all the time it was there in the parlour! Wicked, wicked girl! — and now, when the truth has at last come out, the dragon has gone. Your father took it to Exeter and sold it."

212

"I know" assented Tom. "He bought a large book with the money. But we *must* get the dragon back somehow! What shop in Exeter did he sell it at, Mamma?"

"Unfortunately I do not know. And even if he should return from Dodsleigh to-night, which is not very probable, nothing can be done about it until to-morrow.

"But, Mamma," urged her son, "that will be too late for Nugent to take the letter with him! If he had it, he could give it to Charlotte in Bath — he said he should go straight there from London."

"Not to speak of being able to read it himself at once. But it cannot be helped," reiterated Mrs. Carew with an angry sigh. "Nothing can be done until your father returns."

But was that true? Could nothing really be done before Papa returned? After his mother had gone away, Tom remained in the hall reflecting. He, now the only male in the house, had, as it were — and for the first time in his life — been taken into consultation with her. It made him feel at once responsible and uplifted, and from this conjunction was born a resolution which caused him to go thoughtfully upstairs and betake himself to his own bedroom. There he got out and counted over his small store of pocket-money after which his growing resolution reached maturity. He would go to Exeter this very day and see if he could not recover the letter from Toulon before Nugent's return, and before the Old Toad (which was how he thought of the dragon) was, perhaps, sold to someone else.

213

His plan was to ride his pony as far as Queensteignton and, leaving her there at the inn, take the accommodation coach which plied between that place and Exeter, returning by the same method later in the day. His arm was by now quite sufficiently knit for him to ride; in fact he had already twice ridden the placid Meg since his accident. If she should pull a little, which she very rarely did, he possessed another arm! An idea, a shadowy one, it was true, had already visited him of how he might find the shopkeeper to whom the Old Toad had been sold. His total capital of six shillings and sevenpence would not, he suspected, be enough to buy back the thing, but it would surely be sufficient to bribe the present owner (who ought not really to require a bribe) into allowing him to extract, with whatever mechanical help was required, the missive imprisoned in its interior. If luck favoured him in these two respects, he would be back home before, or not long after, Nugent's arrival, and be able to give into his hands the letter upon which so much depended.

It was an enthralling prospect, with only one drawback, that he could not acquaint his mother with his design, for he was certain that she would forbid him to embark upon it. She would say again that nothing could be done until his father's return. But it could, it must! Lest, however, she should be anxious about him when she discovered his absence, he would let Peggy into the secret, but, taking a leaf out of the departed Arabella's book, he would not do so until he was ready to set out.

II

The bright morning had been succeeded by an afternoon of rain and wind, when the mild and indeed scholarly looking old man who kept the bookshop in the narrow passage almost under the shadow of Exeter cathedral found himself confronting a boy, obviously of gentle birth, who was carrying a small and shabby carpet-bag. For a moment Mr. Whitaker thought that this might prove to be a schoolboy planning to raise money on his lesson-books, in which nefarious course he must certainly not be abetted. But a second glance at the carpet-bag showed that it had every appearance of complete emptiness.

"What can I do for you, young gentleman?" he enquired pleasantly as he came forward.

"Er . . . do you buy china, sir," asked Tom.

Mr. Whitaker smiled. "No, only books, I am afraid. "Why" — again he glanced at the bag — "were you thinking of selling some?"

"Oh no. I want to buy some — at least perhaps not to buy it, but to get a letter out." And seeing that the bookseller, not unnaturally, looked completely at a loss, Tom went on: "My father sold a piece of china in Exeter not long ago, a thing made in the shape of a to — of a dragon. All the time, though he did not know it, there was an important letter which had been pushed inside it. The letter *must* be got out of it at once. But my father is away, and I don't know at which shop he sold the dragon. I thought that perhaps it was here, because I know he bought a large book from you the same day

215

— I mean I expect he bought it from you, because I have heard him mention your name. It was a very large book, called Dimsdale's something or other."

Mr. Whitaker's face cleared. "Then your father, young gentleman, is the Reverend Mr. Carew, Rector of Damarel St. Mary, is he not? I have had the pleasure of selling him books from time to time, and it is quite true that he recently purchased from me the folio edition of Dimsdale's *Memorabilia*. And so you are his son?"

Tom's face had brightened also. Already he felt that he had established some sort of a link with his quarry. "Yes, his younger son. And if I only knew at what shop —"

"Oh, I think I can make a guess at that," put in Mr. Whitaker with some confidence. "Mr. Carew probably sold it at a little shop, not very easy to find, a short distance from the church of St. Mary Steps. I daresay you know that steep street? There is an old dealer up a narrow passage there — his name is Zacharew — who has a passion for old porcelain and gives good prices."

"Oh, thank you, sir!" exclaimed Tom warmly.

"But I must warn you," went on the bookseller, "that you will not find it easy to persuade him to part with his purchase, even if the piece you speak of *was* sold to him. He has the reputation of keeping anything he buys a long time before he will consent to sell it, even if he is offered a high price."

"But that's a very good thing!" returned Tom cheerfully. "It means that he won't have sold the dragon yet. And as I only have a little over five shillings he would not let me buy it back (though I have brought a

216

bag in case he should). I really only want him to let me have the letter out of it, and surely for five shillings he would do that? For after all the letter doesn't *belong* to him, does it?"

"I suppose not," returned Mr. Whitaker rather doubtfully. "It is a nice point, perhaps . . . However, I wish you all good luck, young sir. Pray present my respects to your father the Rector, and say that I hope to have the pleasure of seeing him here again soon. I have a nice clean copy of — but there, I had better write down the name for you."

Tom took the proffered piece of paper, and promised to deliver it. "And thank you very much for telling me about this Zacharew," he concluded earnestly.

And he departed, much encouraged, into the wind and the rain, while Mr. Whitaker stood at the door of his shop smiling, but shaking his head with a slightly dubious air.

The old houses crowded dark above Tom as he descended the steep incline of Step Street. He had in the end to ask his way to the alley up which Mr. Zacharew's shop was situated: and when he reached the narrow passage it did not look a very likely spot for any brisk kind of commerce. Some way up on the left there was, however, a low window with a few cracked pots on a shelf fixed across it, and so, although there was no signboard or name visible, Tom tried the door beside the window. At first it quite refused to open, and his heart sank. Perhaps after all Mr. Zacharew was out. Then, as he pushed harder, the reluctant door opened almost too suddenly, and simultaneously a bell jangled loudly inside the shop.

Almost simultaneously too a little old man came swiftly from some recess shouting fiercely: "Go out, boy! Go out at once! I've had enough of you plaguey young rascals!"

Conceiving that he could not justly be included in this category, Tom stood his ground. The shop, though low in the ceiling, was not nearly so dark inside as it appeared from without, having the advantage of a fair-sized skylight at the back. Neither was it as small as Tom had supposed. There were several good-sized tables spread with an array — or rather disarray — of china objects over which his gaze roamed eagerly, before he brought it back to the little, oddly bearded man not very much taller than himself, who seemed almost on the point of pushing him bodily through the door again. But Mr. Zacharew suddenly appeared to realise that he had not to do with a street urchin, drew back a trifle, and asked, but with suspicion: "What do you want here?"

"Will you please tell me," said Tom, "if my father, Mr. Carew, the Rector of Damarel St. Mary, sold you a china dragon not long ago?"

"And what if he did?" snapped the little man, glaring at him. His unkempt grey hair almost touched his shoulders.

Tom took this as an affirmative. "Have you still got it, sir?"

Mr. Zacharew's bushy eyebrows drew together. "I may have — and I may not. Why do you want to know?"

218

"Because," replied the boy, his heart beginning to beat faster, "there is a — a paper inside the dragon which it is most important that we — that my father should have back."

On that Mr. Zacharew took a long look at him, a very long, appraising and, as Tom began to realise with discomfort, a cunning look. Then he went away to the furthest of the tables on which stood, among other porcelain objects, a bulky Chinese vase about two feet high. From behind this he took up something, and returned. He was carrying the beast so familiar to the Rectory children under the name of the Old Toad.

Tom, who in extreme infancy had feared it, now looked upon its grotesque contours with jubilation. Certainly he had never been so glad to see it.

Mr. Zacharew gave a grim sort of chuckle at the expression on his visitor's face. "I knew there was some kind of paper inside this," and he gave the dragon a shake as he spoke. "I've had one or two tries to get it out, but I've been too busy to go on with them."

"If one had a bent wire, sir," said Tom eagerly, "or even perhaps a pair of scissors —"

"Not so fast, young sir, if you please," interrupted the dragon's present owner, clearing a space on the table near him, and setting it down there. "That's for me to decide. This piece of porcelain is my property now — good Chinese porcelain it is, though the glaze is a bit damaged in places, and it's got a bad crack. And before I come to any decision I must know exactly what is inside the piece, and how it got there."

This proviso did not sound unreasonable. "It's a very important letter from abroad — which a naughty child hid in there. My father must have it back."

"*Must?* Why?"

"Because he has not read it yet — nobody has." (For surely Arabella's baffled attempt did not count.)

"Then how," asked Mr. Zacharew, "does the reverend gentleman know that it is so important? And if it is, why did he not take it out before selling me the piece?"

"Because he never knew that it was in there! It was only this morning that the little girl —"

Mr. Zacharew interrupted him. "Listen, my boy. I don't believe this story of yours, not a word of it! I grant you that there is a paper of some kind in here —" he poked a finger larger than Arabella's into the mouth of his acquisition — "but it's not, to my mind, a letter of any sort. It's — well that's neither here nor there. The point is that this Chinese dragon is now my property, whatever it may have in its innards."

Tom instantly brought out his five shilling piece. "Mr. Zacharew, won't you please take that for the letter, and let me try —"

"Take five shillings in exchange for what may very well be a banknote! Do you think I am crazy, boy? And, come to that, how do I even know that you are really the son of the Rector of Damarel St. Mary. I believe I've heard he is a bachelor. And if this cock and bull story about an important letter was true, God bless my soul, the Rector would have come himself about it!"

"But he could not come — he's away from home," returned Tom, feeling uncomfortably near to tears. "And I promise you it's not a banknote inside, it's a letter from France for —"

"A letter from France! If your father gets letters from France, that we're at war with, then he has no right to do so! Being a parson doesn't safeguard a man who goes in for treasonable correspondence which he hides away like this! Seems to me," cried Mr. Zacharew with real or assumed indignation, "that a magistrate may be the properest person to get out what's in here!" And he gave the disloyal Toad a resounding rap with his knuckles.

Complete despair seized upon Tom Carew. "You are talking nonsense!" he exclaimed. "For if it were as you say, or even if there were a banknote in there, would my father be so foolish as to sell the dragon without taking it out?"

"But you have just told me that he did not know what was in it!" cried Mr. Zacharew in savage glee. "Now, get out of here before I call the watch and give ye in charge!"

"Oh, please listen!" pleaded Tom. "You don't know what may depend upon our getting that letter back! I know my father would willingly pay you much more than you gave him for the dragon, if you would only —"

"I daresay he would!" retorted Mr. Zacharew very grimly. "But he will not get the chance! And you, my boy, won't get back to Damarel St. Mary — if you ever came from there — to tell him so, unless you're out of the door before that clock has finished striking! Out with you!"

A grandfather clock in the corner began a whirring sound as Tom, with a heart as heavy as its leaden weights, backed slowly towards the shop door. It was no use. Now if Captain Nugent Carew, R.N., had only been in his place to deal with this obstinate and horrid old man — but he was not, and could not be. And there on the table in front of him sat the Old Toad, grinning, and digesting that still unread letter from Toulon which might mean everything to Nugent and Charlotte. It was cruel, and bitterly, bitterly tantalizing. Biting back a sob, his eyes still on the Toad, Tom at last turned the handle of the door.

"Get on now!" urged Mr. Zacharew. "And be thankful that the watch is not about, or I might still take a fancy to —"

At that moment, coinciding with the first wheezy stroke of the grandfather clock, there came from the back of the shop a crash which drew a startled exclamation from the china-dealer, and made Tom jump. But he at least could see at once what had happened. Some hard object from outside — a loose tile perhaps — dislodged by the high wind, had just hurtled through the skylight and landed, together with broken glass and a small torrent of water, upon the china vases, candlesticks and figures on the table below.

Mr. Zacharew spun round, gave a cry like some wounded animal's, and rushed to the scene of devastation.

222

But Tom did not pause to speculate whether it was an air from Heaven or a blast from Hell which had brought about this most opportune catastrophe. He acted in fact without conscious thought of any kind. The Toad was in the carpet-bag, and he was running along the alley in the rain almost before he realised what he had done — and before Mr. Zacharew, groaning over a shattered Dresden shepherdess, had realised it either.

The rain was falling so heavily that running did not excite remark, not even the running up Step Street, which no one but the young or the guilt-ridden would have attempted. Wind, too, is stupefying and confusing, and if — which he did not pause to ascertain — Mr. Zacharew were pursuing him with threats and cries, these passed unnoticed by persons who were themselves struggling against the elements with bent heads and deafened ears. Thus all along in his larceny the change in the weather had befriended Tom, for had the stage coach to Queensteignton not been slightly delayed by it, he would not have arrived at the posting inn where it changed horses, in time to catch it. As it was, he was nearly too late.

He climbed into the vehicle with a beating heart and wet shoulders, disposed the little carpet bag as unobtrusively as possible in the straw at his feet, and, to save himself from any awkward greetings or enquiries (for there were sometimes folk from Damarel St. Mary in the coach) pretended to be very sleepy. Inwardly he had never felt less so, torn as he was between elation and a sense of sin — or rather, of fear of consequences.

But of the two elation was the stronger. Had he not merely *borrowed* the dragon, driven thereto by Mr. Zacharew's unreasonableness? He would return it to him to-morrow or the next day, when the letter — Charlotte's letter — had been extracted. Had there only been time, and some convenient instrument to hand, he would have prised the letter out in Exeter itself — or so he told himself — and then restored the dragon to the china-dealer before leaving the city. But he had not been granted either of these requirements.

It was quite dusk by the time the accommodation coach lumbered into the "Courtenay Arms" at Queensteignton where Tom with his carpet bag alighted, and went in search of his pony. The rain had almost stopped, but the wind was just as high. Darkness would almost have fallen before he reached home, and the ostler, who knew him well, remarked: "Yu'm out late, Master Tom. They'll be praaper worrited about ee tu home, I'm thinking!"

"They'll be all the more pleased to see me then, William," replied the young adventurer, reflecting that the best reason for welcome would lie in what he carried — at least it was to be hoped so, for after all no one yet knew what tidings the hidden letter might contain. And he rode cheerfully out of the yard, the carpet bag slung over his right arm. He had not paused to borrow a cord and tie the bag to the saddle, because there was one thing which the equable Meg disliked, and that was anything that bumped about on her back.

There were other things which she did not fancy, and Tom, for the first time in his knowledge of her, became acquainted with them that evening. He had had her for two years (and had ridden since he was a small child), but he had never before been on her back in a half-light and a high wind, with a somewhat enfeebled bridle arm. A stolid animal enough in the daytime, Meg seemed with the waning light to have developed all kinds of unwarranted suspicions. Going out of Queensteignton she shied at a dimly seen milestone which, as her rider reprovingly observed, she had passed dozens of time before without blinking. Then a large puddle, which reflected what light there was in a presumably sinister manner, had to be skirted with care, although there was barely room enough in the road to do so. And when at last they arrived at the stretch of heathy upland known as Upway Common, where the wind was undeniably strong, and wailed with proportionate discordance, that sound, and the tossing branches of a few pine-trees ahead of her, were more than the now unnerved pony could stomach. So she protested against the general eeriness by bucking, an action so entirely out of character that Tom, completely unprepared, left the saddle, carpet-bag and all; and his steed, apparently sobered by what she had done, started at a leisurely pace for home.

CHAPTER
FIFTEEN

When Captain Nugent Carew arrived at the Rectory that evening, he almost concluded that he was not expected there. His rare visits, if announced beforehand, as this one had been, were generally the occasion of a regular family welcome. But this evening the house seemed deserted; at any rate there was no one in the hall — until, after a moment, Peggy came running down the stairs calling his name. Catching her up and kissing her, his lips met a wet cheek.

"What, have you been crying, Peg? Why?"

"Because . . . because Tom has not come back yet . . . and he oughtn't to have gone anyhow. Mamma is displeased."

"Gone? Gone where, child?"

"To Exeter, all by himself, to fetch back the china dragon."

"To fetch it back? But why should it be in Exeter?"

"Because Papa sold it, and all the time there was a letter inside it from France, and Tom's gone to try to get it back."

Her brother stiffened. "What's this?" he asked in a changed voice.

"Oh, my dear Nugent, you may well ask!" said his mother's voice, and there she was close beside him. "It is a tangled and really dreadful tale, arising out of that child Arabella Mounsey's thieving and deceitful ways. (We have had her here you know, for weeks — until this morning.) And your father was called away this morning to Mr. Pelley at Dodsleigh, who is dying. I do not now expect him back to-night. On top of it all that naughty Tom has gone off — But come into the study and I will tell you more fully about it. Peggy, off with you to bed, my child."

"If Tom does not return in a quarter of an hour or so," declared Nugent some moments later, when he had recovered from the impact of his mother's news, "I shall set out to meet him along the Queensteignton road. It is rather nasty weather, and will soon be dark."

"I wish you would, my dear. But there is no horse. Your father has taken Pilgrim, and the mare is out at grass."

"I have legs of my own, my dear mother," replied her eldest son, "and it will do me good to stretch them, after hours of the coach. Let me have a slice of meat, or one of Betsy's pies, and a glass of ale, and I will start."

A letter from Toulon at last! It was partly that thought, partly a real uneasiness about his young brother's non-return, which inspired the swinging pace at which, a little later, Nugent set out in the wind and the gathering darkness. To think that this most anxiously awaited letter had been for weeks, it seemed, in the house, and that no one but that detestable Mounsey brat, who had purloined it, had been aware of the fact! And now it was no longer there, but had been sent away unread! Moreover Tom's gallant but ill-advised expedition to recover it might well have failed, either because he could not wheedle it out of the dragon's new owner, or, worse, because the dragon itself was no longer in the man's possession.

Nugent strode anxiously on, the as yet unlit lantern dangling from his hand. What tidings had the missing letter contained — that was the question which gnawed at him. The miserable Arabella had apparently confessed that it was signed 'd'Esparre', hence it was not, thank God, from the resuscitated Creole himself. One could yet hope, therefore, that 'Tante Ursule' — the presumable writer — was not announcing that worst news of all, his imminent arrival in England to claim his lawful wife.

Every day which had passed since that brief and disastrous interview with Charlotte in the convent parlour, nearly two months ago, had the thought of that possible arrival tormented Nugent Carew (for all his assertions that de Marescot could not be alive) just as every day he had been haunted by the memory of Charlotte's own pitiful, stricken face when he had left her with that curt and unyielding farewell. He was seeing it now as he made a belated stop, in the lee of a hedge, to light his lantern.

It was odd, he thought, as he started on again, that he had not met Tom, and real misgivings for his safety began to invade his mind. There was ample time for the boy to have ridden thus far. Had he missed the

Queensteignton coach at Exeter, or had the bad weather delayed it? He ought never to have gone upon this crazy and unauthorised adventure, even though his motives —

The misgivings suddenly became apprehension. What was this shadowy animal cropping grass at the side of the lane? Even in the very bad light it had much the look of Tom's grey pony, riderless. With an exclamation Nugent strode towards it and lifted his lantern. Yes, it *was* Meg, with an empty saddle and a trailing bridle.

"Tom, Tom," shouted his brother, "where are you?"

There was no answer save a whinny from Meg, who had lifted her head, apparently recognising his voice. Nugent felt very glad indeed that he had set out to meet Tom, and almost equally relieved that Meg had not found her riderless way home to alarm his mother.

"I wish you could speak, confound you!" he muttered, laying hold of the pony's bridle. "You will have to come along with me now, I fancy." This Meg, with nostalgic thoughts of her stable, did not greatly wish to do. But Nugent was determined that she should; if he did not in this way make sure of her, she might yet make her way to the Rectory. Ride her himself he could not, for she was not nearly up to his weight.

So, lantern in one hand, towing the unwilling pony with the other, and speculating most uneasily on what had become of her rider, Captain Carew continued for another half mile or so. The lane would soon cease to run between hedges, would mount and cross Upway

Common. Before he left them he scanned these hedges as well as he could for his missing brother, but in vain. The search, first on one side, and then on the other, was, moreover, delaying his progress. Thinking that he heard the sound of wheels in the distance, he desisted and listened. Sure enough, in a moment or two there approached along the sloping road the lamps and then the dim bulk of what looked like a farmer's gig. He resolved to stop it and to make enquiries, and to this end stationed himself and Meg almost in the middle of the road, holding up his lantern as a signal.

The horse came clopping towards him and was then pulled up. A hearty Devon voice next roared out a jovial query as to whether this was going to be a highway robbery, adding, to some second person in the gig: "That'll likely be the young gentleman's pony," and then to Nugent: "Be you a-looking for anyone, sir?"

"Yes, my young brother. He must have been thrown, I think."

"Aye, that he have," said the owner of the voice.

"Why, have you got him there?" asked Nugent peering through the dusk, and was rewarded by the information that they had picked up a boy back there on Upway Common, lying in the heather.

"Is he much hurt?" Nugent was now at the side of the cart, and the more anxious because there was no sound from the retrieved but as yet unseen Tom.

"No, sir, only a bit dwamlike — stunned, I reckon. Us thought best to get un home, if 'tis young Master Carew from Damarel St. Mary, as Peter here thinks."

"It is he — at least I suppose so. Can I have a look at him?" For by now he could make out that there were three, not two, people on the driving seat, one of them of a smaller size disposed in a limp attitude in the hold of the second man.

"Surely, sir. Peter, hold the gentleman's lantern for him."

Nugent got up on to the step and had a lamplit and partial view of his adventurous younger brother apparently asleep in the arms of the younger farmer. He managed to slip a hand on to his wrist and was satisfied by what he felt there. But the boy did not answer when he spoke to him.

"There's no bones broken, I'm main certain," the farmer reassured him. "And a little while back he was a-talking, though not much sense 'tis true. He'm only mazed by the toss he must 'a taken. Us'll goo straight wi' him to the Rectory now."

"That is uncommon good of you," said Nugent warmly. Where did you find him?"

"Nigh the farthest of they fir-trees on the common, sir."

"I know the place," said Nugent. He reflected for a moment. "Had he anything with him, any package or bag?"

"Nothing as us could see, sir. Though at first when us come upon him he did say something moidered-like about some old toad he'd lost and wanted us to look for it. If he'd 'a had a toad in his pocket certain sure 'tweren't there when us picked him up."

"He had gone to fetch an important letter," muttered Nugent, still on the step; and to see whether Tom had succeeded he began as best he could to investigate his unconscious brother's pockets, with their always unpredictable contents. He found in them a lump of cobbler's wax, some tangled twine, a pocket knife, a button or two, a crown piece and some odd pence, but nothing remotely of the nature of a letter. So he knew that Tom had (not unnaturally) failed in his somewhat quixotic effort. He himself must return immediately to the Rectory and allay his mother's anxiety about the boy's condition, perhaps go for the doctor.

But, just as he was stepping down into the road again, the real significance of the remark about an 'old toad' rushed upon him out of his own childhood memories. Why, of course, Tom had meant by that the china dragon; so had he himself, and Sophia after him, always called it. Then Tom *had* apparently persuaded the man in Exeter to part with, or perhaps to lend, that unusual receptacle, and was bringing it home, letter and all . . . and then had lost the creature in his fall. So the Toad with its momentous contents was lying up there on the common in a furze bush or rabbit-hole — if indeed it was still in one piece! It was imperative that it should be retrieved at once, and by him, not by some stranger, or the letter from Toulon was more lost than ever.

"I think I know now what my brother lost in his tumble," he said to the farmer. "As it is of extreme importance that it should be recovered at once, I will ask you to allow me to tie his pony behind your gig, as you are so obliging as to intend going to the Rectory. I shall get on better without her."

"Aye, tie her on, sir. Will I be taking any message from you?"

"Yes, tell my mother, if you please, that I am searching for what my brother has lost, and if successful, shall be back before long. I cannot say how much obliged I am to you for your kindness."

To offer money for this kindness would, he knew, have been to insult the good man. The embarrassing Meg was disposed of behind the gig, and as the vehicle drew away in the gloom Nugent pushed on as fast as he could in the opposite direction. There was hope now — qualified hope — but also a damnable need of haste, and of good eye-sight.

It took him nearly a quarter of an hour to get from the spot in the lane where he had encountered the gig up to the clump of pines on the heath that tossed gaunt branches against a sky which, this evening, provided them with a suitably romantic background. For, now that the rain had ceased, the flying clouds revealed at moments the presence of a watery moon. Her intermittent light, and that of his own lantern, were all the assistance for a search made more difficult by the fact that Nugent Carew did not know exactly what he must expect to find. Would he see the gleam of porcelain among the stems of last year's heather, or had Tom brought the dragon back from Exeter decently shrouded, and if so, in what? Or was the china monster now in several pieces, and those pieces scattered? In that case, what, in this wind, would become of the letter from Toulon?

After surveying the ruts of the rough road, which held nothing, as far as he could see, but water and small twigs, Nugent began carefully to quarter the ground on either side, peering closely, and holding his lantern low. But he had not proceeded far before he stopped and straightened himself. Through the lamentations of the wind he fancied that he heard a woman's voice, singing. Surely he was mistaken? It must be the voice of the wind itself which he heard. No, there it came again, borne on a gust; and this time, as he held up his lantern, the beam shone on something greyish, which might well have been a woman's garment, disappearing between the pine boles. And with it went, unmistakably, a thin thread of song. Except that this wisp of sound in no way suggested an incantation, and also that such things no longer existed, Nugent might have thought that he had stumbled upon some mild form of a witches' sabbath. Curious, nevertheless, to know the reason for this almost nocturnal performance, he approached the pine clump more closely.

Yes, it was a woman, in a long grey cloak, walking to and fro under the pines and singing softly as she went. Her head was bent, and she had the air of chanting to something which she carried in her arms. Neither of him nor of the rough weather did she take any notice. Nugent Carew was dumbfounded. What a night for such behaviour! The cloak and whatever she had over her head were darkened with patches of rain. She must be mad! Or perhaps he, of all people, had somehow been transported into one of Mrs. Radcliffe's romances!

As he stared and hesitated, the woman came round a tree again, and he had a clearer view of her face as the wind whipped the folds away from it. In the lantern light it was hard to be sure of her age. But she had almost the look of a sleep-walker; and whatever she held in her arms, half under her cloak, half wrapped about with it, was held as a woman holds a baby. Nugent Carew, accustomed as he was to the purely normal and practical, felt singularly helpless; and so it was that he merely stood there watching this crazed female — she must be that — advance towards him and that it was she who spoke first.

"Was you looking for my little baby, sir? I've found her."

The soft voice was not exactly that of a countrywoman, and the little, fleeting smile was sweet.

"Indeed. I . . . I am glad of that," stammered Nugent, still very much at a loss. "Er . . . in that case, would it not be better to go home, madam? You must be wet."

"I have been wetter before now, when looking for my child," answered the apparition. "I do not always find her. But to-night I found her so soon, and now that I have done so, yes, I will go home." She moved a few steps away, then turned round again. "You are so kind, sir — would you like to see her before I go?"

She let slip the front of her cloak, and Nugent saw that what she was clasping to her with such loving care was a small carpet-bag with a bulge in it.

"Poor thing, poor thing!" was his first half-shocked thought. "Quite crazed — she ought not to be abroad." Then, as — always with that heartrending little smile — she held out her burden as though better to exhibit her 'child', Nugent uttered a stifled cry. Why, he knew that little carpet-bag; it had been his father's, and was now Tom's, used for his school books! And it undoubtedly must contain — or had contained — the Chinese dragon and Tante Ursule's letter!

By the time he had come to this startling conclusion the girl or woman was folding the cloak again, with fond little murmurs, over the pitiful substitute for a lost child, or for one who had never existed. In another moment she would vanish into the windy darkness, on her way 'home', wherever that was. Nugent could not possibly allow her to depart with the carpet-bag unexamined — yet how, without the use of force, was he to persuade her to part with her burden for even a moment? But it must be done somehow.

"What a pretty child!" The words came out horribly against the grain. He detested further deceiving the poor creature. But too much hung upon what was inside that bag for him to be over squeamish. "Would you allow me to hold her in my arms for a moment?"

She raised her head and gave him a long look. Nugent could only pray that he inspired confidence. It seemed that he did.

"Yes," she said at last. "Yes, if you have children of your own, and know how to hold a baby."

Captain Carew, who even now could not bring himself to a direct lie, murmured something about being accustomed to young children — which was true, up to a point, for there was always Peggy. His words seemed to satisfy the poor 'mother', for when he had put down the lantern she carefully transferred to his arms the shabby old bag, limp but for a hard object within, and stood watching him with a shadowy smile.

And now what was he to do? Turn and run off with the treasure? He could not bring himself to be such a brute. Moreover the crazed creature would probably rend the night with screams, and although the common appeared empty, her outcries might easily bring someone on the scene.

"Yes, a fine child," he observed, looking down at that old green and red bag, so worn and knocked about, in which he suddenly remembered having, as a small boy, imprisoned the cat. All the time his fingers were trying to ascertain the exact shape of its contents. (Yes, the thing inside did feel exactly as the Old Toad might through an almost thread-bare piece of carpet.) "A fine child, certainly But do you not think that on this wild wet night, she would be the better for a dose of some warming cordial? I am a bit of a doctor, and have my bag down yonder — only a few yards away — so if you will allow me I will just take her there and give her some; fine heartening stuff it is. Meanwhile pray stay were you are, out of the wind; I promise that I will bring your baby back to you in a minute or so."

And without waiting for an acquiescence which he hardly expected, the self-created physician turned and walked quickly down the track towards a large furze bush which he happened to have noticed as he came up.

His action was of course only one degree less horrifying to the poor woman than if he had made off with her burden outright. He was sure that she would follow, and had purposely left the lantern on the ground so that she could not trace him by its light, even if she thought to make use of it for herself. He hoped to get his search over while crouched behind the gorse bush, before she could find him. Stumbling along in haste and semi-darkness, with a wail already sounding in his ears, he found the bush — in fact nearly fell over it — knelt down and opened the old bag. Something hard and light of hue glimmered within. It was, it was the Old Toad!

He pulled it out; it felt quite intact, and when he shook it he thought he could hear a paper jumping about inside, but there was too much noise abroad to-night for him to be sure. About his next step he had to decide very quickly, for already he could hear the woman crying out in a despairing, but fortunately not a very loud voice: "Where are you, sir, where are you? Oh, my child, my Letty!" She had not brought the lantern with her, and it was doubtful whether she could actually see him, but he was not at the end of his difficulties. It was obvious that to extract the letter, if there was one, was impossible, and he could not go off with the dragon itself, because when he restored the carpet-bag to the poor creature it would be unsatisfyingly light and flat, the former a deficiency which even hastily stuffed-in heather would do nothing

238

to remedy. There seemed only one other alternative, so he took it. Feeling for a piece of flat hard ground, he set the Toad on it, and drove his heel iconoclastically down on what he took to be its back. There was a scrunching sound, and when he stooped again his fingers met the sharp edges of an aperture in the porcelain. Was the hole big enough? Yes, he could get most of his hand in — and the hand came out grasping an undeniable paper packet of some kind. The letter was his!

He had only time to stuff it into his pocket, however, when there was the figure, ghostly but insistent, in the dimness on the other side of the bush.

"Sir, sir, I want my child! What are you doing to her?" The voice was almost a shriek now.

"Here she is!" returned Nugent in as reassuring a tone as he would muster, hastily wrapping his handkerchief round the mutilated dragon, and stuffing the end of the linen into the gaping hole, in the hope of stilling the tinkles of the broken bits inside which he had not had time to empty out. He thrust the dragon into the carpet-bag, fastened the latter and stood up.

"Here she is, safe and sound, and I hope the better for what I have given her," he said, thinking ruefully how doubly untrue were his words. "You see that I had no intention of running off with her."

He came round the furze bush and laid the bag in the poor creature's arms. She was weeping now, he saw with remorse. It would be only humane to try to see her home — he presumed she lived in some farm or village — but he dared not, even if she would consent. Moreover he was on fire to get back to the Rectory to read the recovered letter. In addition, she now seemed oblivious of him, holding her recovered treasure close to her heart, and murmuring endearments to it. And when, having fetched his lantern from beneath the pines, he came again to the neighbourhood of the gorse bush, she had moved off into the windy darkness; but the same sound of singing which had heralded her first appearance seemed to show that she had regained her deluded happiness . . . and for that Nugent Carew was profoundly thankful. He wondered remorsefully how long it would last.

The sensible course — and indeed the course which Captain Nugent Carew intended to take, was to walk home as quickly as possible, postponing the reading of the letter until his arrival, more especially as he was anxious for news of Tom's condition. But the letter was clamouring so hard, if not to be read through immediately, at least to be glanced at, that by the time he was back in the lane he yielded. He must have some inkling at once of Charlotte's fate and his own. So, coming in a little upon a convenient copse which bordered the lane, he went a little way into its semi-darkness, found a fallen tree-trunk, sat down upon it, set his lantern on the ground, and tore open Edward Mounsey's covering letter addressed to Charlotte (and most inadequately refastened by the writer's pilfering daughter). He did not trouble to read it; all his attention was given to the enclosure.

"My dear Charlotte," *wrote Mlle d'Esparre.* "I hardly know how to write to you. I almost hope that my previous letter has not reached you, for the news which it contained was alas, completely false. Shamefully deceived myself, I unwittingly deceived you, my poor child! M. de Marescot is not alive after all. He did not survive that murderous attack of which you were witness; he was not picked up alive by two fishermen of the Iles d' Hyères, but was recovered dead from the harbour by two scoundrels of Toulon itself, who for months conspired to gull me into thinking that he was recovering from his injuries under their care in Porquerolles. Meanwhile —"

Nugent stopped. "My God!" he said slowly, and put a hand over his eyes. Was he dreaming this, this which he had asserted all along was the truth — that de Marescot never *had* survived? The news was what he had been desperately hoping the lost letter might contain, yet, now that it was here, staring him in the face, he found that a part of his mind was protesting that it could not be true.

After a moment or two he read on:

"Meanwhile, having found an accomplice to forge his signature, they were obtaining sums of money from me for his pretended use.

This cruel and disgraceful fraud was eventually brought to light by the researches of my notary, who for some time had nourished suspicions, as indeed I had myself, on account of the persistent non-appearance of M. de Marescot in person, and also because we were unable to trace the surgeon from Hyères whom the 'fishermen' said had been attending him. In the end the 'fishermen' themselves were run to earth in the lowest part of Toulon, the whole imposture came out, and as they were then charged with having actually made away with your unfortunate husband, after picking him up in the harbour, they were forced, in order to save themselves, to produce irrefutable evidence of his death. This took place just as you had described in your letter to me from Leghorn. It was proved beyond doubt that it was only M. de Marescot's dead body which these wretches had recovered. Such papers found upon it which they had kept are now in safe custody until the time comes when, as his widow, you are able to claim them."

There was a little more, 'Tante Ursule' expressing a hope that Charlotte would yet find means to communicate with her again, and so forth, but Nugent paid small attention to the end of this epistle. A second time, and again a third, and slowly, he read over the marvellous intelligence which the body of it contained. Nothing to keep Charlotte and him apart any longer, nothing, nothing!

Between this inner exultation and the wind in the trees above him, he never heard a slight crackling of twigs in his vicinity. So that when a man's voice behind him cried triumphantly: "Ha! I've caught ye at last,

Barney Parsons!" he looked round with a start to see a man covering him with a fowling-piece.

"And wi' a lantern too! What impidence!" went on this individual. "Making out your accounts, was you, of what you've poached out of here and Skinner's Wood. Well, you can put 'paid' to 'em now! But don't you stir, or I'll blow your brains out!"

Nugent, who had no wish to be shot by a game-keeper as a poacher, had not, after his first movement of surprise, made any others. He said calmly: "You are mistaken, my good fellow. I am not Barney Parsons — if I caught the name aright — but, as you will see if you come nearer, an officer of His Majesty's Navy."

For he guessed that in the lantern light the fact of his wearing uniform was not fully apparent.

"Are ye now?" was the sardonic yet slightly uncertain reply. The composure, and the tones of his quarry had plainly disconcerted the man with the gun. He came more fully into the lantern light, the muzzle of his piece directed at Nugent on his tree-trunk. But he soon saw that this midnight reader was indeed what he claimed to be; or at least that he was certainly not the poacher for whom he had hastily taken him. He lowered his weapon.

"I'm sorry, sir," he said humbly, touching his hat. "I hope you'll overlook the mistake? — It's Captain Carew of Damarel St. Mary, ain't it? — But I've been after that rascal Parsons so long — though I might 'a known he'd never 'a shown a light nor sit reading a letter —

no, despatches I should 'a said, no doubt — in Shute Copse at eight o'clock at night."

"There's no need at all to apologise," answered Nugent good-temperedly, as he rose from the tree-trunk. "Your master should be glad of your zeal — I rather fancy he is Mr. Wilkins, the new owner of Headleigh Court, is he not?"

"Yessir. Bought it last summer as I dessay you knows; but kep' me on as keeper."

"Mr. Wilkins did well," admitted Nugent handsomely. "And I ought not perhaps to have trespassed on his property," he added, feeling that some explanation of his presence in the copse was called for, "but I was anxious to read a letter which I had not yet had time to do." He was putting that letter back in his pocket as he spoke, and, his head buzzing with good news, did not notice that Mlle d'Esparre's first sheet had been caught by the wind and blown on to some brambles. The game-keeper however, espied it, retrieved it, bent to the lantern to see what it was, and after a second or two handed it to Nugent.

"This'll be yours, sir, I reckon — Oh, thank you, sir — thank you indeed!"

For the naval gentleman, whether he were Captain Carew or no, had tipped him as one might tip a person who would always be associated with the reception of overwhelmingly good news.

CHAPTER
SIXTEEN

Journeys end in lovers' meetings. It is true that the line was not actually ringing in Nugent's head as he set out early next morning for London, but the thought which it enshrined was there. After Whitehall, Bath; after being duly posted as captain of the *Defiance*, the reunion with his dearest Charlotte, in an atmosphere all the more serene and shining because of the thundercloud which had lately darkened their sky, and was now dispersed for ever.

The longish wait in the ante-room at the Admiralty next day passed pleasantly enough for him in the company of a former shipmate, who was just upon the point of leaving it, but stayed to chat with him, to congratulate him upon his prospective appointment and his recent marriage, and to enquire whether any future admirals were yet signalled or due to appear.

"Not yet," answered Nugent, smiling. "I was only married last September." As he said it he reflected that two days ago he could not have made that statement, with any conviction, about a ceremony possibly not valid. In fact he would have winced at any reference to wedlock.

"Captain Carew!" called out the messenger, appearing in the doorway. And as Nugent shook hands with his friend and came forward, the messenger added: "Their Lordships will see you now."

"Their Lordships?" He had expected an interview with the new Secretary, Mr. Evan Nepean.

At one end of the table in the Board Room sat the First Sea Lord, Sir Russell Cathcart, with a couple of his colleagues, the Second and Fourth Lords, beside him.

"Good afternoon, Captain Carew," said he, looking up from some papers. "We should like a talk with you. In fact, had you not been due to report to-day we should have been obliged to send for you."

Nugent was conscious of a sudden prick of uneasiness. Standing there — for he had not been asked to seat himself — he wondered why their Lordships might have been 'obliged' to this step. What could be in the wind? That it was not something pleasant was obvious, not only from the cold tone of the First Lord's voice, but from the expressions of Admiral Goolden and Vice-Admiral Torrey also. And his heart began to sink. He was going, after all, to be passed over in favour of some other captain of equal or even lesser standing who happened to be backed by a person of influence — as not seldom happened in peace-time. And yet he had practically been promised the *Defiance!*

"I will come to the point at once, Captain Carew," said Admiral Cathcart, fixing him with those intimidating eyes of his. "For what reason, and in what circumstances, did you, last autumn, when H.M.S. *Callisto* was paying off at Portsmouth, give permission for a Frenchman named Guillemin to enter the dockyard and make a drawing of her?"

The question — so totally unexpected — had upon Nugent Carew almost the effect of a blow. He stared at the First Sea Lord as if he had not understood the words. Then he pulled himself together.

"Purely out of charity, sir. The man — a Royalist emigrant — was a marine painter trying to make a living."

"A marine painter!" ejaculated Admiral Cathcart scornfully. On his lips the 'p' of the last word sounded like an explosive. "He told you so, I presume — and you took him at his own valuation!"

"Not entirely, sir. He was really a painter. I saw him at work."

"Tchah! That is not what I meant! It was then purely out of this sense of charity of yours that you not only allowed this man access to the *Callisto*, but provided him with a pass which would admit him to any of His Majesty's dockyards?"

"That I never did, sir," returned Nugent indignantly.

"Do you deny your own signature, sir?" snapped the Admiral, reaching forward and slapping down on the table in front of him that page from his pocket-book with the few words, insufficiently weighed, which he had scribbled upon it that bright October morning as he stood with Charlotte and the little Frenchman in the Portsmouth street.

Nugent raised his eyes from it again. "I certainly do not deny writing that, but my sole purpose in so doing was that Monsieur Guillemin, if he were challenged, should have some means of proving that he was authorised to make a drawing of the frigate."

"But there is nothing of that in this paper — no specific mention of the *Callisto*, nor of Portsmouth, nor any limitation as to time! Is that the fashion in which to make out a pass! — Look at it again, gentlemen!" And he slid it along to the Second and Fourth Lords.

They both did so, and Admiral Goolden observed drily: "It is certainly not surprising that the man used this loosely phrased authorisation to obtain access to the yards at Plymouth also."

"Unless indeed," chimed in the Fourth Lord, "Captain Carew, being subsequently stationed at Plymouth, had obligingly provided him with another pass which has not come into our hands!"

This was something unpleasant with a vengeance! With a heart like lead, Nugent began to see not only the *Defiance* vanishing down the wind, but possibly any other command as well.

"I knew nothing whatever, I assure you, of the man's presence at Plymouth. I never —" he checked himself, for he had been on the point of declaring that he had never set eyes on the treacherous Guillemin again, which was not true "Nor did I ever conceive that he would so misuse that pass of mine — meant to be a purely temporary facility — in order to gain access elsewhere"

248

"But you did apparently conceive, Captain Carew," countered the First Sea Lord, "that it was consistent with your duty as a British naval officer to permit, even to encourage, a member of the nation with which we are at war to enter Portsmouth dockyard, and to familiarise himself with the vessel under your command, if with no others?"

"May I point out in my defence, sir, that Guillemin, as I mentioned just now, is a Royalist, one of the party in France to which the Government gives support?"

"That, beyond doubt, is what he told you. But even with your over-sympathetic heart, Captain Carew, it is scarcely possible that you took no steps to find out whether this was true or no!"

"But he was already vouched for, having been introduced to my notice by undoubted Royalists to whom he was well known."

"And who were they?"

"The Vicomte and Vicomtesse d'Esparre."

Sir Russell Cathcart looked down at his papers, turned over a page or two, ran his finger along a line and nodded. (Why, in heaven's name, was all this written down already?)

"And how did you come upon *them*, Captain Carew, and what did you know of *their* antecedents?"

"They —" began Nugent, and halted. He saw now where he stood, and that he would be forced to bring Charlotte into this business. God, what an incredible fool he had been ever to give that permission!

"Yes?" asked Admiral Cathcart.

Hoping to retrieve any impression of reluctance to answer which he might have given, Nugent came out with it boldly. "They are my relations by marriage. Monsieur d'Esparre's sister is my wife. Both have suffered for their Royalist convictions: my wife before her marriage had to flee from Toulon at the evacuation, and Monsieur and Madame d'Esparre had been for some years exiles in Germany. They came to England last autumn. How intimate they had previously been with Monsieur Guillemin I am not certain, but he was sharing their lodgings in Portsmouth when I met them."

"And shared them again in Bath, is it not so?" put in Admiral Goolden.

"Yes, sir." Why, they knew already what he was telling them — seemed indeed to be checking his replies by the papers which were in front of them! Nugent was by this time profoundly uneasy.

The First Sea Lord now leant forward and said, in a tone which showed clearly that this fact at least had not been known to him — "So you have married a French-woman, Captain Carew? Recently?"

In spite of himself Nugent's temper was beginning to rise. What business of My Lords of the Admiralty was it whom he had married! But that he knew it would be quite fatal to his prospects, he would have retorted: "Have you not the date written down there with all the rest?" — and all the more because from the tone of the question he was sure that it was not. Controlling himself, he answered, in a fairly expressionless voice:

"Last September, sir." And, to forestall further galling questions, he added: "In Leghorn, where I first met her. She was teaching in the household of an English merchant there, a kinsman of my father's, having, as I said, fled from Toulon when we gave it up."

"And was this Guillemin a friend of your wife's also?"

"No, sir. She knew nothing of him but what her brother told her when they met in Portsmouth. This meeting," he added, "the first for years, came about by pure chance."

Looking down at his maimed left hand, a relic of Sir Hyde Parker's hardfought and inconclusive action against the Dutch off the Dogger Bank in 1781, the First Sea Lord appeared to brood. "Chance," he muttered "chance, like charity, can be made, it seems, to cover a multitude of delinquencies." He raised his head. "Was it chance Captain Carew, which arranged that this Guillemin should again share lodgings with Monsieur d'Esparre — I should say, your brother-in-law — and this time in Bath?"

"I have really no idea, sir, why the arrangement was carried on," replied Nugent, inwardly fuming. How, and *why*, did the Board of Admiralty know all this?

"It did not strike you that Bath was an odd place for a 'marine painter' to choose as a residence . . . unless he considered that it offered some compensating advantage, such as being under the same roof, and upon intimate terms, with a titled and genuine French émigré?"

251

Nugent stared at him. What advantage, as things were now-a-days with such impoverished exiles, could lie in that?

"No, sir, it did not strike me, because, having no further interest in Monsieur Guillemin's movements, I did not concern myself with his private arrangements."

"A great pity that you did not!" remarked Vice-Admiral Torrey grimly. "You never saw him again, in fact?"

For the fraction of a second Nugent hesitated. Not, again, that he had any intention of lying, but because he was trying to see the implications of his answer.

"Once, sir. In Bath."

"At your brother-in-law's, I suppose?"

"Yes."

"You were by this time, no doubt, intimate with the Vicomte d'Esparre?"

"Hardly intimate. But he had become my kinsman by marriage."

"Would you oblige us with the date and occasion of your visit to him, Captain Carew?" asked the First Sea Lord.

Biting back a curse — why should he submit to this interrogatory! — Nugent answered: "It was the 23rd of January. And it was scarcely a visit. My wife had been staying there, and I went to escort her home."

(They cannot, he thought, know enough of my private affairs to ask: "And did she accompany you?" But if they should, damn them, I shall answer: "Naturally she did!")

252

However, the next question was: "And it was on this occasion that you met Guillemin?"

"Yes. To my surprise I found him there. That was the first intimation which I had that he was in Bath."

But here the inquisition was suddenly broken short by an interruption, welcome for the moment, but almost immediately shattering. For the Second Sea Lord, who had been fidgeting a little, interposed with:

"Don't you think, Cathcart, that the time has come when we should in fairness acquaint Captain Carew with the reason for these somewhat unusual enquiries?"

The First Sea Lord's sandy eyebrows drew together. "Yes, perhaps so. But I fear it will not afford him much satisfaction. — Well, Captain Carew, here it is. Your protégé, the intimate of your French brother-in-law, and vouched for by him, to whom you gave the run of His Majesty's dockyards, is a spy in the service of the Convention. He has been busy sending them the naval information which your complaisance must have made it much easier for him to obtain, and he has just been arrested at your brother-in-law's lodgings in Bath."

A bitterly cold wind was ruffling the lake in St. James's Park. Only the ducks seemed unaffected by it, for the few people passing through did not linger, and the benches disposed at intervals were all unoccupied save one. Upon this there was sitting a solitary naval officer in captain's uniform, who, like the ducks, seemed oblivious of the temperature, and who was staring with a fixed expression at the restless steel of the water.

"That fellow over there must be pretty well impervious to cold," remarked a middle-aged habitué of Brooks's who, with another of the same species, was taking a brisk walk for the sake of his liver. "He was sitting in the same place twenty minutes ago, if I am not mistaken, and, unless one is moving, this wind is enough to chill an icicle."

"Ah well," said the other, "wind is all in the day's work for the Navy."

And indeed the blast might have been a midsummer zephyr for all the physical discomfort it caused Nugent Carew. When the heart is as cold as his, the body's claims to warmth can be ignored. The seas over which he had hoped to sail and fight anew had shrunk to this little piece of water before him, and his promised ship of the line to that derelict toy vessel yonder, lying on its side in the water, and carried fitfully by the ripples towards a landfall of shipwreck.

Not that at any time during the remainder of that scarifying interview over there in the Admiralty Board Room any aspersions had been cast upon his own loyalty. For all the unpleasant stress laid upon his French brother-in-law's intimacy with the spy, none of the three Admirals seemed to have considered him as in any way a willing party to those just discovered activities of the 'marine painter.' Once the encounter was at an end, he found himself free to depart — free to go anywhere he pleased ... except to board the *Defiance*, or indeed the smallest schooner wearing the naval ensign of his native land.

254

The tiny boat was nearly at the edge of the lake by now. Nugent did not know that he had taken command once more of his stiff limbs, and was standing looking down upon it, did not know that he had unconsciously stooped and was picking it up, until his fingers met the sting of the icy lake water. The flimsy, waterlogged sail dripped pitifully; the diminutive pennant at the peak was a mere sodden thread of scarlet. He let the wrecked plaything drop again, and the little splash it made had the effect of rousing him to action. He turned and walked away. Whatever happened he must catch the afternoon coach for Marlborough and Bath.

And, as he turned, his stunned brain began to come to life again. It woke not only to a fuller realisation of how he had undone himself, but to agonised surmises as to Charlotte's position, living as she now was with her brother and his wife, in the very house where the spy had been arrested. The d'Esparres themselves might well be under arrest too, though a stammered question to this effect had brought no information on the point, because Their Lordships had none to give. For, though so deeply concerned in what it might disclose, they were not actually conducting the prosecution of Guillemin — that was the function of the Secretary for Home Affairs. Their business with Captain Nugent Carew had been the part which his incredibly rash permission to the Republican agent had played in the clandestine activities of the latter, a part which could not as yet — which perhaps never could — be fully assessed.

CHAPTER
SEVENTEEN

I

Returning from an afternoon round of parish visiting, the Reverend Peregrine Carew was mediating with keenest pleasure on the subject of his eldest son and that son's wife, now so soon to meet again, with no shadow of a barrier between them. All had come right, and he had been completely justified in his belief that the unfortunate 'Creole gentleman' had not survived. So profound was his joy and relief that, though horrified at his younger son's nefarious action (for which Tom was now paying with confinement to bed caused by concussion), Mr. Carew could not honestly bring himself to regret it, seeing what the stolen, and now shattered and lost dragon had contained. Immediately on his return the previous day, he had despatched to Mr. Zacharew a letter of deep regret and apology for Tom's behaviour, enclosing a draft for the amount which had changed hands over the dragon. In the course of writing it he had said to himself: "If only Tom had waited, I should have gone myself to Exeter after the thing. But would Zacharew have allowed me to buy it back, or even to extract the letter? If he had refused, *I* could not have taken that naughty boy's way out, and run off with it!"

As he now approached his own gate, the Rector's mind, however, turned to the passing last night of his old friend Pelley. His had been a peaceful end, a release from years of ill-heath. One of his last utterances had been to tell the Rector that he had bequeathed him his library, or rather, any books which he chose to take from it; and Peregrine Carew did not find it necessary to put aside as unfeeling the satisfaction which spread over him at the thought of those well-filled shelves. He was pretty sure that they contained a copy of Dimsdale's recently acquired work. Dear me, he reflected, if I had known that one would so soon be left to me, I might never have sold the Chinese dragon at all, since it was mainly because I had that copy of Whitaker's in mind that I did so. And in that case not only would Tom not have had occasion for this illegal proceeding of his — and now be in bed as a result of it (thank God he was not seriously injured) — but the letter from Mlle d'Esparre might have come to light sooner. Unless indeed the want of a hiding place at a crucial moment had led that unprincipled child to destroy it altogether!

So musing, Mr. Carew opened the Rectory gate. A little way inside old George was busying himself, in a rather desultory fashion, with a broom. At his master's footsteps he desisted, hobbled towards him and touched his hat.

"Well, what is it, Cripps?"

"If yu plaze, zur, there'm a little old man a-waiting here in the sweep for to see yu. He won't goo away, nor he won't goo into the house, but keeps a-walking up

257

and down to catch yur Raverunce as yu comes in. Says he have a right to see yu. I'd a swept un away wi' this yere old besom if I could."

A slight tinge of uneasiness shot into Mr. Carew's mind as he nodded to his retainer and continued his progress. Turning the corner with the laurels, the uneasiness became discomfort, for there was no mistaking the identity of the undersized and humpy figure clad in an old coat too long for it, which he then perceived.

"Good afternoon, Mr. Zacharew," said the Rector. "I can guess, can I not, why you are here? I wrote to you yesterday forenoon but you probably have not yet received my letter."

Ignoring this greeting, Mr. Zacharew had shuffled close, and now peered up at him.

"It would have made no difference if I had," he said, with venom. "It's not a *letter* that I want from you!"

"I sent something else besides a letter," replied the Rector stiffly. "But come with me into the house; we cannot discuss private matters here."

Followed by feet which seemed too big for their owner, or were for some other reason slightly unmanageable, and also by certain low-pitched mutterings, he entered the house, ushered the unwelcome visitor into his study, and said, with some appearance of cordiality: "Now, Mr. Zacharew, will you not sit down? You must be tired after the vigil which I hear you have been keeping outside."

Gathering the skirts of his singular outer garment round him, Mr. Zacharew mutely complied, and then looked searchingly round the room.

258

"I can now," went on the Rector, standing in man's natural coign of vantage by his hearth, "make you by word of mouth, as well as in writing, my sincere apologies for my young son's unpardonable behaviour in going off with the piece of china which I had sold to you. I am in hopes that you will accept them, and in addition —"

But Mr. Zacharew, at the word 'apologies', had waved an unclean hand, and now broke in fiercely, "I don't want apologies! . . . I want —"

"Yes, I understand that," interrupted the Rector in his turn. "When you receive my letter you will find that it contains a draft for the sum which you paid me for the dragon."

"Wasted labour!" retorted the visitor implacably. "The draft will be torn up. That's not what I've come for!"

"You mean that you want a larger sum than you originally disbursed? Well, that is a not unreasonable demand. You hoped no doubt to sell the grotesque for more than you gave. But for how much more? The creature was not, as you pointed out at the time, in a perfect state of preservation."

"Sell it for more!" ejaculated the china-dealer. "I'd not have sold it at all for years, maybe never! I bought it for myself. So it's not your money but what your lad stole from me that I want — and I intend to have it!"

"Come, come," said the Rector uncomfortably, aware of the complete impossibility of satisfying this demand, "it is not wise to refuse compensation — and a handsome compensation. As you say you had taken such a personal fancy to the beast, I will pay you up to double the amount you paid me."

"You can't bribe me, Mr. Carew! I wonder you try it, being a parson. I want my lawful purchase back, that you sent your — that your boy stole. If you don't give it up I shall go to a magistrate and get a warrant to make ye!"

"You will find that of little use, Mr. Zacharew," returned the Rector, trying not to show his dawning anger. "No one, not the Lord Chancellor himself, could restore you the dragon, for it was, most unfortunately, broken to pieces during its transit from Exeter." It was praiseworthy of him to resist the strong temptation to add: "My son was thrown from his pony, and in his fall . . ." for that would have been a tacit lie. Not thus, as he knew from Nugent, had the old monster come by his dissolution.

"Broken!" exclaimed Mr. Zacharew, starting up from his chair. "You stand there, Mr. Carew, and tell me that! First stolen and then smashed through carelessness! But at least I'll have the pieces!"

The Rector shook his head.

"I am afraid that you cannot."

"Do you mean to say that young rascal of yours did not keep them — for I suppose he dropped the dragon in his hurry? Where did he drop it? In Exeter?"

This question at least, since he was obliged to give some reply, Mr. Carew could answer truthfully.

"On Upway Common. His pony threw him as he was returning."

"And he left the broken dragon lying there?"

"The boy was suffering from concussion, Mr. Zacherew, and was brought home in that condition by some good farmers who were passing. It was getting dark, and they, naturally, knew nothing of what he might have had with him. He was picked up, if you wish to know, under or near that clump of pine-trees on the highest point."

Mr. Zacharew, stumping about the study, suddenly faced round.

"If these farmers knew nothing about the dragon, and that young rascal was unconscious, how, pray, do you know that it *was* broken?"

Now indeed the hapless Rector was up against a poser. He could not bring himself to say: "Because my elder son went to the Common, found it (but not lying where it fell) and for a certain reason deliberatedly smashed it in order to recover the letter which it contained." All that he could produce in answer was an unconvincing and fundamentally disingenuous: "What could one expect of a piece of porcelain — cracked too — after such a fall? But, as I say" — he went on quickly, "I am offering you double the value of the thing, and my sincere apologies for the whole regrettable transaction."

Mr. Zacharew waved away the offer, this time with both hands, indeed almost with his arms. "Parson or no, I don't believe a word you are saying, sir! The whole thing is a wicked plot of some kind. The dragon never was left on the Common, whether your boy took a toss or not — and that's maybe all a lie too! You'll hear more of this when I've been to a justice of the peace about the theft, and sworn information too about this pretended foreign letter that jackanapes of yours said was inside the creature! Just another lie to get me to let him have the thing in his hands, so that he could make off with it — as he did directly my back was turned for a moment!"

"On the contrary," said Mr. Carew with dignity, "there *was* a letter inside it, and if you had allowed my son — whose subsequent action, I repeat, I in no way defend — to extract it, as he begged, the dragon would still be in your hands to-day."

The china-dealer stood quite still, and subjected the Rector of Damarel St. Mary to the kind of crafty appraisal which he had bestowed on Tom. "Oho!" he said at last. "So there *was* a letter inside, was there? You swear that?"

"I am not in a court of law, Mr. Zacharew," returned the Rector with asperity. "Nor am I accustomed to having my word doubted."

"All very fine, but you may yet have to do some swearing in a court of law! A pretty hole and corner business this is altogether! I think there's those higher than a justice of the peace would like to know what was in a letter hidden away like that, a letter that it was worth larceny to get hold of again!"

Mr. Carew was really angry now. "What the —" (here his naval ancestor nearly manifested himself), "— what, may I ask, do you mean by that? If it is merely an attempt to blackmail me into paying you even more than twice the sum you gave me, then I should advise *you* to keep clear of any magistrate. It is

262

plainly time that this interview came to an end. For the last time, will you accept —"

"I'll accept nothing but the dragon, whole or in pieces!"

Mr. Carew went to the study door. "Perhaps," he said, "you may feel differently when my letter with the draft reaches you. And you have but to say the word now, and I will write you a second draft for the same amount — in exchange, of course, for a signed statement that you are satisfied with the compensation."

"It's no good trying to bribe me!" quoth Mr. Zacharew grimly. "I love my country, I do, and you can't shut my mouth that way about your smuggled correspondence from abroad — treasonable, there's not a doubt of it! You'll get your first draft back as soon as I've received it — I'd not soil my hands even by tearing it up — and soon afterwards you'll have a visit you won't like! Being a parson won't protect you!"

Disgusted, but in reality not much alarmed by this wild threat, and thinking: "The man is quite mad! . . . but I hope he will stop proclaiming his feelings for all the household to hear," the Rector preceded his visitor towards the hall door, noting however his sly glances round the hall. Evidently Mr. Zacharew cherished a hope of seeing his ravished property squatting after all in some remote nook. But he allowed the door to be closed upon him without any further denunciations. Unpleasant and illogical old man! If — preposterous thought — he, Peregrine Carew, had really been involved in anything so incredible as treasonable correspondence, would he not have done anything in his power to avoid the slightest unpleasantness being raised about its hiding place?

More perturbing, in reality, than the dealer's last spiteful outburst, was his stubborn refusal to accept compensation. That did leave the Rectory family in rather an awkward situation. Perhaps, when he actually handled the draft, Zacharew would repent of his obstinacy. Otherwise, Tom might be proceeded against in spite of his father's offer to make good the loss. As matters had turned out, it was regrettable that Nugent's pity for that poor crazed woman had led him to smash the dragon and restore her the pieces instead of bringing it home intact, when it could have been returned to Zacharew undamaged . . . He would go and consult Clavering about the whole affair.

II

Having despatched an excellent meal, two middle-aged bachelors, very dissimilar in character, sat at table next day in a roomy and very comfortable house in the best part of Exeter. They were Mr. Henry Tredgold, its owner, kindly, self-indulgent and with an eye for the foibles of his fellows, and Mr. Frederick Wilkins, newly of Headleigh Court, earnest, sallow and doctrinaire. Although old acquaintances, they had barely met since Mr. Wilkins had acquired his new property last summer; the Epicurean character of the repast provided by Mr. Tredgold might or might not have been intended to celebrate this more protracted encounter. If it had, the giver of the feast must have been somewhat disappointed, for the guest showed himself to be but a moderate and an undiscriminating trencherman.

The two gentlemen, however, were now at the port stage, and Mr. Tredgold, comfortably replete, lazily held up his glass to the light, and enquired of his visitor how he liked his new surroundings and his neighbours. He himself, he observed, knew but few of the gentry out that way — the Claverings of Damarel Place, for instance, and the Herricks. Both of these families, it seemed, Mr. Wilkins had already met, and of both he expressed a qualified approval.

"And Parson Carew?" pursued Mr. Tredgold. "I take it you have made his acquaintance, since, though you are some way off from Damarel St. Mary village, you are I think in the parish."

Mr. Wilkins' thin lips came together more tightly for a moment.

"You know, Tredgold — or perhaps you have forgotten — that I am a free-thinker. It is against my principles to attend any place of worship."

"By Gad, I had forgotten that! (Mind you are not taken up for recusancy!) But you might have met him socially, or even in the hunting-field."

"I do not hunt," replied Mr. Wilkins even more repressively.

"Well, I don't actually know that Parson Carew does, now-a-days. At any rate he is very much liked in the neighbourhood, and respected too. And that, by the way," added Mr. Tredgold, pouring out another glass of port, "makes all the more ridiculous the farrago of nonsense which was sworn against him this morning by that old curiosity dealer near St. Mary Steps."

"And what was that?" enquired Mr. Wilkins.

"Some rubbish about an alleged treasonable letter from abroad concealed in some hollow china ornament or other which this Zacharew recently bought from him. Three days ago (according to the old man), Mr. Carew sent his son, a boy of about fourteen to steal it, which (again according to Zacharew) the boy succeeded in doing. When Zacharew went yesterday to Damarel St. Mary Rectory to demand the thing back Mr. Carew (so he says) tried to bribe him with an offer of twice the purchase money to keep quiet about the affair, alleging too that the ornament in question had got broken during its removal from Exeter. Zacharew is a pretty queer character at any time, but over this alleged theft he seems to have gone completely crazy. But I had to take his deposition." Mr. Tredgold sighed as though the operation had fatigued him, and went on with a humorous sigh. "What extraordinary notions people get into their heads in war-time!"

"You say this dealer stated that a treasonable letter from abroad had been hidden in the allegedly stolen ornament?" enquired Mr. Wilkins frowning.

"More 'allegedlys' than that, Wilkins, if you please! 'Allegedly' treasonable, 'allegedly' from abroad, and 'allegedly' hidden!"

His guest stared at him without showing the slightest reaction to this facetiousness. "This is very odd! Could that possibly be the letter which . . . On what day was this supposed theft committed?"

"On Monday afternoon. What letter do you mean? The port is with you, Wilkins."

The hint went unregarded. "I was wondering," said Mr. Wilkins, leaning forward and speaking with grave earnestness, "whether it can be connected with this theft (which, in that case, would not be so 'alleged' after all) that late that same evening my game-keeper, who was out after a poacher, came in a copse upon a man reading a foreign letter by the light of a lantern. This man —"

"Excuse me a moment! How did your game-keeper know that it was a foreign letter?"

"Because a sheet of it had blown some distance away, and he picked it up, and, being a man of some slight education, recognised that it was not written in English, and indeed saw the name of the place it came from — Toulon."

"Smart of your game-keeper! But continue! What were you about to say when I interrupted you?"

"That the man who was reading this letter wore naval uniform; though Stokes did not see this at first, and even pointed his gun at him, thinking for a moment that he had captured his poacher. When he got a better view of the officer (for such he was) he thought he recognised him as Captain Carew, the elder son of the Rector of Damarel St. Mary — for Stokes has been in the district for years. Indeed he said as much, but, as the naval officer neither admitted nor denied it, Stokes concluded that he had not heard the remark, and did not like to press the point. As he was obviously not a poacher, Stokes then withdrew, after receiving, so he hinted, a handsome vail."

To this tale of nocturnal happenings Mr. Tredgold remarked with a lazy smile that whether or no the trespasser were Captain Carew, a wood after nightfall, and in such wet and windy weather as Monday's, did seem an odd place for a naval officer, or for anyone else, to be reading correspondence.

"If he *was* a naval officer, Tredgold! Coupled with the 'foreign' letter there are all sorts of dangerous possibilities in the episode. In fact I was only waiting until we had quite finished our meal to consult you on the point."

"If you will not have any more port we may justifiably consider it at an end. So pray consult. But first, are you sure that your game-keeper, after one pot of ale too many, did not imagine this little scene, for, if you will pardon me, it smacks of the unlikely?"

Mr. Wilkins shook his head: "Quite sure. Stokes is a most reliable man, and neither drinks too much nor has hallucinations. (Besides, he came away with money in his pocket which was not there previously.) If only we knew whether the officer was Captain Carew or someone else!"

"It seems to me most improbable — almost incredible, in short — that it should have been he, reading a letter from Toulon in a wood at midnight! For one thing, I expect he is at sea, on active service."

"Then who was the officer, and what was the communication from Toulon which he was reading in so clandestine a manner? Do you not, Tredgold, see

268

some sinister connection with the letter stolen that same afternoon, together with the china ornament in which it had been concealed, by Parson Carew's younger son?"

"I can't say I see any connection, sinister or otherwise, but I suppose it is conceivable there may be one," replied Mr. Tredgold, with a tinge of boredom in his voice. "But really, my dear fellow, it is too fantastic to take seriously."

"Tredgold," said Mr. Wilkins almost menacingly, "we cannot dismiss this matter so lightly! Either that man in naval uniform was Captain Carew, or he was not. You admit that?"

"Yes, yes, there's no escape from your logic!"

"If he was not," went on Mr. Wilkins, ignoring this gibe, "then who *was* he? I cannot believe that he was a genuine naval officer; I am, on the contrary, convinced that he was some very doubtful character, some spy who had contrived to procure naval uniform, which you will admit would render his dirty work easier in countless ways. And in any case — in any case," repeated Mr. Wilkins weightily, "I am of opinion that the Admiralty should be informed of the occurrence without an hour's delay!"

"You don't seriously mean that?"

"Indeed I do! Have you forgotten that we are at war? The conjunction of these two very strange episodes, linked together by a letter to recover which, so you tell me, larceny was committed —"

("Allegedly committed.")

"— and which had to be read in secret after dark in a wood —"

("Assuming that it was the same letter, which as yet there are small grounds for doing.")

"— this conjunction convinces me that something exceedingly suspicious is going on under our noses. Possibly a secret landing is being planned in this very county of Devon. No, Tredgold, I have not a shadow of doubt that it is one's duty, as a patriotic Englishman, to warn the Admiralty without delay."

"Why the Admiralty?"

"I should have thought the reason was plain! Because this man was either wrongfully impersonating a naval officer, or was really one — leaving aside for a moment the question of whether or no he was the brother of the lad who is said to have stolen that letter. As a magistrate you *must* take steps, Tredgold; you cannot escape it!"

"No, no, my dear fellow, you cannot expect me, on such flimsy evidence —"

"*Flimsy*, do you call it!"

"Well, perhaps that is rather too strong an expression. But you see, my watchful patriot, that before I can move in any way I must ascertain if there is any truth in the story about young Carew and the china dog or whatever it was. I don't credit old Zacharew's statement about that, and about Parson Carew trying to bribe him, although he swore to it, and no doubt believed what he swore. That will take time; it will mean among other things a visit to Damarel St. Mary Rectory. Then I should have to interrogate your game-keeper; and in the end the odds are a hundred to one that the whole business would turn out to be a mare's nest!"

More thin-lipped than ever, Mr. Wilkins did not answer for a moment. He saw that Tredgold's fatally easy-going nature would lead him to postpone 'taking steps' in a matter which he regarded as of little moment, to the extent of never taking them at all. And to his own zealous, interfering mind the matter was of the utmost urgency. He rose and flung down his table-napkin.

"Listen, Tredgold! Give me a copy of the old dealer's deposition and I will get Stokes to sign a written statement of what he saw. He can come in to Exeter later, and make a formal one before you. I shall go up to Whitehall myself to-morrow. If we let grass grow under our feet . . ."

"Oh, very well," said his host resignedly. His mouth gave a twitch of amusement as he too rose. "If you hunted the fox as a country gentleman should, Wilkins, you'd not feel the need to go upon a wild goose chase!"

CHAPTER
EIGHTEEN

I

When, some twenty-four hours after his vigil in St. James's Park, Nugent Carew reached the d'Esparres' lodging, the door was opened, not by the trim landlady whom he had seen on his previous visit, but by a scared-looking elderly woman of a lower class. She appeared to be deaf as well as frightened, making no coherent reply to his enquiry for Mrs. Carew, but merely jerking a hand towards the stairs and vanishing. And, since Nugent knew the way to his brother-in-law's apartments, he went up without more ado and tapped at his door. Would it be Charlotte who opened it?

It had seemed to him quite likely that he would even find her alone in the lodgings, since it was possible that both Fabien and his wife were in custody. Charlotte herself, surely, could not well be under suspicion, her acquaintance with the spy being so slight. (The fact that it was originally Charlotte herself who, in those early days at Portsmouth, had approached him on Guillemin's behalf in the matter of sketching the *Callisto* he did not intend to reveal to anyone, nor indeed had it any real significance.)

He had to knock a second time before steps — and those a man's — were heard on the other side. The door was opened a few inches, and the Vicomte's d'Esparre's voice, instinct with suspicion, asked: "Who is there?" Then, apparently, he saw.

"Captain Carew!" He opened the door rather wider.

The visitor wasted no words. "Yes, it is Carew. And I know what has happened to the man Guillemin. I am thankful to find that you are still at liberty."

"Come in!" said the Frenchman quickly, and quickly too shut the door behind them both. He looked haggard, hollow-eyed, and, above all, apprehensive.

"You know everything?" he repeated. "All the vile treachery of that scoundrel, that wolf in sheep's clothing, for which *we* must suffer?"

"But you yourselves have not been arrested — and I hope are not likely to be?"

"Not arrested, no," answered Fabien with a contraction of the mouth. "But we are not at liberty either. We must not go elsewhere, my poor wife and I, without permission. Ah, what a misfortune, what an abominable misfortune!"

Nugent made no comment. Words, of which indeed he was rarely prodigal, were coming more sparsely than usual to his lips. He did not even feel a desire to reproach the speaker with his share in the catastrophe which a willingness to oblige a supposedly deserving exile had brought upon both of them, being indeed inclined to believe that his fellow-sufferer was as innocent as himself. He therefore left the subject.

"I have come to fetch Charlotte away," he announced briefly. "A second letter has reached us from Toulon.

The report of de Marescot's survival was false. She therefore is, and always has been my lawful wife."

It seemed to take a few seconds for this good news to penetrate Fabien's absorption in his own calamity. When it had, he seized his brother-in-law's hand with no lack of warmth. "Thank God, thank God! Now the poor girl's distress of mind, which was so painful to witness, will be over. But why in God's name, did my old aunt listen to rumour in that fashion? Had she not, you need never have separated."

"It was more than rumour. She was deliberately deceived, out of mercenary motives. So now, unless Charlotte also is under orders not to leave this house —"

"But Charlotte is not here. Ah, you would not be aware of that, I suppose?"

"Not here?" repeated Nugent, instantly alarmed. "You cannot mean that *she* has been taken into custody, while you —"

"No, no! On the contrary, by not being in this house when that villain was arrested, and still more by her absence when the authorities came again yesterday and questioned us —"

Nugent did not wait for the end of the sentence. "But where is she?" He was beginning to have a strange feeling that his former visit to this place in search of his wife was being played over again with a difference. "Where has she gone? Not, I hope to that convent of hers in Bristol?"

"By no means, Captain Carew. She is here in Bath, and in a better quarter of it than this."

274

"But why?"

"Because," said Charlotte's brother, "a little while ago, desiring, she said, not to be an encumbrance to us" (here Charlotte's husband frowned and muttered 'God knows there was never any need for that!') "she took a post as companion to a rich lady living in Dorrington Square, a Mrs. Tracy Stallingwood. And as I was saying, it is fortunate in the highest degree that she did so, since, having left our roof, she could not be interrogated. The authorities here are in fact ignorant of her kinship with us, probably indeed of her very existence. On the other hand," went on the Vicomte, displaying increasing signs of tension, "I am in hourly fear lest, being ignorant of what has occurred, she may pay us a visit, as she does from time to time. You must not therefore allow her to come near this house, Captain Carew, not even to take farewell of us. It is too dangerous."

"Indeed I will not," agreed Nugent. "I appreciate your natural solicitude on her behalf, and I am not likely to throw away the advantage which she enjoys by having left your roof before this blow fell. What is the name, or number of this lady's house in Dorrington Square?"

"The number is twenty-nine. You should ask for Charlotte, by the way, as Mademoiselle de Soray, which was our mother's maiden name."

"And why, pray has she assumed that?" asked Nugent with some curtness. "Her name is Carew."

"But you must admit, Captain Carew, that there were reasons against her calling herself so!" protested

275

Fabien, not without justification. "As it happens it was again most fortunate that she did not call herself d'Esparre."

"Provided she is not calling herself de Marescot, it is all one to me," replied Nugent, still frowning slightly, and turned towards the door. Then he stopped. After all, this fellow-victim of Guillemin's was Charlotte's brother. "Now as to your own position, d'Esparre," he went on more pleasantly. "Since you are known to be Royalist refugees, I cannot believe that you are really suspected of being implicated in this —" he paused for a moment, and it was his own situation which suddenly stared him in the face — "this disastrous affair. For if you were, you would not be suffered to remain at liberty."

"At liberty!" retorted the Frenchman with bitterness. "What does that liberty amount to, if we may not leave these lodgings — though the landlady at once put pressure on us to find others. Yet even if we were free agents I should hesitate to do so, for it would be most unwise to give the impression of trying to conceal ourselves. But the result of all this disturbance is that, like my poor wife, Mrs. Gibbings finds herself indisposed and has retired to bed. Ah, that scorpion, that crocodile — so affable and hard-working, but all the while, it seems, engaged in collecting information about English ports and naval strength!"

Nugent Carew winced. "How was it that you were so misled about him? I forget if I ever heard where you first met him; not, I believe, in Portsmouth?"

"No, it was before that, in the fishing boat by which we escaped from Holland. He was escaping too — or so he gave us to understand. He . . . he was of service to us financially, for our resources were then at a very low ebb. Afterwards, as he seemed to seek our society, and we, blind fools that we were, had conceived a liking for him — besides being under an obligation — we shared the same lodgings at Portsmouth. Most disastrously this association continued here in Bath; that is to say, Guillemin lived in this house except when away on his clandestine missions. To us, of course, he made great play with the pictures he sold, the new patrons he was finding, and the rest."

Nugent Carew's face grew even grimmer, in the short silence which ensued. It was he who broke it by asking: "And when he was arrested, did he say anything to implicate you?"

"Not in our hearing. And anything he may have said since is as great a lie as ever has been uttered! Should my wife and I, of all people, try to help our enemies the Jacobins against the country which shelters us and is fighting them!"

"Exactly," said Nugent, and turned once more to the door. "That, I am sure, is the view which will be taken of your situation. Your only link with this dirty spy is the fact that you knew him and shared the same roof with him. That is so, is it not?" And then, to his dismay, surprising on his French brother-in-law's face a curious half-guilty look, he added: "If there is anything else, you had better tell me!"

Looking down at the floor and fidgeting, Fabien d'Esparre said in a lowered voice: "There is, I must confess, one link which, if discovered, *would* connect us with this suspected Irish accomplice of Guillemin's in Bristol about whom we were questioned yesterday, and of whom we denied any knowledge. As long as that link remains undiscovered, or as long as Guillemin keeps silence about it —"

"A link with an accomplice in Bristol!" exclaimed Nugent considerably horrified. "But how could you possibly be connected with such a person?"

"Why, through your wife, Captain Carew! Through her whom you claim as your wife!" cried a high female voice behind him. Startled, Nugent turned and beheld in the other doorway Mme. d'Esparre, in a tumbled wrapper, with disordered hair and a high colour on her face. "Your wife — since it seems that she is such after all — who made herself that scoundrel's go-between, carried correspondence for him, was his tool if ever there was one! You must keep her away from us — you must, you must!"

Nugent looked at her for a moment, and then turned away in mute disgust from this half-hysterical accuser. But he was considerably disquieted.

"What in God's name is this tale?" he demanded of Fabien.

He had to wait for an answer until the Vicomte, putting his wife into a chair, had succeeded in calming her, so that the next exchanges were punctuated only with sobs.

278

"I beg you to forgive poor Honorine," he said unhappily, as he came forward again. "She has had much to try her. And, unfortunately, she is only too right. Charlotte *is* the link. All innocently, of course, she played Guillemin's game, assisted him by —"

"Charlotte!" broke in Nugent. "*Charlotte* assist that man! You are raving, d'Esparre!"

"I wish to God I were! But the fact is that when she went to Bristol that time she conveyed at Guillemin's request a little picture of his to a pretended purchaser who lives there, an Irishman in the wine trade, who appears to be an accomplice of his and, like him, in the pay of the Convention."

Nugent recovered himself after a second or two. "Is that all? A picture! What harm could there be in that? What sort of a picture was it?"

"A pretty sylvan scene, most innocent — not a painting of ships at all. But if Charlotte's action had led to nothing else it would have served to mark her out as a channel of communication with this O'Connor."

"Channel of — Nonsense, d'Esparre! I do not wish to sound offensive, but I must say that I think you are losing your head!"

Fabien shook that head very gloomily. "I wish I could think so, Captain Carew. But there is worse. The man O'Connor made an undoubted tool of her by inducing her, when she returned from Bristol, to bring back a letter from him to Guillemin. She was told that it merely contained an expression of thanks and a draft in payment for the picture. What it really held one can but conjecture — and can only pray the law has not discovered! But for the wife of an Englishman to convey anything of the sort could, I sometimes fear, be made to look like complicity — even treason. So far however, no suspicion seems to have fallen upon Charlotte . . . But you see how very important it is that nothing should now come out which could connect her with this house, or with the secret agent who lodged here!"

"Or with us!" cried the Vicomtesse, suddenly turning round in her chair. "Why, Fabien, do you not make it quite plain to Captain Carew that it is you and I, already under suspicion, who are in danger from Charlotte's foolish complaisance? He must not let it be known that she is your sister! Our case is black enough already!"

"But, my dear," interposed her husband, "you yourself urged her to oblige Monsieur Guillemin by conveying that picture to Bristol for him!"

"I may have done so — but how could I know to what it would lead? Any more than Captain Carew himself, the most foolishly complaisant of us all, knew what he was doing when he permitted that monster to go drawing in the dockyard at Portsmouth!" There was vitriol in her tone.

"But I know it now, Madame, I assure you!" retorted Nugent bitterly. "And, if I may be excused, I will go to find my wife, and keep her away from you, without further delay." He bowed and went to the door, seething with anger, less at the attack on himself than at the revelation of the purely selfish motives which, in

Mme. d'Esparre's case at least, lay behind the anxiety that Charlotte should not cross this threshold again.

Fabien hurried out after him, plainly distressed. "Again I must ask you, Captain Carew, to forgive my wife. She is overwrought and ill. I beg you to overlook the expressions she used about the permission you gave, purely to oblige a friend of ours — as we thought him then. I hope you will be generous enough to make allowances for her, since I admit I was hoping to enlist your help, as being yourself in a position immune from suspicion. If you, who know us, were to testify on our behalf, *your* testimony would be listened to!"

"You think so?" returned Nugent with a short and mirthless laugh. "You were never more mistaken! I had not meant to tell you" — and indeed this was no mere figure of speech but the truth — "but this fellow-countryman of yours, or rather what your wife so correctly describes as my foolish complaisance towards him, has involved me myself so deeply in this affair that I have already lost the command which the Admiralty had promised me. Indeed I may even lose my commission altogether. I am therefore the last man on earth whose help you should solicit. But at all costs Charlotte shall be kept out of it."

And with no further leave-taking he ran down the stairs.

II

Round and round the Dorrington Square garden at a brisk pace went Mlle. Charlotte de Soray; with her went

Mrs. Tracy Stallingwood's King Charles spaniel, undergoing exercise on a leash. In addition there went, quite unnecessarily, Captain Ralph Wigram, nephew to the same lady, invalided home from Holland with some pieces of French shell in his arm. Every now and then, on the disingenuous plea that a wounded man merited a little more consideration, this warrior would beseech Chéri's guardian to moderate her pace — for a flirtation, however mild and one-sided, is best carried on at no more than a saunter. So Charlotte, smiling demurely, said at last, with a glance at his beslinged arm, that she would not have thought it possible for anyone having the use of their eyes to deny him consideration.

And having said this, she was obliged to call a halt for another reason. The spaniel, who was young and not yet overfed, had in the course of his restrained activities contrived to tangle his leash round the leg of a stone seat which they were passing. And while Charlotte freed him, Captain Wigram lamented both his inability to assist her, and her inhumanity in hinting that he made a parade of his condition.

"Indeed, Mademoiselle," he concluded, "you are the most heartless young lady, French or English, that I have ever met! Why cannot you model yourself upon my good aunt? She, as you know, sends for more cushions the moment I enter her drawing-room, and would indeed like to see me lying full length upon that purple sofa of hers!"

And upon that 'Mlle. de Soray' gravely indicated the stone seat. "I fear, sir, that this is the only possible substitute here for the sofa — since you insist upon leaving the comforts of the drawing-room."

"That too is unkind, when you know quite well, Mademoiselle, why I have abandoned them for this wind-swept race-course . . . for upon my soul I cannot call it anything else!"

"But yes, sir, naturally I know why you have done so. It is because of your English passion for dogs. You desire to be assured that Chéri is not ill-treated when out of his mistress's sight! I hope that you have satisfied yourself upon that point?"

"Not completely," replied the young officer. "And, since you say that is my object in accompanying you, I must certainly continue to do so — if you really intend to course round the garden once more. For there is not another soul here to supervise your conduct towards the animal — and no wonder, on so chilly an afternoon."

"You are wrong, Captain Wigram," said Charlotte as they set out again. "At least, I can hear that some person is opening the gate ahead of us by which we came in. No, Chéri, you cannot chase that sparrow!"

"That may be, but I shall not allow a newcomer to take my place as overseer. Especially," added Captain Wigram a moment later, "as it is a man, and from what I can see, a naval officer at that . . . I am sure, Mademoiselle, that the confounded dog is pulling too hard for you! Allow me to take the leash."

For something, he could see, was disturbing his companion; she had, quite suddenly, flushed violently, and as suddenly paled. The young man could not know that this change of colour had nothing whatever to do with the control of a tugging spaniel. The fact was that the mere sight of a naval uniform was enough to send a pang through Charlotte's heart; and she could see, as they progressed along the gravelled path between the central sward and the evergreens which concealed the outer railings of the garden, that the figure standing just inside the gate at a few yards distance was so habited. Enough of the uniform, at least, was visible for her to recognise the fact, though the newcomer's actual head and shoulders were hidden by a projecting laurel bough.

"No, no, sir," she replied, ignoring his outstretched hand, and continuing to walk forward automatically, "Chéri does not trouble me, I thank you."

In another moment the obscuring bush was rounded, the naval officer was fully in view; and Charlotte, uttering a name under her breath, stopped dead.

For it was Nugent himself who was walking towards her along the path. It could not be a dream, here in broad daylight in the Square garden! And she could tell by the light upon his face that he had seen her — the light which showed her that this was a very different Nugent from that grim and angry individual who had left her so starkly that day in the convent parlour. Oh, was the bad dream really over?

"You *know* this officer, Mademoiselle?" came Captain Wigram's astonished voice in her ear — though for all the attention she paid it might have been an untimely gnat buzzing there. As for Chéri, but for the involuntary tightening of her fingers upon his leash, he would have attained his desire of pursuing those tantalising sparrows.

'This officer' reached them. A glance at her escort, a 'Your servant, sir,' then he disregarded him entirely.

"Charlotte," he said, without preamble of any kind, looking at her in a way which rendered such a thing unnecessary, "I must speak with you privately, and at once. It is most urgent. Come with me."

He indicated, at the end of the central lawn, a small building between a miniature temple and a summer-house, and offered his arm.

"Sir, this intrusion —" began Charlotte's astounded escort.

"Pray, Captain Wigram, do not hinder this gentleman. He . . . I must ask you to excuse me," said Charlotte hurriedly. Her face, with a lovely colour on it, was quite transfigured, as he could not but notice. "If I might ask you a favour," she went on with an appealing glance, "would you have the kindness to take the dog back to the house with you when you return?" And without waiting for a reply she put into his available hand the end of Chéri's silver-mounted leash.

Thus, deprived of the lady but in possession of the spaniel (who showed a strong desire to follow her) was Captain Wigram left, staring after the two as, very close together, they made their way to the summer-house.

"Good Gad, a pirate!" he ejaculated aloud; adding, after a moment's further observation: "And not the first time he has carried her off, neither!"

285

III

It was cold and damp in the doorless pseudo-temple. A few dried laurel leaves scuttled at intervals about the floor, and in one corner leant a couple of brooms and a rake. A large and very ugly stone urn, motiveless and inconvenient, carved upon with wreaths caught up by rams' heads, occupied its centre. This object and its pedestal did however offer a measure of privacy, and Charlotte, still in a kind of dream, found herself being led behind it, to receive the command:

"Kiss your husband! You have no other!"

And not for one moment did she doubt the assertion. The nightmare was ended. There was to be no more of this sundered, half-dead existence. And she was pardoned — there was no doubt of that — for the suffering which she had felt obliged to cause him. For when, half stifled in his embrace, she murmured something about forgiveness, Nugent stopped her mouth by the most effective method.

They were still standing in this odd semi-concealment when he put into her hand the letter which, after such vicissitudes, had at last reunited them.

"You can read it later, when you are at leisure, my darling girl. It all amounts to this, that the whole affair was a heartless fraud perpetrated on your aunt for money. Monsieur de Marescot never survived that dagger. This separation of ours has been entirely needless. But don't dare to ask me again for forgiveness! It is I who should ask your pardon for letting my sense of injury carry me further than I intended that day at Bristol. I ought not —"

"No, no, you had good reason!" broke in Charlotte. "We were both so unhappy . . . But now we can forget all that, can we not? Oh Nugent, this day more than makes up for it all!" And with a sigh of utter contentment she laid her head against his breast.

"My dearest Charlotte!" he murmured, holding her close. The tone could not have been tenderer, but his eyes (which she fortunately could not see) were anxious. Over this reunion which ought to have been so uncloudedly happy — and which *was* so happy — loomed a new and ugly shadow, obscuring the future just as this hideous great urn in front of them blotted out the view of the cold but still sunlit garden.

It was imperative to get Charlotte out of Bath at once. And he must, he supposed, tell her why. Or could he postpone that disturbing information until they were on their way to — on their way whither? Where could he convey her with the least prospect of her being traced? Home to Damarel St. Mary? No, certainly not. What about taking her on the visit she had not yet paid to his sister Sophia and her husband at Ridborough? It was only sixteen miles away. But that plan required a little thinking over. The first step, in any case, was to detach her from this Mrs. Stallingwood's employment.

"Charlotte," he said, loosening his clasp of her a little, "it is time that we went now and explained matters to this good lady of yours. (It was from her butler, by the way, when I called at the house and asked for you, that I learnt you were in the garden here with that soldier nephew of hers.) I will pay my respects, and you shall take farewell of her with the least possible delay, for I must leave Bath this very afternoon. Can you make your preparations for departure so quickly?"

"Yes, yes — easily! How surprised Mrs. Stallingwood will be!" laughed she. "But you must not be so tyrannical in your haste, my dear husband, as to deny me the time to say goodbye to Fabien."

That speech made it plain that she must learn at once about the shadow. Best perhaps to get it over.

"I am afraid you cannot do that, my love. Let us sit down for a few moments, for there is something that I see I cannot postpone telling you."

"Something which will prevent me from going to see Fabien?" she exclaimed in a tone of alarm. "Oh, Nugent, not that he is ill — or that Honorine is?"

"No, not that, nor anything like it. Sit here." He swept some dead leaves off a wooden bench against the wall of the temple and drew her down beside him. And thus, with the nearest ram's head on the big vase sneering down at them, he disclosed to her the perfidy in which she had so innocently become entangled, and how it was of the first importance to get away before that entanglement had time to come to light.

"For you did, did you not, child, convey a picture from the spy Guillemin to this O'Connor and, worse, bring back a letter to Guillemin?"

"Yes," admitted poor Charlotte piteously. Most of the rapture had gone out of her face, and for the moment it looked quite dwindled and pinched. "But as for the picture, Nugent, 'twas nothing but a painting of a rustic cottage and as for the letter — Mrs. O'Connor when she brought it to me at the convent said it was no more than an acknowledgment and a draft in payment for the painting."

"*Mrs*. O'Connor?" Nugent bit his lip. "You say it was she who brought the letter to you? Was she then by chance the lady who arrived so unopportunely that day?"

Charlotte nodded.

"If only I had known!" muttered her husband. And he added, with patent self-reproach: "Perhaps if I had not gone off so hastily, she might have abandoned her project; and in that case you would never have carried the letter."

Charlotte caught at his hand. "No, no, it was my fault — your going like that! I sent you away! and as for obliging an acquaintance by carrying a letter, not knowing what was in it — why, anyone might do that! Do not look so troubled, dearest! I am sure that all will be well in the end, in spite of the O'Connors and their picture! No one can prove Fabien and Honorine guilty of plotting on behalf of our enemies against England — the very idea is absurd! And much less could I be suspected of it — I who am the wife of the captain of a ship of the line — is not that what it is called? For you were promised one, I know — and perhaps are already appointed to her?"

That he never would be appointed to such a ship now — that at least he need not tell her yet. But Nugent Carew had never in his life made a greater effort to appear cheerful when he was not, than now, when he said as casually as he could:

"No, not yet, my dear," and then, to cut short any further questions, rose from the wooden bench. "Now let us go to this lady's house, and leave it again as soon as possible. I vow I would carry you off straight from this summer-house with nothing but what you are wearing, save that your disappearance would naturally cause Mrs. Stallingwood to raise a most undesirable hue and cry after you." He held out his hand.

"And where will you take me? Back to dear Damarel St. Mary, I suppose?"

"Not at first, I think. To my sister Sophia's at Ridborough perhaps. It is not far away; and it is high time you made Sophia's acquaintance."

"But your sister and her husband will not wish to have a suspect under their roof!"

"My dear girl, the whole point is that you are not a suspect . . . as yet, and please God, never will be! My great object is to prevent you from becoming one."

CHAPTER
NINETEEN

I

She was a great reader of romances, the rich and widowed Mrs. Stallingwood — fortunately for the couple in the pseudo-temple. She even attempted to read them in the French tongue, (hence her desire for a French lady as companion) and for the last week or so, her hand firmly in that of 'Mlle. de Soray', had been wandering, or rather stumbling, through the lush tropical scenery of 'that sweetly touching story', *Paul et Virginie*. In consequence of this predilection for the romantic, the surprise which she had exhibited to Captain Wigram when he returned with Chéri, but without Chéri's guardian, and told her the reason for it, her astonishment when 'Mlle de Soray,' entering at last, escorted by the 'pirate' naval officer, presented him as her husband, shyly avowing that they had been separated by a 'misunderstanding,' now happily cleared up, turned in a very short space to a mood of enraptured benevolence. To think that she had sheltered the heroine of this idyll (for so she regarded it) for a month, and had known nothing of her real story.

"And you pretending, my dear, that you were single — and all the while married to such a distinguished-looking officer — a hero as well, I have no doubt! La, I never read a tale more moving! Captain Carew, you will honour me, will you not, by accepting my hospitality until to-morrow, at least?"

"I fear, Madam —" began Nugent.

"But you cannot be so brutal as to snatch away this naughty — this charming deceiver" (here she beamed upon Charlotte) "to-night!"

"With the deepest regret, madam, I fear that I must," replied Nugent. He was quite determined that Charlotte should not spend the night anywhere in Bath. And, a few further attempts on the part of the captivated lady being met with polite but undiminished firmness on his part, she gave way, sighing out:

"A second honeymoon! Yes, naturally you are all impatience for that! Pray ring the bell, Ralph, and my maid shall pack Mrs. Carew's trunk without delay." For it was naturally not given to Mrs. Stallingwood to know that, owing to her hasty flight from Damarel St. Mary, the newly-discovered heroine possessed neither any receptacle large enough to be dignified by that name, nor sufficient raiment to fill it if she had. "No doubt, Captain Carew, as you are not taking the mail-coach, you have already ordered a post-chaise — or perhaps have your own in waiting outside?"

"Neither, Madam, I am afraid," replied Nugent. "But if you will excuse me I shall go now and procure one. I saw some posting-stables not far from here."

"That would be Johnson's, I presume," commented Mrs. Stallingwood. "But I do not recommend them; no one hereabouts hires from them. And if you go yourself you will deprive me still further of your society for the short time which remains. Let me send on your behalf to the people I always employ when I do not use my own carriage; you will be sure then of the best attention. All that is required is a message by the footman to mention your destination."

But that was exactly what Nugent did not intend to impart to any person in Mrs. Stallingwood's house. Yet he could not bring forward this resolve as a reason for refusing a kind offer. He had to say, with what good grace he could muster, that, deeply sensible though he was of Mrs. Stallingwood's civility, he could easily see to the matter himself since he had, in any case, one or two hasty purchases to make. So having (as a diplomatic blind) ascertained the name of the stables which she recommended, he took temporary leave, regretting that he could not contrive to warn Charlotte not to mention Ridborough as their destination. (But on the other hand he had already begun to modify his plans about Ridborough.)

The door had hardly closed behind him when Mrs. Stallingwood turned to Charlotte.

"Come closer to the fire, my dear," she cooed, patting the seat of a pink and purple chair in her nearer vicinity. "And now, tell me, if you will, more of your history — your true history! Where did you meet your distinguished husband — in some very romantic circumstances, I am sure? And where is your real home, if it is not impertinent to enquire? About the misunderstanding, now so happily at an end, I will not be so indiscreet as to ask," she concluded archly.

With Captain Wigram also in close attendance, Charlotte told them something of her past history, which, from the view of romance, was satisfying even to Mrs. Stallingwood. But she did it almost mechanically. She was too happy to be upon her guard, nor did she in her inmost self believe that there was much necessity for it. Her whole being was so flooded with joy that the haste to leave Bath which possessed Nugent seemed to her of small moment, although she was its cause. And it was not until the attentive and still enraptured Mrs. Stallingwood asked whether she and Captain Carew were going far that night, that she felt a sudden prick of caution.

"I really do not know how far, Madam. I have left it to my husband."

"But as you are, I assume, returning to his home in Devonshire" (and the now more wary Charlotte mendaciously allowed this assumption to pass) "I fear you will have to post as far as Shepton Mallet — for I know of no inn fit to lie at in Radstock. And that will be — a matter of nearly twenty miles, will it not, Ralph?"

"You are right, my dear aunt," responded that young gentleman. "That is, if Mrs. Carew is indeed taking that road."

Charlotte looked up at him (for he was standing) and was suddenly uneasy. Could he possibly have been still in the Square garden within earshot of Nugent's concluding mention of Sophia and her home? But she dismissed the idea, for, after all, neither his look nor his tone seemed charged with any particular significance. Probably he only meant that it was not the more usual

294

route by Wells and Bridgewater, taken by the mail-coaches.

"Oh, as to that," she said smiling, "I am no longer my own mistress! I must go where I am bid." And here the King Charles, always partial to her, becoming so insistent in his pawing demands to be taken on her lap, she set him there and caressed him, with some hopes of turning the conversation from post-routes.

The move was attended with more success than she had anticipated or indeed desired. Mrs. Tracy Stallingwood gave a sudden delighted exclamation. "There now! For the last few minutes I had been casting about in my mind for some little memento which I might perhaps persuade you to accept, my dear, as a souvenir of your stay with me. Now the problem is solved! I beg of you, Mrs. Carew, to take the sweet dog home with you. He is devoted to you already, and you, I perceive, will greatly feel the parting from him. I shall feel it even more, but I know that he will be happy in your care — will you not, Chéri, my angel?"

"Oh no, madam!" protested Charlotte hastily, and with some vigour. She was touched, but taken aback, being by no means desirous of this travelling companion, and convinced that Nugent would be even less so. "I could not possibly deprive you of him; and he is naturally much more devoted to *you!* Now, Chéri, go to your mistress!" And she set him down upon the floor.

But the spaniel, raising his snub nose, and gazing up at her with deep reproach in his prominent eyes, immediately showed his intention of returning to her lap.

"Ah, now, Mrs. Carew," observed Captain Wigram, stooping over her, "I see indeed that there was never any call for me to supervise your treatment of the animal. It must have been greatly to his liking. My aunt is right; he must certainly become your own property. Lucky dog!"

"But indeed, indeed —" Charlotte was beginning, trying to fend off the redepositing of the favoured animal on her knee, when the door opened to admit her husband.

And after that matters moved swiftly. Farewell of Mrs. Stallingwood was of course taken in the purple, pink and gold drawing-room, but Captain Wigram inevitably attended the pair to the chaise. And it was he who, despite his one-armed condition, relieved the footman of Chéri, whose basket had already been placed within, depositing the dog on Charlotte's lap at a moment, when, by a perhaps fortunate coincidence, Captain Carew was giving some final instructions to the postillion.

"Is it too much to hope, Mrs. Carew?" he asked in a low voice, "that Chéri will sometimes remind you of this morning's promenade together, so strangely — and for *you* so happily — cut short?"

Charlotte was flustered. "But did your aunt really mean — oh dear! I am afraid — I would rather not . . ." But her half-hearted and bewildered attempt to return the unwanted livestock was frustrated — if it could ever have succeeded — by the young officer's withdrawal

296

from the door to make way for her husband, who, after shaking hands with him, mounted briskly in and shut the door. Next moment the dimly-lit chaise was in motion, and Nugent Carew turned to his recovered wife with a deep sigh of satisfaction.

"Thank God! At last we are off. Very kind of Mrs. Stallingwood to press us to stay the night, but it would not have done at all — cold evening though it is. I hope you are well wrapped up, my dear?" Feeling in the semi-darkness whether the rug over her knees was properly tucked round her, he stopped in astonishment.

"Good God! what have you got there? Not, surely, a *dog*."

Chéri himself replied in the affirmative with a short, sharp bark. He had already settled himself on the seat between them and did not wish to be disturbed.

"But, my dear Charlotte," said Nugent, peering down, "what on earth possessed you to encumber yourself with this animal?"

"You once said," responded she with a ripple of mirth, "— it was when Tom came home for the Christmas holidays — that if I wanted a spaniel you —"

"But do you mean to say that, at this juncture of all others, you have bought —"

He stopped, as Charlotte slid both hands round his arm and laid her head against his shoulder. "*Je ne fais que plaisanter, mon très cher!* Indeed I am not to blame. I did not want him in the least and tried hard to refuse him, But Mrs. Stallingwood insisted. Chéri is a present from her, a memento."

"But, my dear girl, a present can be refused! Travelling as we are, wishing above all to attract no attention —"

("And that is so delicious!" murmured Charlotte to herself.)

"— What did you say? — Charlotte, you do not seem to realise our situation!"

"But yes, I do! And this need for secrecy about our destination — which I find truly enchanting — that is just why I could not refuse the gift. For Mrs. Stallingwood thought that we were going home to Devonshire, where the little dog would naturally be no trouble, nor indeed cause much on the way thither. And so I had no good reason to give for refusing Chéri, unless I should have told her that as we were fugitives from justice it was not convenient to have him with us."

"You allowed her, then, to think that we *were* going to Devonshire! Good girl!"

"When you praise me, my husband, for what was so nearly a lie, then indeed I feel that I begin to be a suspected person!"

"But that you are not — and, please God, never will be!"

"And the poor Chéri — to everyone else in that house, you know, except Mrs. Stallingwood, he was 'Cherry' — will not make me so? See, Nugent, he was not comfortable on the seat, and now he wishes to go to sleep on my lap!"

"It is you I want to look at, not your lapdog," retorted her husband, slipping his arm round her. "But it is so confoundly dark in here!"

"No doubt it will be lighter chez Madame Sophie. And then you can look at me as much as you like."

"I must tell you that we are not going to my sister's after all — at least not to-night."

"But where, then? Is this all a part of your plan for saving me from the law?"

"I suppose it is. Listen, my dear. I did not wish the livery stable to know that I proposed to go to Ridborough Hall, lest (though I admit the possibility is remote) we might be tracked there through their knowledge of the fact. Nor, on reflection, did I think it wholly wise for us to present ourselves unannounced at my brother-in-law's. He may have other guests. So I have told the postillion that, though we are actually upon our way to Chippenham (where, I may say, I have not the slightest intention of arriving) we shall go no further to-night than Bradworthy where there is a good inn, so I have heard. There I shall dismiss him. Now Bradworthy, though it is upon the high-road to Chippenham, happens to be only about six or seven miles across country from Ridborough. To-morrow morning I shall get hold of a horse and ride over to see Sophia. After that I shall know better how the land lies, as we say, and make my dispositions for you accordingly."

"Nugent, how clever! But, mon Dieu, what trouble I continue to cause you! First all that false rumour about poor Monsieur de Marescot — but that was not my fault — and now this business of the Irish couple in Bristol! Alas, I am to you nothing but a nuisance — if that is the correct English word?"

"It is an English word — but not the correct one, for it does not apply to you in any way. My dearest, my own Charlotte, nothing else is of any account, so that I have you back!" He caught her to him almost roughly. "Take off your bonnet, so that I can kiss you properly — Oh, confound that dog!"

II

It lasted, that second honeymoon, with all its heightened happiness and oblivion of the world outside, until next morning. For fugitive though Charlotte might be (at least in Nugent's eyes) the circumstances had a distinct flavour of a *voyage de noces*. The Blue Dragon Inn at Bradworthy was unexpectedly large and comfortable, providing at short notice an excellent dinner before a blazing fire, in a sitting-room as private as anyone could have wished. Even the undesired presence of the King Charles added to the general impression of ease and normality. To Charlotte the interior of the Blue Dragon was that evening a good substitute for Paradise, a region where there was no place for qualms about a possible angel with a flaming sword; while for Nugent who, even in this enchantment, could not altogether stifle an apprehension of the hand of the law stretching out to clutch at this recovered bride of his, that very apprehension seemed to make her dearer, more to be protected at any cost. It was not in fact until he was falling asleep beside her, with the spaniel snoring lightly at the foot of the bed, that the remembrance of his own plight recurred to him. Yet it did not keep him from slumber.

But the cold morning light, in which he woke early, cast a more realistic hue over the situation. The first problem was his sister Sophia and her probable reaction to the proposal to leave Charlotte in her care. Should he tell her the truth, or merely say that, being in the neighbourhood, he had thought it a good opportunity for his wife to pay her a visit, and, at last, to make her acquaintance? In either case (always supposing that Sophia could and would give her sister-in-law hospitality) Charlotte should be tolerably safe, tucked away at Ridborough Hall. (How hard, nevertheless, it would be to leave her there!)

But for himself . . . no amount of planning could solve *his* problem. His career was irretrievably damaged, if not ruined. If only he had some person of influence to speak for him! Yet not the highest in the land could now undo his own criminal folly, which in Their Lordships' eyes — and he could hardly blame them — had blotted out in an hour his past good record of service, and swept him from the quarter-deck of the *Defiance* before he had ever set foot there. Nevertheless he intended to go straight back to London from Ridborough, and haunt Whitehall in the not very robust hope that time — and the circumstances of war — might induce the Board to take a more lenient view of his case.

Though reluctant to wake Charlotte, still sleeping like a child, he rang at last for hot water, made enquiries about hiring a horse, and ordered breakfast for himself in half an hour. It would in any case be wiser for Charlotte to take hers later on in seclusion upstairs. Awake soon after this, and still sleepy, Charlotte acquiesced, and lay watching her husband shave.

"Were you not saying something about a horse just now?" she presently asked. "Must you go to Ridborough Hall so early?"

"I fear so. I must learn as soon as possible whether I can leave you in Sophia's care or no."

He heard her sigh. "I wish . . . I wish your sister would say No! I wish Mr. Devenish's house was full of visitors! Then I need not be separated from you — unless my company is too dangerous!" And suddenly she sat up in bed, her eyes shining, tendrils of amber escaping from the edge of her lace nightcap. "Nugent! I have an excellent idea! You will very soon be taking command, will you not, of the ship of the line which was promised you? You admitted last night that you had come straight from London, not from Plymouth, and London means, I am sure, the Board of Admiralty?"

Her husband did not answer, and as she could see from the bed that he was just scraping the corner of his chin, she waited for no reply, but went on, hugging her knees like a child:

"When you go to take command of her I shall accompany you as a midshipman — like Mr. Vernon! I am tall enough."

There was a moment's pause. "A disguise, my dear Charlotte," said Nugent, trying with a very heavy heart to meet her mood, "a disguise will hardly serve to allay the suspicions which I have hopes of your otherwise escaping."

"I should take care not to be found out! . . . But I suppose you are right. Yet it would have been a delightful plan, and would have enchanted Mrs. Stallingwood if she ever came to hear of it. But tell me, dear husband, if I am accepted at Ridborough Hall how long must I stay there?"

"That is a question I can scarcely answer offhand. It will naturally depend upon circumstances."

"*En bien*, if you cannot yet tell me when it will be safe for me to join you — as myself, *bien entendu*, not as a copy of Mr. Vernon — you can at least tell me at what port I must do so. For there will be much to do there, will there not, before your ship has her full crew and can put to sea?" For by this time Mrs. Nugent Carew knew something of these matters.

"Yes, yes," said Nugent hastily. "Much to do — and therefore plenty of time for you to join me."

"That is good," remarked Charlotte contentedly. "But where *shall* I join you when my period of . . . of quarantine is over?"

The razor slipped a trifle. "At the moment," replied Nugent as carelessly as he could, "I cannot be quite sure. Nothing is settled as yet."

"Not settled? *Mais, mon ami*, what do you mean by that? What is it that is not settled — which ship you are to command, or where that ship will be in harbour?"

Purposely indistinct, Nugent murmured something about 'still at sea,' and 'the exigencies and uncertainties of war'.

"Oh, how tiresome for you, my dear!" A measure of relief was however audible in his wife's voice. "But if this ship intended for you should be unduly delayed, or sent elsewhere, the Admiralty will naturally give you another in its place?"

"The number of sixty-fours is not unlimited. Lie down, Charlotte, or you will take cold."

Charlotte did not obey. "But" she protested, wrinkling her forehead under the cap, "a sixty-four had been definitely promised to you in the spring. You told me so in that letter I had from you before I . . . before I left the Rectory!"

"Promises are notoriously like pie-crust," came from the neighbourhood of the mirror.

"Pie-crust? I do not understand."

"Made to be broken." And though he tried to say it lightly, Nugent's voice betrayed him.

There was a dead silence, in which, since he dared not turn round and look at her, he busied himself in dabbing at the tiny cut which he had inflicted on himself. Then at last Charlotte spoke, in tones of intense indignation.

"You mean that the Admiralty have broken theirs! Oh, abominable! After keeping you, with all that you have done in war, these five months half-idle, and then not to carry out what they had undertaken! Is that what you call the 'fair play' which you once told me was so dear to your nation! For the rest of my life I shall never again trust the word of an English official!"

304

He had not guessed that she could be so vehement; he had forgotten that in her veins there ran, after all, the warm blood of the South. He had to turn round.

"You must not say that, Charlotte! It is not warranted by the circumstances. One has to learn, in the Navy, to . . . be patient and wait."

"But no, not in war-time!" she retorted. "Here every sailor is needed, for fighting, for convoys, for guarding the shores. Is not England an island? You cannot deny that!" And as Nugent made no reply, but turned back to the dressing-table and began to wipe his razor, she added after a moment: "Is it then out of patriotism that you have *agreed* to wait . . . once more?"

"Sailors and soldiers, my dear girl," he answered, "do not *agree* — they obey."

Charlotte sighed deeply, and leant her head on her hand. "*Hélas*, I suppose that is true! Have the Admiralty then appointed you again to a mere frigate? I hope at least that it is a finer vessel even than the *Callisto* — for you told me once that there *were* finer?"

Another silence. Sick at heart, Nugent mechanically examined his chin in the glass. There was no escape from it: he would have to let her know the truth. But before he had even started to pick his words there came a sudden flurry and a patter; and there was Charlotte beside him in her night-gown, gripping his arm with both hands.

"Nugent! *Pour l'amour de Dieu!* Something has gone amiss! Tell me, tell me at once what it is! Surely, since the Admiralty do not know of my action, it cannot be because of that letter which I brought —"

"No, no, my dearest girl," said he with emphasis. "No, it has nothing to do with you! I told you that you were not yet suspected of anything. It was my own incredible foolishness at Portsmouth which has undone me."

She dropped her hands. "Foolishness? What foolishness?"

"Do you not remember that it was I who gave permission to the spy Guillemin to make a sketch of the *Callisto*? But for God's sake go back to bed — you will catch your death of cold!"

"Permission to sketch the *Callisto*," echoed Charlotte, visibly paling. "But surely . . . that was such a small matter . . . how could it . . ."

"Guillemin used the permit I gave him in order to visit other dockyards also, Plymouth among them. I am responsible — at least in part — for his activities. The Board could not overlook that."

She was staring at him in horror. "Then . . . do you mean that they would not appoint you even to a frigate . . . that you have as yet no ship at all? Oh Nugent, my dearest, it is not that, surely?"

"That, unfortunately, is the situation," he answered in an expressionless voice, though the words it was plain, came from a dry throat. "A lesson not to be too ambitious." He looked down at her, forcing a kind of wintry smile. "If you will not go back to bed of your own will I shall carry you there!"

And as she did not move, but continued to gaze at him dumbly, he put his threat into execution. But, since she would not lie down, his attempt to heap the bedclothes over her was not very successful, and this second upheaval of his couch disturbed Chéri, who gave an angry bark and jumped to the floor.

Then, sitting bolt upright, Charlotte delivered her ultimatum.

"You will not need that horse, Nugent. I shall not consent to be left behind at Ridborough Hall, I am coming with you. Because it is I who am responsible for this blow, for it was I who asked you for that permit!"

"Child, child, do not be absurd!" said her husband, moved and startled. "To blame yourself is nonsense, for if you had not been Guillemin's innocent spokesman, your brother would have been, or the man would have asked me himself. You *must* be guided by me, and stay awhile with Sophia!"

She shook her head vehemently. "While you are —"She broke off. "What *are* you proposing to do next?"

He sat down on the bed, just as the doubly disgusted Chéri had decided to return there. "To go back to London. After a little Their Lordships may conceivably relent."

"Then I shall come back with you. No, not as a mid-shipman, nor even as a cabin-boy. As a maid-servant if you prefer — but in your company by some means or other!"

"You can't, my dear, you can't!" he said, seizing her hands. "I implore you for your own sake to fall in with my plan, and go to Sophia!"

"No," she replied with astonishing determination and composure — she was, he saw, not in the least hysterical — "I will not. I refuse! And if you take me there by force I shall run away again — like Arabella!"

And he could only gaze at her rather helplessly, while she went on: "If indeed you were on the point of going to a new ship I would agree. I would stay quite meekly for a while with your sister, because I should know that you were happy and busy. But it is too much to ask of me to remain hidden away there while you drag out your days on a doorstep in Whitehall, and I cannot share those days! It is true that you have lately come, perhaps, to think of yourself as having no wife —"

"No, that I never did!" he interposed with emphasis.

"All the more, then, can you realise that you have one, and that she has the right to share your bad fortune as well as your good. I am coming to London with you, Nugent, and you cannot prevent me!"

CHAPTER
TWENTY

Although still youthful and elegant, Chéri the King Charles spaniel loved his comfort, and was used to spacious rooms, a special cushion, adulation, and food more succulent and plentiful than was good for him. For the last two days, however, these amenities had been singularly lacking; indeed the only link remaining with the old princely existence had been the person whose lap he was wont to frequent. And now, after yesterday's long and tiring journey, even that person had deserted him, and he found himself this morning quite alone in a strange bedroom which did not appeal to him.

It was, though naturally Chéri was unaware of this, a bedroom in Batt's Hotel in Dover Street, whence his new owner and her husband, though they had only arrived there the previous night, had already set out to look for more modest quarters, on the score both of expense and of privacy. Not only was Captain Nugent Carew expecting daily to learn that he had been put on half-pay, but he was feeling with some bitterness that lodgings in an obscurer spot were more fitting for a disgraced naval officer than a hotel in the centre of London. There was also the question of the strict seclusion he considered desirable for Charlotte's safety. And, happening to bethink him of a certain petty officer in a ship in which he himself had served several years ago, who had announced the intention, after his discharge, of setting up with his wife, a Londoner, lodgings suitable for gentle-people in that city, and also by a lucky freak of memory contriving to recall the name of the street in Soho which had been indicated, he was now setting out with Charlotte to find the dwelling of Mr. and Mrs. Goodbody, in the hope that they might be accommodated there for the present.

It was Charlotte's first sight of London, and Nugent at least was unhappily aware of the inauspicious circumstances under which the introduction was taking place. He had hoped to show it to her one day in very different ones. She, however, undamped by this thought, if indeed it had occurred to her, or by the fact that it was a dull and rather cold March day, was brimful of interest and excitement as they made their way along Piccadilly.

"To think that this is London! *Sais-tu*, Nugent, I have never seen a large city before!"

"Had you never been to Paris?"

"No, never. It is a long way from Arles, you know. It is true that I had been to Marseilles once or twice. What is that wide street and what is the building at the end? I should like to look at it closer. May I?"

"It is St. James's Palace. It is out of our way, but if you wish to look at the exterior, my dear, you shall."

He did not altogether relish walking down St. James's Street, either on her account or his own, but he met no one whom he knew, and any eyes which rested on the attractive auburn-haired young lady on his arm were certainly not accusing her of treasonable activities.

After they had looked at the old red brick building, and Nugent had told her something of its history, they proceeded eastwards along King Street and debouched into the dignity and space of St. James's Square. As they traversed its upper end Charlotte looked about her with admiration.

"What fine houses! And, look, Nugent, at that lady over there with the little spaniel! It might almost be Chéri, it is so like him!"

For up the steps of a house at the opposite corner was going a lady leading a King Charles spaniel the very counterpart of her own.

Her husband followed her gaze. Then his expression changed. "If your dog has run away, I hope he knows better than to go to that particular house," he said briefly. "It belongs to Admiral Sir Russell Cathcart, the First Sea Lord."

And, evidently anxious to leave it on his lee as soon as possible, he strode on in the direction of Duke Street.

"*Oh!*" breathed Charlotte, and, half fascinated, half repelled, lingered a moment looking at the dignified façade, and watching the lady, of whom she could see only the back, being admitted. It was rather like having pointed out to one the abode of an ogre — though it was consoling to know that, besides the ogre, someone dwelt there who was human enough to possess a pet dog.

She hastened to overtake her husband. "I wonder who the lady was — the Admiral's wife, or his daughter? Is he married?"

"I believe his wife died many years ago. I have no notion whether he has a daughter or no," was Nugent's somewhat curt reply; and the two went on up Duke Street.

The little street in Soho, that once fashionable neighbourhood, parts of which were fashionable still, was quiet and respectable. Enquiries after a couple named Goodbody soon resulted in the discovery of two persons of that name. But these, to Nugents surprise, turned out to be not husband and wife, but two elderly men, solemn, ruddy faced and puzzlingly alike.

"You see sir," said the ex-petty officer, who had recognised him at once, "my wife died last year, and so my twin brother Henry come here to live with me and help me. And he having been in service in good houses, we has everything as well looked after as in poor Matilda's day, and we haven't lost in custom by the change. But at the moment, I'm happy to say, the rooms happens to be vacant. Might I have the pleasure of showing them to you and your lady, sir — they're on the next floor?"

This explanation had been given to the accompaniment of some nautical adjurations from a large grey parrot which Charlotte had been delighted to observe in a corner of the Goodbody's own parlour; after which they followed the spokesman to a decent and cheerful set of rooms above, which they looked over. Charlotte asked their prospective landlord who did the cooking, to which he responded: "My brother Henry, ma'am."

"You have no woman to help you?"

"We don't find it necessary, ma'am."

Charlotte's face lit up. "Then I can cook for my husband sometimes!"

Mr. Goodbody was deeply shocked. "Oh, no, ma'am," he protested, "that wouldn't be at all fitting for you, a Captain's lady! We do everything that's necessary in the house, me and Henry, I assure you, ma'am, besides him cooking and me laying the table and serving meals."

"If my wife agrees," said Nugent, looking at her, "we will take the rooms," and Charlotte signifying assent, it was settled and Mr. Goodbody, much gratified, departed downstairs again.

"Not very grand quarters, but clean and tolerably cheerful," observed Nugent surveying them.

"I like them very much," pronounced Charlotte gaily. "And, however excellent may be the cooking of Monsieur Henry Goodbody — is not that rather a droll name? — I shall insist on cooking for you sometimes, *mon mari*, in this new home of ours! It is my right! There is a small empty room no larger than a cupboard next to your little dressing-room. In there, if you will buy me a chafing-dish, I shall prepare you some delicacies."

"I am still doubtful of the wisdom of having allowed you to accompany me to London," observed her husband, not very relevantly.

"Because you will be obliged to eat the dishes I shall cook for you?" queried Charlotte, laughing. "You will find no cause for regret on that score, I promise you!"

And Nugent smiled too. He had been, he still was, secretly enchanted by the stubbornness which she had displayed two mornings ago at the Blue Dragon, when, though he had felt that it was weakness in him, he had given up the attempt to bend this new Charlotte to his will, and had 'allowed' her to accompany him.

"Then I suppose I must promise to eat anything which you choose to set before me! Well, now we must return to the hotel and prepare for the transfer of our baggage."

II

When he went to the Admiralty next day, Nugent had no intention of seeking an interview with any official. He judged that such a step would be premature, so he merely handed in a card bearing his present address, with a brief: "Kindly see that the Secretary is notified of this." He was just turning away when the messenger who had received the card glanced at it and exclaimed:

"I think, sir, that the Assistant Secretary would like to see you. He gave orders that if you called he was to be informed of it."

Nugent's heart gave an almost sickening leap. Surely this summons must mean a turn in the ill tide of his affairs? And this interpretation seemed to be borne out by the fact that, for the first time in his experience of visits to the Admiralty, he was not called upon to wait, but was conducted straight to Mr. Lampard's presence.

The Assistant Secretary's handsome, greying head was bent over some writing, but directly his visitor was announced he laid down the pen and rose. Such slight intercourse as Nugent had had with him had always, within official limitations, been of a very friendly nature.

"Good morning, Captain Carew. Your call is most opportune. I was anxious to see you about a certain matter, but did not know whether you were still in London."

"Do you mean, sir, that Their Lordships . . . is it too much to hope that they have reconsidered —" began Nugent.

Mr. Lampard slightly shook his head. "The matter in question has not as yet come to their ears. I trust indeed that it need never do so. In which case," he added with the glimmer of a smile, "it need never be known, either, that I have, perhaps, exceeded my duty in keeping them in ignorance of it until I could have a word with you in person. Pray sit down, Captain Carew, and I will lay the facts before you. I am sure that you will be able to explain them satisfactorily."

Bewildered and disappointed, Nugent obeyed. Leaning forward on his writing table, his two hands clasped together, Mr. Lampard began to enlighten him.

"Yesterday afternoon a gentleman from your part of the country, a Mr. Wilkins, insisted upon seeing me, having, so it appeared, failed to gain access to Mr. Nepean. He sent up written word that he had some

315

very important information to give relative to plans for a hostile invasion of these shores. Although I thought he would have done better in that case to call at the office of the Secretary of State for Home Affairs, I consented to see him, on which his choice of the Admiralty for his revelations became apparent. He had come, it seems, to warn My Lords of what he termed the treasonable actions of you and your family, and especially of yours!"

"*What!*" exclaimed Nugent starting forward in his chair. "Wilkins, that newcomer, that insufferable prig, dare to accuse —"

"Wait, wait, Captain Carew, and don't jump to conclusions!" exclaimed the Assistant Secretary. "Wait until you hear how I found this earnest gentleman ridiculous, and the written information he brought with him so preposterous, that I have followed my own judgment, and have so far kept the whole matter to myself. His assumptions being so absurd, it was indeed not fair to do otherwise until an opportunity had been given you of hearing his charges. Not, of course, that I wish to arrogate to myself any judicial functions."

"Treasonable actions!" repeated Nugent hotly. "The man is insane! What, in God's name, can he have twisted into treason? What does he accuse me of?"

"First, on the testimony of his game-keeper, of having been found late at night reading a foreign letter in a copse on his estate. Secondly (and this nonsense, which seems to me even wilder, is embodied in a copy of a sworn deposition made before a magistrate in Exeter) of being somehow concerned as well in the purloining of this letter (or at any rate of *a* letter) through the agency of your younger brother, from the informant, a dealer in Exeter, to whom your father had sold a china ornament in which it was — God knows why — concealed. Added to which, when this dealer went to remonstrate with your father, the reverend gentleman tried to bribe him — or so the dealer says — to keep silence over the transaction because of the secret letter. I must admit that I never heard a more ridiculous tale. Mr. Wilkins had, I thought, a very large bee in his bonnet. So, matters standing as they do between My Lords and you, I was not anxious to lay this silly charge before them unless it were absolutely necessary; and I have also refrained from taking up the time of the Secretary over it. He has enough to do as it is."

Mr. Lampard's tone conveyed the impression that he almost considered these 'charges' of Mr. Wilkins's to partake of the nature of a joke. They were very far from appearing so to Nugent Carew, who sat frowning and inwardly cursing Mr. Wilkins for a damned meddling busybody. So angry and indignant was he that he had scarcely room to feel gratitude for the Assistant Secretary's even more than friendly attitude.

"This Mr. Wilkins," went on Mr. Lampard "— I suppose you are acquainted with him — seemed to me a most curious specimen of a country squire. He told me that he had posted all the way from Devonshire at his own expense purely because he was 'possessed with a consuming patriotism'. I am afraid that I put down both him and his game-keeper as endowed with a consumingly lively imagination. The sworn deposition of this Exeter china dealer is, however, a little more difficult to get over."

There was a pause. Nugent removed his gaze at last from the dolphins wreathed about the Assistant Secretary's ornate ink-pot.

"Yes," he agreed in a curiously flat voice, "it *is* difficult, because (save for the statement about my father's attempt at bribery, which must be completely false) the deposition is true. So is the game-keeper's statement."

"Good God!" exclaimed Mr. Lampard, falling back in his chair, and staring almost with open mouth at his visitor. "You cannot really mean, Captain Carew, that the letter in question was really concealed in an ornament sold to a dealer, and then that a brother of yours — No, no, the tale is too fantastic!"

"I know that it seems so. But I cannot deny it."

"And you *were* the naval officer reading this communication in a wood after dark? I remember, I believe, that the game-keeper had said he was not sure of your identity, and this Mr. Wilkins in consequence made a great deal of play with the possibility that the individual whom the man encountered might have been wearing a naval uniform to which he had no right, and was even perhaps a French emissary in disguise!"

Nugent gave a mirthless laugh. "Wilkins need not have given so much rein to his crazy suspicions. It was I myself in the copse, and no emissary from France or anywhere else! (But, by the way, the time was nowhere near midnight.) Being overcome with impatience to

318

read this letter — a purely private one, I assure you — I had mistakenly yielded to the temptation to do so at the first opportunity."

"The first opportunity! Does that mean that you had only just recovered it? But I thought that your young brother . . . This is all uncommonly perplexing! And is it true also that the letter was from abroad?"

"Yes, that is true also."

"But it is beyond my comprehension how this china ornament comes into the story!"

"I do not wonder at that, sir," said Nugent frowning. "But if you have patience to listen to the tale of a child's misdeed I will make it clear to you." And in those august precincts he thereupon unfolded the narrative of Arabella Mounsey's exploit. Potentially grave though its results were, Mr. Lampard could not wholly suppress a smile.

"You have been very frank, Captain Carew," he said at the end. "I think my superiors might well be annoyed if I troubled them with this tale of a naughty little girl's prank, and the consequent storm in a tea-cup — or, should I say, in a china dragon?" And as Nugent's expression showed the relief he felt, Mr. Lampard went on more gravely: "At the same time I must warn you that the fanatical Mr. Wilkins, if he considers that his disclosures are not receiving the attention they merit, is quite capable (or so I think) of bombarding My Lords directly, or approaching the Secretary for Home Affairs. If the former should happen I might find myself regarded not too favourably by Their Lordships, and even by Lord Spencer himself, for not having laid the matter before them when it was first brought to my notice. I should of course give them your explanation of the episode, which has completely satisfied me . . . in all save one respect, the actual tenor of the letter itself. Mr. Nepean — in the event of Mr. Wilkins moving again — would probably — nay certainly — wish to know that.

"The letter, sir, was on a purely private matter. I give my solemn word of honour as to that."

Mr. Lampard looked down, and fidgetted a little with his pen. "But you must surely realise that such a description of the nature of its contents might well sound like an evasion? I don't say that it does to me," he added quickly.

"It is God's truth nevertheless, Mr. Lampard."

"But do you not recognise, Captain Carew, that it might be urged that 'of a purely private character' is exactly the statement which would be made, in a parallel case, about any document whose real nature it was desired to conceal!"

"I cannot help that, sir," replied Nugent stubbornly. "The letter had no bearing upon anything under the sun save my own most private affairs. It was sent on to me from Leghorn by a kinsman of my father's, a well-known merchant there, Mr. Edward Mounsey, the father of the little girl who has caused all this bother, and a man above suspicion, as any enquiry would establish."

Mr. Lampard was looking at him more gravely than he had hitherto done. "You will not then consider

320

producing this letter — or avowing its contents — should you actually be called upon to do so?"

"I am afraid not."

"You realise how much your refusal might prejudice you?" What an unnecessary question! Of course he realised it, realised it even passionately. But, sufficiently obstinate already by nature, Nugent Carew was also in the grip of a deep and instinctive revulsion against the idea of being forced to reveal to any outsider that the legality of his marriage had ever been in doubt. Moreover the revelation would bring in Charlotte, whose existence he desired to go as unremarked as possible.

"I must hope that Mr. Wilkin's zeal has been satisfied, sir," was the reply he found. "Do you know if he has remained in London?"

"No, I am in ignorance of his whereabouts — But once more," said the Assistant Secretary "if he renews his charges I counsel you to be prepared to sacrifice your private feelings, and to produce this mysterious letter, however intimate its character. I hope, of course, that the necessity to so do may never arise."

Nugent got to his feet. "I must not take up any more of your time sir. You have shown me extraordinary kindness, indeed I cannot adequately thank you for it. Yes, if that pestilential fellow renews his charges in another quarter, I will undertake to reconsider my attitude about the letter; that might be forced upon me after all. In any case I am most deeply sensible of my obligation towards you. I only hope that you yourself will not be blamed for the course you have taken in withholding the results of Mr. Wilkins' 'patriotism'."

"Only if he is as persistent as he is wrong-headed," responded the Assistant Secretary, as he too rose. Then, holding out his hand, he said with a little smile: "Can it be that there is something in the air of Devon conducive to that state?"

Nugent looked at him for a second or two before he understood.

"You mean, sir, that I am wrong-headed too? Perhaps I am. Your forbearance the more deserves my gratitude. I assure you that you have it in full measure!" He hesitated a moment, and then added: "Is it permitted, before I take leave, to ask whether anything further has come to light about the activities of that scoundrelly French agent?"

He had the weakness (as he knew it to be) to refer thus anonymously to Guillemin, because the thought of bringing out his name in these precincts was too painful.

Mr. Lampard's expression darkened; in fact it became sombre. "If you mean, has it yet been ascertained whether or no he succeeded in sending the plan of the improved Medway defences out of the country before his arrest, we still do not —"

"The Medway defences!" broke in Nugent, appalled — yet hardly believing that he was hearing aright. "Good God, what is this?"

Unqualified surprise appeared on the Assistant Secretary's visage. "Why, were you not aware what had happened? Did not Their Lordships — but I am forgetting. That was five days ago, and they did not then themselves know of the disaster."

For one moment Nugent felt a cold so mortal invading his very vitals that he gave an audible gasp, and one hand went out instinctively towards the back of the chair from which he had risen. That action and his sudden pallor caused Mr. Lampard to say with concern:

"I see that this news is a shock to you. Will you not sit down again for a moment?"

And Nugent Carew had no course but to comply, and sat there silent, a hand over his eyes. "I did not know that new defences . . ." he said at last, but got no further.

"They have been in contemplation for some months, and had just been drawn out in their final form. If by some miracle — for I begin to think it will need one — it can be proved in the course of the next few days that a copy of them has not been transmitted to the Convention, it may still be possible to proceed to carry them out."

"But if they *have* been sent abroad, then Chatham is in continued danger until different dispositions can be taken! This is worse than anything I had imagined!"

"I cannot pretend but that it is a grave situation. The existing defences, as you must know yourself, need supplementing. Yet the new scheme cannot possibly be put into operation while there is any doubt about its having been communicated to the enemy."

"This is the end of me," said Nugent Carew, more than half to himself. "I might as well resign my commission at once." He rose, and standing rather stiffly, looked directly at the Assistant Secretary. "I should not like to leave you under the impression, Mr. Lampard, that the only thing which weighs with me in this is my own situation. My unpardonable short-sightedness has ruined me, but on my soul, what horrifies me most is the injury I have done to my country. I was told no details at all by Admiral Cathcart, only that the man Guillemin had been arrested for spying."

"Just so. Neither the First Sea Lord nor anyone else knew then about his having made a copy of the Medway defence plans."

"Am I to understand that he somehow obtained access to them here in Whitehall? That seems incredible."

"No, that was not the case. The plan was temporarily abstracted at Chatham, where for the time being it was lodged in the Admiral's possession. Even then it was not stolen in the sense of being carried off for good. It vanished for one night — as afterwards appeared — long enough for it to be copied. For it was only the small scale general plan, the master plan, which was taken — and restored."

"Then," said Nugent with a glimmer of hope on his own account, "there must have been an English confederate of some kind also. And how, Mr. Lampard," he went on, the hope spreading a little, "was this abstracting and copying of the plan traced to Guillemin, especially if it was, apparently, only discovered after his arrest?"

"That is rather too lengthy a story to go into now, Captain Carew. But it comes to this, that through a series of mischances the fact that the plan had been missing for most of one night did not come out till afterwards. (I must explain that it was on the ground of less serious activities that Guillemin was originally arrested.) And that Guillemin, who had been seen sketching in Chatham, though never actually in the dockyard, was at the bottom of the theft is indisputable. If he had not contrived to elude arrest it would have been carried out there, and not at Bath. The question is whether he managed in the time to despatch the copy to France, and by what means. As nothing in the nature of a plan was discovered in his room at Bath it seems probable, unfortunately, that he succeeded."

"I wonder," observed Nugent out of a dry mouth, "that *I* was not arrested the other day in the Board Room itself! I should have thought that the First Sea Lord — But I am forgetting, he was at that time ignorant, you say, of this disastrous development. Tell me the truth frankly, Mr. Lampard: should I not prepare myself for the hour when a warrant for complicity is issued against me?"

"No, my dear fellow, no," answered Mr. Lampard warmly. "There is no thought of such a thing, I assure you!"

"Then," said Nugent feverishly, "I am free to do what I can to retrieve my criminal folly. Can you give me no clue — is there no way in which I could help to find out what has become of the copy of the plan?"

"None at all, I fear. The Office for Home Affairs has been doing all it can in the matter. It will be most difficult to prove satisfactorily that the spy did *not* succeed in getting it out of the country."

"If only I could," said Nugent between his teeth, "I would choke the truth out of that vile impostor, even if I myself had to be hanged for doing it!"

Mr. Lampard shook his head. "Personally I sympathise with your desire. But, as you well know, English justice does not admit of such methods with prisoners. No, I am afraid there is absolutely nothing you can do, except to pray that it may somehow be proved that Guillemin had not time — or at any rate, did not succeed — in despatching his copy of the plan to France."

For once Charlotte had not heard her husband's return. She was consolingly absorbed, in the little back room in which she had already installed her chafing-dish, in making against supper-time a certain delicacy familiar to her childhood which was to be an addition to the fare provided by the brothers Goodbody. But when, a little later, flushed with success, she came into the living-room, and saw him sitting by the hearth with his head buried in his hands, and not stirring at her entrance, she stood a moment as motionless herself. Then she stole quietly to his side and knelt down by him.

Supper was over. It had been a rather silent meal, in the course of which Charlotte had been so touched by Nugent's rousing himself to pay tribute to her cooking, that she nearly burst into tears. At the end an effort had to be made by both of them to seem to be conversing in a normal manner when one of their landlords came to clear the table. Before the operation was completed Nugent had vanished into the adjoining bedroom.

It was a chilly evening, but not so chilly as Charlotte's heart. She had heard, with an emotion little short of horror, about the coping-stone of Guillemin's treachery, for in the end Nugent had told her, though he had kept silence about the mischief Wilkins had set on foot. In what a net of misfortune had she entangled him — for all this came from her plea in those early happy days at Portsmouth on behalf of the impostor! She shivered, and removing Chéri from her lap, bent and poked the fire. Then she glanced at the clock on the mantelpiece. What could Nugent be doing in there? He had been in their bedroom quite a long time, and though at first she had heard him moving about, now all was silent. At last she got up went to the door, opened it and looked in.

Her husband was standing at the dressing-table with his back to her, but the candle-lit mirror showed her only too clearly what he was about. He was cleaning a pistol.

For one terrible second Charlotte felt as though the floor had crumbled under her feet, and that she was falling into some unknown depth. Next moment she was at the dressing-table clutching his arm and crying out in horror:

"No, Nugent, no, *no*! I will not let you! Put the dreadful thing away — give it to me!" Then she saw that the weapon's fellow was lying on the dressing-table near its case — they were a pair of small travelling-pistols — and with one hand she snatched it out of his reach.

"My dear girl," exclaimed Nugent, astonished, "why all this agitation? I found these pistols badly needed cleaning — my servant at Plymouth seems to have neglected them . . . Charlotte, what in God's name is wrong?" For, clinging to him with an almost frenzied grip, his wife was now sobbing hysterically against his shoulder.

And then the meaning of it all broke upon him with a shock. "Charlotte, you surely did not imagine that I was thinking of making away with myself! I cannot seriously think you so . . . so misled!"

"But I was," she gulped. "Seeing you with that pistol . . . and after what you had told me . . . Oh, my dear, my dear!"

He put down the fire-arm and held her close. "How could you think," he said reproachfully "that I should take such a cowardly course — leaving you alone and unprotected — above all now, when you are in danger? You have little to pride yourself upon to-day in your husband, but at least I am not so bad a one as that! Now sit down here, and try to forget that you ever imagined such a thing!"

Trying to stifle her sobs, Charlotte subsided into a chair. "Oh, forgive me!" she said spasmodically. "It was only that I was frightened, coming upon you with that thing in your hand . . . Oh, Nugent, it is *I* who ought to use a pistol on myself! All this misfortune which has come upon you so undeservedly is my doing — all of it, from first to last! If you had never married me you would never have known of Guillemin's existence. And it was I who asked you for that permission on his behalf — you cannot deny that! And the two disastrous letters from Tante Ursule, with all the complications they have caused, those would never have been written if —"

Kneeling beside her, Nugent tried to check her self-accusations, but she went on despite him: "And if I had not gone away to Bristol because I was afraid to face a meeting with you, Guillemin could not have given me that picture to take with me, and I should never have become involved in his plans, and caused you this anxiety about me! Yes, it is I who am the cause of everything! In your heart you must know it. But you have never reproached me . . . you are too good to me!"

And Charlotte began to weep anew, while Nugent took her in his arms assuring her that it was ridiculous for her to blame herself, since he himself had never for a moment thought of doing so. Finally he induced her to dry her eyes and to return with him to the living-room, leaving the objects which had provoked this outburst still lying incongruously upon the dressing-table. And, as they sat close together by the fire, he told her what it appeared he thought he had already mentioned at supper, that he intended to set out for Chatham early next morning — not that he imagined any result could come of his visit, but that he felt impelled to make it. The journey was the reason of his looking over his travelling pistols, because he would have to traverse Blackheath, a region of ill repute among travellers when night drew on.

"You are right to take some protection against robbers. But," added Charlotte with a pale smile, "you cannot shoot Guillemin, for he is in prison. Ah, if only you could have captured him at Chatham single-handed, before he copied the plan, and taken him as prisoner to the Admiralty! How they would have welcomed you!"

But it was no use dwelling upon such a fairy-tale, and Charlotte's voice died away into silence, Nugent staring into the fire, while the spaniel at their feet whimpered in a dream concerned, perhaps, with an equally glittering and impossible 'if only' of the canine consciousness — some tempting sparrow which was eluding him. Charlotte's eyes rested on him; she drew her brows together and studied him attentively for some time without moving. Then, suddenly, she drew a quick breath and glanced up at her husband.

"Is it far to Chatham?" she asked.

"Only about thirty miles."

"Thirty miles. That makes sixty altogether. Then, if you stay there awhile you will scarcely be able to return before night?"

Nugent roused himself. "That is possible, though I assure you, my dear, that I shall do my utmost to be back to-morrow night. As you know I very much dislike leaving you alone for any length of time just now, in case you should have been traced."

"But if that had been so," she protested, "we should surely be aware of it by now?"

He shook his head. "One cannot be certain. And it is, I know, useless for me to go to Chatham at all . . . but I cannot keep away. There must be something I could do, or discover!"

There was no hope, only desperation, in his voice. In silence Charlotte slipped her hand once more into his. He returned the pressure, but nothing more was said between them. When the fire grew low Charlotte got up to mend it, and afterwards knelt there, looking sorrowfully at him, absorbed in his own bitter reflections.

But she too was thinking hard, though if her husband had looked at her then he would not have found it so easy to guess the subject of her cogitations. Nor indeed did she wish him to do so.

CHAPTER
TWENTY-ONE

As he had planned, Nugent left early next morning for Chatham, adjuring Charlotte to go out as little as possible — he would obviously have preferred her not to do so at all — and above all not after dark. He promised to be back the same evening if he could. And Charlotte bade him farewell with feelings which might well, she told herself, be those of a faithless wife anxious to take advantage of her husband's absence in order to prosecute an amour. For during the night she had finally made up her mind to carry out the daring, the really impudent scheme, the first idea of which had come to her as she had sat looking down at the little spaniel dreaming in the firelight.

Since she intended, if possible, to keep Nugent (like any deceived husband) entirely in the dark, it was obviously of the first importance to embark upon her plan as soon as possible after his departure. But that, unfortunately, was impracticable. She could not well present herself at the Ogre's castle before he set out for his important work at the Admiralty, as she presumed was his daily custom; it would be a most unpropitious moment. She must therefore wait until he should have returned (as she fervently hoped was also his habit) for dinner, at three o'clock or thereabouts. And again she must hope that he did not dine much later than three, for it was always possible that some change in Nugent's plans might bring him home in daylight. A further and more delicate calculation had also to be made, since she could not, naturally, present herself too near that consecrated hour, when the Ogre might be presumed to be at his hungriest. About half past two, perhaps, would be the best moment. Even then, unless all the saints whom she had ever invoked came to her aid in a body, she might not even succeed in crossing the threshold of that house in St. James's Square, at that or any other time. And, once inside . . . but she must leave that to her guardian angel. There was nothing else that she could do.

She determined to obey Nugent's wish by remaining indoors all morning at least. Part of the time she spent in brushing Chéri's silky coat with unnecessary assiduity, telling him meanwhile, evidently to his satisfaction, how he was going to serve as a magic key. Then she went over every detail of her own toilet. She must wear her best — a modest best, it was true, but much of it bought in Bath. It was so important to make a good impression when — a thought to make her shiver — she stood, seeking admission, upon *that* doorstep. Much worse tremors assailed her, however, if she allowed herself to think of standing actually in the presence of the house's inhabitant — if indeed she ever achieved that terrifying privilege. What would she not have given to believe that there was a chance of being admitted to that of the sympathetic Mr. Lampard at the

Admiralty. But she felt that any female would be ruthlessly turned back from even the outer defences of that stronghold. And she did not know this Mr. Lampard's private address, as she did Admiral Cathcart's, nor had she dared to ask Nugent if he knew it. It was unlikely that he did, so that she would have aroused his suspicions, perhaps, and for nothing. Moreover the Assistant Secretary could not, she supposed, wield anything resembling the First Sea Lord's authority. She remembered having heard her soldier father say: "In a desperate situation, it is the enemy's strongest position which should be attacked. He will probably not be expecting it." Well, this was a desperate situation, if ever there was one, and she was going to follow his advice!

It was a fine but cold afternoon, threaded through with a wind strong enough to ruffle Chéri's coat when she set out with him under her arm. She walked fast, not really so much on account of the temperature, as in order that the time of her transit from Soho to St. James's should be as brief as possible, giving her less opportunity of wavering in her purpose and turning back. In consequence she arrived in the Square almost before she realised it. Then, more slowly, and summoning all her courage, she mounted the steps of the house which Nugent had pointed out with such disfavour. Once up, quaking, but uttering a prayer, she lifted the formidable knocker.

Not till it had fallen did she realise, with dismay, that she was not really aware of the name of the actual owner of the other King Charles. (But it was too late to

334

turn back now.) And if she played for safety, and asked for 'the lady of the house', she was, surely, much less likely to be admitted.

A short, tense delay, and the imposing door was opened by an elderly manservant. His gaze, at first impassive, showed a sudden unmistakable surprise as it lit upon the black, brown and pearl of the little animal under the arm of the young lady before him. For a moment his mouth fell open a little, and he seemed about to say something. But training prevailed, and he remained mute, waiting to learn why he had been summoned.

Charlotte took the plunge. "Is Miss Cathcart at home?"

"I believe so, Madam."

(Thank Heaven, there *was* a Miss Cathcart then!)

"Will you ask her if she would receive me? I have come upon a matter of some importance."

"If you will please to enter, Madam, I will enquire."

So there she was, inside the Ogre's residence, admitted with due deference to the lofty if rather narrow hall, and not left there either, but conducted to a sort of ante-room at the side. Here, as the butler (if he was one) still lingered, Charlotte remembered that she must give her name, and, since she possessed no visiting cards of her own, was obliged to say, "I am Mrs. Carew — Mrs. Nugent Carew."

When he had withdrawn she sat down with as great an assumption of composure as though she were not alone, and stroked Chéri. Had she not schooled herself to the part she must play? Yet in reality her pulses were thudding. Suppose Miss Cathcart refused to give an interview to a quite unknown young female — with or without a King Charles spaniel?

But no! "Miss Cathcart will receive you, Madam." The second stage of her bold venture had begun.

The room into which she was ushered was a light and spacious apartment, full of handsome furniture. A large brocade-covered sofa was drawn up in front of the fire, presenting its back to the room, and from the further side of this rose a lady of a spinsterish appearance, wearing a dress of the latest material made up in the style of ten years earlier. She came forward — but not very far. The sight of what her visitor was carrying caused a reaction even more marked than that shown by the man-servant. She stopped dead, the look of enquiry on her young-elderly face turning to one of complete bewilderment.

Charlotte had sufficiently studied her own opening gambit. "I trust, Madam, that you will pardon me," she said, with a nice mixture of aplomb and diffidence. "I have ventured to call upon you to ask whether this little spaniel is, perhaps, yours?"

Before Miss Cathcart could reply, before the astonishment had died out of her eyes, that question was answered once and for all in the negative by a short and furious barking from the neighbourhood of the fire; and round the barricade of the sofa rushed her own King Charles, transported with fury at the presence of another. Roused by the challenge, Chéri instantly replied, beginning to struggle violently in his mistress's arms. The ensuing uproar had one good result, for in the subsequent securing, holding and more or less successful pacifying of the champions by their respective owners, a good deal of the formality of a meeting between two complete strangers was thrown to the winds.

When at last Miss Cathcart was able to hear, and then to make her own voice heard, she appeared full of gratitude, and expressed herself most deeply obliged to Mrs. Carew for the trouble to which she had put herself.

"My dear little Monarch, as you can see — and hear" she went on, "is not lost, and never has been, I am thankful to say. But where was this little beauty found? He has not the appearance of a lost dog!"

"Oh, he . . . that is to say . . . I have brushed him well," stammered Charlotte, rather taken aback. She had, she now perceived, somewhat too rashly taken for granted that since (as she well knew) Miss Cathcart could not claim Chéri as hers, she herself would quietly resume unchallenged possession of him. But that might not be so easy. She thought it best, therefore, to pave the way to this result by adding, as composedly as she could: "If no other person claims him, I shall be very glad to keep him myself," hoping that Miss Cathcart would be satisfied with this solution.

At that moment, luckily, her hostess became more occupied in pressing her visitor, who was still standing, to seat herself on the sofa beside her. So Charlotte, still retaining Chéri firmly in her arms, complied, and Miss Cathcart resumed her former seat. Here, after first glancing nervously at her own pet, who was rolled into a sulky ball in his basket, she put out a somewhat bony hand to stroke his rival.

"One must indeed hope, Madam, for your sake, that the real owner will not come forward to claim him from you — though indeed she must be sorely lamenting her loss. If I am not being too inquisitive, may I ask in what part of London he was found?"

There was that awkward question a second time! Charlotte fenced.

"I am a stranger to London, Madam, and do not know the name of the district from which he came." (And of Chéri's birthplace — wherever that was — this was true.)

"You did not, I see, find him yourself?"

"No. He was given to me — I may say, pressed upon me . . . by a lady," prevaricated Charlotte. "But, as I say, I do not know London well."

She guessed that it was almost upon Miss Cathcart's lips to say: "You are indeed a foreigner, are you not?" For, well as Charlotte could handle the English tongue, she had no illusions that she spoke it with the accent and intonation of a native. Miss Cathcart, however, did not venture so far as this — and indeed, for the mistress of a house of this type she had a manner singularly lacking in assurance. Having presumably denied herself this comment, she now seemed to be somewhat at a loss how to continue the conversation, thereby forcing upon Charlotte the conviction that she and Chéri ought now to take their leave. But that happened to be the one thing she was determined not to do . . . yet. So she found herself at the point where she would have to

338

burn her boats and intimate, with what tact she could, to this unassuming daughter of the First Sea Lord that it was really her father with whom she hoped to have speech. And what would be the most natural way of leading up to this thorny topic?

Glancing about her in the silence which now reigned, she suddenly observed upon a wall, amid other large engravings, a mezzotint of what appeared to be a furious naval engagement, the usual welter of splintered masts floating spars and half-drowned men. On this she deliberately fixed an interested gaze, and, seeing her visitor looking so intently at the picture, the hostess was almost constrained to make a remark of some kind about it.

"A fine engraving of a sea-fight, is it not, Madam?" she observed. "Yet I find it unsuitable for a drawing-room, and I could wish my uncle would hang it in his library instead."

(*Uncle!* She was not a daughter after all!) "Your uncle is perhaps a sailor?" queried Charlotte, all innocence.

"Yes. He is on the Board of Admiralty — the First Sea Lord, in fact."

"The First Sea Lord! One of your great English naval captains, then! How much I should like to set eyes upon him!"

"Oh, but that —" returned the great naval captain's niece, with a suggestion of an uneasiness bordering upon alarm, "— that would not, I fear, be possible!"

"No, naturally not," agreed the guest. "An Admiral so highly placed does not receive unknown ladies. And in any case he is no doubt from home?"

Miss Cathcart glanced at the clock. "At present, yes. But he usually returns about this time to dine, unless he is detained at the Admiralty by very urgent business. On his entrance he always goes straight to the library with his papers and so on, and I am afraid that I could not possibly suggest ..." She did not finish the sentence, but gazed rather unhappily at this would-be admirer of the great man.

"She is afraid of her uncle" thought Charlotte. And that put an end to her own slight chances of gaining an admission to his presence sponsored by her. But now that she herself had learnt that Admiral Cathcart was not in the house, yet was presumably on his way there, she was all impatience to leave this room. Might she not possibly have the luck, if the saints were really bestirring themselves, to come face to face with him in the hall as she departed? Failing that, could she not, once outside the front door, linger a little on the door-step, and so intercept him ... even though he might be hungry? It seemed the only chance remaining to her. She could make it appear that she was just going away; and Chéri, the 'reason' for her ever having come, would be under her arm.

Murmuring that she must take her leave, she made a movement to rise, which caused Chéri, at the moment insecurely held, to jump down with a joyful bark on to the Persian rug in front of the fire. Instantly springing from his basket, Monarch launched himself anew at the invader of the sacred territory, and for the second time the air was rent with the yappings of conflict, while a single agitated blur of sable and chestnut rolled itself

340

madly about that product of Eastern looms. Themselves uttering cries, the two owners instantly precipitated themselves once more upon the furry maelstrom. And so, between snarls, barks, their own adjurations and their endeavours to separate its component parts, neither of them was aware that the door of the drawing room had opened, and that someone had advanced behind their backs to the scene of conflict, until a man's voice startled both of them into turning round.

"Good God, Georgina, what is the meaning of this pandemonium? I heard it even in the hall! . . . What, two of 'em? Dammit all — get hold of their tails, get hold of their tails! Here, let me try — Ah, bravo, Madam!"

For Charlotte, fully as anxious as Miss Cathcart that neither little dog should injure or be injured by the other, had succeeded, more by luck than skill, in clutching some portion of one of them — she knew not which. And a moment later Admiral Sir Russell Cathcart, half angry, half amused, was holding out the other wriggling warrior by the scruff of its neck, and saying:

"I told you, Georgina, what would happen if you got another of these ridiculous creatures — unless it were a bitch. Now, you little beggar, be quiet!" And with that he threw his prize — it was Monarch — on to the sofa, where he remained snuffling and glowering.

"But indeed, Uncle Russell, I have not got a second spaniel," expostulated Miss Cathcart, flushed and discomposed. "The other little dog —"

"It is I who am the culprit, sir," explained Charlotte nervously, the dishevelled and panting Chéri once more in her arms. "This spaniel belongs to — that is to say, it was I who brought him here. I regret very much that he should have caused such a disturbance."

"Far more likely that it was that creature on the sofa which caused it, Madam," was the First Lord's reply. He was plainly no dog-lover. "You were, no doubt, unaware that my niece already possessed one of the little whelps. But I am unmannerly. Present me, Georgina."

Sir Russell Cathcart, seen at last, was in appearance totally unlike what Charlotte had expected — neither burly and red-faced, nor lean and hard-bitten. He looked much more like a judge than a sailor. Of middle height, and a little inclined to corpulence, he had a long, pale, sagging countenance, set with a quite terrifying pair of pale blue eyes. At sight of them a further qualm ran through Charlotte. She braced herself to meet their hostility when he should hear her name.

At first, as his niece announced it, Admiral Cathcart merely bowed and said mechanically: "Your servant, Madam." But the next moment he had directed that searching gaze at her and was repeating:

"Mrs. Carew? Mrs. Nugent Carew? Then you are . . . the French wife?"

"Yes, sir," said Charlotte meekly.

"And how, may I ask, did you come here, Madam? *Why* have you come here?"

"Because, sir, I have some information to give you."

"The deuce you have! Information as well as a quarrelsome little dog!" Seeming to find the situation humorous, the First Sea Lord gave vent to a sardonic kind of crow, which was probably meant for a laugh, and turned to his niece. "You should have warned Mrs. Carew, Georgina, that that whipper-snapper of yours would not tolerate another of his kidney."

"But, Uncle," protested Miss Cathcart, puzzled and upset, "I had not the pleasure of Mrs. Carew's previous acquaintance. She very obligingly came here to bring this stray spaniel, thinking it was mine."

"Thinking it was yours?" Once more those penetrating eyes were turned for an instant on to the so obliging visitor . . . "And if you had never met before," went on their owner, addressing his niece again, "how did Mrs. Carew know, pray, that you had a spaniel of this breed, and why should she imagine into the bargain, that you had lost it? I fancy there is more in this than meets the eye of a female as guileless as you, Georgina?"

And he looked again, and longer this time, at Charlotte, who, in an effort to sustain his gaze, unconsciously hugged Chéri rather tighter than he appreciated.

"I think I had better investigate this matter," pronounced 'the great English naval captain' at length. "If you will accompany me to another room, Mrs. Carew, I will give you five minutes to present this 'information' . . . Ah, I see that you and your 'stray spaniel' do not wish to be parted. Bring him with you then; a second set-to in here will be too much for Miss Cathcart."

He crossed the room forthwith, and held open the door. Half quaking, half elated, Charlotte passed through; the Admiral preceded her across the hall, opened another door and stood back, indicating that she should enter.

The successful intruder then found herself in another room as lofty, but neither so spacious nor so light. One wall was lined with bookcases, there was a massive carved mahogany table in the middle bearing writing materials and a few papers, a fine pair of globes in one corner and over the mantelpiece a portrait of a naval officer of about forty — presumably Sir Russell Cathcart at an earlier stage of his career. A bright fire was burning.

"Be seated, if you please, Madam!" And Charlotte, depositing the now quiescent and probably exhausted Chéri on the floor beside the designated chair, complied, though she would somehow have preferred to stand, as the Admiral continued to do.

"And now, Mrs. Carew," continued he, "having, as I strongly suspect, obtained admission to this house by a stratagem, you are, I suppose, going to admit that your 'information' is only another ruse, a pretext for seeking an interview in which you hope to make an appeal on behalf of your husband? For I cannot easily conceive for what other reason you have come here."

"I assure you that it is not a pretext, sir," said Charlotte earnestly. "I have genuine information in my possession."

344

The Admiral's compressed lips denoted complete scepticism. "About whom or what?"

"About the French spy — Guillemin." And as the Admiral said nothing, but stood looking at her with that expression unchanged, she went on: "Is it not a fact that the authorities are anxious to learn by what means he communicated, when in Bath, with an accomplice in Bristol named O'Connor? Or have they by this time discovered it?"

Was there not at her words a slight change in Sir Russell's demeanour? She could not be sure. But at any rate he replied after a moment.

"Evidence on that point would, I think, be welcomed. You affirm that you can provide some?"

"Yes, sir. I can tell you, on the . . . on the best authority, who acted as a bearer of information from one to the other."

This time the Admiral looked at her still more attentively, and, without removing his eyes, pulled up a chair and sat down.

"Ah, yes," he said slowly. "You have, as I remember, close ties with the French émigré gentleman at whose house Guillemin was arrested. Then, if you are in possession of certain facts, you must do your duty, my dear Madam, as an Englishwoman, which you now are."

What did his suddenly altered tone and expression — and his words — imply? For a moment Charlotte was puzzled; then she guessed. Admiral Sir Russell Cathcart, with his judge's face, thought that she was proposing to inform against Fabien himself, and was encouraging her in that unnatural course! For a moment she was hard put to it to keep back her indignation; then, though flushing hotly, she bit her lip and fought it down. Above all things she must keep cool.

"Are you referring, sir, to my brother, the Vicomte d'Esparre?" Her voice did shake a little, nevertheless. "It is true that Guillemin lived in the same lodgings, but neither my brother nor his wife, both of whom are convinced Royalists — exiles for that reason — were anything but his dupes. They had not the slightest suspicion of his real activities."

Perhaps she had been mistaken after all. For the Admiral merely replied: "That, I am informed, appears to be the case, as far as can be ascertained — Yet *you* appear to know something!"

"I have that misfortune," said Charlotte. "Or perhaps, from the point of view of the English government, the good fortune."

"You really make me curious, Mrs. Carew," said her host, drawing his chair slightly closer. "You actually know who served as a go-between with the confederate in Bristol who has escaped arrest? Who was it?"

Wishing that he had remained further away, for she felt the impact of his personality a trifle less at a distance, Charlotte, after studying the carpet for a few seconds, replied: "I must first say, sir, that I take a serious personal risk by telling you."

The Admiral raised his sandy eyebrows. "But how is that, Mrs. Carew? You are under the protection of the law of this country." And he sounded really surprised.

Charlotte dropped her eyes once more. "I am not so sure of that protection," she murmured. "And so," she went on after a moment, "since I run a risk, and the information is really needed, I thought ... I wondered ..." After all, now the crucial moment had come, it became practically impossible to put her speculation into words.

Her attempt to do so appeared unnecessary. "Am I to understand, young lady, that you are trying to strike a bargain with me?" There was a good deal more than surprise in the First Sea Lord's voice now.

"Yes," said Charlotte more boldly, since the word was out. "I know that it is monstrous of me, but —" and here for the first time she made a gesture — "it is more than I can bear to see my husband so heart-broken!"

"You choose a very odd method of trying to mend that organ," retorted Admiral Cathcart. "Let me tell you that your suggestion almost amounts to blackmail, which is a crime very seriously regarded in this country!"

"Blackmail? I do not know that word, sir," said Charlotte, looking straight at him and his frown. "But — as I said — I knew that I was running a risk. I thought that I might find myself in prison in the end (but not because of this 'blackmail'). Nevertheless I felt ... that I ought to do what was right."

" 'What was right!' You conceive it right, Madam, to set a price on information which, whether it prove of much or little value, it is your duty to give! — that price being, I suppose, that the Board of Admiralty should

347

turn a blind eye on your husband's grossly imprudent conduct?"

"A person who does his duty, especially in the face of difficulties, is sometimes recompensed," hazarded Charlotte. "And the return I hoped for was not for myself."

There was a silence while the First Sea Lord studied this female casuist who had invaded his house. But she was not looking at him. He had laid a hand on the arm of his chair; it was the hand with the two fingers missing, and Charlotte's eyes, falling upon the mutilation became rivetted to it.

"You are either a very bold or a very innocent young woman," said Admiral Cathcart at last. "Before we go any further I must ask you a question. Am I right in presuming that it was your husband who put you up to this manœuvre?"

At that Charlotte did look straight at him. "Oh no, *no* — indeed no! He has not the faintest notion that I even intended to come here!"

"Then I am to understand that he is also unaware of your possession of the information you speak of?"

For a moment Nugent's wife hesitated. It would be much simpler — though false, but that she was past caring about now — to say that he was ignorant of it. But an aspect of the situation which she had not sufficiently considered was breaking upon her. If she were skilful enough could she not contrive to make at least part of the 'manœuvre' redound to his credit? At any rate she would try. So she replied: "He knows it now, sir, but he only learnt of it recently. When he did,

348

he naturally thought that the authorities should be informed of what I knew, if they were still in ignorance. But he saw that . . . in short that I was afraid of the consequences to myself — I will explain why in a moment, sir" (for it looked as though the Admiral were about to interject some remark). "So we waited a little to see how things were going. Then I . . . became more courageous, and knowing that in his heart he wished me to give this evidence, I . . . took advantage of his being absent from London for the day, and came here. But he does not know that I have done so, and never, never would it occur to him that I should try — very wrongly and foolishly, as I see now — to make a bargain of the matter."

(If that did not work, nothing would. It was the best she could do.)

Sir Russell Cathcart was still studying her hard; of this she was fully aware, and she now sat with her eyes cast down, her fingers nervously gripping each other. The fire crackled; Chéri at her feet got up and curled himself the other way round, and her thoughts wandered back to the affray in the drawing-room — unreasonably, for this vital moment, here and now, should be absorbing all her attention — and yet it had become curiously unreal . . . She heard the Admiral's chair move slightly and guessed that he had risen.

"I am glad to see, Madam," came his voice, exceedingly dry, "that repentance — if you are indeed repentant — has not led you to bring out your pocket-handkerchief! That is something. I detest women who weep the moment they are in difficulties.

Listen, Mrs. Carew! I cannot possibly make a bargain with you, especially as your evidence may turn out to be quite worthless. But I undertake that, if it proves to be of any real value, your action in coming forward of your own free will shall not be overlooked, and your husband's case shall be reconsidered with as little delay as possible." He coughed, and added in a manner which suggested annoyance with himself: "A most un-English and reprehensible transaction! But, note you, I only say 'reconsidered'!"

"Oh, thank you, thank you, sir!" exclaimed Charlotte with a gasp. "Yes, I understand . . . I cannot thank you enough!" She did yearn now for the use, however temporary, of her banned pocket-handkerchief, but dared not risk losing such merit as abstention from tears had procured her. "Yes, not a bargain, but kindness — generosity, on your part!"

"No, not entirely that either," said the Admiral, reseating himself. "For I do not say that, in spite of his serious lapse, the Board might not have found your husband *some* employment before long. We are at war, and he has not yet been struck from the active list. Remember, if you please, that I have promised reconsideration only — and that contingent upon the value of this information of yours. Well, now let us come to the point. Who was the individual who acted as Guillemin's intermediary with the Irishman O'Connor, and how did you get wind of him?"

Charlotte drew a long breath, and with prayers to all the heavenly host, laid down her trump card — trusting that it was one.

"Because it was I myself who acted as messenger!"

She could at least congratulate herself upon its immediate effect. The Admiral appeared so astounded that it was a moment or two before he found speech. When he did he was frowning, but the frown was half incredulity.

"You, Mrs. Carew, you yourself! You were in the affair — and now turn King's evidence!"

"I do not know what that expression means," replied Charlotte with perfect truth. "But I can swear to you, by any oath you wish me to use, that I conveyed Guillemin's little painting to Mr. O'Connor, and Mr. O'Connor's letter to Monsieur Guillemin in complete ignorance that I was taking part in anything wrong, and merely to oblige each of them in turn."

Those pale, alarming eyes were searching her face relentlessly now. But she could meet them, for was she not telling the absolute truth? And the Admiral seemed to realise that — at least she hoped so — for at last he relaxed his attitude, the frown disappeared, and leaning back in his chair he said:

"Proceed then, if you please, with your story. What painting, and what letter did you convey?"

So Charlotte did proceed. By the time her short recital had ended its hearer was pacing slowly up and down the library. It was impossible to tell what he was thinking. After about a minute of this quarter-deck exercise he came and stood near her again.

"What did you say, Mrs. Carew, was the date of your visit to Bristol?"

Charlotte reflected, in order to be sure that she was answering correctly. "I went there on the 21st of January and returned to Bath on the 25th."

The Admiral uttered an impatient "Tchah! Too early, by Gad! Weeks too early! And you never served a second time as go-between?"

She shook her head. "I never had occasion to visit Bristol again."

"And have you no notion who took your place as messenger — if indeed anyone did?"

"I am afraid not. I knew very little indeed of Monsieur Guillemin's doings when I was staying with my brother. Part of the time he was absent, part of it sketching in Bath."

Had her disclosure missed fire after all? For Sir Russell Cathcart's initial astonishment seemed to have given place to something very much like disappointment.

"You did not *refuse* to act again, I suppose?"

"No; it was never suggested. As I have said, sir, I think it was only when he learnt, on the very day itself, that I was upon the point of going to Bristol for a few days, that it occurred to Monsieur Guillemin to use me as his messenger."

The First Sea Lord resumed his pacing, but it did not last long.

"In my opinion," he pronounced, returning to his former place near Charlotte, "the entrusting of that picture to your hands was a commission whose real importance lay in the fact that it established you with the Irishman as a channel of communication — all the more desirable, perhaps, that you were ignorant of what you were doing. It was the letter — the pretended money draft — which his wife induced you to take back with you to Bristol, which was the real crux of the matter — and I fear it will never be known now what that letter contained. But in any case the transaction took place too early to afford any clue to what it is most necessary to know — weeks, in fact, before —" But here Sir Russell pulled himself up, and walked away again, unaware that his visitor could well have finished the sentence for him by saying, "weeks before the copying of the Medway defence plans, you mean."

But Charlotte had no cause to plume herself upon that perspicacity. Her heart was indeed sinking lower and lower, for the counters of her 'bargain' were showing up for what they were — almost worthless. And would not the First Sea Lord most certainly feel that he was in consequence dispensed from keeping his part of the contract — which in any case he had declared would be contingent upon the value of what she had to tell? She had done Nugent no good, but even, possibly, harm.

The arbiter of destiny had now seated himself behind the big writing table, and was dipping a pen in the inkpot.

"In spite of the date of your visit to Bristol, Mrs. Carew," he said, somewhat abruptly, "the Office of the Secretary of State for Home Affairs will wish to be informed of what you have just told me. Steps must be taken about that."

"Must I go to see someone there too?" asked Charlotte, in a voice which she had no need to try to render weary and dispirited.

But to her relief the Admiral, now writing fast, replied with emphasis, though without looking up: "No, my dear Madam, you will not. Lord Portland's Office can well send someone responsible here to question you. After dinner, that is. I shall despatch a note there at once. Meanwhile you will do me the pleasure of dining here with my niece and myself . . ." He signed and sealed the letter, and went to the bell-pull. "Miss Cathcart's maid shall attend you at once."

Charlotte was much startled and touched. "You are very kind indeed, sir," she said a little tremulously. "Especially as my information seems . . . of so little use. I thought, indeed I honestly thought, that it was of value, but . . ." Her voice tailed off, and, to hide the sudden tears in her eyes, she picked up Chéri and bent her head over him.

"Not going to cry after all, I hope?" enquired her host, glancing sharply at her as he gave the bell a tremendous tug. "It will be time for that pocket-handkerchief of yours when the Home Office official finds your information worthless. I am only a plain sailor" — even at so tense a moment this self-portrait struck Charlotte as hardly accurate — "but I cannot help thinking that with a little further dredging something of value might be brought up. And a good dinner will not, I think, come amiss to you after so much agitation over . . . spaniels. — God bless my soul, it is past three o'clock already!"

CHAPTER
TWENTY-TWO

"Oh dear, what an unfortunate occurrence!" lamented poor Miss Cathcart to herself as she nervously stabbed her needle in and out of her tambour work. "I have acted very unwisely — but what else could I do? And Uncle Russell will be so cross and sarcastic at dinner! By the way" (she had glanced at the clock) "why is it not yet announced? That will anger him still more!"

Agitated by the thought of this further crisis, she left her needle sticking in a large yellow pansy, and rose with the intention of ringing the bell in order to make enquiries. But before she reached the pull the door opened and the butler appeared.

"Sir Russell wished me to inform you Madam, that it is by his orders that dinner has been delayed. It is to be served in ten minutes from now, and Mrs. Carew will be partaking of it. Sir Russell further desired me, Madam, to send your maid to attend her and to furnish her with anything she may require."

"Mrs. Carew is staying to dinner!" murmured the startled lady under her breath. "Very well, Manton. Ask Carter to come to me."

"What *can* have happened to Uncle Russell?" she asked herself a quarter of an hour or so later, noting her formidable relative's expression — for him, almost benignant — as he carefully detached the liver wing from one of the chickens before him for the guest. (It was true that he had already angrily banished the sirloin to the sideboard because it was 'as usual' overdone. Another banishment which had more quietly taken place was that of the visitor's King Charles, now temporarily relegated to the servants' hall.) Mrs. Carew is certainly attractive, thought Miss Cathcart, but I have never known the Admiral influenced by a pretty face. Even poor Aunt Rachel can never have been in the least beautiful.

As for Charlotte, thus unexpectedly feasted at the Ogre's table, she knew better than to ascribe this surprising hospitality to any charm of her own, or even, as matters had turned out, to the value of the disclosure which she had made. She assigned it partly to Admiral Cathcart's wish to give the Office for Home Affairs any crumb of assistance, however meagre, in its efforts to unravel the Guillemin affair; and partly to a dislike, natural in a gentleman, of subjecting a woman to another trying interview without offering her a meal. Of this meal she was indeed unfeignedly glad, although she could not eat half of what was pressed upon her, so that the Admiral rallied her upon her lady-like appetite. (Not, she observed, that his niece was much of a trencherwoman either.) At the conclusion of the repast Sir Russell insisted upon her taking a glass of port with him. Foreign wines like sherry and claret were all very well, he pronounced, but they were negligible compared to good port; which from the context it almost seemed that he regarded as a vintage of British origin. Yet he had not himself drunk much wine with his dinner, differing in that respect from what Charlotte had always heard was the custom of Englishmen.

She had not quite finished her glass when the butler entered and announced to his master in discreet but audible tones: "A gentleman from the Office of the Secretary for Home Affairs to wait upon you, sir. I have shown him into the library."

"Already!" observed the Admiral. "I must have aroused the curiosity of Lord Portland's people to some purpose! Take in the port and a couple of glasses, and say I will be with him very shortly."

He finished his wine and rose. "Take Mrs. Carew with you to the drawing-room, Georgina. I will have her summoned when her presence is required."

Three or four minutes later, therefore, Charlotte found herself alone for the second time with Miss Cathcart, Monarch — now undisputed ruler of this territory — and her own sense of guilt towards that self-effacing lady, whose personality during the meal had been so obliterated by that of her uncle, that Charlotte had felt she was barely present at all. Now, as she resumed independent existence on her drawing-room sofa, Charlotte, seated by her, addressed her with apologies.

"May I hope, Madam, that you will forgive my subterfuge about the spaniel? I never, I must confess, thought that you had lost yours. But I happened to see him one day when I was passing the house, and he so closely resembled my own, that I thought I might make use of the likeness to gain entrance. It was inexcusable, I know ... but I was so desperately anxious, on my husband's account, to speak to Admiral Cathcart, and I knew that I could not hope to do so at the Admiralty itself."

Miss Cathcart's resigned expression did not change and there was no resentment audible in her reply.

"No, Sir Russell would never have received you there," she said. "And as your recent interview with him here seems to have put him" — (here she checked herself, and substituted), "to have passed off so well, I am sure I am very pleased that you were able to contrive one. And now it seems that you are to have a further interview with some one from the Home Office? I trust that also will go off as Sir Russell would wish."

"Indeed I hope so too," rejoined Charlotte, noticing that the phrase had not run 'as you would wish.' Poor lady, she thought, I suppose her uncle's good or bad temper is the most important matter in her life. If he had not in the end shown himself so amiable, I fear she would not so easily have forgiven me for the trick I played on her. And, asking to be allowed to look more closely at Miss Cathcart's needlework, she expressed an admiration which was as genuine as her preoccupation with what might be going forward in the library would admit.

Proceedings there had opened with the Admiral's expression of pleasure at finding whom the Home Office had sent, for Mr. Philip Esdaile, distinguished and intelligent in appearance, was one of their senior officials. "Very good of you to have come yourself!" said Sir Russell as he shook hands.

"I thought that as I am supposed to know most about this miserable espionage case, I had better do so," replied Mr. Esdaile.

"I am very glad, very glad indeed to see you. Has the port — Ah, here it is! Pray be seated, Mr. Esdaile. I hope you will not in the end charge me with having brought you here on false pretences. But a — a person has come forward who a few weeks ago acted as intermediary between the man Guillemin in Bath and O'Connor in Bristol. And though this person has little to tell, and though the date of the transaction is too early for it to have had any connection with the business of the Medway defences, I thought that your Office might wish to put some questions."

"Most certainly; and we are greatly obliged, Sir Russell, for the opportunity. Your note gave us to understand that the person in question was in your house at this moment. Is that so?"

Sir Russell nodded. "That is the case. And not under lock and key either, as you probably assume."

"Ah, I understand!" said Mr. Esdaile. "The informer came to turn King's evidence!"

His host gave a half sardonic little smile. "In a sense, yes. But the term is in reality hardly applicable, since I am satisfied that she acted in ignorance of what she was doing."

"*She!*" Mr. Esdaile was so startled that, presumably afraid of dropping it, he hastily put down his glass upon a table at his elbow. "It is a woman, then!"

"A woman, and a young woman, and, if one is to believe her, a mere catspaw in the matter. Nevertheless her testimony may have some importance."

But the visitor's face had fallen. "A mere catspaw," he said reflectively. "H'm." He took a sip of port. "Then, if I may say so, her evidence is hardly likely to be of great value. She surely cannot have much to reveal if she acted in ignorance of what she was doing."

"I admit that may be so. But I am trusting to your acumen, my dear Esdaile, and to your somewhat wider knowledge of the ramifications of this unfortunate business to elicit something or other which may be of use. By the way, has anything further been discovered since yesterday about that scoundrel O'Connor's actions just before he decamped — more particularly in relation to the Medway plans? Are you any nearer finding out for certain whether the copy Guillemin made has left the country or no? Nothing further on that crucial point had been communicated to the Secretary when I left the Admiralty a while ago."

Mr. Esdaile looked grave. "We have not yet been able to find proof one way or the other. There is, however, one piece of information now in our possession which has not yet, I think, been passed on to Mr. Nepean. You have doubtless been told, sir, that O'Connor had destroyed all his papers before he escaped; but that, it appears is not strictly true. One or two letters have now been found, and among them one, unfortunately not dated, signed 'Peasell', informing him that he would receive 'what he was to expect', through the usual medium. The presumption is strong that what he was to expect was the copy of the Medway plan, which, as you have heard, would ordinarily have been sent by him to France by way of Ireland — though in the circumstances he might have taken it himself when he fled from Bristol. If only we knew what that 'usual medium' was, the knowledge would greatly assist our investigations."

"It cannot have been my present visitor," muttered the Admiral. "Mrs. Carew, unless she is lying, acted as intermediary on that one occasion only, weeks before the plan was abstracted."

"Mrs. Carew!" repeated Mr. Esdaile, obviously experiencing a second surprise. "Carew! Is not that the name of —"

"Yes. A damned fine officer too! It angered me greatly that he could be so inconceivably misguided. She, the 'intermediary' is his wife. By the way she is French — the sister of that émigré fellow in whose house Guillemin was lodging. She had been staying there too. But that relationship, I suppose," he added in an afterthought "is no news to you."

"But it is, Sir Russell, I assure you! Captain Carew's wife a sister of d'Esparre! I had no idea of it."

"Had you not? I have known it for some days," returned the First Sea Lord with a certain satisfaction. "Got it out of Carew himself that day we had him before us at the Admiralty."

Mr. Esdaile was looking reflective. "Has it not occurred to you — to Their Lordships in general — that this marriage might be held to throw a rather different — possibly a rather unwelcome — light on the Guillemin affair?"

Sir Russell Cathcart stared at him. "I cannot say that it has; and I have had plenty of time to digest the knowledge. In what sense do you use the word 'unwelcome', Mr. Esdaile? Have you then proofs, after all, that this French émigré was in any sense an accomplice of Guillemin's?"

"No, no. His protestations of ignorance appeared, and still appear, perfectly well founded."

"Then I don't see what you are driving at. If the brother has satisfied your people of his innocence, and the sister has satisfied *me*, what the devil can it signify that she is married to Carew?"

Mr. Esdaile did not appear disturbed by this bluntness. "Only that the relationship appears to account for the readiness with which Captain Carew so incautiously gave the pass to Guillemin."

"Naturally. The deduction is not hard to make," returned the Admiral a shade tartly. "But it is time I asked Mrs. Carew to come here herself." On the way to the door he paused. "By the by, who is the person who signs himself 'Peasell' (which I think was the name you mentioned just now) when writing to O'Connor? Sounds like an Englishman, God forgive him!"

"We take 'Peasell', Sir Russell, to be an anagram of 'Apelles', the Greek painter. Guillemin had used the name on other occasions."

"Apelles? Was that the fellow who gave out that his paintings of fruit were so lifelike that the very birds

362

pecked at 'em? Apelles indeed!" And, uttering his crow of a laugh, the First Sea Lord left the room.

Mr. Esdaile rubbed his chin thoughtfully. If Sir Russell Cathcart could not or would not see the implications of this marriage connection, then it was no use arguing with him. One would do better to reserve one's judgment until one had seen the French wife, d'Esparre's sister.

The Admiral's voice could now be heard through the half-closed door, adjuring someone in the hall not to be nervous. The Home Office, it appeared, had fortunately sent him a *gentleman!* Mr. Esdaile suppressed a smile.

There then came in, somewhat nervously, a young lady entirely unlike the idea which, even in so brief a time, he had formed of 'the French wife' in question. He rose and bowed, the young lady dropped a curtsey, and the Admiral installed her in a chair near his own.

"Now, Mrs. Carew, tell Mr. Esdaile all you told me — and more, if you can. Do not hurry!"

Having taken a good look at her new interrogator, Charlotte decided that she need not be unduly alarmed. So, fortified by the Admiral's support and his excellent dinner, she embarked for the second time on her recital. Nor did Mr. Esdaile alarm her during its course, not even when he entered into the question of her relations with her brother, how long she had stayed with him (fortunately he did not ask the true reason of that stay) how much she had then seen of Guillemin, and so forth. She was not, in fact, a quarter as nervous as she had been with Admiral Cathcart. Mr. Esdaile's questions rather helped her than otherwise. In response to them she gave as full a description as she could of the little water colour, and of all the circumstances of Guillemin's commissioning her to carry it to Bristol.

"At any rate," observed Sir Russell at this point, "the painting was not of a ship of any kind, as appears to have been usual with that scoundrel."

"Quite so," agreed Mr. Esdaile. "Nor, according to Mrs. Carew, was it in oils. Can you give us any explanation of those facts, Madam?"

"I remember, sir, hearing my brother say that Monsieur Guillemin had found that there was less market of late for pictures of vessels, and that he was giving up those subjects, and taking to water-colour scenes, which found a better sale."

"Such, no doubt, as the four or five which were found in his bedroom after his arrest. And so, Madam, having learnt that you were going to Bristol, he took advantage of that fact to request you to convey the water-colour in question to O'Connor, as he did not care to risk sending it by post or carrier. It is possible, of course, that the errand may have been contrived by him merely as a pretext for putting you into touch with O'Connor, so that when the time came the latter could send a letter back by you."

"Precisely what I said!" interjected the Admiral.

Mr. Esdaile slightly inclined his head as a tribute to this perspicacity. "How did Guillemin receive that letter, Madam?" he resumed. "Did he show any anxiety or eagerness on the point — did he indeed seem to know that you might have one for him — enquire about it in any way?"

364

"No, sir, not at all. He merely took it from me when I handed it to him, and thanked me warmly for my kindness in conveying it, and the trouble to which I had been put over the painting." And here Charlotte found herself adding, for she could not help it: "I . . . Monsieur Guillemin was always so courteous and cheerful that I . . ."

Looking more than ever like a Lord Chief Justice, Sir Russell said severely: "The worst kind of villain! Your people never laid their hands after all on that letter, Esdaile? No, I remember, no papers of any kind were found in Guillemin's possession."

"Unfortunately, no, Sir Russell. But now, Madam, to revert once more to the painting. Can you tell us any more about its reception by the O'Connors?"

Charlotte reflected for a moment.

"Only that they — and Mrs. O'Connor in particular — made much of my kindness in bringing it, and that she especially was full of admiration for it, and spent some time discussing with her husband where they should hang it to the best advantage. So that it somewhat surprised me when I returned for my —"

"Returned?" broke in Mr. Esdaile quickly. "When did you return, and for what reason? I thought you said you only went there on that one occasion?"

"You never told me anything about returning, Mrs. Carew," said the Admiral reprovingly.

The culprit coloured. "Forgive me, sir! I had really forgotten the little incident until this moment . . . I found, after leaving, when I had gone some way back towards the convent — perhaps ten minutes or so of

365

distance — that I had dropped my pocket-handkerchief. And as it was one I valued I went back to ask if I had left it behind. Mrs. O'Connor herself took me into the parlour, and we found it at once. It was than that I happened to notice that the picture had already been removed from its frame."

"But how did you know that?"

"Because the glass and frame were lying on the table, but the painting itself was not there."

"Did you remark on this fact?"

"No, sir. But Mrs. O'Connor must have seen that I had observed it, because she told me the reason for the removal — that the picture was being put into a better frame. She begged me not to inform Monsieur Guillemin of this, lest he should be offended."

"H'm," remarked Mr. Esdaile thoughtfully. "I wonder, I wonder if he would have been! . . . Was Mr. O'Connor in the room too?"

"Not at first. But almost immediately I heard him outside calling for his wife (he did not know that I had returned) and asking why she had left him just then. I remember that he spoke of a kettle of hot water, and the mixing or pouring of something in which he needed her help. Then he came in, and, on seeing me, stopped rather suddenly, and said no more about it. Mrs. O'Connor explained that her husband had a fancy for trying his hand at cooking — though I should never have thought so, from his appearance."

Mr. Esdaile had been listening with the utmost attention. "Cooking? *Cooking!*" He leant forward in his chair. "Did O'Connor also actually use the words 'pouring', or 'mixing'?"

"He used both, sir. I could not have imagined it, for it was so odd to connect him with kitchen matters."

"Quite so. And when he saw you, he broke off and seemed disconcerted?"

Charlotte tried hard to recall her exact impression. "Perhaps one might say so," she replied slowly. "But at the time it seemed natural to me that he should be, a trifle, because he might not wish to have this hobby of his, so unusual in a gentleman, mentioned in front of a stranger."

"That," agreed Mr. Esdaile with emphasis, and almost grimly, "I can well imagine. He would dislike it even more than your observing that the picture had been removed from its frame." And then he added, as if to himself, "Great Heavens, if that should be the key!"

"You are devilish mysterious, Mr. Esdaile!" remarked the First Sea Lord, with some impatience. "What key, and to what riddle, is afforded by a frame without a painting, or an Irish spy who has a fancy for cooking?"

But Mr. Esdaile did not reply. Instead, he directed a doubtful glance from Sir Russell to Charlotte, and back again. The girl instantly got from her chair.

"You do not wish to speak further in front of me, sir? That is only right. If you will excuse me, Messieurs, I will withdraw."

"No, no, quite unnecessary —" the Admiral was beginning, and then, observing that Mr. Esdaile did not support his protest, he appeared to change his mind, and muttering: "Very proper feeling on your part, Mrs.

367

Carew," went across to the door, Charlotte following him.

But Mr. Esdaile was coming after her. "Before you leave us for a few moments, Madam, there is one question I should like to put. Did the O'Connors seem in any way unwilling that you should leave the house after this little scene? Did they seek to detain you in any way?"

"Oh no, sir," answered Charlotte, surprised. "Not in any way. It would have been strange, would it not, if they had!"

"Not so strange, perhaps, as it appears."

"But I should have been in the way had I remained any longer."

"Yes, you would undoubtedly have been in the way." He smiled, but his tone was grave. "My apologies, Sir Russell!" for the Admiral, fidgeting, was waiting by the open door.

When he returned, after having ushered Charlotte once more into the presence of his niece, Mr. Esdaile, standing by the fire with a smile on his face had just finished writing something in a notebook.

"Well, sir?" enquired the First Sea Lord. "What is this wonderful key of yours?"

In two words, one of them exceedingly brief, Mr. Esdaile told him.

Half an hour or so later Charlotte and Chéri were rumbling back to Soho in the hackney carriage which the Admiral had insisted should be procured for her. Five o'clock had struck before she finally parted from

Mr. Esdaile, with instructions on no account to leave London at present, as she must hold herself at the disposal of the Office of Home Affairs, in case it should be necessary to question her further.

Sir Russell himself had put her into the hackney coach. Whatever had passed between him and Mr. Esdaile during her temporary absence from the library had clearly pleased the Admiral not a little. Indeed his parting words to her, if somewhat enigmatic, had been reassuring.

"They say the real gist of a lady's letter is to be found in the postscript. I am hoping that the same is true of your evidence, Mrs. Carew. Good-bye. Perhaps after all you have not done a bad day's work!" There was a frosty twinkle in his eye. "But," he added, as Chéri began to celebrate their departure by barking, "don't bring that 'stray dog' here again!"

'Perhaps after all you have not done a bad day's work.' That was all she had to go upon. But surely that statement was as much as she could have hoped for — nay, more! Now her chief preoccupation must be to keep her intervention a complete secret from her husband. Ought she, for instance — once more like a guilty wife, returning, this time, from a rendezvous — to stop the coach and alight from it a little before reaching their lodgings, in case he should have come back already and should ask her what she was doing in one? But it was impossible that he should have returned by this time from Chatham, thirty miles away, unless he had spent no time there after all. Nevertheless, she

369

stopped the vehicle, for she had no desire to arouse a possible curiosity even in the Goodbodys.

By the time Nugent did appear it was she who was impatiently waiting for him. It had been dark for some hours when he came in, grim and dispirited, having neither discovered nor accomplished anything, save that he had met with a certain naval officer of his acquaintance who held some position at Chatham which Charlotte did not fully grasp. "And he," said Nugent wearily as he sat down to the table, laid with covers for two "— dear girl, you should not have waited supper for me — he thinks it impossible that, in this time of war, my services should be entirely dispensed with . . . even after the calamity which I have brought about. He knows old Vice-Admiral Ellam, and would get him to speak for me if he thought that would be of any avail; but Ellam was put on the retired list six or seven years ago. He would not have the slightest influence with the Board, and the new Secretary, Mr. Nepean, probably never heard of him."

In her acute sorrow and sympathy for her husband it was all that Charlotte could do not to burst out with the news of her afternoon's achievement — as far as it had been an achievement. But no, a thousand times no! When restitution and advancement came, it was imperative that he should not know that she had any hand in it. All she could do at the moment was to ply him with food and drink.

"But, my dear, look after yourself!" he protested. "For I warrant" — and the glimmer of a smile appeared on his lips — "that, being alone, you dined off some mere omelette or something equally unsatisfactory!"

"Oh no!" returned Charlotte instantly — and unwarily. "I had an excellent dinner, I assure you!"

"Indeed? And what did our good landlords provide for you?"

Such a simple and natural enquiry — and so dangerous to answer! Suppose — although it was not very likely — he were to refer in some way to this imaginary meal and its bill of fare in front of one of the Goodbodys! It would naturally bring out the puzzled response. "But your lady, sir, did not dine at home to-day!" And then Nugent (who had told her to go out as little as possible) would naturally want to know where she had partaken of this excellent meal! Oh dear, what a difficult path was that of subterfuge — beset on every side with snares!

She had to scramble out of this one as best she could. "You must not be too inquisitive, *mon ami*," she answered with a little laugh. "My good dinner was of my own providing, but it was something more substantial than an omelette, although I cooked it myself. Now, enough of that subject. It is more to the point that you should eat well after your journey. And the journey itself; this dangerous Blackheath? You met no robbers there, I hope?"

CHAPTER
TWENTY-THREE

I

How slowly the day had passed! Every hour Charlotte expected a summons from Mr. Esdaile for further questioning: hoped for it, if it meant further advantage to Nugent, but feared it too, because, unless he happened to be out when it arrived, she would be unable to hide yesterday's doings from him. The mere mention of a visit to the Office for Home Affairs would bear only one construction for him — that some connection had been traced between her and Guillemin, and she would therefore have to reveal the true state of things. But apparently Mr. Esdaile did not require her presence to-day.

Nugent also was restless, as well as low-spirited. He went out in the morning, came in and tried to read, and wrote a letter or two, repeating the same procedure in the afternoon. Between four and five o'clock, when he was again writing and Charlotte sewing, the scene had all the outward appearance of a peaceful domestic interior, even though the couple were not in their own home. And, glancing up at the end of his letter, the same thought occurred to Nugent Carew himself. There sat his young wife, newly restored to him, busy with her needle near the window, the light bright

372

behind her, the spaniel sleeping at her feet. It was still balm to his wounded spirit that she should have insisted, even at possible risk to herself, on sharing with him what could not be other than a period of disheartened waiting. And the reality of what was to be shared in London was even worse than he had ever anticipated. He had not known, that morning at the Blue Dragon, that he was ultimately responsible for the conveyance to the enemy of the Medway plans!

The bitterness of his disgrace and of his own self-condemnation came over him in a flood as he looked at her, and, without meaning to do so, he came out with the words:

"I am a pretty poor husband for you now that we *are* reunited!"

Looking up almost with a start, Charlotte dropped her work, sat down opposite to him at the table, and laid both her hands over his.

"Do you not know," she said, looking at him with great tenderness, "that in my eyes you could never be that — not if you were only . . . what do you call those men who collect rags and paper . . . a *chiffonier!* And" — a different note came into her voice — "is there not in your Shakespeare a character who says some words like these: 'We know what we are, but we know not what we shall be'? I shall yet see you an Admiral — in my heart I know it!"

He bent his head and put a kiss on the hands which covered his. "If it were not for your trust and belief —"

"But, Nugent," she broke in, "you are wrong to speak as though I were the only person who trusted you! You know that is not so. To begin with, you have in full the trust of your parents; even if they knew of what you have learnt from Mr. Lampard it would make no difference. You have written to them, have you not, and explained that we were coming to London for a little while?"

"Yes," said her husband with a sigh. "I wrote a line that morning before we left Bradworthy without of course mentioning the reason why I was not bringing you back at once. I was in fact thinking of writing a short letter to my father now, since I was not then able to give him an address in London, but I find that I have come to the end of my writing-paper. I will go to that stationer's a couple of streets away and buy some before he closes his shop. Would you care to accompany me, for a little fresh air? You have not taken it at all to-day, which is unusual."

Charlotte glanced at the clock; no summons was likely to come for her at this hour. "Yes, I will certainly accompany you, for I shall just have time, while you make your purchase, to go to a little shop not far from the stationer's, where the other day, when it was closed, I saw a flask of olive oil. (I think the proprietor must be an Italian.) I do so long to taste olive oil again. Chéri can have a little exercise also."

"He does not seem greatly to desire it," commented Nugent, casting a look at the deeply slumbering King Charles. ('And well he may not, after yesterday's battles!' thought Charlotte with half-guilty amusement) and went to array herself for going forth.

374

She parted from her husband at the stationer's and went on, with Chéri, in quest of her olive oil. The little shop in which she had seen it was situated not more than five minutes away, in a still more obscure street. She found it, made her purchase, and, having exchanged a lively conversation in his native tongue with the proprietor — Italian, as she had guessed, a little fuzzy-pated man from the South — emerged with her flask of oil to rejoin Nugent.

But she was not to rejoin him yet. A little way outside the shop were standing two men who had the unmistakable air of waiting for someone. She had not observed them as she entered. As she came towards them it was clear from their faces that the someone was herself; indeed she heard one of them say to the other in a hoarse undertone: "That's her — that's the little dawg!"

Charlotte did not like the look of these two loiterers, though their clothes were not torn or dirty, but even neat, after a peculiar style. She liked still less the fact that they were evidently not going to allow her to pass without demur — and pass them she must. Indeed one of them, the shorter, came forward touching his forelock.

"We 'opes as you'll forgive the liberty, ma'am," he said, in the same hoarse voice, but quite respectfully, "but we'd be greatly obliged if you was so kind as to tell us where you got that remarkable pretty little span'el from?"

"Aye, that we should," concurred the taller of the two.

Surprised and indignant, Charlotte jumped to the conclusion that she was somehow being accused of having come into possession of Chéri in an unlawful manner.

"The little dog is my own property," she said with dignity. "I . . . I cannot see how this is any concern of yours." And, shortening Chéri's leash, she pulled him away from his intended investigation of the legs of these persons. If only they would move aside and let her pass!

The shorter man was now addressing her again, but still in tones much nearer the wheedling than the threatening.

"Me and my mate is dawg-fanciers, ma'am, and we'd give a great deal if we could get hold of a little dawg or two of that breed! We could sell 'em well, to ladies like yourself for instance. If you'd just tell us where the little span'el was bred, you'd be doin' two pore men a good turn indeed!"

Probably the only way of getting rid of these obnoxious individuals — since there was no one visible to whom she could appeal — was to comply with their perhaps not unreasonable request. But Charlotte first picked up the subject of this conversation.

"The spaniel was given to me by a lady in Bath. I do not know whether he was bred there, but I suppose it is probable."

"Ah, *Bath!*" said the first man with emphasis; and seemed to ponder. "Bath's a long way off, Matt," remarked the other, shaking his head.

"Aye, it is. Do you know, ma'am, where the lady bought him?"

"Not in the least."

"Per'aps she bred him herself?" suggested the taller man.

"No, I am sure she did not. I cannot tell you any more. I am afraid. Will you kindly let me pass?"

Neither of them moved, but the man called 'Matt' said eagerly: "Suppose you was to give us the name and address of the lady in Bath, me or my mate would write to her, and if she's as kind as you, ma'am, she'd likely tell us where she got him. A dawg and a bitch like that to breed from — well, it'd be the making of us in our perfession!"

His 'mate' seemed to be eyeing Chéri so hungrily that Charlotte became convinced that, if she did not comply, one or other of them might in a moment snatch the coveted animal away from her and make off with him. Hastily she said therefore:

"The name of the lady is Mrs. Tracy Stallingbridge," and added the address. "Now I cannot talk to you any longer; I must rejoin my husband." And, whether rendered cautious by the mention of a male protector near at hand, or because they had got what they wanted, the two dawg-fanciers did then move aside for her, and she walked quickly past them followed by voluble thanks in those husky voices.

And followed too, she was almost sure a moment later, when she had reached the cross street which would lead her back to the stationers, by the owners of the voices in person, for as she turned to her right to go along it, a hasty sideways glance showed her that the two men were certainly coming her way. They meant to

377

find out where she lived in order that they might later steal Chéri! She was convinced of it! It was a punishment for having pretended yesterday that he was a lost dog! So directly she had turned the corner and was out of their sight she fairly ran, the dog becoming every instant heavier, and her reticule weighed down by the flask of oil, bumping and swinging on her arm. But she had not far to go, for almost immediately, to her great relief, she saw Nugent walking towards her.

"My dearest girl," he exclaimed as she hurried up, out of breath, "why are you running — and carrying that lazy dog, too! Give him to me!"

"If I had not carried him I doubt if he would be here now!" panted Charlotte as she relinquished her burden. "Quick, quick. Let us get back by the shortest way possible — down that little street over there — so that when they reach the corner they will not see which way we have gone!"

"They? Who?" asked Nugent, bewildered, turning nevertheless with commendable docility as Charlotte almost tugged at his arm.

"I will tell you everything when we get back," said she as they hurried down the side street. "Two men — dog stealers — Oh my poor little Chéri! Hurry, hurry!"

In a few minutes they were back in their lodgings, and Charlotte could subside into a chair. Her husband, still puzzled, deposited the cause of this agitation in her lap. "And now, perhaps, you will be more explicit about these dog stealers of yours. Surely they did not attempt actually to snatch the animal from you?"

"No, they did not try to do that; they were not even rude or threatening. They only wanted to know where Chéri came from, so that they could find a spaniel like him to breed from. At least, that was what they said. But I think that was only a pretext. I am sure that they really wanted to find out where I was staying so that they could steal him at their own convenience. If they had taken him then, they knew that I should have screamed or called for help."

Her husband drew up a chair and sat down by her. He was suddenly looking perturbed. Charlotte had not thought that he cared so much about the dog — save possibly on her account.

"I must understand this better," he said gravely. "What did these men look like? Were they for instance wearing red waistcoats?"

"Red waistcoats? No! Do dog-fanciers usually wear them? I do not know how to describe their appearance or their clothes, except that they were poorly dressed, but clean, and spoke as your English lower orders speak. Oh, Nugent, I shall be afraid to take Chéri out with me any more — but afraid to leave him behind also!"

"I am not concerned about the dog. It is you. What exactly did you say to these men, for I suppose you were obliged to say something?"

"Yes, I was obliged to do so," answered Charlotte, puzzled. "I do not think they would have let me pass if I had not told them what they wanted to know — where Chéri came from. At first I thought that they

379

were hinting that he was not lawfully my own dog. So I said that he had been given to me by a lady in Bath."

Nugent gave a smoothered exclamation. "You did not, I hope, tell them the lady's name, or where she lived?"

"But why not?" asked Charlotte, more and more astonished at his attitude. "As I could not possibly tell them where Chéri had been bred, I said that I thought Mrs. Stallingbridge might be able to do so . . . Ought I not to have done that?"

"A thousand times no!" said he with vehemence — and added, half to himself: "But it is my fault — I should never have allowed you to go about unescorted!"

"I am very sorry, Nugent, if, as you seem to think, Mrs. Stallingbridge will be annoyed at receiving a letter from one of these men — if indeed either of them can write. It was to get rid of them that I gave her name. And yet I have not, I fear, succeeded! Poor Chéri! but you shall be well guarded." And she stopped over him and stroked his soft coat. "Now I must take off my bonnet."

But when she lifted her head again she was astonished at Nugent's expression. Why should he be so concerned over the possible annoyance of a lady whom he had only met once, and would never see again?

"What is troubling you, my dear one?" she asked.

"This — that I fear you will have to leave London at once."

Charlotte's astonishment was ten-fold increased. This was carrying matters too far! "You mean, in order

380

to save Chéri from being stolen? But surely we could think of some other plan for his safety! . . . Moreover, I cannot possibly be away from London now!"

He shook his head. "It is no matter of the dog's safety, my dear girl, but of your own. You have fallen into a trap — for which I do not in the least blame you. The fault is mine, for ever letting you go about alone. Listen, but do not be unduly alarmed. Those men who accosted you just now had, I am convinced, nothing to do with selling or breeding dogs. That was all a blind, a device for getting an opportunity to ask you a few questions. It is through your possession of that wretched spaniel that you have been traced from Bath, and those men were undoubtedly Bow Street runners in disguise who have been trying to find you. Your telling them that it was a Mrs. Stallingbridge who gave him to you, which was just what they were hoping to hear, put into their hands the last link in the chain."

Charlotte stared at him without speaking. For a moment she did feel a pang of alarm — but only for a moment. The notion seemed to her quite wide of the mark. Bow Street runners — whatever they were — no!

"I cannot think you are right, Nugent!" she protested. "How could I be traced through poor Chéri? That would mean that Mrs. Stallingbridge had become suspicious of me after our departure, which is surely impossible — and that she gave information."

"It is not impossible that she answered questions, if she were asked them by the proper authorities. No; unless I can hide you away at once you may find yourself subpœnaed — that is, cited to appear — in

381

Guillemin's case. We must make some plan at once. Yet I do beg you, my dear, not to be unduly alarmed!"

His entreaty did not seem very necessary. Charlotte, though she was wrinkling her brows, showed little sign of apprehension. Indeed she somewhat surprisingly said, though with a certain hesitation: "Have you never in your heart of hearts thought that I ought to be so cited — or rather that I ought already to have come forward, to tell how I took that picture to Bristol, and brought back a letter?"

To that her husband did not give a direct answer, but, looking away, and thus missing the quality of the gaze she had turned upon him, he answered: "It is too late now to debate that question. Moreover, to be candid, my fear has been not so much that you might have to appear as a witness, but that you might even be arrested for complicity."

"Oh no, I am sure that I should not — now!" exclaimed Charlotte with vivacity.

"How can you tell, child? And why do you say 'now'? The situation is the same — save that it is worse!"

"I . . . I meant," said Charlotte, hastily correcting herself, "now that some days have passed."

"During which, as you can see, you have been traced! Where can I send you," asked Nugent, beginning to walk up and down the room, "that these runners will not follow you?"

"But they have followed me — almost to this door. Oh, Nugent what would be gained by my leaving London now?"

"Much, because after all — thanks to your own quick wit — they are still not sure of the street. Yet they have only to go from house to house in the immediate neighbourhood until they find one which contains a dog like that!" He cast a by no means affectionate look at Chéri. "But the question is, where can I send you at short notice? To Sophia? But how should I acquaint her beforehand? I must think it over, and decide quickly."

Ruefully leaving her husband to these unnecessary cogitations, Charlotte went to take off her out-door garments. If Nugent felt himself to be in a quandary, she knew herself to be in a worse one. She had two very good reasons for not leaving London: firstly, that she was under official orders not to do so, and secondly that since her complicity was now voluntarily made known to the authorities she stood surely in no danger of arrest. To be called as a witness at the trial would not now alarm, though the publicity would distress her. Yet neither of these excellent reasons could she bring forward to Nugent without breaking her self-imposed vow of silence, taken entirely for his sake. She must none the less find some means of avoiding banishment. For banished she must not be, when her work was perhaps only half done. Moreover if, in contravention of Mr. Esdaile's instructions, she was found to have fled and left no trace, all her testimony might be invalidated, and Nugent left in a worse plight than before — married to a French wife who had made a fool of the First Sea Lord and a senior official of the Office for Home Affairs! No, she *must* remain, remain even if she had to disclose yesterday's doings. But she would be driven to extremities before she did that!

The argument about her departure prolonged itself through the rest of the evening, Charlotte combating any plan which was raised, relying on the fortunate circumstance that Nugent ascribed her obstinacy to her natural wish not to be separated from him again. There was, it is true, a moment in which he betrayed sufficient exasperation to remark that the only course seemed to be to drown the spaniel, so that the house could not be identified by his presence. (But he immediately apologised for this brutal suggestion.) Another fortunate circumstance was that it was much too late to take any steps that evening for Charlotte's despatch to the refuge upon which he had at last decided — a quiet little hostelry of which he knew at Staines. In the morning, he announced, he should go out early and make enquiries about the means of transport thither.

So when they went to bed, it was clear to Charlotte that she would be driven to her last line of defence, which seemed to her a reasonably strong one. For she proposed to find herself to-morrow morning too seriously indisposed to get up, much less to undertake a journey to Staines or anywhere else.

II

Just about the time that Charlotte was parting from her husband at the stationer's, three men, two standing, one seated, were bending over a long narrow table at one end of which lay three small unframed water-colour landscapes. The scene was a small room in the Office of the Secretary for Home and Colonial Affairs. A fourth water-colour was occupying the attention of the seated man, who wore spectacles, and was very intently and methodically passing over its surface a small flat brush, which he from time to time dipped in a little dish full of a clear pinkish liquid. Several other dishes or saucers with contents slightly differing in colour lay to hand; and, because it was late afternoon and the room did not admit a great deal of daylight, a lamp burned on the table close to him.

Under this treatment almost all the left-hand half of the little picture, which seemed originally to have portrayed a woodland scene of some kind, had become a featureless and streaky blank; and as the brush travelled steadily and still more encroachingly from top to bottom of this martyred work of art, Mr. Philip Esdaile, who was one of the two persons standing, said in a slightly disappointed voice: "Nothing there, evidently, Carrington."

The man with the brush laid it down against the edge of the dish. "Shall I leave this one now, sir, and proceed with another?"

"Pray do so." And at this the third man, moving to the far end of the table, took up one of the remaining pictures and brought it back. This represented a ruined and ivy-clad castle on a height, against a thunderous sky. Mr. Esdaile and he scanned this Gothic conception closely for a moment or two.

"I begin to fear, after all," said the former, "that we shall draw blank, either because this device never was resorted to, and we are in consequence following a false trail, or because these particular four paintings are merely what they appear to be, and no more. Indeed, why should Guillemin, who contrived that so little that was incriminating should be found in his quarters, have kept them if this were not so?"

"In which case," said his colleague, handing the water-colour to the seated operator, "the Admiralty's fears about the Medway plans will be confirmed. Do you still feel convinced, Esdaile, that the picture which this Mrs. Carew, as you tell me, conveyed to the Irishman — and which from her evidence it is plain that he was upon the point of treating as Carrington here is doing this one — did not itself bear the plan upon it?"

"You are forgetting, my dear Payne, that when Mrs. Carew conveyed that painting to Bristol, Guillemin had not got access to the plans. They had not in fact left Whitehall for Chatham."

"Of course! I am becoming scatter-brained! I wish however that we knew what information *was* conveyed by that picture which she took?"

"That," replied Mr. Esdaile equably, "I fear we never shall know. Yet, thanks to O'Connor's haste to bring it to light, and to what Mrs. Carew happened to overhear, the picture has at least acted as a pointer."

"Or as a blind," muttered Payne, and bent once more, like his companion, to look at the obliteration of the second scene.

The expert had begun by putting a wash from another saucer over its whole surface. This had the effect, not of diminishing, but of intensifying its tones.

386

"I suppose that will have to dry a little," observed Mr. Payne, "before you can start upon your next stage?"

"The drying will only be the matter of a few minutes, sir."

"I am afraid that this probably *is* a waste of time," said Mr. Payne as he went to join Mr. Esdaile, now turning over the remaining sketches. "Or perhaps Carrington has not hit upon the right reagent, or whatever it is called."

"He is very experienced, you know, in dealing with sympathetic ink and the like."

"But why should Guillemin have chosen water-colour to disguise his drawing of the plan? Paper becomes quickly sodden when treated with liquid. Oils, now . . . Yet I suppose the scraping of the canvas which would be required in that case would have suited him even less. By the way, talking of oil-paintings —" And Mr. Payne inaugurated a short discussion on lines more purely artistic than their recent one had followed.

All at once there was an exclamation from the man at the table.

"Mr. Esdaile, sir! Mr. Payne! Something's coming up, or I'm a Dutchman! (Excuse my freedom!) But there *is* something here!"

In an instant the couple were stooping eagerly over the table. A slice of the tempestuous sky, a slice of ruin, and a considerable outcrop of crag had vanished. And in their stead, faint but quite perceptible, showed some thin brownish lines already turning black, part of a design the major part of which was still concealed.

"By God, Esdaile, I believe we have it! Go on, go on, Carrington!"

"But in heaven's name go carefully!" added Mr. Philip Esdaile.

CHAPTER
TWENTY-FOUR

I

"I was right, you see, Torrey," observed Sir Russell Cathcart with emphasis. "The Toulon fleet has come out! I knew it would. Naturally the French are impatient to retake Corsica."

He was standing next morning squarely in front of the fire in his room at the Admiralty talking to the colleague who did undeniably resemble the typical sea-dog — Vice-Admiral Torrey, the Fourth Sea Lord. It was early, and the business of the day had hardly yet begun.

"I only hope, then," grunted the Vice-Admiral, opening his snuff-box, "that Hotham will make mincemeat of it!"

"I doubt it," returned the First Sea Lord — and with justification. They were very soon to learn in Whitehall that Lord Hotham had let slip the opportunity of an operation so thorough, and had been well satisfied with a much less drastic carving up — though Captain Horatio Nelson, in the *Agamemnon*, had later done his best to remedy this defect in the case of the *Ça Ira*. But that also was still unknown.

"Now if the Mediterranean command had not been taken from Lord Hood —" went on Sir Russell, without, however finishing the sentence. Instead he poked the fire vigorously. His companion, however, was well aware that he had thoroughly disapproved of the supersession of that fine senior officer, the result of a disagreement with the First Civil Lord.

A clock struck the half-hour while Admiral Cathcart was still battering at the coals. "Egad, I must be off!" exclaimed Vice-Admiral Torrey, and, snapping shut his snuff-box, he left the room, while Sir Russell, after a final warming of himself, went slowly towards his writing-table.

He had not sat down there before the door opened and there was Torrey again. "Just met a messenger bearing the First Lord's compliments; he wishes to see us both without delay if possible."

The unexpected summons suggested some urgent matter. "I wonder what is afoot so early," muttered Admiral Cathcart as he followed Torrey out. "At this time of day Lord Chatham would still have been abed!"

For the previous First Civil Lord, elder brother to Mr. Pitt though he was, had the misfortune to be an incorrigibly late riser. To Lord Spencer, who had succeeded him last summer, no such reproach could be addressed; and though he lacked experience of naval affairs and was inclined to be obstinate, as in the affair of Lord Hood, he at least brought zeal to his new post, and was later to display efficiency. But as there was also a new Secretary in Mr. Evan Nepean, whose appointment dated only from mid-March, when he had succeeded the septuagenarian who had held the post so long, there was about both men (one in the late thirties, the other in the early forties) in the eyes of the older Sea Lords, a certain flavour of the new broom and its proverbial activities.

There was also, in Lord Spencer's room, a physical atmosphere of noticeably lower temperature than in the First Sea Lord's, and Sir Russell Cathcart, who liked a fug, emitted an audible "Br-r-r!" as he entered. On the other hand, the mental temperature was distinctly higher, for it was clear that Lord Spencer himself, and the new Secretary, the only occupants, were in a state of what in civilian circles would have been termed excitement, as they stood together by the great writing-table, intently studying something which the First Lord was holding.

As the two admirals came in he broke off what he was saying and looked up.

"Good morning, gentlemen. It is good of you to come so promptly. You will I know, forgive the abruptness of my summons when you see what I have here!" And he held out a sheet of thick paper stretched upon a framework.

Admiral Cathcart took it from him and looked at it for a moment. "God bless my soul!" he exclaimed loudly "The Medway key plan!" He turned the thing over, and saw from the back that it was, or had been, a picture. "Then Esdaile's guess was correct! Thank Heaven for that. Look, Torrey!"

"Yes," said Lord Spencer with a gratified air, "Mr. Esdaile of the Office for Home Affairs has just brought it to Mr. Nepean. Their experts succeeded yesterday in bringing out what was under the water-colour drawing.

Naturally it must be closely compared with the original in order to make sure that we are not being duped in some way, and that it is a genuine copy — *the* copy, in fact, which we feared might already be in the hands of the enemy."

Admiral Torrey, who had been examining the plan more closely, here gave it as his opinion that there was little room for doubt on that score. He was, he said, fairly familiar with the plans, and believed that the drawing would be found to correspond exactly with the real key plan.

"But what," suggested the First Lord, "if the spy, for safety's sake, has taken the precaution of despatching another copy to France by this curious method, or, more probably, by some other?"

"Mr. Esdaile, my Lord," explained the Secretary, "when he brought the drawing to me, gave me some good reasons why it may, with the highest degree of probability, be considered the only copy."

"Did Mr. Esdaile," put in Admiral Cathcart, "happen to tell you what originally gave him the idea of having the paintings which were found in Guillemin's quarters examined and tested?"

Mr. Nepean shook his head. "No, sir."

"Do *you* know what it was, Sir Russell?" asked Lord Spencer.

The First Sea Lord gave his frosty smile. "I have a very good notion. It was a mere hint — not even intended as a hint — from an unexpected quarter. But this is beside the mark. When this plan has been carefully compared with the original, we shall, I presume, be able to proceed with the dispositions for the Medway defences already resolved on, and to cancel the later and less effective plans which had to be drawn up in substitution for them?"

"Certainly, and with the greatest alacrity. And, in the matter of verification, the first plans have been returned from Chatham, have they not, Mr. Nepean?"

Even before the Secretary had time to answer in the affirmative there was a tap at the door and in came, rather hurriedly, Mr. Lampard.

"Forgive my unceremonious entry, my Lord!" said he. "But as I knew that Mr. Nepean was with you, and as this signal of a most urgent character has just been received from Spithead, I thought I was justfied in disturbing you." And he tendered a paper to his superior.

The Secretary opened and read it. He gave an exclamation under his breath and brought the paper over to Lord Spencer. And when the First Lord too had read it, a look of dismay came over his face.

"Good God! How distressing — and how exceedingly unfortunate! Captain Metcalfe of the *Redoubtable* has just had a dangerous seizure — is in fact unconscious, and may never, the surgeons say, regain consciousness at all. And the *Redoubtable*, as you know, must join Sir Robert Fortescue's squadron with the least possible delay!"

A silence filled with concern fell upon the room. The First Sea Lord, knitting his brows, seemed, according to his habit, to be seeking counsel of his Dogger Bank legacy; Vice-Admiral Torrey, still holding the recovered

393

copy of the plan murmured: "Poor fellow!" under his breath; the two Secretaries looked at each other questioningly, and Lord Spencer finally came out with the query which was in all their minds:

"Who is there capable of taking Metcalfe's place at such short notice?" No one answered, and he went on: "We shall have to make a transfer of some kind. Is the Second Sea Lord here this morning?"

Admiral Cathcart lifted his head sharply. "In view of the vital need of haste, my Lord, would it not be an advantage to appoint an officer who was immediately available — one on the spot — I mean, in London at the moment?"

"Most certainly! Every day's delay in getting the *Redoubtable* to sea hampers Admiral Fortescue's operations, as you are well aware. But do you know of any officer now in London who possesses the necessary qualifications for the command of a sixty-four?"

"I do, my Lord. Captain Carew, late of the *Callisto* frigate," replied the First Sea Lord imperturbably, yet with a certain just perceptible set of the jaw; and he put his hands behind his back.

Drawing his breath sharply, Vice-Admiral Torrey stared at his colleague in amazement, and Mr. Lampard turned and did much the same.

"Any officer recommended by you, of course, Sir Russell . . ." murmured Lord Spencer thoughtfully. The name, even if he had recently heard it in an unfortunate connection, did not appear to strike any unwelcome note in his mind. "One must not, naturally, be over-hasty. But Captain Carew being in London at this moment . . ."

II

Charlotte had started to establish her position as a temporary invalid about a quarter past six that morning, when, waking and realising that her husband was awake also, she began a series of little restless movements and sighs which soon had the desired effect of drawing from him an enquiry as to their cause.

"I do not feel very well," responded she in a small voice. "My head aches. But no doubt it will pass off. I will try to go to sleep again."

In the hope that she would do so, her spouse did not plague her with questions, and, having planted the good seed, the embryo sufferer promptly resumed her slumbers.

Later, she merely opened her eyes and smiled palely at Nugent as he bent over her before betaking himself to his little dressing-room. But the moment he was gone she slid out of bed and hastily surveyed herself in the mirror. Alas, she was neither appropriately pale, nor flushed with fever. A moment's hesitation, and she rejected the notion of supplying either of these deficiences by means of powder or rouge, since Nugent might detect their presence, and returned to bed. When he came in again shaved and dressed, and made solicitous enquiries as to whether she felt better, she shook her head, but added bravely:

"No doubt I shall feel less giddy as the day goes on. But just now . . . my head swims if I even try to sit up. At present I fear I could not walk a step without falling."

Nugent looked down at her in puzzled concern. Did or did not a faint suspicion that she might be malingering just brush his mind in passing? Charlotte could not tell.

"Do not try to walk then, my dear — at least not yet," he said. "Perhaps when you have eaten your breakfast . . ."

"Breakfast?" murmured Charlotte with a distaste which she was far from feeling. "Yes, I suppose I must try to eat something — otherwise I might faint in the coach. But I cannot swallow much."

"I hope you do not feel that you will be unable to travel to-day?" asked he, now plainly uneasy. "You know how urgent I hold it that you should leave here."

"Able to travel?" echoed the sufferer faintly. "This afternoon, perhaps. Pray do not force me to try this morning!"

Nugent coloured a trifle. "I do not want to force you to anything, you know that, Charlotte. And indeed, if your indisposition continues, I must bring a doctor to see you, and perhaps procure some woman to look after you."

A physician was the last person Charlotte desired to interview. "I am sure neither will be necessary," she replied, bringing the brave smile again into play. "This headache and dizziness will pass in a little time. Go, my dear, and have your own breakfast."

He went, he brought her some on a tray — there being no female in the house to fulfil this office — and, when he had finished his own, came back balanced (she thought) between real concern and a very faint suspicion which he did not like to put into words. So (her heart smiting her) she urged him to go out and make enquiries about stage-coach or chaise, able to encourage him in this course since she had the whip-hand of the situation. It depended entirely upon her co-operation whether any arrangement which he made could be carried out. So he went; and, having secured a reprieve from immediate banishment, the schemer went on nourishing a faint hope that something — she knew not what — might occur to make exile quite unnecessary even when she had 'recovered'. Suppose for instance, that some good fortune should bring Nugent this morning into contact with the two 'dog-fanciers', still probably hanging about in the hope of stealing Chéri! Then he would surely discover that she had been right about their profession, and he wrong!

He had been gone perhaps half an hour when she heard steps approaching her door from the living-room. There was a discreet tap, and the voice of a Goodbody — she knew not which, for they were practically indistinguishable — asking if the Captain were within.

"No," answered Charlotte, raising her own voice a little, "he has gone out. Do you want him, Mr. Goodbody?"

"There's a letter come, Madam, from the Admiralty by messenger, and as it is marked 'Immediate' we thought as the Captain should have it at once."

Charlotte's heart gave a great jump. "From the Admiralty! Give it to him, pray, directly he returns. He will not be long."

"Very good, Madam." The steps receded.

The Admiralty! What, what could the letter contain? Good news or bad? Charlotte wished now that she were up and dressed, so that she could study Nugent's face as he read it. Perhaps when Goodbody had given it to him he would bring it in here to read. But she doubted this.

And she was right. Ten minutes or so later she heard his step in the living-room, and almost imagined — but knew that it was imagination — that through the door she could hear the letter being torn open. She *was* sure that she heard him give an exclamation. Then there was silence; a long silence, it seemed, and her heart sank. It must be still more bad news. Had it been good, he would have entered quickly to share it with her.

At last she heard him approach the door; it opened and he came in. Forgetting her 'indisposition' she sat up in bed, eagerly scanning his face. And she saw that he looked dazed.

"I have just had this letter from Mr. Lampard," he said in a voice which also sounded bewildered. "I find it . . . very difficult to believe. Read it, Charlotte."

He laid it on the bed, and, as she caught it up, walked slowly, and as if he scarcely knew what he was doing, back through the open door into the sitting-room.

Charlotte read:

"Dear Captain Carew,

"I hasten to acquaint you briefly with the good news. The copy of the Medway defences plan had *not* been sent to France; it has been discovered, drawn in some kind of sympathetic ink, underneath one of the water-colour paintings found in Guillemin's room at Bath. Acting upon some as yet undivulged source of information, the Office for Home Affairs subjected these to tests, and the key plan was revealed. The First Lord and the Secretary, who have just learnt these facts, are naturally very greatly relieved — as I know you will be.

"I have also another piece of information which may startle as well as encourage you — though I have doubts as to whether I should pass it on at this stage. It is this. Owing to the sudden dangerous illness of Captain Metcalfe of the *Redoubtable,* that vessel, which is just on the point of sailing to rejoin Admiral Fortescue's squadron, must immediately have a new captain posted to her. And with my own ears — though I admit that at the time I could scarcely believe them — I heard the First Sea Lord put forward your name to Lord Spencer. Naturally I cannot say at this juncture whether the appointment will go through, after what has occurred, but Sir Russell Cathcart's support always carries weight — and the plan has *not* left the country after all. I think therefore that the auguries are hopeful, and if this turns out to be the case I shall be the first to offer you my most unreserved congratulations."

For a moment the shock — the double shock — of joy almost brought on a real attack of giddiness. Charlotte gave a little gasp and shut her eyes. When she opened them Nugent was standing by the bed. "Oh, my darling, my darling!" Her eyes full of tears, she flung her arms round his neck. "It is . . . Oh, I do not know what to say! In one letter — two such pieces of news! My heart is too full!"

He held her close, in silence, until after a moment he said under his breath: "I believe my own is also."

Disjointed but glorious thoughts were whirling through Charlotte's mind. It will all come right without my part in it being known! . . . then there *was* something odd about that picture I took to Bristol . . . who could possibly have dreamt that Admiral Cathcart of all people . . . wonders will never cease . . . what a happy day . . . now I can get up, because Nugent cannot possibly send me off to this Staines now! She released her clasp, Nugent gave her a long silent kiss, and raised himself. As he did so the letter slid from the bed to the floor. He stooped and picked it up, looked at it with a slightly puzzled expression, and said: "Here is a postscript, written along the side, which I had not seen."

"What does it say?"

"I was just about to close this letter," *he read out*, "when Mr. Wilkins forced his way in, and on

400

finding that no notice had been taken here of his 'information' —"

But here Nugent ceased to read aloud and went on silently — to Charlotte's disappointment. Then he looked up with a frown.

"Confound the fellow!" he said. "I am afraid I may have to go to the Home Office without delay."

"The Home Office?" asked Charlotte, pricking her ears. "But . . . are you sure that it is you they want? May I not see the postscript?"

"Why, my dear, you do not imagine it is *you*! Why should you — Ah, I see, you were fearing that they had discovered your part in aiding Guillemin! No, it is not that, thank God! Nor is it the Office for Home Affairs which is requiring my presence; it is Lampard advising me to go there without delay. That miserable Wilkins —"

"But who is Wilkins?" interrupted Charlotte. "And what is this 'information'?"

"Something," answered Nugent in a careless tone, "that was not worth troubling you about. The man has a bee in his bonnet, as we say. I suppose I must follow Lampard's advice. But first, as you seem to have recovered, and I am so anxious —"

"No, no!" she exclaimed. "The Home Office first! Yes, this wonderful news has cured my headache. Where is my pocket-handkerchief?" And as she sought for it, half laughing, half crying, a memory came to her, and she added: "I hope you do not hate women who cry? At least you have never said so!" She then dabbed at her eyes and murmured: "Captain Carew of the *Redoubtable!* I said you would be an Admiral one day!"

"My dearest Charlotte, you go much too fast! I am not yet posted to the *Redoubtable*, and it is more than likely that the appointment will not go through. You see Mr. Lampard doubted the wisdom of raising my hopes in the matter. But there is a chance. And with regard to the first part of his letter, as I can, I hope, be as patriotic as the insufferable Wilkins, it is even more to me, in my heart of hearts, to know that the Medway plan is safe."

"Wilkins again! But what can he do? Nugent, you must let me see that postscript!"

With some reluctance he handed her the letter again, reflecting however that it did not reveal the fact that, but for Tante Ursule's letter about the decease of M. de Marescot, there would have been no 'information' to give. And Charlotte read aloud:

"I was just about to close this letter when Mr. Wilkins forced his way in, and on finding that no notice had been taken here of his 'information', left for the Office for Home Affairs. I strongly advise you, therefore, to go there yourself without delay, since his allegations at this juncture might just tip the scales against you."

She laid down the letter. "What are the 'allegations' of this Wilkins? I do not know the word, but it seems to mean something unpleasant. Nugent, you have been

402

keeping something from me, that is plain! Later you shall confess, but now — do not waste a moment in going to the Office for Home Affairs, as the kind Mr. Lampard advises. The best person to ask to see would —" She clapped her handkerchief quickly to her mouth and then made a feint of blowing her nose with it. And luckily her husband, who had taken up the letter and was re-reading the postscript, did not realise how nearly she had come out with a name the knowledge of which she would have found it very difficult to explain away.

He finished reading in silence, and said: "Yes, I think I should go. But I do not like to leave you. Those runners —"

"In that case," put in Charlotte, smiling, "you should not have left me just now to find out about the coach for Staines!"

Nugent smiled too. "You have me there. And the coach, as I have not yet told you, leaves at two o'clock."

"So, if I am well enough, you are really going to be so heartless as to send me away now, just when the news of your appointment to the — what is her name? — the *Redoubtable*, may come at any moment!"

For a moment Nugent was diverted from the Staines plan. "I cannot conceive," he said with vehemence, "what induced Admiral Cathcart, of all people, to suggest my name! It is almost incredible, after his attitude that day! He must, like poor Metcalfe, have had a seizure of some kind. I am almost inclined to believe that Lampard was mistaken — that he must have heard amiss in some way —"

"No, no, no!" broke in Charlotte, nearly bouncing in the bed, as no genuine invalid ever bounced. "He would never have done such a cruel thing as to report Admiral Cathcart's words unless he were sure of them! So do not allow this sinister Mr. Wilkins, whoever he is, to defeat such surprising goodwill . . . whether it is due to a seizure or no! Pray go at once. And meanwhile I will get up, for this marvellous news has indeed cured my headache. And about this afternoon coach . . . we shall see."

III

Grievous as it must ever be to have one's nobler traits underrated, to be an unappreciated patriot is particularly galling. Poor Mr. Wilkins left the presence of the Assistant Secretary of the Admiralty fuming with anger and irritation. Nothing, nothing had been done since his previous visit in the way of acting upon his valuable information, save that, so he had elicited, Captain Carew, being in London, had admitted to his identity with the man reading a letter in Shute Copse. Yes, but what had that letter contained? That Mr. Lampard could not or would not reveal — and Mr. Wilkins strongly suspected that this was because he could not. Efforts to go above the fellow's head, and to gain access to either the Secretary or the First Lord had been in vain; both were much too busy, he was told, with more important matters. Well, there were other people who would pay more attention to his warnings than the ungrateful minions of the Board of Admiralty.

He only wished that he had gone to Lord Portland's office in the first instance.

When, more than an hour later, for he had some unavoidable business to transact in the meantime, he did arrive at the Office for Home Affairs, Mr. Wilkins was pained to discover fresh evidence of the indifference of Government officials to their country's good, in the unconscionable length of time he was kept waiting. And then he was only interviewed by an underling who seemed incapable of realising the urgency of his visitor's errand, merely making notes of what he said, and promising that these should be passed on to the proper quarter. But at this such alarming ebullitions began to take place in Mr. Wilkins that the underling was intimidated into seeking the aid and countenance of a superior, and returned saying that Mr. Esdaile himself would see the gentleman.

The name meant nothing to Mr. Wilkins, but he noted the underling's deferential utterance of it, and when he perceived the superior appointments of Mr. Esdaile's official room, not to speak of the air of authority which, unassuming as it was, invested its occupant, he felt slightly mollified.

"Pray be seated, sir," said Mr. Esdaile with courtesy, "and let me hear what you have to say in support of this testimony of treasonable practices among your neighbours in — Devonshire, is it not? I must premise, however, that I find it hard to believe that Devon gentry —"

"Wait, sir, until you have heard what I have to tell!" broke in the impetuous patriot. "Moreover, to the best of my knowledge, it is only one family in the district which is implicated. But, disgracefully enough, it is that of the parson of the parish, the Reverend Peregrine Carew."

"*Carew!*" repeated Mr. Esdaile, as one familiar with the name. "What Carew is that, and what has he been doing? He is, you say, a parson?"

"Yes, the incumbent of Damarel St. Mary. But it is his two sons who have been most active. The elder, the more dangerous because of his age and position is, I regret to say, a Captain in His Majesty's Navy; the other, who may be regarded as his tool, is a mere schoolboy."

Mr. Esdaile was looking at him very hard. "A Captain in the Navy? Do you know his Christian name?"

"I believe it to be 'Nugent'. As to what they and their father have been about, I am convinced it will be found that they have entered into correspondence with the enemy, relative probably to an attempted landing on the Devon coast. The whole affair centres round a mysterious letter from abroad which Captain Carew was caught reading secretly at midnight in a wood. To show that this clandestine behaviour is not mere hearsay, I must tell you that I have just heard from the Assistant Secretary to the Admiralty that Captain Carew has admitted to reading a letter in those highly suspicious circumstances."

"Oh, so you have already been to the Board of Admiralty about the matter, Mr. Wilkins?"

"I have been there twice — and received scandalously little attention either time! Yet this business may have all kind of ramifications affecting naval affairs. I have come at my own expense all the way from Devonshire —"

Mr. Esdaile held up a restraining hand. "One moment, pray. Mr. Wilkins." He gave a quick glance at the clock. "I will give you what attention I can spare if you will kindly confine yourself to essentials. Did you yourself find Captain Carew reading this mysterious letter which, by the way, if he has admitted to reading it, even in unusual circumstances, it is conjecturable that he had a perfect right to read."

"The history of that letter, sir —" And with these words Mr. Wilkin launched himself upon the eddying flood of his narrative.

CHAPTER
TWENTY-FIVE

It was hard to believe! The Medway plan safe; and Sir Russell Cathcart — of all men — proposing him for the command of the *Redoubtable! Both* pieces of good news, surely, could not be true, thought Nugent Carew as he hurried down the stairs into the street. When he had gone out earlier this morning it had been raining; now the wet cobbles were glistening in the sun. So, in that interval, had life changed for him — or, at least, showed every prospect of changing.

And yet there was still that pest Wilkins, whose infernal meddling activities he was now hastening to quash. But for Lampard's warning he would much have preferred to ignore them entirely. But, as that good friend had truly written, a trifle might tip the scales against him. He could not afford even the hint of a fresh black mark against his name. Satisfying though it would be to cross swords with the informant in person, he was not likely to have the chance, since Wilkins must have had ample time after leaving the Admiralty to present himself at the Office for Home Affairs and to have departed again. It was even possible that, had some zealous official at the latter taken his testimony against a naval officer seriously, Mr. Nepean had by this time been made aware of what the Assistant Secretary had hitherto kept to himself.

Up in Mr. Esdaile's room Mr. Wilkins had finished, having landed, out of breath, on the further bank of his narrative some five minutes ago. He had been listened to with patience and courtesy, and had, he felt, made a real impression on this important official of the Home Office. Mr. Esdaile had just promised that due steps should be taken at once to investigate the matter, the key to which plainly lay in the contents of that 'letter from abroad'. And what they were no one could say save Captain Carew himself.

"But that," observed Mr. Wilkins on a note of sour triumph, "is the last thing he will ever venture to do!"

Mr. Philip Esdaile did not comment upon this prediction, as he rose from his chair. He had had enough of the patriot, and wanted to rearrange his thoughts, which, on the subject of persons bearing the name of Carew, were more various than Mr. Wilkins was aware.

"I am much indebted to you, sir, for coming here," he was beginning — and was interrupted by a tap at the door . . .

"Would you see a Captain Carew, sir, sent here by the Assistant Secretary to the Board of Admiralty?"

It would have been difficult to say which of the two men was the more surprised, but it was probably Mr. Frederick Wilkins.

"Certainly," replied Mr. Esdaile with alacrity. "I will see him at once. This is a most opportune coincidence, is it not, Mr. Wilkins?"

Mr. Wilkins did not seem entirely to concur. He took up his hat and cane, not without a certain haste. "I was already upon the point of departure, sir. It would be better, would it not, if I left you alone together?"

He had no doubt calculated that this could conveniently be done, since the messenger would have first to fetch the applicant from some waiting-room. But this was not the case. Captain Carew stood already in the doorway, looking straight at him; and to say that this expression was hostile would have been a considerable understatement. So, bending upon him in return a gaze charged with lofty indignation, Mr. Wilkins laid down his hat and cane again with calm, as one disdaining to elude the encounter, even if he could have done so.

Nugent Carew came in. He wasted no words on any preamble. "Have I permission, sir," he said, addressing Mr Esdaile, "to ask this gentleman to repeat to my face the story about me which he has no doubt been telling you — or rather, the libellous interpretation which he has been putting upon it?"

"Am I to understand, Captain Carew, that you knew of Mr. Wilkins's presence here this morning?" asked Mr. Esdaile in some surprise.

"Only because Mr. Lampard has just informed me by letter of his intention to bring his lying allegations to this office, sir."

"I know my duty better than Mr. Lampard seems to know his," snapped out Mr. Wilkins, who appeared to be going to make full use of this confrontation, since he could not avoid it.

410

"Gentlemen," said Mr. Esdaile pacifically, "it is clear that we have now, by good fortune, an excellent opportunity of investigating these charges and, let us hope, of disposing of them. But this will demand calm. I suggest that you both seat yourselves."

Calm was not the most conspicuous element in the reception of this suggestion.

"You must forgive me, sir," responded Nugent very stiffly, "but I do not sit down in the same room with an informer — even with one who has nothing to inform about!"

"Neither will I, as a lover of my country, sit down in the presence of a man who is plotting to betray her!" retorted Mr. Wilkins. "Nothing to inform about, indeed! What of that foreign letter you were caught reading late at night in Shute Copse, the letter which, because of its secret and treasonable nature, was concealed and then feloniously abstracted from its hiding place by your young brother?"

"I have yet to learn, Mr. Wilkins," retorted Nugent Carew in a very steely voice, "by what authority you claim the right to control the private correspondence of my family! *Has* your office, sir," — he turned to Mr. Esdaile — "issued any kind of warrant to this man?"

"The law," riposted Mr. Wilkins with great promptitude, "requires every citizen, even in peace-time, to assist in the apprehension of —"

"Gentlemen," broke in Mr. Esdaile once more, "you are wasting time — your own and mine. As I see it, there is only one method of clearing up this situation satisfactorily, and that is, that Captain Carew should make known the contents of the letter in question, and offer some explanation of the unusual circumstances which seem to have surrounded its reception and perusal."

So, like a horse that has refused a fence, Nugent Carew found himself once again being forced to face the obstacle which he had so emphatically declined to clear at Mr. Lampard's invitation. But this time his refusal was even more absolute.

"The contents, sir, had to do solely with my own private affairs. I give you my most solemn word of honour for that. Nothing in the world shall make me communicate them to this meddling fool!"

"What did I say?" ejaculated the gentleman so characterised. "He dare not!"

Mr. Esdaile looked annoyed. "But I was not for a moment suggesting to you, Captain Carew," he said, ignoring this persistent gadfly, "that Mr. Wilkins should be one of the recipients of your confidence. I was about to request you to lay the information before me as representing the Office for Home Affairs, but in private. I do not doubt your solemn assurance, but a little reflection will convince you, I think, that such a course would be in your own best interests."

Fate was an implacable rider. There was nothing for it but to swallow his immense aversion to the course proposed, and agree. For a man under a cloud, as he was, any other action would be completely crazy; it would be cutting his own throat.

"Very well, sir," he replied, standing very erect. "If you will dismiss this country gentleman turned spy upon his neighbours, I will tell you what was in the letter."

"And expect to be believed?" cried Mr. Wilkins, wrought up to the last pitch.

"Captain Carew will no doubt be able to produce the letter itself," interposed Mr. Esdaile quickly, almost fearing a brawl in his room. His apprehension was not lessened when with a cackle of ironic laughter the gadfly observed: "That would indeed be a considerable feat of legerdemain! Why, it must have been in ashes these ten days!"

Without even looking at his accuser, Nugent advanced to Mr. Esdaile, took out his pocket-book, opened it and drew out a letter. "The sooner, sir, you see fit to rid this room of a presence which cannot but be offensive to you also, the sooner will this letter be in your hands." Then, turning his back upon the presence in question, he walked to the window and stood looking out, so torn with anger which he could only just keep under control, and with mortification at having been forced to give way over the letter, that he certainly saw very little through the panes, or heard with what expressions the odious Wilkins was ushered out.

"Now, Captain Carew!"

He turned and saw that Mr. Esdaile, having just shut the door, was looking at him.

"Let us get this distasteful business over. I regret that I should be obliged to ask to see that letter, but Mr. Wilkins's allegations have made it unavoidable."

"Added to my own folly over the man Guillemin," said Nugent harshly. "For naturally that is known to this office — though not, I trust, to Wilkins?"

"Your unfortunate kindness — shall we call it — to that 'marine painter' *is* a matter of knowledge to a few of my colleagues, Captain Carew — but only to a few. It has certainly not been passed on to Mr. Wilkins, nor can he have got wind of it by other means, or — or we should certainly have heard of it," finished Mr. Esdaile, with the shadow of a smile. "Now, will you not sit down?"

Nugent complied. "Before I hand you this letter, sir — which, you may be surprised to see, is not addressed to me, but to my wife — I must explain the circumstances which led to its being written, as well as the unfortunate adventures which befell it upon arrival. I shall be as brief as possible."

And he kept his word. The second narrative to which Mr. Esdaile listened that morning was no river in spate like the first. Concise though it was, it was clear enough, if, in its later passages, decidedly out of the common.

"But, by the way, sir," said the narrator in conclusion, I presume that you are willing to accept this letter as being the identical one which the game-keeper saw me reading that night? If you think it necessary to bring him up from Devonshire to identify the outer sheet — which is all that he saw — I am quite willing . . . He will certainly not know enough French to read any of it," he added to himself.

Mr. Esdaile shook his head, as he received and unfolded the letter. "Quite unnecessary." And he too added something half to himself. It was: "All this coil from the escapade of a naughty child!"

Reading French with ease, as he obviously did, and desirous, equally obviously, not to give the impression of relish in another man's private affairs, he ran his eyes rapidly over Mlle. d'Esparre's Ulysses of an epistle, glanced at Mr. Mounsey's covering letter, and handed both back.

"You have completely satisfied me, Captain Carew. I also understand your most natural reluctance to disclose this very intimate personal concern to any stranger."

"Thank you, sir," said Nugent, appreciating both tone and words.

"I consider that this letter completely disposes of Mr. Wilkins's baseless allegations against you. There remains, however, in connection with it, an accusation made against your father by this dealer in Exeter — Mr. Wilkins left a copy of his deposition with me — that the reverend gentleman tried to bribe him."

"Which I would stake my soul he never did!" cried his son hotly. "He may have offered the man more in compensation for the loss of the dragon than he received from him in the first place when he sold it to him — but that is not bribery!"

"He may very well have done that; and it certainly is not bribery. In any case, a charge against Mr. Carew of wishing to conceal the letter because it was treasonable necessarily falls to the ground once it is proved that the letter was not so. The behaviour of your younger brother ... well, strictly speaking —" Mr. Esdaile smiled, but did not finish. "A fine would meet his case, I imagine, if it were brought before a magistrate."

"I suppose," then observed Nugent with some hesitation, "that you will, in order to substantiate its innocence, be obliged to pass on the gist of that letter to the Board of Admiralty, since Wilkins first lodged his charges against me with them — with Mr. Lampard. (I refused, by the way, to show him the letter the other day.) He alone at the moment knows of the Wilkins affair."

"That," observed Mr. Esdaile, "is peculiarly satisfactory, from your point of view. I shall therefore communicate its contents to Mr. Lampard alone — if indeed it be necessary even to take that step. It may be enough to say that you have shown me the letter, and that I am perfectly satisfied as to the baselessness of any charge connected with it. And now, my dear Captain Carew, I trust you will not think me impertinent if I offer my sincere congratulations that your marriage with so charming and intelligent a young lady as Mrs. Carew has not been broken. That would have been a calamity."

Nugent stared at him. "My wife *is* charming and intelligent," he said, puzzled, "but ... I do not understand who can have told you so."

Mr. Esdaile himself looked slightly surprised. "But I had no need of any such information, my dear sir, having, as you know, spent a considerable time in what

I might almost call conclave with her and Sir Russell Cathcart at his house, the day before yesterday!"

Nugent gripped the arms of his chair. "*What* do you say? A conclave at Sir Russell Cathcart's — and my wife there! I have not the faintest notion what you are talking about, Mr. Esdaile!"

And now Mr. Esdaile was more than surprised; he was taken aback.

"But," he almost stammered. "I took for granted that Mrs. Carew had gone there with your approval, in order to disclose the involuntary part which she had played —"

"*Never!*" broke in his visitor. "I knew — I know — nothing about it. My wife go, unknown to me, to see the First Sea Lord! It's impossible — there *must* be some mistake!"

"But, my dear Captain Carew, I tell you I went to St. James's Square to question her, in answer to a summons from Sir Russell himself. And to a most valuable discovery did her answers lead! Indeed it is to what she had observed on her visit to the O'Connors in Bristol that we came on the track of the method through which Guillemin had planned to transmit the copy of the Medway plans to the enemy; hence our discovery of the copy itself, which confirmed us in our hope that it had not left the country. So you can realise what a service Mrs. Carew's visit to Admiral Cathcart (which must have been something of an ordeal for her) has rendered!"

Nugent had listened to him with a dazed expression. He now rose.

"I must believe you, naturally. But I . . . I have not yet fully grasped this startling news." And indeed this was evident. "My wife had never given me any hint that she contemplated such a step!"

"And has not informed you of it afterwards! Ah well, she may have thought you would have disapproved — though indeed she was only doing her duty in disclosing this information."

"I suppose I am to blame for not having volunteered it myself. But it amounted to so little — she was a mere catspaw."

"That was clear — yet she had seen and remembered an incident which turned out to be of the greatest importance."

"In fact she has done something to wipe off a part of the black mark against her husband's name!"

"If you like to put it so, Captain Carew. Nor would it be an exaggeration to say that the Admiralty — indeed the whole country — is in her debt. And by the way," went on Mr. Esdaile, who had also risen, "I had to request her not to leave London yet awhile, as it was possible that we might wish to question her further. But since her information led us in the right direction, I do not think that will now be necessary. I had intended to write to her to-day to that effect; but perhaps you will be good enough to convey my compliments, and inform her that she is now free to leave London if she wishes."

"I will do so, sir," said Nugent, following him to the door. "What you have just told me explains," he added with a half-wry smile, "the opposition she has been showing to my wish that she *should* leave . . . I cannot sufficiently thank you for your kindness . . . for your attitude throughout!"

"I hope that your luck has now turned," responded Mr. Esdaile cordially. "And so," he added, half-smiling, half-grave, pausing with his hand upon the door-knob, "I trust that you will not seek out any further encounter with Mr. Wilkins. Misguided as he has been, I do not think he was actuated by any personal spite against you. Some persons in these days have invasion and treason on the brain — though not many go so far as to accuse a naval officer of your rank of complicity."

"No, Mr. Esdaile, I have no further concern with Wilkins — none whatever. Good-day, and again I thank you most sincerely."

No, he certainly had no further concern with Wilkins! He had almost forgotten about him — almost forgotten that he had just cleared himself, at such cost to his own pride, of the man's allegations. One subject, one person only, filled his mind as he walked homewards — Charlotte! Unknown to him, she had actually bearded Admiral Cathcart in his private house, deliberately choosing for the purpose the day when he himself was absent at Chatham. And from this amazing action of hers had flowed the discovery that the Medway plan was safe . . . and also, for it was impossible not to guess at some connection, though he could not see clearly what it was — the First Sea Lord's astounding proposal of him for the command of the *Redoubtable*. His head was really going round. Was this the refugee girl whom he had married last autumn, bringing her from a life of uncertainty and hardship to the calmer existence in which he was eager to cherish and protect her?

A sound of shrill and continuous barking greeted him as he opened the door of the lodgings. That spaniel of hers was evidently downstairs in their landlords' quarters without his mistress, for she would not have tolerated this noise, especially in the Goodbodys' own parlour, whence it proceeded. The door was ajar, so he looked in and perceived Chéri testifying whole-heartedly to his disapproval of the cold-eyed, clambering grey parrot on its perch, and his determination neither to Avast nor Belay, as unceasingly adjured to do.

Where was Charlotte, then? Surely she had not been apprehended and removed — *now?* (Fool, why had he not taken the opportunity of mentioning his strong suspicions about the 'dog-fanciers' to Mr. Esdaile, who might have thrown some light on the matter!) Nugent ran up the stairs. Good God, there was some person in the living-room with her — he could hear a man's voice! He was only just in time then — perhaps indeed too late.

But before he could turn the door-handle he heard Charlotte laugh. And the man laughed too. What the devil could this mean? Nugent threw open the door and walked in.

And in the middle of the room, holding Charlotte by both hands, and looking down at her with much affection, stood, of all people, his own father.

"My dear sir, what a surprise — what a very pleasant surprise!" exclaimed Nugent, as both turned towards him.

"Is it not delightful?" smiled Charlotte. "Mr. Carew only arrived about five minutes ago."

"But how," asked Nugent, as he grasped his father's hand, "how did you discover our whereabouts in London?"

"I remembered," answered the Rector with a tinge of complacency, "that you had mentioned putting up at Batt's Hotel when you went to town last autumn. So I went there in search of you. The rest you can guess."

"I cannot quite guess however, delighted as I am to see you, what has led you to take this journey? — But pray, my dear father, be seated!" And he pushed forward an arm-chair.

"There were two reasons," responded Mr. Carew, complying. "One was my desire to see our dear Charlotte as soon as possible — since there was nothing in your letter from Bradworthy to intimate when you proposed to bring her home. The second was that I had been made a little anxious by that letter — not indeed by anything which you had written, but by what you had not. I had a suspicion that your business at the Admiralty was not going quite smoothly. And Charlotte tells me" (he smiled across at her) "that I was correct in my impression, though she has not revealed to me what was amiss. I understand, however, that all is now miraculously put right."

"Yes — at least I have reason to hope so. And 'miraculously' is the appropriate word. You could not have found a better. But a miracle, as we all know," added Nugent, looking hard at his wife, "does not work itself."

Charlotte tried to meet that look as if she did not understand its significance, but she found it impossible, and, flushing hotly, turned away.

"Indeed, that is quite true, as I have recently discovered," assented his father.

"What, have you likewise been in need of a miracle-worker, sir?" enquired Nugent, still with his eyes upon his own.

"Yes, indeed I have," replied Mr. Carew rather ruefully. "I found myself in considerable trouble after your departure accused of treason and attempted bribery and I know not what by that crack-brained old Zacharew to whom I had sold the Chinese dragon. Scandal, in fact, was very nearly brought upon the Rectory."

"Oh, sir, you had not told me that!" exclaimed Charlotte in a voice full of self-reproach. "Then I, alas, was the cause of it! Tante Ursule's letter —"

The Rector put up a hand. "No, no, my dear, the trouble had nothing to do with you! I must assign, I fear, a good deal of it to Tom's escapade — for which, I am glad to say, he now seems physically none the worse."

"But did Zacharew actually bring those fantastic charges against you, sir?" protested Nugent. "I was aware, from the accusations which that pestilential fellow Wilkins has been making against me, that

Zacharew had sworn information against you in Exeter, but not that anything had come of it!"

"Indeed, thanks to Clavering's good offices, nothing has. He was the miracle-worker in my case. But Wilkins, my dear boy, what had Wilkins against you?"

"That is exactly what I should like to know," observed his daughter-in-law under her breath.

Nugent caught the remark. "Charlotte," he said at once, "do you know that your spaniel is downstairs barking himself hoarse at the parrot? I think you should stop it before he drives the bird to attack him."

"I will," said she without hesitation. But from her expression it was plain that she guessed the reason for this suggestion. And indeed, as Nugent held open the door for her, she murmured meaningly: "That Wilkins! And you told me he only had 'a bee in his bonnet'!"

Nugent ignored this thrust. "Wilkins," he explained to the Rector as he closed the door behind her, "has proved a confounded nuisance to me, but no more. I will tell you of it another time. I did not wish Charlotte to learn of his activities, because she would probably had felt that his interference too could be laid at her door, whereas it was actually my own impatience which brought it about. But tell me, my dear father, how you, or rather the Squire, succeeded in routing Zacharew?"

"Clavering very obligingly went and interviewed his acquaintance Mr. Tredgold, the Exeter magistrate before whom Zacharew made his deposition. After that he visited Zacharew in person, taking with him a large and apparently valuable Chinese jar, which I had often seen at Damarel Place, and, to tell truth, had thought very ugly. This he induced that odd old man to accept in place of the vanished dragon, and even, I believe (for I was not present) to accept with enthusiasm. Matters thereupon went no further; nor would Clavering allow me to pay him a penny for this substitute, which he said he had been longing for years to get rid of . . . But all this is as nothing compared to your good fortune, my dear Nugent, for which indeed I thank God! Charlotte is given back to you — your undoubted wife, as I always believed her to be — and in addition you are at last to be posted to a ship of the line! What is her name?"

"The *Redoubtable*," answered his son. "At least, there is talk of it. The appointment is not yet made. I expect to learn before nightfall whether or no I have been selected." He paused, and his eyes turned towards the door. "But there is no shadow of doubt that the other, the far greater prize, is mine already. You will stay and dine with us, will you not, sir?"

So Nugent knew! But exactly how much did he know — or guess? Now that their pleasant meal together was over, and Mr. Carew had departed, the reckoning was upon her. Nugent was at the moment accompanying his father to the door downstairs, for to accompany him back to Dover Street was inadvisable, lest an urgent message from the Admiralty should arrive meanwhile. So, holding rather tightly to the back of a chair, Charlotte stood waiting for his return.

424

Now he was in the room, had closed the door carefully, and turned to face her, wearing his quarter-deck expression. But that she had expected.

"And now, Charlotte, will you kindly tell me exactly *what* you did during my absence at Chatham, and by what means you secured an interview with Sir Russell Cathcart in his own house? I know now that you had one."

Charlotte bent her head in acquiescence. There was a constriction in her throat, but the ordeal had to be faced. Falteringly at first, then gaining more confidence, she gave an account of her visit, suppressing only one aspect of it. When she had ended, her husband stood and looked at her for a moment or two without speaking.

"Well, Madam!" he said at last. "I am forced to address you in this manner, for upon my soul I feel that I do not know you sufficiently to call you anything else!"

This was not encouraging. Nevertheless Charlotte fancied that she could detect a glint of amusement in his eyes. She might be deluding herself, yet she risked a reply in much the same vein.

"My name, sir, is Charlotte Carew — as you have always asserted."

"And rightly asserted," said he. "It is not the name which has changed, but its bearer. This is a Charlotte Carew who has gained the approval of the First Sea Lord and has also, I gather, earned the gratitude of this country for her services."

Wishing Admiral Cathcart to be brought in as little as possible, Charlotte fastened on the second point. "And why not of this country?" she asked quickly. "Has she not been told more than once that she is now an Englishwoman?"

"She is now," corrected Nugent, "a young lady whom I have not met before — not, at any rate, the one whom I married last year in Leghorn!"

Charlotte caught her breath. If he felt like that . . . But there was a good answer to the accusation.

"We had not then known each other very long, had we?" A note of pleading had crept into her voice. Yet, as some instinct, right or wrong, still whispered to her that some portion of this stern displeasure could, surely, only be assumed, she added, half-smiling: "You must also remember, my dear husband, that until the ceremony I was a French subject, and make allowance for a sudden change of nationality!"

Far from lightening the atmosphere, however, this half serious remark seemed to have the opposite effect.

"That, my dear Charlotte, as you well know, is a mere quibble! And, in any case, no English wife would have done what you did — and without her husband's knowledge or consent!"

Something sharper than mere apprehension struck at Charlotte's heart. Nevertheless she could not bring herself to take up the role of the erring wife, to fling herself down and entreat forgiveness at any cost, she who had successfully faced a real ordeal on her husband's behalf. She looked away, and said, sadly enough, though the words were half-jesting: "Then, if I have ceased to be French, and yet am not a true Englishwoman, how am I ever to hope for absolution?"

In the silence which followed the sleeping spaniel gave a muffled yelp, and down the little street some itinerant vendor could be heard calling his wares. Into Charlotte's mind shot a half-despairing remembrance of the consul's office at Leghorn which had seen their marriage, of those homeward-bound days in the *Callisto*, of her first sight of the English coast, of the old house at Damarel St. Mary. Were those bright memories, so recently won, all now to be tarnished over with pain?

If she had looked then at her husband, and seen the change in his expression, she would have learnt the answer to that unspoken question, and to her spoken query as well. Nor would she have been so much taken by surprise when, suddenly abandoning his position by the door, he caught her in his arms.

"On quite different grounds, my dearest Charlotte. Because I love and admire you with all my heart."

The elder Goodbody's too-discreet tap went unheeded. So, since the missive which he bore was marked "Most Urgent," he opened the door, began to enter, and incontinently withdrew again.

"You clumsy fool, to go a-bursting in like that, just when the Captain was taking leave of his lady!" was the reprimand which he administered to himself.

But that was precisely what the Captain was not doing.